Books by Joseph Souza

THE NEIGHBOR

PRAY FOR THE GIRL

Published by Kesington Publishing Corporation

THE NEIGHBOR

JOSEPH SOUZA

KENSINGTON BOOKS
http://www.kensingtonbooks.com

KENSINGTON BOOKS are published by

Kensington Publishing Corp.
119 West 40th Street
New York, NY 10018

All Kensington titles, imprints, and distributed lines are available at special quantity discounts for bulk purchases for sales promotion, premiums, fund-raising, educational, or institutional use. Special book excerpts or customized printings can also be created to fit specific needs. For details, write or phone the office of the Kensington Special Sales Manager: Attn. Special Sales Department. Kensington Publishing Corp, 119 West 40th Street, New York, NY 10018. Phone: 1-800-221-2647.

Kensington and the K logo Reg. U.S. Pat. & TM Off.

ISBN-13: 978-1-4967-1621-7
ISBN-10: 1-4967-1621-3
First Kensington Hardcover Edition: May 2018
First Kensington Trade Edition: August 2018
First Kensington Mass Market Edition: April 2019

ISBN-13: 978-1-4967-1622-4 (e-book)
ISBN-10: 1-4967-1622-1 (e-book)

10 9 8 7 6 5 4 3 2 1

Printed in the United States of America

To Marleigh, Allie and Danny
for their love and support.

ACKNOWLEDGMENTS

Publishing a book requires the help of many and for that reason I have certain people to thank. First, there's Bryan Wiggins and the entire Pine Cone Writer's group. Their support for my work has always been unwavering and enthusiastic, and I couldn't have gotten this far without them. Julie Kingsley never blinked an eye whenever I needed another set of eyes to look something over. Tim Queeney gave me fantastic feedback on the novel and was generous with his time. A shout out goes to my agent Evan Marshall. He was a big believer in my writing and was always there for me when I needed him. Much thanks to my editor, John Scognamiglio, whose keen editing eye greatly improved this novel. And I couldn't have done it without my wife, Marleigh, and my kids, Allie and Danny, Their love and support means the world to me.

LEAH

Monday, October 12, 8:12 a.m.

I FINISH THE STORY I'M READING ABOUT THE MISSING girl and place the paper down. Two weeks have passed and still nothing about her. She and her boyfriend were walking back to campus when the attack happened. The only thing he can remember, before passing out, is a vaguely recalled racial slur. The police are calling it a possible hate crime and I couldn't agree more.

The starlings are at it again, streaming in waves over the field behind my home. They rise and fall like a bedsheet drying in the wind. They keep me spellbound this morning as I sip coffee on the back deck. It's October and unseasonably warm. I watch their flights of fancy as Mr. Shady, our impetuous cockapoo, stares at me from behind the sliding glass door, paws brushing madly against the glass.

My neighbor walks out onto her deck, dressed impeccably in a matching blue skirt and blazer, leather briefcase in hand as if about to leave for work. Clarissa catches sight of the starlings and freezes to watch them. Although we've been neighbors for the last three months, we've barely gotten to know each other. I'm hoping that will soon change.

I raise my head up above the cedar railing, hoping she'll take notice of me. She seems completely mesmerized by the aerial display, and for a brief second I think I see the hint of a smile on her face. The transformation is dramatic and most welcome. But then her daughter comes running out, laughing and shouting, and it breaks her concentration. Clarissa spins around, in full maternal mode, and catches me staring at her. I lift my cup, unable to shake the queasy feeling that I've been caught doing something I shouldn't.

"Hello, Clarissa," I shout in a singsong voice. "Beautiful morning, isn't it?"

She gives me a tepid wave before ushering her daughter inside. Embarrassed, I sit back and watch as the murmuration disintegrates like one of those dying dust devils dancing across an Iowan cornfield.

I pick up the paper and read where a candlelight vigil is to be held tonight on the campus of Chadwick College. I dump the remainder of my coffee over the railing and stand with renewed purpose. My breakfast of egg whites and wheat toast sits uneaten on the plate, and so I toss it in the trash. It seems that every morning my breakfast sits untouched in the trash. I'm always so busy rushing around and taking care of everyone else's needs that I often neglect my own.

There's plenty to do before we attend the vigil tonight. I need to call and make sure Clay can sneak out of the brewery for a few hours. Then there's lining up a babysitter. Finishing the laundry. Getting dinner ready for the twins.

I go back inside and rinse out my coffee cup, happy that the kids are off to school. I relish the few hours of free time I have to myself. I stare at the Gaineses' property through the kitchen window. It's a decent view from here but not as good as the one I have from upstairs.

Our two houses are the only finished homes in this cul-de-sac. Theirs is slightly bigger than ours, with a larger lot and upgrades that we could have had but for the money. The builders completed it three months before our home was built, obviously taking more time for the sake of craftsmanship. Our house, on the other hand, lacks that finished touch and meticulous eye for detail.

I had high hopes when we bought it. I expected boatloads of families to be arriving soon after we moved in, filling the neighborhood with energy, youth, and vitality. But they never came. It feels strange being one of only two families living in this abandoned development. We're like reluctant college roommates forced by chance to get along.

So why no other families? There were rumors about shoddy construction, unsafe well water, and possible radon contamination. I overheard someone at the pharmacy say that the contractor had gone out of business. Clay examined the house up and down and from every angle. He had radon and well water tests done. Everything came back normal. Yet rumors started to spread about lawsuits from aggrieved buyers looking to reclaim their deposits.

I stare out the window, yearning for something better. People. Activity. Engagement. Three of the lots have only foundations. Two homes were framed, shingled, and then left to rot. The rest are just vacant, weedy parcels screaming for occupancy. It makes me sad to look out and see our unfinished neighborhood and realize what might have been. Maybe one day more families will come, but each day that passes makes that harder to envision. And selling this place is not an option. The neighborhood's tainted. We're like the *Titanic*: way under water.

The front door to the Gaineses' opens and Clarissa walks out holding her children's hands. I step back from the window so that she doesn't see me. Her kids are a few years younger than Zack and Zadie.

Clarissa glances over in my direction and I duck beneath the sink, panicked that she might have seen me. She's tall and striking and I find myself intrigued by her demeanor and form. Peeking over the sill, I can't decide if she's a raving beauty or merely interesting to look at. She's one of those people you can't take your eyes off. Despite being of African-American descent, she's light skinned and appears like an amalgam of the world's ethnicities rolled into one exotic species.

The hot water streams out of the faucet and scalds my hand, and I howl as I pull it back. Only then do I realize that I've been rinsing my cup out for the last minute. I shut the water off and continue to watch as she gathers the children into her Mercedes. The children are a handful this morning and Clarissa struggles to maintain control of them. Once she gets them seated and buckled, she slips behind the wheel and speeds off.

Sadly, I'm once again the only person left in this neighborhood. It's terrible to feel abandoned, adrift, as if I'm the last person on earth. It feels vaguely apocalyptic. It reminds me of what might happen someday if we continue to harm the planet.

Mr. Shady rises on his hind legs and rests his paws on my shin, reminding me that I'm not alone. He wants his morning walk, and if I forget, he gets anxious. In many ways, Mr. Shady has been a godsend to this household, even if he doesn't really like me. I try not to take this slight personally. After all, he's only a dog. The runt of the litter. But I get so lonely being in this house, day after day, staring over at the Gaineses', that it's nice to have another living thing around to keep me company.

He stares up at me when I converse with him, craning his neck this way and then that way and then this way again. Often, I think he understands what I'm saying. And sometimes I think I know what's in that doggy brain of his. It reminds me of the kind of relationship I had with my twin sister so many years ago.

CLAY

Monday, October 12, 8:27 a.m.

THE STARLINGS WERE THE FIRST OMEN OF THINGS TO come. Leah's obsessed with them just like she is with that missing girl. She couldn't stop talking about those birds the first time she saw them, certain that they were communicating to her. Honestly, I think she moved us into this shitty neighborhood because of them. I had no say in the matter, which is another story altogether. Then again, I didn't really care where we lived or the style of house. One neighborhood was as good as the other in this small town. I moved her and the kids all the way cross-country only to allow her to sign away our lives on the basis of some birds.

So that's where we stand right now. Living in a broken neighborhood that no one wants to move into. No friends to speak of. Neighbors who want nothing to do with us. Upside down on the house. What a mess.

I can understand why she misses Seattle.

I was hoping our relationship would get better once we moved to Maine. A quieter life. Slower pace. Community and friends. Little to no crime (aside from that missing girl). Decent schools for the kids. I initially thought I wanted to live in Portland, Maine, because of the burgeoning beer scene. But then I realized that Portland was much like Seattle: crowded and overpriced. The land of hipster doofusville. After escaping from one urban environment, I thought it was time to try something different and move to a more rural area.

It must sound odd to people when I tell them that we moved from Seattle to Maine. Seattle's the place where everyone wants to live. Hiking and boating. Scenic vistas. Lots of coffee and beer scenes. But like any popular city, it grew too expensive. Traffic stagnates on every road and interstate. The craft beer market is oversaturated with brewers large and small. So I asked myself: why fight it? Why keep living in a shoe box when we can move to Maine and have a bigger house? Use the equity in our Seattle home and put a down payment on something nicer. Open my own brewery and sell beer to all the craft bars in Portland.

To be fair, Leah didn't want to move here. Her parents lived just outside of Seattle, and while she wasn't close to them, she did maintain occasional contact. It took weeks of convincing and cajoling before she reluctantly agreed to go to Maine. Then it was all a matter of execution.

I first laid eyes on Leah as we marched through downtown Seattle, protesting against Bush and the Iraq War. I was supposed to be meeting another girl there, hoping to start a relationship with her, but for whatever reason, it never materialized. It didn't matter. There were plenty of other cute girls in the crowd, as well as grizzled old Seattle hippies reliving their youth. But of all the thousands of people in attendance that day, I couldn't take my eyes off that one girl. Leah. She was chanting and holding up a protest sign, and because I didn't see any guys hovering around her, I made my move.

She was stunning back then, before the stress of marriage and kids took their toll. We made casual conversation, stopping every so often to chant antiwar slogans. Our eyes met and she smiled flirtatiously at me as we marched. By the time we reached Chinatown, I looked over and to my dismay she was gone. I was furious at myself for taking my eye off her and not getting her number. Someone was up on a podium and delivering a fiery speech mocking George Bush. I looked all around for Leah but couldn't find her. Just my dumb luck to connect with a cute girl and then lose her in the crowd.

Then, by chance, I was at the dog park a week later with my twelve-year-old black lab. I was about to leave when I saw her. What were the odds? It was Leah from the protest march. Her chocolate lab rushed up to Brewer and the two dogs began to sniff each other out. I waved to her and she waved back. We conversed for over an hour while our dogs wrestled and played in the park. That was the start of our courtship.

A few friends warned me about Leah when we first met, advising me in the gentlest way to cut my losses. To *run* like the wind. Who listens while in the throes of love? I do still love her. Or at least I think I do. And she still loves me. Or at least I think she does. I want a future here in Dearborn, Maine. We've talked about attending marriage counseling and about opening the lines of communication and being more honest with each other.

"Honesty": now, *there's* a loaded word.

I really would like to be honest with Leah and tell her the truth about certain things that I dislike in our marriage.

Like how I hate making love in the dark. Or how she insists on scheduling these sessions a month in advance, scribbling it down on the calendar in hieroglyphics. Oral sex is completely off the table, and that needs mentioning. Sure, part of that is my fault. But a lifetime ban?

I also hate when she obsesses about things. Like those damn birds. Can't get her mind off them. When we moved here, she sat for hours and watched the movers unpack all her china and silverware. Climate change too. She can't stop talking about it. The missing college girl—that's been a big obsession of hers lately. There's our black neighbors, whom she watches out the window. Who gives a shit if they don't want to be our friends?

But the biggest issue is that we've grown apart and we can't seem to communicate the problems our divide has caused. No longer do I care about politics and literature. Maybe I did once but not anymore. Maybe I'd convinced myself I cared in order to be with Leah. I'd never been all that suave with women up to that point, and I certainly didn't want to lose this stunning girl because of my perceived ignorance. But now being married all these years, with two children to support, I'm able to drop the pretense and embrace my true nature.

All of this has left us broken in a way I cannot fix. I know that I can't escape my marital problems by moving across the country. Something has to break. But what more can I do? I thought Leah would change once we settled here. She didn't. I thought that she'd be happier and more spontaneous. She isn't. Yes, she did change in certain ways, but she's changed for the *worse*.

Still, a man has his needs. Isn't that what they always say? That a man will start looking elsewhere if he's not getting his needs met at home. So I turned elsewhere. I'm ashamed to admit this. After moving my wife and kids three thousand miles away, I did the worst possible thing a husband could do. I broke my marriage vows. That I didn't intend it to happen says nothing about my moral culpability. I screwed up and I make no excuse for my behavior.

For that reason, I can't be totally honest with her.

I need to make sure that Leah never finds out. . . .

That the girl I had an affair with is the same girl who went missing.

LEAH

Monday, October 12, 10:56 a.m.

I NEED TO FIND SOMETHING MORE MEANINGFUL IN MY life besides being a mother and wife. There's only so much mindless laundry and housecleaning one can do. Most days I can barely wait for the kids to come home just so I can have someone to keep me company. Zack usually goes straight up to his room and buries his head in one of his science fiction books. At least Zadie still enjoys hanging out with me and giggling about silly little girl things.

The prospect of my first Maine autumn makes me giddy. I gaze out the window and see hills and mountains rolling across the landscape. Not like the majestic, snowcapped Cascade Mountains but nice all the same. The burgeoning foliage appears like the aftermath of an artist's brush. I grab the leash off the hook and Mr. Shady goes wild with excitement, spinning around and around as if chasing his own tail.

I gather up some paper bags and head out. Mr. Shady stops and sniffs at every leaf, rock, and twig he comes across. As we walk around, I envision this empty subdivision as if it were the last remnant of a lost civilization. On the opposite side of the street sits a grove of trees, thick and mossy. Mr. Shady stops to check out a scent along the path. Since moving here we've seen deer, eagles, turkeys, and even a young moose strutting through the fields behind our neighborhood. We must be careful though. The coyotes will snatch Mr. Shady up if we leave him outside for any length of time.

We pass one of the bare concrete foundations. How sad to see it like this. That the developers would leave these lots in such woeful condition depresses me.

I stop at our locked mailbox and pull out the contents. Three bills and an ordinary-looking letter with no return address. Now, who could that be from?

My mind traces back to the missing girl. What was she like? What were her hopes and dreams? They reported that she grew up in New York City. I think how devastated I'd be if something bad like that happened to Zack or Zadie. I'd spend the rest of my life searching for them. No way I could ever rest knowing that they might still be out there.

Mr. Shady leads me around the circle, pulling excitedly at the leash, wanting to take off into the nearby fields and chase squirrels and small varmints. Instead, I stop in front of the Gaineses' house and stare up at their farmer's porch. It's a lovely porch. It wraps around the house and gives them a nice view of the fields and nearby hills. No one is home and so I can stand here and admire it for as long as I like. I often think I could walk naked around this neighborhood and no one would notice. Or care.

I remember standing on their porch three months ago, after we'd just moved in, a homemade pie in one hand (I actually bought it at the local bakery) and a bottle of wine in the other. This, despite the fact that *we* were the new neighbors on the block. I thought it a nice gesture, especially since they hadn't yet approached us. I knocked on the door and Clarissa's husband appeared, looking dumbstruck at the sight of me. His face broke out in a warm smile and he graciously accepted the gifts proffered. But then he didn't invite me in. What the heck? Nor did he ask how we liked living in our new neighborhood. Or how our children were adjusting to their surroundings. His children were playing in the background and making quite a ruckus, so maybe it was a bad time for me to show up unannounced. But I wish Clarissa had come to the door instead. I often look back on that day and think that our families might have gotten off to a better start if she'd been the one to answer.

Something comes over me and I find myself walking up the stairs and onto their porch. It's not the first time I've been up here. I laugh and wonder why I continue to do this week after week. There are a couple of rocking chairs on the far end and some potted plants hanging from the wood ceiling. A folksy sign says THE GAINESES.

Mr. Shady stands perfectly still next to me. It's as if he knows that we're in a place we shouldn't be. The boards creak underfoot as I tiptoe across them. What a beautiful farmer's porch. I only wish we had one. I lean down and peer through the first window, taking in their artful decor.

What would I say if someone discovered me up here, a Peeping Tomasina—the Aramaic name for twin? I'd say that I was being neighborly. That I saw a suspicious person lurking around the house and was merely checking to see if everything was okay. Yes, that's what I would say, even if I'm the suspicious person in question. Most neighbors would do the same, right? It doesn't much matter to me, anyway, because I know I'll never get caught. Clarissa and her husband rarely return home before dinner.

I walk the length of the porch, stopping occasionally to peer into one of the windows. For some odd reason this thrills me. Much more so than watching them from my bedroom window. I move to the last pane, near the corner of the house, and am afforded a full view of the living room. It's simply incredible, far more elegant than our humble furnishings. Leather sofas and hammered nickel lamps. Cherrywood side tables. And the place is immaculate. Not a toy, wrapper, or shred of laundry littering the gleaming oak floor. For that reason alone, I'm jealous.

But what impresses me most is their collection of African-themed art: masks, terra-cotta figurines, and colorful paintings depicting the African experience. Framed pictures hang on every wall, and I wonder if they are real or merely artful reproductions. How can she keep such a neat and tidy home while working full time and with two young children running around like that? Because no matter how hard I try, I can't seem to keep the bobby pins, dolls, crayons, and assortment of miniature toys from sneaking back downstairs in the middle of the night. They hide in the creases of our couch and along the floor, waiting for my bare feet to be impaled by them. They subvert every effort I make to keep the house clean.

I feel slightly naughty peering inside, but I never tire of the view. I get the same adrenaline rush every time. Although I'm not seeing anything of particular interest, I'm thoroughly enjoying myself. It's fascinating to observe someone else's life when they're not around. I feel like an ethnosociologist studying a newly discovered tribe's habitat. Maybe it's the boredom of being a housewife or the simple fact that I'm so alone in this new town that I'm going crazy. I can't lie to myself; I'm desperately in need of a friend.

Before I can process my emotions, I lift the sill only to discover it's locked. Good. Now I won't be tempted to go inside. It's a criminal offense, silly. Mind your own business, Leah. You're a college-educated woman with two children and a loving husband. You're not a stalker. You don't covet your neighbor's stuff.

Mr. Shady barks and I tap his moist black nose with my finger. He stops immediately and titters. I should turn around and go straight home, but something always prevents me from doing so. Mr. Shady stares up at me, wagging his tail anxiously. Or maybe it's nerves. He wants to get off this unfamiliar porch and return home to his comfortable bed, brimming bowls of brown beef pellets, and freshly filtered water. He's a dog imbued with reasoning, intelligence, and good judgment, I reassure myself.

But I'm not ready to leave the Gaineses' porch just yet. I feel a sudden urge to see more, to know more about these people. I grasp the handle, completely against my better judgment, and to my surprise the door opens. It always does.

It frustrates me that the Gaineses have not yet welcomed me into the neighborhood. Is it a race thing? A matter of class? It's obvious they're better off than we are, especially after Clay sank every penny of our savings into his brewery. He's so busy with his IPAs, stouts, and lagers that he doesn't seem to care that our neighbors haven't reached out to us yet. We moved three thousand miles away so he could follow his dream of opening a brewery, and then this happens. Or doesn't happen. So where does that leave me? The kids?

I partially blame Clarissa for this estrangement. Oh yes, she's friendly enough whenever we run into each other on the street or at the supermarket. I don't know why her aloofness bothers me so. Maybe it's because she seems like the kind of person I could become good friends with: she's smart, progressive, cosmopolitan, and a mother like me. She gives me her undivided attention whenever we speak briefly on the street. She puts her hand on my forearm and seems concerned about what I have to say. Do I bore her? I often feel like I go on too long when I talk to other people, saying whatever pops into my mind. I dread the awkward silence and the dead-eyed stare. Yet once we're back in our respective corners, it's like we're strangers again. My invitations to dinner get politely declined for one reason or another. A gulf lies between our two households and I don't know why or what I've done to cause this.

A breeze rustles through the trees as I stick my head gingerly inside the foyer. I want to go inside, walk around and check everything out, but something prevents me from doing so. It always does. I glance at my watch. Darn, I've forgotten that I've scheduled Clay in a few minutes. Before closing the door, I snatch a tiny African wood carving off a side table and stuff it into my pocket. It marks the first time I've ever taken something out of their house.

I stare down at Mr. Shady and reassure him that we are done here and that it's time to go home. He spins around in anticipation, getting tangled up in the leash. My hand holding the envelope is shaking with excitement. Kneeling down to free him, I hear the sound of flapping wings and notice that the starlings are at it again. I smile as they soar overhead, angling toward the dense woods across the street.

I rip open the letter and read it.

You mustn't be so hard on yourself, Leah. You were only a child when it happened.

My heart races with fear and I crumple the paper and stuff it into my pocket along with the carving. Who sent this nasty note and why? I start to get light-headed. Just thinking about it fills me with anxiety, as does the figurine I've stolen from their house. Mr. Shady stares up at me with an accusing look. Or am I imagining this? The landscape begins to spin as I reach down to keep from falling. But it's too late. I let go of Mr. Shady's leash and everything goes black.

CLAY

Monday, October 12, 11:30 a.m.

I RACE HOME FROM THE BREWERY. LEAH HATES WHEN I'm late for our monthly scheduled trysts, despite the fact that she seems as eager to be done with it as I am. Sex with Leah is far from satisfying and I often wonder if it's worth the effort. It's been this way for a long time. With so many things to do at the brewery, it seems counterproductive to be here. I could work straight through the night and still not be done with all of my tasks.

I park in front of the house and bolt up to the front door and inside. I call out her name a few times, but there's no reply. Great. She's out for a walk or jog and has completely forgotten about our scheduled quickie. I scribble a happy note for her with a permanent marker and leave it on her novel. Then I race back out to the truck before she returns.

Whew.

It's weird that I'm so relieved. Most guys would give their left nut to dash out of work and have a nooner with their wife. But work is the only thing keeping me going these days. It's been a lifeline and my only means of staying sane. Moving to Dearborn and starting this brewery has given me a reason to live, and to pretend to be happily married.

Things have been rocky as of late and not all these problems have been Leah's fault. I've contributed mightily to the decline in our marriage. But things will soon change. I plan to be a better husband. I *need* to do better. At least for the twins' sake. They deserve to have two loving parents raising them, especially after I moved them away from the only home they ever knew.

Once back in the brewery, I revel in my narrow escape. A celebratory beer is called for. I sit in my tiny, cluttered office and knock back the first of many that I'll quaff throughout the day. Quality control is how I rationalize my drinking. Thankfully, there'll be no talking after ten boring minutes of sex. No cuddling with Leah while my mind makes a list of all the things that need to get done. No listening to her go on about climate change or the missing college girl. I haven't yet told Leah that the girl and her boyfriend were at the brewery the night she disappeared. Leah would freak if she knew. She wouldn't stop asking me questions. Her obsession with this case is driving me insane.

I have one main rule with Leah: what she doesn't know won't hurt her—unless she finds out. Then I'll be the one hurting.

LEAH

Monday, October 12, 11:35 a.m.

I LIFT MY HEAD OFF THE DECK AND THE FIRST THING I see is Mr. Shady staring at me with those big brown eyes. He sits dutifully by my side, keeping a close watch over me. He has stayed by my side the entire time, loyal to a fault. Maybe he doesn't hate me after all. Or maybe he doesn't hate me as much as I'm led to believe.

I reach out to pat his head, but he shrugs off the gesture and beckons me with quivering legs. A few orange leaves lie sprinkled over the porch like nature's footprints. I glance at my watch and see that I've been out for over eight minutes.

"Such a good boy staying with me like that." I pat his head, but he snaps at me. "Okay, Mr. Sourpuss, suit yourself."

I pick myself up off the porch and walk Mr. Shady back to the house, relieved that no one has seen me passed out on my neighbors' porch. Of all the times to have an anxiety attack. Serves me right for stealing into their house and making off with one of their art pieces.

I open the front door to my house and see the note that Clay has left me. He didn't wait very long before heading back to the brewery, and in some ways I'm relieved. He signed the letter with hearts and kisses. So sweet.

Mr. Shady collapses on his pillow, head on paws. He watches me for a few seconds, but inevitably his eyelids close and he begins to snore.

I pour a tiny glass of wine to settle my nerves, turn the radio on NPR, and open my Jane Smiley novel to the bookmarked page. A few minutes pass before the news comes on. I lay the book down on the coffee table and listen. The missing girl's boyfriend comes on, begging the public to help find her.

The reporter returns. The police admit that they've discovered a lacrosse stick by the trail, with the victim's blood on it. They've only now released this information, hoping to keep emotions from running high on campus. It certainly looks to be a hate crime. Two black students out for a casual stroll, one beaten, one kidnapped.

Mr. Shady raises his head, sees me getting emotional, and lets his chin fall back on his paws. For some silly reason I feel partly responsible for this crime. My whole life, I've taken for granted my status as a white woman living in a country that affords people like me such a privileged status. Sometimes I feel ashamed because of my heritage, my colonial ancestry, and how we enslaved black people.

I eagerly look forward to the vigil tonight. Just thinking about it makes me happy, makes me feel like I'm making a difference in this world. I'll raise a candle against racism and hate, and hope that everyone in town comes together as a community. More than anything, I need that girl to be found, alive and well, and for her to see how much she is valued by the people in Dearborn. I don't know the girl, yet as strange as it sounds, I suddenly feel as close to her as I do my own children.

CLAY

Monday, October 12, 12:07 p.m.

A VIGIL, SHE SAYS. CAN YOU BELIEVE THIS? I HANG up the phone. A candlelight vigil is the last place I want to be tonight. It means I have to stop drinking beer and switch to coffee instead. Sure, I'm pretty lit right now, but that comes with owning a brewery.

I hate going on that campus, even if a lot of my business comes from the students, faculty, and staff there. The lot of them are a bunch of pretentious assholes who wouldn't know a good beer if their life depended on it. The next dickweed who asks me for a lemon wedge in their Bavarian Weiss is going to get an earful. Education is a good part of my job. Teaching people the true nature of beers and how to properly drink them. Teaching them not to be sheep.

They're calling this attack a hate crime. It may have been a hate crime, but in my opinion all crime is a hate crime—and trust me when I say that there were many people in town who hated Mycah Jones.

Hating Mycah is probably the nicest thing one could say about that girl, and thinking that I have to honor her tonight makes me sick. I'll keep my opinion to myself, of course. This is Leah's thing. Vigils and protests and occupying shit are right up her alley. If it will make her happy to stand with a bunch of brainwashed kids and their airhead professors, it's a cross I have to bear.

LEAH

ZACK AND ZADIE WILL BE HOME SOON. MOST DAYS they take the school bus home. Oftentimes, Clay picks them up and drops them off before returning to the brewery. I told him about the vigil this evening, and by the sound of his voice, I could tell he didn't want to go. It took a little persuading on my part, but in the end I convinced him that our presence there would go a long way to creating goodwill in the community.

I feel as happy as a gooey duck under two feet of Puget Sound mud. I place a frozen turkey tetrazzini into the oven and then pour myself a third glass of Chablis. I've folded all the laundry, put the dishes away, and read two chapters of my novel. I've picked out my outfit for tonight: a somber black dress with a V-neck. Understated jewelry and black leather boots.

Our future in Dearborn seems so much brighter now. If only I didn't miss home so much.

How I miss my old life in Seattle. Taking the kids to their playgroups and conversing with all the other mothers. It was my primary means of socializing. I never had many close friends growing up, so I eagerly looked forward to our thrice weekly playgroups. We all shared the same political beliefs, and every so often we would meet for coffee or go out somewhere and converse over glasses of wine.

I even miss the rain. In Seattle it's more like a constant mist. I also miss the never ending cover of clouds that blankets the region nine months of the year. We lived in a tiny bungalow in Ballard and within walking distance to shops, parks, restaurants, and great pubs. A long time ago, Swedish immigrants settled in Ballard and made it their home. I miss the Swedish market and the annual lutefisk-eating contest held every summer. I miss taking the kids to Golden Gardens Park and listening to the seals' incessant barking. I miss walking around Green Lake and swimming with the kids in the warm water, and then cooling off with ice creams at Häagen-Dazs.

We had the perfect life in Seattle and I never wanted to leave.

I can't wait to see my two little monsters and hug them to death. My love at this moment feels singular and pure. Loving one's kids is the greatest gift a woman can be blessed with in this life.

My own childhood was not as idyllic as my children's. I never felt truly loved by my parents in the way I love my own children. But my sister and I made up for their apathy by developing a tight bond. We truly loved each other and were inseparable whenever I was home. Being twins, we could communicate without talking. Not a day goes by when I don't think of Annie. I miss her terribly and wish she could see how wonderful my life has turned out. It would be so cool if she could have lived long enough to meet Clay and the kids.

The sun moves lower in the sky. Soon we will turn the clocks back and lose a precious hour of our lives. A distinct chill is beginning to fill the air. Then the snow will fall and blanket the countryside. I've heard all about Maine winters and can hardly wait to experience one. The snowier, the better. Maybe winter will change my mind-set and make me appreciate this part of the country. I see myself snowshoeing and sledding. I've studied the L. L. Bean catalogs for so long now that I know every model's face and dress size. I've often pictured myself as one of those All-American Bean girls: rosy cheeks and woolly white sweaters, sitting by the stone fireplace with my handsome hubby after a day of skiing, a cup of hot cocoa warming in my cold hands.

I pour myself another glass of wine as I check on the turkey tetrazzini bubbling away in the oven. The pleasant smell wafts up to my nose and makes me happy. It smells delicious as it permeates the air. When it's done, I transfer the tetrazzini to some glass cookware to make it appear home cooked, grab the cardboard boxes and aluminum trays it came in, and stash them deep inside the recycling bin so no one sees them.

Cooking, admittedly, was never my strong suit. At least in Seattle all the supermarkets sold wonderfully prepared meals at a decent price. Meat loaf and mashed potatoes and chicken dinners with two sides of vegetables. Clay never noticed when I purchased prepared food for dinner, and if he did he never said anything about it.

I mix a salad, wondering what kind of family Mycah Jones came from. Chadwick's campus is less than a mile away, and if a kidnapping and assault can happen in this small college town, then it can happen anywhere. I sip my wine and read more about the case in the newspaper. When I'm done, I put the paper down and concentrate on setting the table. The wine has made me slightly dizzy and so I tell myself to take it easy.

It's nearly three o'clock when I hear a car pull up outside. I peek out the window and see Clarissa parking her Mercedes in the driveway. She's home early today. She gets out and unfastens the two children from their car seats. Almost immediately, they start running and screaming at the top of their lungs, their energy knowing no bounds. Clarissa looks particularly stressed as she walks behind the car and begins to pull plastic bags out of the trunk.

Plastic?

Doesn't she know about climate change? Or plastic's onerous role in depleting the ozone? She tries to grab too many bags at once and one of them splits apart. Groceries spill over the blacktop, cans rolling down to the street, eggs cracked, and bright yellow yokes streaking across the driveway.

This is my opportunity to help.

I run out with my reusable bag and help pick up the groceries, making a mental note of the items she purchased: canned vegetables, mac and cheese, Hamburger Helper, beer, wine, crappy chicken nuggets, and two packages of overstuffed Oreos. Her food choices surprise me; I never would have suspected her as the type to buy Oreos. She strikes me as a stern and disciplined mother when it comes to her family's nutritional habits. I pictured her carrying bags of organic apples, kale, free-range chicken, and grass-fed beef. I can't help but be slightly disappointed by all this.

Clarissa looks flustered as I run over and pick up the groceries. I help her carry them inside, where she instructs me to place the items on the granite island. I go back out and help her bring in the rest of the bags while her two little ones run around the house and scream like banshees.

"You'll have to excuse my children. They're all wound up this afternoon," Clarissa says as she takes the groceries out of the plastic bag and places them on the counter.

"I have children too, remember?" I stare at all the plastic bags on the counter, trying not to appear judgmental.

"Something on your mind?"

"Not really," I say. "It's just that . . ."

"Go on. Say your piece."

"The sight of plastic bags makes me anxious."

"For real?"

"Our planet is in dire straits," I say, trying not to lecture. "I have some extra reusable bags at home if you ever need one."

Clarissa laughs. "Thanks, but I have plenty. I simply forgot to bring mine today."

"I find it helpful to keep extras in the trunk just in case."

"I'll certainly remember that," she says as she puts away groceries.

"I know it sounds crazy, but I'm really concerned about the future of our environment."

"Think you're the only one?"

"I didn't mean to imply that you weren't."

"Just because I forgot my bags one time doesn't make me a climate denier."

"I know, and I'm sorry." What the hell am I saying? I remind myself to take it easy on the wine. "The plastics they use today are incredibly toxic. Did you know that sea turtles confuse plastic bags for food, which ends up blocking their digestive tracts?"

Clarissa stares at me before breaking out into a fit of laughter. Her response hurts my feelings. I fail to see what's so funny about destroying the planet and killing sea turtles.

"I'm sorry."

"I don't find that funny, considering our planet will die soon if we don't take immediate action."

"Yes, you're right. I'll make sure to use my reusable bags from now on. And I'll certainly remember the plight of those poor sea turtles next time I shop."

"I'm sorry if it sounds like I'm lecturing you, Clarissa. I get so worked up about this issue at times."

"No, you're right. I should be more mindful of these important matters." Clarissa scrunches her plastic bags into a ball before stuffing them into a drawer. "Anyway, thank you for helping me."

"That's what neighbors are for."

"How did you even know my bags broke?"

"The oven's by the window. I was checking on my turkey tetrazzini when I looked out and saw your groceries spill over the driveway."

"Must be nice to stay home and make home-cooked meals for your family."

I can't tell whether she's poking fun at me or truly envious of my situation. Then again, I'm always one to see the good in people, so I let her comment pass.

I glance around her home. It's more elegant and refined than what I saw through her window earlier in the day. I wonder if she'll notice that one of her wood carvings is missing. Why did I take it? The thought of what I'd done fills me with guilt, and I promise myself to return it to its rightful place the next time I'm in here.

Her kids run into the room and chase each other around the kitchen island. I stand awkwardly as Clarissa herds them toward a side door, where I presume a spacious playroom awaits them downstairs. How lucky they are to have a finished basement. For some reason, I suddenly feel like an imposition. The children's voices fade away as they scramble downstairs. I wonder whether I should go home or stay a few minutes longer to say good-bye.

Clarissa appears at the top of the steps, looking tired and frazzled. The expression on her face is one of surprise—that I'm still here? Maybe she expected me to see myself out.

"Thanks so much . . . ." She pauses awkwardly, pointing a finger at me.

"It's Leah." I try not to sound offended.

"I'm so sorry, Leah. I'm absolutely horrible with names." She uncorks a bottle of Riesling and pours herself a glass. It takes her a few seconds before she realizes that she hasn't offered me one. "Would you like wine?"

"Maybe just a little." I gesture with forefinger and thumb, although I'd be happy with a full glass.

"Cheers," she says.

"Cheers." I clink her glass, noticing the macadamia-nut-sized diamond on her finger.

"Don't mind me, I'm a little off today."

"Any reason why?" I ask.

"It's been three years since we moved here from Atlanta and I still miss it."

"I know how you feel. We moved from Seattle this summer and I miss it every day."

"I've never been to Seattle. Hear it's a wonderful place."

"It really is a beautiful city." I raise my glass again. "To two homesick moms."

"To homesick mommas," she says, toasting. Then she shakes her head and looks away.

"What is it?" I ask.

"I have so much to do this afternoon and I don't even know where to begin."

"What's up?"

"There's a vigil tonight on campus for the missing girl."

"Yes, I heard about that on the radio."

"This crime has everyone on edge. We've got grief counselors at Chadwick working around the clock. People are just so upset."

"The police also reported that they found a lacrosse stick near the crime scene with blood on it."

"I heard that as well. There's a rumor spreading around campus that someone on the lacrosse team may have been involved with Mycah." She sips her wine. "If you ask me, that team is made up of a bunch of spoiled, rich, white kids."

"Do you believe the rumor?"

"Anything's possible. There's been so much racism in this school's past that nothing would surprise me." She takes another sip of wine. "Have you been following the case?"

"Like everyone else in town."

She finishes her wine and stares at me.

"So are you going?" I ask.

"If I can find a babysitter." She glances down at her cell phone. "Our usual girl can't make it tonight and neither can her backup."

"Why not?"

"They're attending the vigil with some friends. Seems like everyone in town is going to that event."

"That's a good thing, right?"

"Of course it is, but not so much for me. I'm supposed to give a speech tonight."

"Really?" This impresses me but I try not to show it.

"Not if I can't find a babysitter on short notice."

"What about your husband?"

"Russell's a tenured professor at the college. He has to attend."

"I see." I sip my wine, careful not to drink too much lest I make another stupid comment. "Good sitters are hard to come by these days."

"Tell me about it." She stares at me over the rim of her glass. "Would you be willing to . . . ? No, I can't impose on you like that."

"Willing to what?" I know what she's going to ask.

"I just couldn't."

"Try me."

"Is there any way you could watch my kids tonight?" She pours herself another glass. "This vigil shouldn't last too long."

Does she really think that I'm so heartless as to not want to attend? Is it because I'm white? Or that I'm not in any way affiliated with Chadwick College? Certainly, this hate crime transcends campus life. Do I look like someone who is so cold and callous as to not care about racial injustice and hate crimes in my own community?

"I'd really love to help you, Clarissa, but my husband and I are also planning to be there."

She looks surprised. "Of course. I should have assumed as much."

"I suppose I could ask my sitter if she'd be willing to look after two more children."

"Goodness, that would be so helpful if you could. Of course, we'll help pay any additional costs."

"I can't guarantee that she'll do it."

"I totally understand. But it would be so helpful if you could somehow convince her how urgent this is. My kids are usually well behaved."

Well behaved? "I suppose it couldn't hurt to ask." I know our babysitter will happily watch two more children if I ask.

"You don't know how much this means to me, Leah. Thank you so much."

"That's what friends are for, right?" I sip my wine, a feeling of goodwill coming over me. The wine is cold, dry, and delicious, and I could easily drink a few more glasses, but she doesn't offer me another. "Can I ask you something?"

"Sure."

"How well did you know the missing girl?"

The question seems to catch her off guard. "Not that well."

"What is it you do at the college, anyway?" The alcohol has loosened my tongue and made me bolder than usual.

She pulls out her phone and checks her messages as if already bored with my company. "I was hired as the college's chief diversity officer. I'm the first in the school's history."

"That's wonderful."

"It's only a half-time position for now, but I also teach some courses as well. This semester I'm teaching Race and Gender in America."

"Such an important and timely subject," I add. "What exactly does a diversity officer do?"

"Make sure the various minority populations are represented on campus. I ensure that all students' voices are heard by the administration." She seems slightly agitated, which makes me uncomfortable.

"Has it been a problem in the past?"

She looks up at me as if I've asked a stupid question. "Chadwick has historically been a bastion of white male privilege. They only began accepting women sixty years ago. My job is to change the perception of race, gender, and privilege on campus, and to help recruit bright young minorities to the school."

"A truly worthy goal."

"Did you know that the author Robert Cornish graduated from Chadwick?"

"From what I read, he represents everything wrong with twentieth-century literature," I respond.

"*Force of Will* is such a racist novel. They should ban it from every library in this country."

I remember how much I loved reading *Force of Will* in college, and it suddenly fills me with guilt.

"So you can see why I have to attend this vigil tonight, especially considering that I'm one of the keynote speakers."

"Have you prepared a speech yet?"

She laughs. "What do you think? I'm still not sure what I'm going to say. But I'm pretty good on my feet, if I do say so myself."

"Wonderful." I clap happily. "I'm sure you'll be magnificent."

"Considering the tragic circumstances, I'd say it's not *that* wonderful."

I curse myself for making such a stupid comment. "I was merely speaking to your ability to bring people together through the use of words."

"What I'd really like to do is get my hands on the bastards who committed this crime. It wouldn't surprise me in the least if it was one of those privileged frat boys on the lacrosse team."

"I heard over the radio that members of the team were in town that night."

"There's a dive bar they like to patronize called the Monkey Pub. The college has pampered them for too long now. Their parents donate lots of money to Chadwick and because of that they're considered hands-off by the administration. Their coach is a pompous ass too."

"Why don't they fire him?"

"Because he produces winning teams. His players all graduate, get jobs on Wall Street, and end up donating millions back to the school. In his seventeen years at Chadwick, he's won five national championships. The administration is too chickenshit to fire him."

"But winning isn't everything, right?"

"That's what I've been saying since I arrived here, but apparently the administration doesn't agree with me."

"They should put their priorities in order. Place more emphasis on equality and social change rather than merely wins and losses."

"He's a sneaky one, Coach Williams. He always manages to recruit a few token minorities so he can appease the administration and make it look like he's more diverse than he really is."

Clarissa's phone rings. She answers it and turns to me. After a few seconds, she tells me that she really needs to take the call and would it be all right if she brings the kids over later, assuming our babysitter can watch them. It seems a rather abrupt end to our discussion, but I nod in agreement. My wineglass is half full. It would look boorish if I guzzled the remainder down while she's staring at me. As soon as she turns her back, I drain my glass and head out.

I feel slightly giddy as I stagger back to the house. It's been a grand day thus far and I experience a sense of joy that I haven't felt in a long while. Mr. Shady starts to bark as soon as I approach the front door. I stumble inside and collapse on the couch, praying that my chance encounter with Clarissa will be the start of a long and meaningful friendship.

CLAY

Monday, October 12, 6:30 p.m.

I GRAB AN EXTRA-LARGE COFFEE AND A JELLY DONUT
on my way home from work. My head's a mess. I over-
did it this afternoon and ended up drinking more than I
should have. As usual, quality control's to blame.
Hopefully, Leah will be too busy getting ready for this
vigil to notice the sad condition I'm in.

Some of the jelly spills on my shirt as I navigate my
way home. I try to clean it off with a napkin, but it
leaves a blotchy red stain that resembles blood. Or
worse: lipstick.

Leah's gabbing nonstop the moment I walk through
the door. I can tell from her flushed cheeks and the fran-
tic way she's moving around that she's also been drinking. My lucky day. When she gets like this, she's usually
too distracted to notice anything else. I down a quick

beer while I'm waiting for her to get dressed. The kids are sitting at the kitchen table, having a snack and trying to ignore their drunken parents. Once they're done eating, we excuse them from the table, and they dash up to the safety of their rooms.

Do I feel guilty about drinking in front of the kids? Truthfully, no, but I do feel bad for them when I'm drunk and slurring my words. Or when Leah's trashed and acting stupid. I've always had a fondness for beer, and it never really seemed to matter when the kids were little. They just thought it was the same goofy old dad when I was sloshed. Now that they're older and can connect the dots, and can tell when we've had a few, it's become an issue. Leah's drinking has certainly increased in the last year, ever since we decided to move to Maine. Her drinking worries me more than anything. Maybe it's the uncertainty of moving here that caused it. Or maybe it's because our relationship is not where it should be. Nothing good can come out of talking to her about it. She'd forcefully deny it. She'd point to my excessive drinking and call me a hypocrite for calling her out. My biggest fear is that something bad would have to happen before she realizes that she has a problem.

I hear a loud knocking. My next-door neighbor Russell appears at the front door. What's this? We're responsible for taking care of his kids too? Great. After a brief chat at the door, he leaves just as our babysitter pulls up in the driveway. Leah greets Molly with detailed, written instructions that would put most technical manuals to shame. Molly continues to nod her head so rapidly and with such enthusiasm that it appears to me as if she has some sort of neurological disease. As soon as Leah is satisfied that she understands her rules, we head out.

I'm exhausted and the coffee has only made me sleepy. I've been working twenty-four/seven for the last six months and it's starting to wear on me. Don't get me wrong. I absolutely love making beer. It's been my life-long dream to open my own brewery. But a person can only do so much before the body and mind begin to break down.

A parking space opens up two streets away from Chadwick's front gates. The sidewalks are filled with people of all ages heading toward campus to pay their respects.

"Isn't this amazing?" Leah says, clutching my hand.

"It's a vigil. I don't think it's meant to be amazing."

"I mean to see people from all walks of life coming together. Just think how we could effect real change in this country if we were all on the same page."

And by that she means if things were run *her* way.

Honestly, I feel allergic to politics these days. Politics means nothing to me. The system is so corrupt it's left me jaded and cynical. Leah believes that I still share her progressive views, and at one time I did. It's how I met her. But no more. I've given up caring about social justice, equality of income, and LBGT rights. Does that make me a rube? Maybe. I can't even bring myself to vote.

"Hurry, Clay. We need to get there before it starts."

LEAH

Monday, October 12, 6:52 p.m.

I'M ALL JITTERY AND NERVOUS AS CLAY AND I GET OUT of his pickup truck and make our way toward campus. It's the same pickup truck he uses for his brewery, and it even has the words FRESH BEER on the side, which strikes me as a bit tacky for the occasion. Still, it's the last thing on my mind. My head is spinning from all the wine I consumed earlier in the day. Thankfully, a long shower and a couple more glasses of wine helped calm my nerves.

I clutch Clay's callused hand to keep me steady. I certainly don't want him to know I'm slightly drunk. The night is cool and crisp and the trees above rustle in the October breeze. Up ahead I see hundreds of lit candles flickering in the night. The closer we get, the better we can hear the murmur of the crowd. It's both exciting and nerve-racking to be part of such an important event. Reporters and news cameras appear every-where.

Russell had dropped the children off with Clay while I was taking a shower, and by the time I came down, Molly had already arrived. I gave her brief instructions and made sure everything was in place. The children immediately began playing with each other soon after being introduced. It always amazes me how easily children can get along with one another. There's rarely any judgment or suspicion. I often wish adults could act in the same manner, but inevitably things change with age, and we become more defensive, skittering back to the safety of our tribe.

Clay's odor tonight horrifies me, although I try not to make a big deal out of it. He reeks of grains, hops, and sour yeasts. I wish he'd showered beforehand, but at least he took time off from the brewery to be with me. When he quit corporate America to brew beer, I was appalled by his decision. He hated being locked up all day in a cubicle. The loss of his salary was a blow to our finances, but coming home each night reeking of beer was the worst. It took me years to come to a grudging acceptance of that particular smell.

"You're shivering, Leah. Are you okay?" Clay asks.

"I'm nervous."

"We can turn around and go home if you want."

"I bet you'd like that."

"No, I came here to support you."

The surrounding buildings are all lit up. I've jogged around this campus more than a few times, passing students lugging backpacks around, all of them look-ing like mountain climbers ready to scale Everest. We pass Prescott Hall and I see banners hanging out the windows, decrying racism and sexism, and promoting LBGTIQ rights. I see another that reads BRING BACK MYCAH!

"I understand the LBGT part, but what do the *I* and *Q* stand for?" Clay asks.

"*I* is for 'intersex' and the *Q* means 'queer' or 'questioning.'"

"Intersex?"

"People born chromosomally one sex but have the opposite genitals."

"And why the *Q* if you already have *G* for 'gay'?"

"Because a person can identify as queer or questioning without necessarily being gay."

"You seem to know a lot about this stuff." Clay laughs. "They should have a *C* for 'confused.'"

"Kids are way more accepting these days."

"I suppose, but I'm old school when it comes to college." He turns and stares at me. "How do you know all this?"

"I just do," I say. "Don't you think it'll be a better world when Zack or Zadie go off to college?"

"I'm not so sure, the way things are going."

"You'll still love them, right? However they turn out?"

"Of course. Whatever letter they choose to be, I'll always love them."

"Very funny," I say. "No person should be attacked because of his or her racial makeup or how they identify."

"I came here, didn't I?"

"I wanted you to come to this vigil because you want to be here, Clay. Because you want to effect change and create a more equitable society."

"Yeah, that too," he says, more to appease me than anything else.

I squeeze his hand as we pass the library and then the admissions office until we arrive at the quad. It's such a beautiful campus, especially at night and with hundreds of people holding candles in support. A stage has been set up in front of Gordon Memorial Chapel. All around me people are huddled together in solidarity, anticipating the start of this vigil. Voices whisper in hushed tones. People hold up signs with the words BRING BACK MYCAH and RACISM with a red line through it.

Someone passes us candles and we light them from a neighbor's wick. Once they're lit, I grab Clay's hand again. It feels rough and calloused, yet protective at the same time. I love his big brewer's hands. Looking into his eyes, I can tell he's been drinking. It's part of his job, or so he tells me. He claims that he needs to be doing quality control throughout the day. Like a chef tasting his food. I know he's right, but I still don't like that he drinks all day, every day of the week. If unchecked, it could turn into a real problem.

Then again I should be the last person to lecture him about drinking, especially after consuming nearly a bottle of wine earlier in the day. But that's an anomaly, not something I do on a regular basis.

Without warning, the crowd starts to sing "We Will Overcome." It's a beautiful moment and my voice gets lost in the chorus echoing off the buildings enveloping us. It's a moving tribute. I turn and look at Clay and notice his narrowed lips and furrowed brow; he's not even pretending to care. It hurts my feelings that he won't even try for my sake. He's wearing the same grubby clothes he wore all day at the brewery. It even looks like he has lipstick on his collar, although I know he'd never cheat on me.

After a few student speeches decrying the history of racism on campus, Clarissa takes the stage to mild applause. She's dressed in a stunning orange and blue African bazin and head tie. Her caramel complexion radiates against the flickering candlelight. Dangling from her ears are gold disks with the continent of Africa stamped out of the middle.

She speaks and her powerful voice resonates across campus, becoming almost unrecognizable to me. Its eloquence echoes far and wide, and I can't quite believe that this is the same harried woman I spoke to just a few hours earlier.

She speaks about Mycah in the past tense, as if the girl is dead. She speaks about her as if she's a martyr for the cause, recognizing her contribution to social justice and racial equality. Then in the next breath she calls for a moment of silence, asking people to pray for the girl's safe return.

Everything happens in a blur, and before I know it, we're marching through campus, singing a protest song and holding up our candles. It nearly brings me to tears. Clay shuffles next to me, silent and brooding, eager to head back to his truck. It frustrates me that he refuses to fully participate. He's the one who moved me three thousand miles across the country. Ripped me away from my comfortable surroundings to live in this frigid, hostile state.

How I miss the Pacific Northwest and the Puget Sound. The smell of pine trees and the gentle mist that falls much of the year. I miss the mountain ranges that rise up on both sides of the city, giving Seattleites their spectacular views. I miss talking politics with my group of stay-at-home moms, and drinking lattes as our children play together in the parks.

We straggle back to the car afterward, Clay pulling me faster than I care to go. The occasion is somber, powerful, and I don't want to tarnish it with haste. Truthfully, I don't want the night to end. For the first time since moving here, I feel a part of something bigger.

"That was beautiful," I say once we're back inside the truck.

Clay turns and looks at me oddly, nodding in a way that is meant to be dismissive. I've noticed that his attitude has changed over the last ten years. No longer does he care about the social issues that we once shared. Age and fatherhood have narrowed his views in a way I don't find appealing. All his interests have converged on to one thing: beer.

"Didn't you find the vigil moving?" I ask.

"It was okay."

"Just okay?"

"Yeah. Okay."

"You don't think it was a beautiful tribute?"

He laughs.

I cross my arms and turn away from him. "I could tell you didn't want to be there."

"Jesus, is this going to turn into another argument?" He turns on the radio and the news comes on.

"I was just asking a simple question."

"Look, Leah, I'm sorry that girl has gone missing. But the truth is, I found the whole thing laughable."

"In what way?"

"Nothing they said or did will bring that girl back. In fact, the whole event turned into one long political statement about how minorities are being oppressed in this country."

"It's true."

"Bullshit. They turned that ceremony into a civil rights movement. They made it seem like all white people are racists for merely existing. Anyone could have kidnapped her. It could have been a bunch of black gangbangers who took Mycah, for all we know."

I'm stunned by his comments. It strikes me as odd that he said her name, as if he somehow knew the girl. Then again, maybe he did know her. She was of legal drinking age. It's entirely possible she was a frequent visitor to his brewery.

"Did you know her?"

He laughs nervously. "I knew who she was."

"How so?"

"She came to the brewery on occasion with some of her friends. I stopped a few times and talked to them. And trust me, you have no idea of the kind of crazy shit that goes on on that campus."

"I didn't realize you knew her."

"I didn't really know her. Just to say hi. I recognized her one day when they put her picture in the newspaper."

"And you never thought to tell me?"

"I didn't think it was a big deal."

"Why wouldn't you? You knew how interested I was in the case."

He shrugs like a little kid.

"What in the world did you talk to her about?"

He's about to explain when his mouth goes slack.

The truck accelerates down the empty road as he turns the volume up on the radio. What is he doing? I turn to complain, but he shushes me with a finger to his lips. This demeaning gesture makes me feel like a little girl again. I turn to protest when I hear the reporter's voice over the radio.

Mycah Jones was pregnant. . . .

LEAH

Monday, October 12, 8:37 p.m.

I'M SHAKEN BY THE NEWS AND ONCE HOME POUR MY-
self a glass of wine. Molly said the children played
beautifully together and were no problem. Clay paid
Molly her usual fee plus some, and then she drove
off, leaving four sleepy kids watching *Toy Story* in
our living room.

Although I'm furious with Clay, I can see that he is
exhausted from working all day, not that exhaustion
has ever stopped me from arguing before. The kids are
happily ensconced in the living room, sprawled over
the floor in their pajamas, heads resting on pillows
while watching Woody and Buzz. I don't want to ruin
the good mood. A particular vision forms in my head
of our families growing close, hanging out on snowy
nights while the kids play board games in the other
room. I see the four of us going through bottles of wine

and beer and reveling in our intelligent and witty conversations, bragging about how beautiful our children are.

Clay, as if apologizing for his earlier behavior, offers to stay up with the kids until the Gaineses come to take them home. Instead, I tell him to go to bed. My goodwill this evening is based entirely on selfish motives. Besides, I'm too hyper to sleep. I want to meet Clarissa at the door and praise her for delivering such an amazing speech.

The movie is almost over by the time I collapse on the couch with my third glass of wine. Zack has already fallen asleep next to Willie. Zadie is drifting in and out of consciousness. Only Sasha is still bright eyed and fully engaged in Buzz and Woody's epic adventure. I love *Toy Story* as much as the children.

But tonight I find it difficult to concentrate on the movie. All I can think about is the missing girl and the child she's carrying. Various theories come to mind. The news reporter didn't give any more details about the case, and her boyfriend doesn't remember anything about the assault other than that vaguely recalled racial slur. Maybe Cordell is behind his girlfriend's kidnapping. It's entirely possible that she conceived in order to prevent him from leaving her.

After I polish off my third glass of wine, my eyelids succumb to gravity. Sometime later I find myself being awakened by the familiar chime of the doorbell. I jerk my head up and look around the living room in panic. The movie menu is playing over and over on the flat-screen. All the kids are asleep, stretched out in their pajamas in awkward poses. I step over Zack's body and check myself in the mirror above the mantel. Holy crap, I look horrible. The doorbell rings again. Through the window I see that all the lights are on in the Gaineses' house. Cars are parked in their driveway and all around the cul-de-sac.

What's going on?

I stand by the window as the doorbell rings two more times in succession. Are the Gaineses having a party without me? Not that I'm in any mood to socialize with complete strangers: I'm tired and still processing the news of Mycah's pregnancy. I need to put the children to bed. But seriously. This get-together angers me. An invitation would have been nice, considering that I was the one who arranged for our babysitter to watch their kids. But then I realize that it's not too late and that Clarissa is possibly waiting outside to invite me over for introductions. Oh yes, and refreshments. I laugh at my silly predilection for rushing to judgment. Certainly, she's going to ask me over and introduce me to all her wonderful friends. It's late, so I promise myself to stay for just one drink.

Happily, I check myself in the mirror one last time. My hair is frizzy along the edges and sticking up everywhere. The creases around my eyes appear more pronounced than ever. I straighten everything out as best I can, ready to congratulate Clarissa on giving such a magnanimous speech. But when I open the door, I'm stunned to see Clarissa's husband standing there in his dark blue suit. He's tall and well built and at least a decade older than his wife. He reminds me of that famous basketball player the way he carries himself. He's confident to a fault. Almost arrogantly so. I stare at him and wonder why Clarissa didn't come over here and pick up the kids herself.

"Hey there. I'm here to pick up Sasha and Willie?"

"Yes, of course. Come inside."

He steps across the threshold and I close the door behind him. Flustered, I can't remember if we've been formally introduced. Then I remember the time I brought over pie and wine. He stands quietly, content not to chat, gazing around our cluttered living room as if it's the last place he wants to be right now. So embarrassing. It takes me a few seconds to remember his name. Russell. When he sees his children sprawled out on the floor, he goes over and picks Willie up and cradles the boy in his powerful arms. I gently wake Sasha. She sits up and yawns, stretching her skinny arms above her head.

"Wake up, Sasha. Your father's here," I whisper.

"Okay."

"Did you like the movie?"

"What movie?" She yawns again.

"*Toy Story*."

"Uh-huh."

She rubs her eyes and I help her stand. It pleases me that our kids got along so well. But then I remember the Gaineses' party tonight and the fact that we weren't invited, and I become all ruffled again. This obvious slight stings me. Should I say something to him? I open my mouth to inquire about the get-together when I hear Clay's voice calling out.

"Hey, Russell," Clay says, standing at the foot of the stairs in his pajamas.

"What's up, man?" Russell says to Clay. "Thanks for watching the kids."

"No problem," says Clay, selfishly taking all the

credit when I was the one who offered Molly's services.

"We didn't watch them, actually. Our babysitter did," I say. "We were at the vigil tonight. Just like you."

"Oh. That's cool."

"Wasn't it beautiful?"

"Yeah, real nice vigil." He grabs Sasha's hand and smiles stiffly at me as he turns to leave. "Have a nice night."

"Throwing a party tonight?" I ask.

He turns and stares at me as if I asked a personal question. "Having a few close friends over. We'll try to keep the noise down." He winks at Clay, and that condescending gesture irritates me.

"Would you please tell Clarissa I thought her speech was amazing?"

"Will do," Russell says.

"So what's the occasion?" I ask.

"Occasion for what?"

"The get-together."

"We're having some people over from the college. People who knew the missing girl," he says, struggling with the door. Clay walks over and opens it for him.

"How's Clarissa? She seemed nervous when I was over at your house this afternoon," I say.

"You were at my house today?" he asks, looking surprised.

"We had a few glasses of wine together. I arranged for our sitter to watch the kids." I shoot Clay a glance.

"She's good." He turns to Clay and says, "Take care, man. See you around."

I wait for Clay to shut the door. He looks at me

sleepily, his ripped Pearl Jam T-shirt scrunched over his slight paunch. It bothers me that he seems to know Russell better than I know Clarissa.

It suddenly occurs to me that the Gaineses didn't chip in for the babysitter. Clarissa said they'd help off-set the cost, and then they didn't. It's not about the money. Had they invited us over for a quick drink and introductions, I would have let it go. Been totally fine with it. But they didn't even do that and it infuriates me.

Clay comes over and puts his arm around me in a curious manner, swiping a misplaced hair out of my eye. His breath repulses me and I turn slightly away from him. I have no intention of making love to him tonight, if that's what he's after. I'm angry, sad, and confused. I'm a good person. I can't believe the Gaineses are having a party next door without us.

"What?" Clay says.

"I'm not in the mood for *that*."

"Mood for what?"

"You know."

"What's the matter with you?"

"A girl has gone missing, is possibly dead, and our next-door neighbors are having a party. Doesn't that strike you as odd?"

"They're colleagues and sharing some stories about her."

"They didn't even pitch in for the sitter."

"You're going to make a stink over a lousy twenty bucks?"

"They make way more money than you do."

"Do you know how much Russell and his friends spend at the brewery?" He removes his arm from my shoulder. "He takes his staff and colleagues there every Friday afternoon for beers."

"God, I'm so sick of hearing about your stupid brewery. Could you please put me first just this once?"

I stomp up to my room, forcing him to put the children to bed by himself. Besides, I know he's right and that I'm being petty and selfish. I can't tell him the real reason I'm so mad. He doesn't understand how lonely I've been or how much I want to move back home. Or how badly I want Clarissa to be my close confidante and friend. What is it about her that's causing me such turmoil? Why do I so want to please her? If she only took the time to know me, to know my family, I'm sure that we could become good friends.

Once under the blanket, I bury my head in the pillow and try to muffle my sobs. Tomorrow will be a new day. A better day, I hope. It has to be. I realize that I need to learn more about the missing girl if I want to become friends with Clarissa. I need to do a little digging around and see what I can find out about this mysterious Mycah Jones.

LEAH

Tuesday, October 13, 7:45 a.m.

*I*T'S A GLORIOUS FALL MORNING AND THE SUN'S RAYS pour through the wood shutters. Clay's side of the bed is empty. He's been going into the brewery before dawn each morning in order to get a jump start on the day.

I wake my blue-eyed monsters and tell them to get ready for school. I'm not angry anymore. Clarissa's slight only makes me more determined to show her my worthiness. It may take some time, but she'll eventually come around and see what a good person I am. She'll understand my commitment to progressive causes and racial equality.

I prepare breakfast and make school lunches. Mr. Shady's bowl is empty, so I fill it with pellets. I brew up a fresh pot of coffee, take out my favorite "World's Best Mom" cup, and pour it to the top along with some cream and sugar. I stop for a moment and stare out the window. All is quiet in the neighborhood. The guests have long gone and the unfinished development returns to its bleak denouement.

The colors along the nearby hills are deepening. I move to the sliding door, expecting to see the starlings, but to my disappointment they're nowhere in sight. As I step onto the deck, my breath lingers in the brisk fall air. The sky is baby blue and laced with ribbed clouds. To my delight, three deer prance around in the field behind us. But I miss the starlings and their twisty transports. They feel like an integral part of me now, connecting me as much to this town as they do to something greater in the universe.

I glance over at the Gaineses' deck. Clarissa is nowhere to be seen. She's probably inside, getting the kids ready for school. I wonder if she knows that I'm out here and is too embarrassed to face me.

Zack comes down, his hair sticking out in every direction. I wet it down with water and gel so that it will lie flat. I run a comb through it, flipping the bangs up so that he looks somewhat stylish, but he quickly flattens it back down with his hands. Zadie sits quietly at the kitchen table, dressed in a blue skirt and blouse, her long blond hair combed into a neat ponytail. I'm always awed at how beautiful my children are. It's incredible to think that they came out of this body.

The twins eat their breakfast, gather their backpacks, and the three of us walk silently down to the bus stop.

It still amazes me that I had twins after two years of fruitlessly trying to have children. We'd always discussed having children, and we both agreed that two would be our limit. Then we tried, whenever we could, and failed for nearly two frustrating years. I nearly gave up when the startling news came that I was pregnant. And twins at that. In one fell swoop we had an entire family. I wept with joy. It meant that Clay and I could stop pressing and relax. The news came at a very good time in our marriage. The strain of trying to produce a child had begun to tear at the frayed edges of our relationship. The twins changed everything. I didn't feel compelled to have as much sex after they were born, and I believed Clay shared these feelings.

Twins beget twins, they say. It runs in the family. A long time ago I had a twin, but I try not to think about her so much these days. Or I hadn't thought about her until that mysterious letter arrived yesterday. It forced me to think about poor Annie again. The doctors claimed she had the mind of a two-year-old, but I never believed that silly diagnosis. I intuited that she was far more intelligent than she let on. Was I the only person who could see this? Who understood her?

The twins and I stand like statues until the bus arrives. I kiss them good-bye and then watch as it motors off with its precious cargo. As soon as they're gone, I realize how abysmally lonely I am and how much I miss human contact. Alone, I cease being Leah the dutiful mother and wife. When I'm alone I become the other Leah. The Leah from a long time ago whom I've been trying to forget.

I often wonder about what part of me I'm trying to forget. Is it the sad little girl who was too overprotective of her twin sister? The teenage Leah forced to live with relatives who clearly didn't want her? Maybe the young adult Leah who found it difficult to make friends and spent much of her college years holed up in the library and studying.

There are things I did that I'm certainly not proud of, and I hope Annie didn't hold it against me. If she could only see me now she'd know that I'm a good mother and person. Family life has changed me for the better. My experience with my own children has convinced me that I would never be like my parents. I would raise my kids differently and tell them every day how much I loved them. Not a day would pass when they'd doubt my love for them. Never would they question their love for one another or experience the turmoil that Annie and I had to go through.

I turn toward the deserted cul-de-sac and head back up the hill. I know I should go home and take Mr. Shady out for a walk, but instead I head over to the Gaineses' house. All the cars are gone, the kids shipped off to school. Alone again, my mind stirs with theories about the missing girl.

I look back one last time to make sure no one is watching. Certain that I'm by myself, I climb the stairs until I'm standing on their porch. Oddly, this never gets old. The door opens as usual and a sense of excitement fills me as I slip inside their house. What I'm doing is so wrong, yet I can't seem to help myself. I can't help being that Leah from a long time ago.

Everything looks exactly as it did yesterday except for the missing figurine. After being snubbed last night, I'm glad I took it. I walk around the living room, brushing my hands over metal sculptures and African tribal masks. Her taste is so refined that it nearly makes me cry. I walk over to the kitchen island and swipe my hand across the smooth granite countertop. I peek into their oversized fridge. Every shelf is filled with meats, cheeses, and expensive treats. I grab a nearly full bottle of Pinot Grigio, remove the cork, and take a long, delicious swig. It's way too early to start in on the wine, but I don't care now. Getting slighted by her last night still stings and I will do whatever I want, when I want.

I sit at the kitchen island for a few minutes and enjoy more of their wine.

Sometime later, up the stairs I go. I've never explored the second floor. The kids' rooms are neat and orderly. I slip into the master bedroom. A tinge of jealousy fills me at first glance. It's much bigger than ours and has an attached full bathroom with a hot tub. It's spotless and classy. There are family photos hung along the walls. Camping in the woods. Hiking up a mountain trail. At the beach. I open a few drawers but find only clothes. It thrills me to be going through Clarissa's things. She deserves such shabby treatment after the terrible way she snubbed me last night.

And then I find it, and it gives me the biggest thrill to date. A white dildo lies under her clothes and along the bottom of the drawer. I laugh hysterically. I'm no prude, not much of one anyway, but this really surprises me. I've heard about women who use such things, but up until now have never actually met one. I run my fingers along the rubber shaft, wondering how someone could possibly insert such a device into their body. I'm trembling with excitement knowing that I'm holding something taboo and so intimately connected to Clarissa. Does her husband know she keeps a *white* dildo instead of a black one? What does owning a white dildo say about her? That she prefers white men to black? Maybe the store was sold out of black ones. The irony causes me to laugh as I place it back under the folded clothes where I discovered it.

What else can I find? I snoop inside her nightstand until I come across an even bigger prize: a diary. It's clearly Clarissa's, judging by the pink color. I hold it in my hand as the first effects of the wine begin to worm deep into my cerebral cortex. Titillation fills me. I want badly to read it, but the darn thing is locked. How I'd love to know all her fears and innermost thoughts. If only I could open it, then maybe I could understand what makes her tick.

I shake it in frustration, but it fails to budge. I search frantically for the key, moving all the clothes aside in order to find it, but it is nowhere to be seen. I move to the drawers and search inside. As I'm doing this, the sound of a car door slams outside, causing me to freeze. *This is not supposed to happen.* I move to the window and see Clarissa's car parked in the driveway. I can't believe she's come home so early, the one day I chose to snoop around. In all the time I've been watching her, she's never returned at this hour.

What am I going to do?

The front door opens and closes. Panicked, I scramble around, trying desperately to put everything back in its place. I hope she won't come up to the bedroom.

I hear her voice downstairs and realize that she's talking to someone on the phone. Kneeling next to the bed, I remain perfectly still. But then the sound of her footsteps coming up the stairs fills me with dread. Her voice becomes louder the higher she climbs. I search for a place to hide. It's then that I notice that the top drawer of her nightstand is open. *Darn.* It's too late for me to close it without being seen. I slip under the bed and slide to the middle of the floor.

The mattress sags once Clarissa sits on it. She's crying. Her words are muffled, but I can tell that she's involved in a heated discussion. What's wrong? She stops sobbing and stands next to the bed. Her high heels come off. Then her dress and shirt fall to the carpet. Her bra and underwear come off next until I presume she's naked. Is she going to take a shower?

She says she misses someone. But who?

I realize I have to pee. Oh God. The coffee and wine have caught up to me, and I squirm in discomfort. Clarissa moves to the dresser and opens one of the drawers. She removes something that I cannot see. I try to look over my extended toes, but instead I tap my forehead against the overhead board. Ouch. Something lands on the floor to my right. I turn and see the long white head of the dildo pointing toward me. She leans over to pick it up but accidentally kicks it further under the bed until the dildo is resting against my arm.

Clarissa falls to her knees and I can clearly hear the sound of her voice. The words coming out of her mouth are dirty and sexually provocative. Her hand feels along the floor for the dildo. I grab it by the head and push it within reach of her hand. Her long nails tap along the oak floor and I notice that she has taken off her wedding ring. It takes a few seconds, but then she finds it and jumps back onto the bed.

Safe for now.

My bladder is pulsating and I'm afraid I might let

go. Above me the mattress is bouncing inches from my face. Clarissa moans loudly, shouting that she's a nasty whore and a dirty ho. A nigger bitch in need of a lesson. It pains me to hear such foul language coming out of her mouth.

I want to pee so bad it hurts, yet I'm also dispirited by her dirty little secret. Clarissa pleasures herself just above me, and for whatever reason, I can't conform this behavior to my perception of her. I've never before used a dildo and have no intention to ever start. Clay and I make love twice a month, scheduled on the calendar and in a darkened room. He's pleaded with me to try other positions, other "acts," but I keep telling him that I'm not ready for it. The one time I tried to please him, he came too early and I gagged and ran out of the room. He apologized profusely, but I stomped out of the bedroom, humiliated and sick to my stomach, swearing to never attempt that "act" again. I showered and gargled for over an hour, trying to get that taste out of my mouth. I didn't speak to Clay for three days, and it took quite a long time before he won back my trust.

Clarissa moans and finally lets out a shrill scream. Then there is silence. The silence seems far stranger than her loud cries of pleasure, and I imagine her sex toy lying on the bed next to her, glistening with bodily unguents and fluids. But it doesn't last. She goes into the bathroom. I hear the shower running and in less than five minutes she's back in the room and getting dressed. Her phone rings and she picks up, strapping on her high heels as she talks. I slide over, trying to make out what she is saying, but realize that she's speaking in hushed tones.

Once she's put on her heels, Clarissa stands and faces the bed. She ends the call and walks around to the other side. I'm so engrossed in her movements that I momentarily forget that I have to pee. She faces the nightstand and makes a strange noise that sounds like a gasp. She stands there for nearly a minute before slamming shut the top drawer that I'd failed to close. A few minutes later I hear the front door close. The Mercedes roars to life and then races out of the cul-de-sac. The sound of the motor eventually fades into the background.

Shaking with fear, I stay under the bed until I'm sure she's gone. Part of me still thinks she's inside the house, waiting to lash out at me for spying on her. Or maybe she parked down the road and is in hiding, hoping to ensnare me once I slip out the front door.

After thirty minutes I slither out from under the bed and into the bathroom. My bladder finally lets go and it's a welcome relief. I sit on that toilet for what seems like a long time, until I feel empty inside. I'm filled with a tremendous guilt for sneaking in here and spying on my neighbor. I wait another ten minutes before deciding to leave. I spray the room with freshener until it smells like a tropical rain forest.

Once home, I shower for over an hour, trying to erase the memory of Clarissa grabbing for that dildo. I'm still trembling when I emerge, my normally pale skin red and shriveled. Never in my life have I invaded a person's privacy in such a devious and criminal way. Yet part of me still trembles with excitement from this newfound discovery. What I have done is sick and a complete invasion of her privacy, yet it doesn't bother me as much as I thought it would. I'm so pathetically lonely that I'll do just about anything to be liked and accepted. And what better way to do this than to become friends with Clarissa. She could open a whole new world for me, and if it requires a little underhanded behavior to accomplish this, then so be it.

CLAY

Tuesday, October 13, 10:13 a.m.

I'D BEEN WORKING LONG DAYS AND NIGHTS AT THE brewery when my relationship with Mycah first began. Leah and the kids were still in Seattle at the time, preparing for the big move. Time and circumstance converged to create the perfect storm for my cheating ways.

The first few months at the brewery were the most difficult. I ran into some unexpected problems with asbestos-wrapped pipes and faulty drainage. We gutted the inside, and with the help of a local asbestos crew, we worked night and day to put it back together. A local carpenter rebuilt the oak bar in the tasting room using salvaged wood, and he framed the walls and ceiling. After the new wiring, plumbing, and French drains had been installed, I began to assemble the stainless steel kettles and brewing equipment.

I was sitting against the exterior of the building, having my first coffee of the day, when I saw this angelic-looking thing walking in my direction.

She stopped and smiled at me as I puffed on a cigarette (I'd started smoking again). Unable to take my eyes off her, I gladly returned the attention. Hell, I couldn't remember the last time a beautiful girl smiled at me like that. For a brief moment I felt desirable again.

"Hey, you," she said.

"Hey."

"Mind if I bum a smoke?"

"These things are bad for you, if you haven't noticed."

"Oh, I've noticed. But there's a lot worse habits one can have than smoking."

I pulled one out, lit it with the end of mine, and passed it to her.

"I never should have started when I was in high school," she said.

"I recently fell off the wagon."

"Expensive too."

"And you can forget about your breath."

"Not the best habit to have when you want to kiss someone."

I laughed at her brashness. "Anyone in particular?"

"Maybe." She walked over and stuck her head inside the garage door. "What's it going to be?"

"A brewery."

"For real?"

"One thing I never lie about and that's beer."

"I know people who lie about more important things."

"What's more important than beer?" I laughed. "Are you a connoisseur?"

"Who doesn't like a cold one every now and then?"

"Most ladies prefer wine or fruity cocktails."

"Who said I was a lady?"

"My sincerest apologies."

"No worries," she said, waving her hand. "So tell me, is it hard to make?"

"Beer making's a very simple process, yet extremely complex at the same time, if that answers your question. Would you like a tour?"

"Thought you'd never ask."

"You'll have to bear with me; it's still a work in progress."

"Isn't everything in life a work in progress?" she said, holding out her hand. "Mycah Jones."

"Clay Daniels, president and CEO of Rustic Barn Brewery." I grabbed her hand in my own and felt a distinct thrill.

I moved aside to let her enter and showed her around. There wasn't much to see, as I hadn't finished installing the kettles and fermenters. The sophisticated electric panel used to control the brewing system sat idle on a workbench. The tour was relatively quick. I didn't want to bore her with the mundane details of brewing, but she seemed genuinely interested in what I had to say. We made our way into the unfinished tasting room, where I'd installed the refrigeration system. We pulled two stools up to the oak bar. A few nights earlier I'd kegged one of my experimental brews and hooked it up to the tap. Moving behind the bar, I poured her a beer, making sure to top it off with a nice head. I passed one glass to her and then poured one for myself.

"It smells yeasty," she said, nose in her glass. "Like fresh bread."

"That's the noble hops you're smelling." I lifted my glass. "Cheers."

"Cheers." She raised a toast and drank.

"What do you think?"

"Wow. It's so clean and crisp." She pressed her lips together in a way I found unbelievably sexy. "Shouldn't you have asked to see my ID first?"

"I was always taught never to ask a woman's age."

"You were taught well." She took another sip. "I'm not sure what else I'm tasting here, but it's complex."

"There's a bit of a grassy hop flavor with a slight bitterness. Also a touch of pils malt near the finish."

"Your palate's obviously more refined than mine."

"Brewing beer's been my passion for quite some time now." I lifted my glass and studied the amber liquid.

"Dude, this beer is amazing." She smiled at me with the most beautiful green eyes, and I had to admit it felt awesome to be the object of this girl's attention.

"So what do you do?"

"I'm a student at Chadwick College, majoring in social justice."

"What does that qualify you to do?"

"I hope to be a civil rights lawyer someday."

"Very admirable, although you'll not have much time for beer while in law school."

"It's all about making time for the things we most desire in life."

"So true."

"Damn straight, beer man." She drained the remainder of her beer. Once it was empty, she hopped off her stool and headed toward the exit. "I'll see you around."

"You know where to find me."

"Clay Daniels, brewer and patriot." She hitched her bag over her shoulder and disappeared from sight.

I walked over to the door and watched as she moseyed down the sidewalk, her white summer dress rippling in the wind. I felt intensely happy after the brief encounter. She'd lit something inside me that I thought had long been extinguished. It came as a revelation that I could feel so damn good about myself. What had I been missing all those years?

Yes, I missed my family in the most abstract sense. I loved Leah, but I also knew that once we were back together, I'd quickly become irritable and need my space. Leah, with all her quirks and odd behaviors, could wear a man down. She was high maintenance. Needy. Obsessed about the craziest of things. She often drove me crazy about the most inconsequential matters.

Maybe it's my imagination, but it seems as if my children resent me for having moved them from the only home they ever knew. Not so much Zadie, but certainly Zack. He's constantly rebuffing my affection. I thought he'd eventually come around, but so far he hasn't. He refuses to hug or kiss me. In fact, he rarely even talks to me unless I take him aside and force the issue. Then he sits quietly, staring past me until I leave him alone. Thankfully, Zadie still loves me, showering me with hugs and kisses whenever I come home.

I sit in my abandoned brewery, regretting that fateful day I met Mycah Jones. A fresh beer sits on the concrete floor beneath my feet. I'm exhausted from sanitizing fermenting tanks and loading sacks of grain.

Any day now, I expect the police to walk in here and start questioning me about my connection to Mycah. They'll ask me about her disappearance and how well I knew her. But I can't tell them anything. I need to keep that part of my life secret if I want my family to remain intact. Otherwise, this secret will spread like cancer and destroy us. And if that happens, my life will be over.

LEAH

Tuesday, October 13, 11:08 p.m.

*C*LAY COMES HOME QUITE LATE AS I SIT IN THE LIV-
ing room, reading my novel. I love Jane Smiley but
can't quite get into this one. Maybe it's my frame of
mind. Or maybe the book really is a stinker. Every
author has one. Oftentimes I feel like I'm the main
character in a bad novel.

Clay's tired and mindless of my presence, stum-
bling around in the dark and acting weird. He gives me
a perfunctory kiss on the top of my head and then
grabs a beer out of the fridge. By the way he moves, I
can tell he's been drinking again. He's getting worse. I
think the pressure of running a business is starting to
weigh on him.

He grunts something unintelligible and I badly want to
tell him what happened over at the Gaineses' house today.

But I know better. Mr. Shady wakes up and stretches for a few seconds before strolling over to greet his master.

"How was your day?" he asks.

"Uneventful. Went for a run. Zack and Zadie had a good day at school. Zack, as usual, went up to his room and stayed there until dinner."

"What the hell's wrong with him?"

"It might take some time for him to get adjusted to his new home."

"Damn kid." He gulps his beer and scratches Mr. Shady along his backside. "I don't think Zack loves me."

"Of course he loves you. He's just going through a difficult phase now."

"Between you and me, I think he's being a stubborn little asshole."

"Shhh. He might hear you."

"I don't really care if he hears me."

"You're drunk, Clay."

"I'm tired and cranky."

I mark the page in my book and place it on the coffee table. "Have you heard anything more about the missing girl?"

"Jesus, Leah, do we have to talk about that right now? It's so goddamn morbid."

"That's the problem, Clay; you don't talk to me about anything except beer, which I hate talking about."

"Isn't it enough that I went to that stupid vigil last night and was made to feel like a white supremacist?"

"I thought it was a beautiful ceremony."

"Please. That entire event was merely an excuse to make a political statement. They barely mentioned the poor girl's name."

"I moved all this way for you, Clay. Why can't you at least play along so I can fit in here?"

He seems taken aback by my words, but instead of standing to hug me, he puts his beer down and scratches Mr. Shady's butt.

I turn and walk upstairs to the bedroom. The hell with him. He's drunk and acting selfish. I have no intention of sleeping in the same bed with him tonight. I grab a blanket out of the closet, grab his pillows, and toss them down the stairwell. He can stay down there all night and get as drunk as he likes for all I care.

Despite what happened this morning, I feel I made some progress in my grand plan to befriend Clarissa. Tomorrow, I'll try again. There has to be more to this Mycah Jones story than what the police are telling us.

And I plan to find out.

LEAH

Wednesday, October 14, 7:37 a.m.

I SLEPT TERRIBLY, TOSSING AND TURNING ALL NIGHT, without Clay by my side. Mr. Shady greets me at the base of the stairs this morning, spinning in anxious desperation while waiting for his walk. But I don't feel like walking him. I open the sliding door leading to the patio and watch as he bolts out to the backyard and does his thing.

The morning is overcast and cold. A brisk wind blows down from the north. I cinch up my robe as Mr. Shady circles the yard in search of a good place to poo. He wanders aimlessly over to the Gaineses' backyard and plops his butt down over their manicured lawn and lets go. Clarissa will be furious when she sees it and will know that it was our dog that pooped there. I'm underdressed and too tired to go out in my bare feet to scoop it up. I remind myself to pick it up later after she leaves for work.

Mr. Shady scoots back inside the sliding door, and I chastise him loudly, squeezing his wet snout in my hand.

"Bad dog, Mr. Shady. You're not supposed to poo in our neighbors' yard." I tap his moist nose as he stares up at me. "I'm going to send you to the doggy pound if you keep it up. Do you know what they do to bad doggies at the pound?"

Mr. Shady stares up at me with a terrified expression.

I let go of him and he scampers into another room, far away from me.

Upon turning, I see Zack and Zadie staring at me from the kitchen table. Zadie has a finger in her mouth and is frowning.

"You're not really going to send Mr. Shady to the dog pound, are you, Momma?"

"Of course not, honey. Momma was just mad at him."

"They'll put him to sleep," Zack says.

"Shut up, Zack," Zadie says, punching her brother in the arm.

"Ow! She hit me," Zack complains.

"Keep your hands to yourself, Zadie."

"Zack was being mean to Mr. Shady."

"It's the truth," Zack says. "That's what they do to dogs at the pound."

"But what if Mr. Shady heard you?" Zadie says.

"Dogs don't understand us," Zack says spitefully.

"Oh yes they do," says Zadie. "Isn't that right, Momma?"

"Sometimes they do," I say. "Of course I would never send Mr. Shady to the pound."

"Zack could have hurt Mr. Shady's feelings," Zadie replies.

"It's stupid to punish a dog for going to the bathroom," Zack says. "Dogs act on instinct."

I laugh. "Since when have you become an expert on dog behavior?"

"I watched this show on dogs and they said that the punishment must be given the moment the act occurs or else it can seem random and cruel."

"Mr. Shady knows that pooping in our neighbors' yard is wrong."

"Pooping," says Zadie, laughing.

"Dogs are incapable of bad behavior," Zack continues. "They act according to instinct and pack behavior."

"For God's sake, Zack, are you eleven or thirty-seven?"

"Are you making fun of me?"

"I'm sorry, hon, I'm just tired," I say, walking over and wrapping my arms around him. He tenses up as I squeeze him to my chest. "I love you."

"Do they put unwanted kids to sleep too, Mommy?" Zadie asks.

"That's the dumbest thing I've ever heard," Zack says.

"No, dear, they don't," I say.

"Good. I was beginning to get worried," Zadie says.

What did Zadie mean by that? Is she feeling unloved? Unwanted? I've done my best to raise these two and protect them from the worst the world has to offer. When they were little and growing up in Seattle, they were always smiling, happy children. But now they're growing up and nearing their teen years, experiencing and feeling strange things that come with this age. I know I'm a good mother. And Clay, despite his drinking, loves his monsters to death. I bet it has something to do with moving across the country and settling in a foreign place. Hopefully, it's temporary and they'll return to their happy selves. I'll redouble my efforts in giving them all the attention they need. My goal is to return to those happy days when they were young and full of joy and so adorably cute.

I pour cereal into their bowls. Zack eats his without milk. It's reassuring to know that my child prodigy tests off the charts. His pediatrician claims that he manifests behaviors symptomatic of Asperger's, although it's not a full-blown case. I do love him, even if that love is sometimes skewed in the abstract.

Unrequited love pains me, especially from my own son. It's made worse by the fact that Zadie is so unusually loving and outgoing. The contrast in the twins is alarming. I try so hard to be sympathetic to his needs and to what he's going through. It's possible he's experiencing social anxiety. The move to Maine has been difficult for all of us, but especially for him, a boy used to routine and habit.

Afterward, they walk down to the bus stop by themselves. I'm too tired to take them. Truthfully, I'm relieved now that they're gone. I have precious little time to myself. In a few hours I'll be lonely again. I'm finding I don't want to be around the twins as much. For some odd reason they depress me. They wear me out and leave me exhausted. They often make me feel as if I'm a terrible mother. Worse, they remind me of my twin sister, Annie, whom I miss so much.

It's funny to think that we were identical twins because we looked nothing like each other. The reason for this was Annie's disability. It affected her muscles and bone structure, causing her limbs to become useless, twisted appendages. Her face was misshapen and her mouth forever contorted to one side of her face. Because of this she couldn't speak, the words unable to form over her spastic tongue. Despite these handicaps, we shared a bond that no one could break. She could read my mind just as readily as I could read hers. It was the one sure thing about us being identical twins, and we relished our unspoken pact.

I stare out the window, waiting for Clarissa and the kids to drive away. I don't care anymore about the morality of sneaking into her home and invading her privacy. I feel so lonely that I'll do virtually anything to be accepted. I wish Clay would shower me with more attention. Maybe treat me like one of his beers.

Ten minutes pass before Clarissa walks out the door, a child clasped in each hand. Wedged under her armpit is a leather briefcase. For some reason she looks different this morning, as if she threw her outfit together at the last minute. Yet she looks stunning. Her face is scrunched tight, and she looks pissed off about something. This is a side of her I've not yet seen. But after finding her dildo yesterday, it thrills me to know that she has a naughty side. That she uses a *white dildo* to get herself off. The secret knowledge of this puts me in a very advantageous position.

Mr. Shady paws at my pant leg for a walk. I tap him away with my foot, signaling that there'll be no walk this morning for being such a bad doggy. He's not my pet, anyway. Yes, I was the one who wanted a dog when we moved to Maine. Then for some strange reason Mr. Shady became attached to Clay. The little ingrate. I'm the one who walks and feeds him every day. Clay comes home late at night, and it doesn't matter how many biscuits or scraps I've slipped the dog throughout the day, he inevitably runs up and cuddles in Clay's lap. At night, he sleeps on the mattress, curled behind Clay's knees. Of course, he's nice to me when it's just the two of us here alone. He has no choice but to be nice to me. I suppose he tolerates me more than anything else. Maybe he thinks he's doing me a favor by allowing me to walk him around the neighborhood.

Mr. Shady barks and I nudge him away with my foot. But he refuses to give up.

"Go away, Mr. Shady. I'm not taking you for a walk this morning."

He lowers his ears, sticks his tail between his hind legs, and scampers off into the living room. Usually, I'd care about his hurt feelings, but right now I don't give a darn.

I turn on the radio and hear more news about the missing girl. Mycah Jones was three and a half months pregnant the night she was taken. Three members of the lacrosse team were brought into the station for questioning and then released. They were in town that evening and drinking late into the night at a frat bar. One of the players was seen staggering around the center of town near the time of the crime, a lacrosse stick in hand. The players claimed they'd just come from a scrimmage and didn't have time to lock up their gear.

The news finishes and a song comes on by the Barenaked Ladies. I'm intrigued by this new development and want to know more. It keeps my mind occupied. I want to know what happened to this poor girl. I want to know more about Clarissa and her hopes and dreams. It occurs to me that if I want to know more, I'll need to take it upon myself to find out. Dig around and be proactive. The facts won't jump up out of thin air and magically appear to me. I'm certainly not afraid to be assertive when the situation calls for it, to go after the things in life I need.

I've waited in this empty house long enough. It's been over thirty minutes since Clarissa departed. I head out the front door, glancing furtively around to make sure no one sees me. Then again, I'm the only person in this neighborhood. I scamper up the porch and brashly open their front door. All is quiet, so I make my way upstairs. There'll be no wine drinking today. No ogling her furniture or art collection. I know exactly what I need to do and where to find it.

Her pink diary is exactly where she left it. I pull it out and then run my hand along the smooth bottom of the drawer, lifting out her satiny undergarments. There are some coins and what I imagine to be earrings. Then I feel it. A small metallic object with a jagged edge. I pull it out and realize, to my delight, that it's the key to her diary. This makes me so happy. It's as if I'd located a clue to an unsolved murder mystery.

I plop down on the bed and consider the morality of what I'm about to do. Oddly, it doesn't feel like an invasion of privacy. It feels quaintly spiritual, a way of connecting with another human being on a deeper level. We all have secrets. I have mine. She has hers. Having secrets is a trait that all humans share. Therefore, there can be no "real" secrets if we all have them.

I insert the key into the lock, hear the mechanism

pop, and open the book. There are ten pages dated and filled with entries. She's written something for each day. I imagine there must be dozens of other diaries stored in this house, detailing her life journey. But I'm not interested in them right now. I'm only concerned about the one in hand.

I read the first page, slightly disappointed by the pedestrian content. I expected something more profound and insightful. Not exactly Jane Smiley, but something with a bit more literary flair. She seems far more creative than this trite rehashing of the day's events. Kids, work, daily chores. Nothing heartfelt or emotional. But then I read page four and nearly fall off the bed. It hits me so hard that I must close my eyelids and calm myself down. I slowly open my eyes and reread the passage.

Tuesday, October 6
I woke up early as usual, the kids screaming and Russell in an exuberant mood, kissing me all over and apologizing for his shitty behavior last night. I shoved him away from me and served the children their breakfast, which consisted of a crappy bowl of cookie cereal drowned in milk. Then I did my best to ignore Russell until he left for work. Doesn't he know that his cheerful demeanor only pisses me off even more? WTF? He thinks he can make things right by acting all nice and romantic after humiliating me last night. The hell with him. Does he really think he can put his hands on me like that, and that I won't be angry come morning? Hell no,

I'm not letting that happen again. I keep telling him that I won't stand for it anymore, and that I'll leave, but then he pulls out his ace card and that shuts me up.

I feel trapped. I feel so lonely and objectified, like one of those Southern slaves servicing their master, only this master is black like me. If people only knew the truth about him and my marriage, then this delusional cruise ship we call the Happy Gaines Family would start to take on water and sink. The children don't deserve this. They don't know yet how to swim.

I skip a few more diary pages, my heart racing, and come to this.

Thursday, October 8

Is that why he had to go off at night and screw that little tramp? Because she did the nasty stuff that I refuse to do? Did she think she was better than me? Did she really think I didn't know that she was seducing her professor? Yeah, girl, I was on to you. And Russell knows I won't leave him. Because if I ever do, he'll expose me. But now I can expose him as well. Expose him as a lying, cheating son of a bitch who preys on his female students.

But seriously, who will give a damn that an intelligent, progressive black man like Russell Gaines cheats on his wife? It's a badge of honor these days to mess around. MLK, JFK, and Jesse Jackson did it, and they're icons. Bill Clinton, the first black president, screwed anything that moved. It's not fair that society glorifies these philanderers.

But what I've done is unforgivable in Russell's eyes. Bad, bad, bad for me if people find out. I'm sure I'll never live it down. But what other choice did I have at the time? It's who I am. It's been living deep inside me ever since I was a little girl.

I can barely control myself. What has she done? What is her secret? There's only a few pages left in the diary and I need to know. It's like some riveting best seller that I can't put down. Jane Smiley on steroids. Why won't Clarissa name names? Be more specific about who her husband slept with and how he's degrading her.

After a few more pages of trivial content, I turn to the last page, praying that there'll be something juicy and revealing.

Tuesday, October 13

It happened again last night. Twice in one month. The last time he struck me that hard was over a year ago. I can't take it anymore. I just can't. But I know I must. For the sake of the children I must stay strong.

I feel like killing myself and ending all the pain. But then I stepped onto the deck yesterday morning and saw all those magnificent birds and it reminded me that there's more to life than simply pain and suffering. A greater force is watch-

ing over me and I must surrender to it. God is real and good. Let's see how things play out. I will look for signs from God. Like those birds.

Oddly, I glanced over and saw that my neighbor was waving to me. Had she been watching me the entire time? It sort of creeped me out. I waved to her to be nice, trying not to look so worried. Maybe God sent her to this neighborhood to help me. I'm so lonely it hurts, and she seems like such a nice person, with a lovely family. She's pretty too. She almost looks like one of those delicate birds. I feel terrible for not being more friendly to her, but considering the circumstances I'm in, it's probably best she not be around Russell. Maybe one day I can open up to her about my problems. No, that's unlikely to happen. I can't risk it. I just can't risk losing everything.

The detectives are swarming around campus, asking about Mycah. They'll find the truth about her soon enough. She's not the martyr everyone is making her out to be. There's a side of that girl that will soon be made public, and it will come as a big surprise to people.

I so badly need help. God, please help me!!! I'm afraid and feel all alone. I miss Atlanta and all my friends. If there was only someone I could trust, a close friend I could open up to and explain the injustice being done. How that woman ruined my life and turned my husband against me.

That is the last page. How could she stop there? I flip through the remaining pages to see if maybe she scrawled something else, but all the pages are empty.

I stick the diary back in the drawer exactly where I found it. The key too. I run downstairs and check the patio door and realize that it's unlocked. I sneak out into the yard because it's easier to keep out of sight back there. Mr. Shady's mess greets my nose as I sprint over and slip inside the house. I'm intrigued by her entries. I need to know more about the connection between Clarissa and the missing girl, and what her husband has done to deserve such vitriol.

I collapse on the sofa and realize that my hands are shaking. What strikes me most is that Clarissa needs a friend as much as I do. So why is she pushing me away? I must convey to her, in the subtlest manner, that she can confide in me, and that I would never violate her trust. Russell's abusive behavior needs to stop. Should I report him to the police? I want to be a good friend, but at what point do I put our friendship aside and report a crime?

She must have a reason to keep this quiet, and this is something I know about. Russell is holding something over her, and if she speaks up, he will take the kids and deny her visitation rights. But what has she done to deserve this?

My cell phone rings, transporting me back to the dull existence that is my life. I look at the caller ID and see that it's from the twins' school. I don't want to speak to the staff there. I don't want to know what odd thing Zack has done this time. It seems he's in the guidance counselor's office every two weeks. But to ignore it would make matters worse.

"Hello?"

"Mrs. Daniels? This is Susan, the principal at Woodrow Wilson Elementary. I think you better come down here."

"What happened?"

"It's Zack."

"What has he done this time?"

"I think you better come over so we can discuss it."

"Okay, I'll be right there."

CLAY

Wednesday, October 14, 11:59 a.m.

*D*ETECTIVE ARMSTRONG PULLS UP NEXT TO THE brewery while I'm inventorying my supply of grains. He's already questioned me once, although briefly, about what happened the night Mycah Jones disappeared. I told him everything I care to share. That it was busy at the brewery that night, standing room only in the tasting room. Part of me thinks I should come right out and tell him the truth about our affair. But if Leah finds out what happened, our marriage will be over. She'll take the kids and move back to Seattle, and I'd lose the brewery and everything I worked for.

I look over and see Ben sanitizing the brew kettles. The plan is to brew another fresh batch this afternoon. This one will be a winter beer infused with vanilla beans, cinnamon sticks, and extracts from hazelnuts, raspberry, and cranberry. The finish will be chocolaty and robust, and I expect it to be a big hit when it premieres next month.

There's a knock at the garage door. Ben walks into the tasting room and lets Armstrong inside. I remember our last interview the morning after the girl went missing. We sat in a nearby coffee shop and I answered all his perfunctory questions. Ben walks the detective through the tasting room and into the heart of the brewery. I shake the man's hand and lead him away from the kettle.

A sheen of sweat begins to form over my forehead from scrubbing tanks all morning. I'm prepared to admit the truth if he forces the issue. The guilt is killing me, and in many ways it would be a relief to get this off my chest. Maybe Leah will forgive me and we can grow closer because of it. Or maybe not. It's a chance I'd rather not take.

Armstrong gazes around at all the shiny equipment. I pick up a scrubber brush and grip it in my gloved hand. At my feet is a bucket filled with hot water and bleach. Ben, a young man of few words, resumes sanitizing the kettles and fermenters. He's gotten so much better at the job these last few months. I've even given him a raise, despite ruining a fifty-gallon batch of my prized Czech pilsner.

"Sorry to bother you again, Mr. Daniels."

"No problem." He's a small and compact man with close-cropped black hair. "Armstrong, right?"

"You have a good memory." He glances around the brewery. "Quite a setup you have."

"It's an electric brewing system. State of the art. Beer practically makes itself."

"Excuse my ignorance, but I know nothing about brewing. My brother-in-law once roped me into brewing a pale ale with him, but I made a mess of it."

"You should give it another shot. It's cheap, fun, and you get to make the kind of beer you like."

"I'm afraid I'm not much of a beer drinker to begin with," he says. "So what's the biggest difference between your system and the old style?"

I wonder if he's merely making small talk, but I feel obliged to answer. As much as I love talking about beer and the craft of brewing, I have no desire to go into details with a relative novice. I'm nervous about being questioned and way behind schedule. Any minute now one of the local farmers will be showing up to haul away our spent grains so they can feed it to their hogs.

"The electric system regulates the mash temperature more accurately than with a flame. This allows me to brew a more consistent product each and every time." I laugh. "I hope I'm not boring you with the details, Detective. It's a much more complicated process than that, but that's the gist of it."

"Makes me wish I liked beer." He peers into the stainless steel brew kettle.

"I can't believe you're a cop and you don't like beer."

"Afraid not. It might come as a surprise, but I don't like donuts either."

"They might need to send you back to the police academy."

He laughs. "I suppose you could say I'm a bit of a health nut."

"You're not one of those vegans, are you?"

"No, I'm not that fanatical."

"The problem is you haven't had a really good craft beer yet. I'll make a convert of you soon enough."

"Perhaps." He takes out his notebook. "I'm more of a wine drinker."

"Come to the tasting room some night and I'll set you up with a sampler tray. You might be pleasantly surprised."

"I might take you up on that offer. Of course, I can't accept gifts."

"Don't worry, you'll be paying through the nose for my beer."

Armstrong smiles and I get the distinct impression that he's one of those guys who will never like beer. "I have a few more questions to ask you about the night Mycah Jones went missing."

"I told you everything when we met for coffee."

"Bear with me for just a few minutes. I'm merely trying to connect some dots."

"I'll help you in any way I can." My stomach churns as if my innards are being twisted into saltwater taffy.

"You said the tasting room was crowded the night she went missing and that Mycah Jones and her boyfriend were sitting by the fireplace." He points his pen toward the gas insert.

"Yes, we were very busy that night. Customers were lined up everywhere."

"Business that good?"

"That night it was."

"Had you seen them in here before?"

"A few times."

"Did you notice anything unusual that night?"

"Nah. I was too busy running between the brewery and the tasting room. Bree was pouring that night."

"You didn't overhear any arguments or see any unusual behavior?"

"Far from it. Everyone seemed to be in a really good mood. Honestly, Detective, we never have any problems in here."

"No one was drinking too much or acting crazy?"

"This isn't a dive bar that serves five-dollar pitchers of Natty Lite. I charge six dollars for the cheapest glass of beer. My clientele are connoisseurs and decidedly upscale. We ID everyone who comes through the door, regardless of how old they look. Keeping prices high is a good way to keep out the riffraff."

"And yet Mycah Jones and her boyfriend were here that night, and both of them are students at Chadwick College."

"I don't discriminate against race or college students. Everyone of legal age is welcome here."

"Did you know her?"

"Only to say hello sometimes when she came in. I remember her because they put her picture up on the TV."

"I ran a check on her credit card. It seems that the victim visited your pub quite often. The night she disappeared, she charged over thirty dollars to her Visa."

"Okay."

He pauses to look at his notes. "Did you know that she was an outspoken activist for Black Lives Matter?

It's probably why she had so many detractors on campus."

"College kids, right? They're all protesting something or another these days."

"The administrators at Chadwick tried to keep it all hush-hush, but we've learned quite a bit recently, including the fact that she was fourteen weeks pregnant."

"Yeah, I heard something about that on the radio, but I've been way too busy to keep up on it."

"She was attending Chadwick on a full scholarship."

I hear something calculating and rehearsed in his tone. Is he implying something? Does he suspect that I'm withholding information? Or that I was the one who impregnated her?

"They paid their tab and left without incident, Detective. What more can I tell you?"

"Her car was parked in the back lot the next morning."

"Maybe they drank too much and decided to walk back to campus. Considering that Chadwick is less than a mile down the road, I'm assuming they made a sensible decision."

"A sensible decision that possibly cost her her life."

"Sensible in that she knew better than to drink and drive."

He studies his notes again. "Did you talk to them that evening?"

"We chatted briefly. They wanted to buy me a beer, but I rarely drink when I'm working." My nose grows an inch.

"What did you talk about?"

"I probably asked how they liked the beer."

"How long have you been in town, Mr. Daniels?"

"The brewery opened in June. I spent most of the winter and spring getting it ready to open, commuting back to Seattle once a month to see my wife and kids. They stayed on the West Coast until our house was built in Deerfield Estates."

"That's the unfinished development on the outskirts of town. I heard the contractor just up and left," he says.

"One and the same."

"So you were here most of the summer?"

"Like I said, since last winter."

"If you don't mind me asking, Mr. Daniels, why did you move to Dearborn?"

I stop scrubbing and glare at him. Like my personal life is any of his goddamn business. "Seattle is a very expensive place to live and we couldn't afford to move out of our tiny bungalow and into something bigger. The twins were getting older and needed more space, and my son was diagnosed with a mild case of Asperger's."

"Sorry to hear that."

"No need. He's an extremely smart kid, but there were certain educational functions that weren't being met in his old school. We researched Maine and discovered that the educational system here in Dearborn was one of the best in the state."

"Yes, it's a fine school system."

"I figured I could open a brewery in town and do it much cheaper than I could in Seattle. The Portland beer scene is exploding and there's lots of demand. So that's how we ended up here."

"Interesting."

"Is there anything else?" I say, gesturing with the scrubber. "I've got a lot of work to do here."

"I suppose I have all the information I need for the moment," he says, closing his notebook. "Oh, one more thing while I'm here. I asked your pourer and she said you left the tasting room for about an hour that night. Would you mind telling me where you were?"

"I was wheelbarrowing the spent grain outside and loading it into the bins. One of the farmers was planning on picking it up in the morning, and I hate leaving it exposed and attracting all the mice and rats."

"And that took how long?"

"Roughly an hour, but I'm not entirely sure. Whatever it took to get the job done."

Armstrong thanks me and leaves. I resume scrubbing the inside of the tank with renewed frustration. I hate lying. More bleach. More scrubbing. I move from tank to tank, the muscles in my arms aching, the sweat pouring down my face. I need a break. No, I need a *beer*.

Mycah returned to the brewery a week after we first met. I'd be lying if I said I had stopped thinking about her. Often at night, tired and sore, and after sampling too much of my product that day, I would lie in my cheap hotel bed and think about her. What an exotic creature. So utterly and completely different than Leah. There was something about her that intrigued me. Never in my life had I dated a black girl (nor did I hold out any hope that this situation would change). When you're tired, lonely, and frightened about your financial future, you tend to focus on things outside your comfort zone. For some odd reason, my mind wouldn't let go of her. Of course, I never expected to see her again. I never expected her to walk into my unfinished brewery late at night while I was soldering copper pipes.

I'd left the door unlocked, as I always did. She sauntered in with a leather bag tossed haphazardly over her shoulder. At first I was confused. I had to remove my welding helmet in order to see better. But then I caught sight of her in the full light and my heart beat a little faster. She looked beautiful in the most slapdash way. She wore a tweed baseball cap with her raven hair tied up in pigtails. The look was both hot and sophisticated and gave me a whole new perspective on her. She was carrying a white bag from a nearby burger joint that was wildly popular with the college kids. The bag was saturated with grease.

"You've returned," I said.

"I was in town and saw your light on. You do know that it's just past eleven."

"I tend to lose track of time when I'm working."

"You must be starving to death," she said, standing over me and giving me a great view of her legs. I rose to my full height. In high heels, Mycah was only a few inches shorter than me.

"Come here to tease me?"

She laughed. "Don't flatter yourself, brewmeister. I come bearing a late night cheeseburger."

My face blushed. "I didn't mean it like that."

"Relax." She held out the bag. "Bet you're starving after making beer all day."

"Haven't eaten since noon." I reached into the greasy bag, past the fries and packets of ketchup, and pulled out a warm, pillowy burger wrapped in yellow wax.

"Not yet." She put her hand on my chest to stop me and I felt the rhythmic beat of my heart like a Harley Sportster bombing down the road. "I'll trade you for it."

"What would you like to trade?"

"How about one of those delicious beers you brew?"

"A beer for a burger? You strike a hard bargain." I unwrapped the wax paper. "I have plenty of beer. The question is, do you have enough burgers?"

"A double bacon cheeseburger and a large fries isn't enough?"

"My beer's worth *way* more than that."

"The pleasure of my company must count for something."

"I guess you have me there."

I led her into the tasting room. She sat at one of the wooden tables while I poured two mason jars of Rustic Barn Red, a beautiful burgundy-colored ale brewed using five different malts, three hops, and a specially cultured yeast. I poured thick heads, and when I brought them over, Mycah had already spread the burger out over the yellow wax paper. The aroma emanating from the burger tantalized me. In the middle of the table she'd dumped out the shoestring fries and covered them with a large dollop of ketchup and chipotle mayo.

"Here you go, madam," I said, setting the jar down in front of her.

"Thank you, good sir." She took a sip, leaving a mustache of foam over her upper lip.

"Where's your burger?"

"Not hungry."

"Then what brings you here tonight?" I asked.

"I went out with a few friends for drinks, saw your lights on, and thought I'd swing by and say hello."

"I think you're using me for my beer."

"Is that what you think?" She laughed, and it was a beautiful laugh that echoed throughout the empty tasting room. "You can read me like a book, Clay Daniels. Where else in this crappy little college town can I get a beer as good as this?"

"Nowhere."

"Exactly. Besides, you think I'd come here to use you for your body?"

The forwardness of her words shocked me, and I experienced a sensation of unease mixed with pleasure. I'd never met anyone quite like this brash young woman. I downed half my beer, kept my mouth shut, and then wolfed down the burger and fries.

"You have foam all over your lip," she said.

I went to backhand it off, but she grabbed my hand and cleaned it off with a napkin. Then she did something that caught me off guard. She leaned over the table and kissed me, lingering for quite some time. It was one of the most sensual kisses I'd ever experienced. When she sat back down, I knew I'd crossed a dangerous line. It shocked me. Had I been giving her mixed signals? Although I knew better, I was too weak to resist her advances. Many things pair nicely with beer, but keeping one's sexual desire in check is not one of them.

I remember thinking at the time that a woman like her might never come my way again. And it wasn't like I had a vibrant, healthy sex life with Leah. Mycah had taken hold of me with that one kiss and gripped me in her sexy tentacles. I knew that I would need to steer clear of her if I wanted to remain happily married. It would be futile to resist her temptations.

And now to think that she's gone.

LEAH

Wednesday, October 14, 12:07 p.m.

I DON'T WANT TO BE HERE, SITTING IN THIS PRINCI-
pal's office with the stained ceiling tiles, menacing
laptop computer, and reams of student files. Fields
and pastures beckon out the window and all I want to
do is run barefoot through them. My mind is roaming,
scheming, improvising like a jazz pianist. All I can
think about is Clarissa and that missing girl. I've for-
mulated a plan to learn more about Mycah Jones.
Now all I have to do is go through with it.

I wish I could work up some effort to care about
Zack and his various issues. But I just can't. I know
that's cruel to say, but he's been chipping away at my
maternal instincts ever since Clay moved us to Maine.
It's like a flesh-eating bacteria working its way to the
bone, inching closer to the marrow where all empathy
lives.

Without warning, the principal enters the office, with Zack by her side. Susan is a stern-looking woman, almost masculine in her demeanor. Her hair is close-cropped and spiky. I suspect she's a lesbian but have no proof, nor do I really care. Despite my unease with her authoritarian nature, I do like her. She projects strength and confidence. She's not one to be trifled with, and her students seem to like and respect her.

"Hi, hon," I say to Zack, but he fails to respond or look up at me. I turn my attention to Susan. "What seems to be the problem?"

"Zack and his classmates were required to do a report on a book of their choosing." She gazes down at Zack, and I can't tell if her expression is one of sympathy or disgust. "Zack chose to do his on *Mein Kampf*."

"Hitler's autobiography?" I'm momentarily embarrassed by this. "But why?"

Zack looks up and shrugs. "You wouldn't understand."

"Try me." I want to shake some sense into him.

"I wanted to know why he killed all those people."

"In all my years as a teacher, and now as a principal, I've never had a student choose this book for their report."

"It's a historical document," Zack says.

"The contents of that book are offensive and highly divisive." She turns to me. "Zack is an intelligent and curious boy, but I think this is something we need to keep our eye on."

"Of course." I feel shell shocked. What if word gets out that my son's a Nazi sympathizer?

"I'm afraid that he doesn't quite understand the devastating effect the book had on the world."

"It's a historical document," Zack complains. "That's the point of the assignment—I do understand."

"Zack," I say, "that book was the blueprint that led to millions of Jews being killed. Just being seen with it makes you look bad."

"It's only words."

"Words are important," I say.

"A lot of Germans loved Hitler."

"I'm not going to discuss this with you, Zack. I think it best you choose another book to do your report on," Susan says.

"Censorship is destructive to free thought," Zack says as if he's quoting from memory.

"I had no idea he was reading such trash. I promise that it won't happen again," I say.

"You're stifling my intellectual growth," Zack complains.

"We're trying to teach you to become a critical thinker," Susan points out.

"Sounds like brainwashing to me," Zack says.

"Someday you'll understand," Susan says.

"I'm smart enough to know the difference between right and wrong," Zack says, resting his chin on his fist.

"We'll have the final say on that."

"Fascism," Zack says. "Guilt by association."

"Does anyone else know about this?" I ask.

"Just his teacher and myself, unless he's been speaking to other students about it."

"I don't speak to those morons."

"Is he being punished?" I ask.

"I thought it best we have this discussion and leave

it at that. I merely wanted to keep you abreast of the situation."

"Hitler also believed in censorship," Zack says.

"This discussion is over."

"Is he free to go back to class?" I ask.

"As long as he understands the rules."

"Dictatorship."

"Go back to class, Zack," I say. "And be good."

He leaves the room without even a good-bye. I'm so embarrassed that I can't wait to escape this office. After a few parting words with Susan, I exit the building and run to my car.

I find the proper font and then print out a photograph of myself. Once it's arranged in the form of a press badge, I take it to one of the stationery stores and have it laminated. Add a string to it, hang it from my neck, and just like that I'm a news reporter from the *Tacoma Tribune*.

I drive to the campus. I can hardly believe what I'm about to do. Me, of all people, trying to pass myself off as a reporter. But this is nothing new; I've acted boldly before. Being assertive empowers me and gives me a sense of purpose. If I want to change my life, then I must be the one to make it happen.

I make my way down to the campus and park along one of the lovely side streets. I adore this section of town with its tree-lined streets and cute bungalows. Before leaving the car, I gather my hair up in a bun and put on a pair of wire-rimmed glasses. Glancing in the rearview mirror, I notice that they make me look more sophisticated. Like an intellectual. I put on a felt fedora and then walk toward campus.

It's chilly outside. I'm glad I wore my gray, double-breasted peacoat. The campus looks completely different during the day. A few students meander along the narrow paths, eyes glued to their cell phones as they pass. Above us the bright foliage contrasts brilliantly against the rich hues of the brick buildings. Chadwick is such a beautiful college. It resembles the stereotypical New England campus of my favorite novels and films. It makes me wish I'd gone here as an undergraduate.

Without warning, the quad fills with students like a desert riverbed after a torrential downpour. They scurry along the paths that zigzag throughout campus, lugging backpacks and staring down at their phones as if it's the Pied Piper leading them astray. I pass a stone church with an impressive steeple and spend a few seconds admiring its majesty. There's a bronze statue of Ebenezer Chadwick up ahead. On the plaque it says that he was from a prominent landholding family and at one time was an officer in the militia. I glance around, wondering what building Clarissa works in. Maybe I should try to find her and ask her out to lunch. But it's not likely she'd accept on such short notice.

The mob begins to dwindle down as students head to their next class. A large clock chimes, striking the hour. Across campus I see what looks to be an administrative building. A few students sit on the granite steps, texting, reading, electronic buds stuffed in their ears. I look for the easiest prey, the one who will provide me the most information with the least resistance.

I approach a harmless-looking student who looks

like he's barely out of high school. I tell him that I'm a reporter from Tacoma working on a story about the missing girl. I ask where the lacrosse players live and he informs me that the upperclassmen live in a series of frat houses just off campus. Who knew frat houses still thrived in this day and age? Their mere existence reminds me of the days when sexist attitudes and white male privilege prevailed. I see a frat house and I automatically think *Animal House. John Belushi wearing a toga and smashing a guitar.*

I walk across campus, far to the south, leaving the quaint buildings and athletic fields behind. I arrive on a street with impressive white houses, some with faux pillars and balconies. There are Greek letters over the entryways. Some have porches with easy chairs. Students walk up and down stairs and toward campus. I ask someone where the lacrosse players live, and when they ask why I want to know, I show them my fake press credentials. They point me to the Alpha Delta Phi house, directly across the street.

My body is racing with nervous energy as I make my way up the steps. It's a beautiful white house with four massive pillars and an expansive porch with three alternating balconies overhead. The door opens and three young men wearing backpacks sprint down the stairs before I can ask them anything. I stand awkwardly at the door, my hand gripping the brass knocker. Summoning up the courage, I knock three times and wait. It takes almost a minute before someone answers—a ridiculously tall Adonis with long, flowing, blond hair. I assume he's a lacrosse player. He stares down at me as if I'm lost.

"Can I help you?" he asks.

"I'm a reporter working on the Mycah Jones story."

He looks around nervously. "We're not interested." He starts to close the door.

"I'm not here to vilify you. I only want to find out what happened to her."

"Look, I'm really sorry she went missing, lady, but this is total bullshit, putting the blame on us."

"I'm sure you're right. I'm not here to blame you."

He freezes and looks at me. "What paper do you work for?"

"The *Tacoma Tribune*." I show him my fake badge with the woman's name lifted off the paper's Web site.

"Don't they have any missing persons in Tacoma you can write about?"

"There are certain aspects of this case that make it intriguing on a national level," I say, making it up as I go.

"Like the fact that she's an oppressed minority and we're all racist white dudes from affluent backgrounds? For your information, I grew up in a middle-class household outside of Detroit."

"Then tell me your side of the story."

"That's the thing. I don't know what happened to her. None of us do."

"Don't let them label you. Control the narrative and get ahead of this story before it controls you."

"Hold on a sec."

The door closes and I pace nervously on the porch. What am I getting myself into? Am I crazy to impersonate a reporter? Is it a crime? I walk past the wicker chairs and hanging swing. Alongside the house sit some empty kegs stacked three high. I wander back to the front of the house and sit on the rail. A few minutes pass before the door opens. This time another guy appears. He's tall, but with short black hair combed over to the side and his bangs spiked. He's good-looking but not as handsome as the blond Adonis who answered earlier. He waves me inside and I follow him to the back of the house, passing an ornate spiral staircase. We arrive in a large room with overhead lighting, beaded leather sofas, and a baby grand piano off in the corner. The lid is raised. He motions for me to sit across from him. Between us is a coffee table on a hand-knotted Persian rug.

"Bill said that you're a reporter and want to talk to us about Mycah Jones."

"Yes."

"I'm Tanner, the president of this frat."

"Nice to meet you, Tanner." I introduce myself using the reporter's name.

He leans over the table. "It's absolute bullshit what they're saying about us."

"Oh?"

"There were about seven or eight of us drinking in town that night, but we had no reason to go after Mycah Jones, despite her sorry-ass behavior on campus."

"Sorry in what way?"

"She's been nothing but trouble ever since she arrived at Chadwick, always trying to stir things up and drive a wedge in the student body."

"What has she been doing?"

"Pushing all this nonsense about racism and gender inequality on campus. Where do they come up with this shit?"

"Is it true?"

"Maybe in the past this place had issues, but certainly not now. Minorities are treated no different here at

Chadwick than anyone else. In many ways they're treated better, and the rest of us are held to a higher standard."

"Have you ever considered that maybe your perception of campus life comes from being a privileged white male?"

"What are you talking about?" He looks at me as if I'm crazy. Have I pushed him too far?

"I'm just playing devil's advocate," I say. "So why do the police think that someone on the lacrosse team might have something to do with her disappearance?"

"When Mycah became president of the student body, she purposefully singled out the lacrosse team as the representation of all that was evil with Chadwick. We were easy targets. We're white, mostly come from good families, and are the embodiment of the school's past. But we're not all spoiled rich kids. Many of us come from working-class backgrounds. My father works as a cop in Maryland."

I jot all this down like I'm a real reporter. He's eager to talk, so I don't want to interrupt him unless I absolutely have to.

"Here's the irony. Mycah comes from money. Her father's supposedly some rich investor in Manhattan. Last year she organized a protest in front of our frat house and brought along every oppressed minority group with her: LBGT, blacks, socialists, Hispanics, Asians, whoever felt they were oppressed, which is just about everyone these days. They tried to run us off campus by saying they felt 'threatened' by our existence. Can you believe that?"

"Obviously she didn't succeed."

"That's because some of the alumni promised not to donate any money to Chadwick if they kicked us out. Mycah wrote an editorial about it in the school newspaper, detailing how minorities on campus have for years been suffering from institutional racism. She pushed for gender-neutral bathrooms and safe spaces on campus. The bitch—excuse me—even got elected president of the student body by guilting white students into supporting her. Personally, I think the election was rigged by the administration, but no one can prove it."

"She obviously feels strongly about these issues."

"People like her can never be happy unless they have something to rail about. So they keep manufacturing lies in order to keep their message relevant or else it will fade into the background. Perpetual crisis, I call it. Eventually these morons will need to grow up and get a life."

His words sting, forcing me to momentarily reexamine my own assumptions. But before I have a chance to reflect on it any further, he continues.

"The final straw came when she took a selfie of herself next to the statue of Ebenezer Chadwick. In it she was holding a lacrosse stick in front of the Confederate flag and was wearing a Chadwick sweatshirt. She tweeted it using the hashtags #ChadwickRepublicans, #WhiteMalePrivilege, and #EbenezerScrooge."

"Maybe it was a joke."

"She said she was only trying to make a humorous statement, but even the administration made her apologize for the photo. Unfortunately, it only made her more popular with certain groups on campus, completely dividing the student body. But at least she was forced to step down as president."

"Were there many students on campus who didn't like her?"

"Hell yeah. But many more did. She even wrote an editorial blaming white males for global warming and climate change. Can you believe that?" He shakes his head in disbelief. "Now the entire Greek system is on probation and may be done away with because of her lies."

"Do you think any of her detractors would try to harm her?"

"I think some would like to, but I don't know anyone who would actually go through with it. The players on this team are all great guys. And trust me, no one wanted anything to do with that girl's drama."

"I'll bet there were some players willing to overlook her faults."

"Yeah, she's smoking hot. That's part of her appeal. It's all in the marketing, right?" He laughs. "Unfortunately, she's been backed to the hilt by Chadwick's new director of diversity despite the fact that Mycah tried to get her fired."

"Tell me more."

"I forget her name. They hired her a few years ago to help smooth tensions on campus after all this political-correctness bullshit started getting out of control. I was a freshman at the time. The president claimed they hired her to attract top minority students, but I think it was more to keep the lid from blowing off this school."

"So they brought in more minorities?"

"What do you think?" He laughs. "They instituted

this new policy where students whose parents make under sixty grand get to attend Chadwick for free."

"It's called equal opportunity," I blurt out, instantly regretting it.

"Tell that to my parents, a cop and teacher, who are struggling to help pay three college tuitions. And now I have student loans up the yang."

"Do you know this diversity officer's name?"

He leans back against the sofa, looking like a future CEO or hedge fund manager.

"I can't remember. Her husband was hired as a tenured professor in the African-American studies program. I think her position is half-time. She also teaches a few courses in the department."

"Did you attend the vigil the other night?" I ask.

He fidgets nervously. "The whole team was there. As much as us guys didn't like Mycah personally, I never wanted anything bad to happen to her. It wouldn't have looked good if the team didn't show up. It would have given the administration another excuse to screw us over."

I jot it all down, excited, feeling as if I'm a real reporter breaking a story, a story that will never get printed. I thank him for his time before leaving. My endorphins are popping and streaming. I can't believe what I just accomplished. Maybe I should have been a journalist instead of an English major. The adrenaline rush that comes over me is like nothing I've ever experienced. I feel so intoxicated with power that I don't want to return to my old humdrum existence as mother and wife.

I drive home in a state of giddiness. But that falls

away as soon as I walk through the front door. My boring life returns in full force like a blunt slap in the face. Soiled breakfast dishes sit in the sink and on the counter. Piles of laundry await folding and putting away. Soon the children will be home and the usual pattern of my drudgery will begin all over again.

LEAH

Thursday, October 15, 7:42 a.m.

BEFORE GOING TO BED I WAITED UNTIL ALMOST eleven o'clock for Clay to come home last night. I was exhausted and fell quickly to sleep, but I heard him stagger in just after midnight. He tossed his clothes on the floor and collapsed heavily into bed. Even from my side of the mattress, I detected the stale scent of beer on his breath. It oozes from his pores and gives off a stench that never fails to repulse me.

The children are at the table and eating breakfast when he staggers downstairs. He pulls up a chair and takes us in. Despite shaving and showering this morning, he looks like hell. His hair sticks up in every direction and his skin appears blotchy, as if he slept on a hairbrush. Despite his pitiful appearance, I marvel at how handsome he is. At times he reminds me of one of those disheveled detectives in those TV crime dramas. Nevertheless, I'm still angry with him. I need help around here. Chores are piling up and I can't possibly do it all myself. The twins need him. They need their father's love and attention more than ever. Doesn't he realize this?

I scramble three eggs in a pan, caramelize his turkey sausage, and scrape butter over his whole-wheat toast while he reads the paper. I set his coffee down in front of him. He manages to mutter, "Thank you," under his breath as I let Mr. Shady out to do his business. Once Mr. Shady comes back inside, I sit down across from Clay and stare at the children. Zack is reading a comic book. Zadie is moving her head back and forth while softly singing a song from the movie *Frozen*.

"You came home pretty late last night," I say.

"I know and I'm sorry. I'm so behind on everything at the brewery that it's pathetic."

"We need you here, Clay. The kids need their father."

"I know, babe. Just give me a little more time to get a handle on things."

"I can't parent them all by myself. You should probably hire another person to help you and Ben."

"I'm not quite there yet, but once we start turning a profit, I promise you I will."

"You'll wake up one day and Zack and Zadie will be grown up and off to college, and then you'll be sorry."

He sighs and puts his head in his hands in frustration.

"You forget that I was a single parent for almost

eight months while you were out here setting up your brewery."

"I know and I can't tell you how much I appreciate what you've done for our family." He reaches out and clasps my hand. "Just give me a month or so to get straightened out and I promise things will get better."

I sip my coffee and stare at him. "I had to speak to Zack's principal yesterday."

"Oh?" He turns and watches as Zack flips the page of his comic book. "What did he do now?"

Zack keeps his eyes glued to the muscular super-hero.

"Speak up, son. You must have done something if your mother had to go down and speak with the princi-pal."

"I'm guilty of reading a book," Zack says.

"*Mein Kampf*," I add.

"*Mein Kampf?*" Clay wrinkles his face before burst-ing into a fit of laughter. "Holy shit."

"It's not funny," I say.

"It was for a book report. I read that *Mein Kampf* was banned in Germany, so I wanted to see what the big deal was," Zack says. "I wanted to find out why the German people liked Hitler so much."

"Sounds like a reasonable explanation," Clay says, biting into his toast. "Kid's into history."

"He's way too young to be reading *Mein Kampf*," I say. "Do you know the stigma that could attach to him if other students find out about this? They'll label him a Nazi and he'll be teased and bullied throughout school. It could even affect your business, Clay."

"Okay, kiddo, maybe you shouldn't be reading that sort of thing," he says, running his hand through his son's hair. Zack jerks his head away as if repulsed by his father's touch. "What's the matter?"

"You know I don't like to be touched."

"Sorry for showing some affection."

"You're never around anymore," Zack says.

"I'm trying to support our family and provide you with a nice home."

"Whatever. You know I don't like being touched."

"When did this start happening?" Clay turns and glares at me.

"I don't know," I say.

Zadie starts to sing louder.

Zack stands as if to leave. "It's just a stupid book. I don't know why you two are making such a big deal out of this."

Clay walks over and gives me a peck on the cheek before fleeing out the door. I load the dishwasher, clean the table, and wipe down the kitchen counter. The kids gather their book bags and take their lunch containers out of the fridge. There's a *Frozen*-themed lunch box for Zadie and a *Jurassic Park* lunch pail for Zack. I usher them to the front door and wave good-bye, happy to have them gone. Happy to be finally alone with Mr. Shady and my myriad of thoughts.

Although I should be cleaning, I sit down with a second cup of coffee and stare out the window. The blinds are open, affording me a full view of the Gaineses' home.

I can't wait for Clarissa to leave. I'm going to slip into her house once she leaves and start reading the latest entry in her diary. I'm getting closer to some truths. I finally feel like I have a distinct purpose in life—which is to locate this missing girl. How could Clarissa not want to be my friend once I find her?

Clarissa's right on schedule. Same routine as always, except for one thing. She's wearing sunglasses today. Did Russell strike her last night? I bristle with rage. The poor thing. No wonder she's pushing me away. She walks her children down to the car and buckles them into their seats. Then she backs up and speeds out of the neighborhood.

Mr. Shady jumps up the moment I stand. It's been two days since I've taken him around the neighborhood, and I have no intention of giving him a proper walk this morning. Maybe later, after I accomplish a few things, but not now. He barks knowingly, as if he can read my mind.

I stand over him as he sits by my feet, whimpering in fear. "Go be a good boy and lie down."

I sneak out through the sliding glass door and around the back until I'm standing on her porch. Her sliding door is locked today and I shudder at the implication. Is she on to me? Does she know I've been sneaking inside and reading her diary? But there's no way she could know. There's no mail deliveries or busybody neighbors snooping around, and I'm certain that no one saw me coming or going. I creep around to the front of the house, and to my relief, the door is unlocked.

There'll be no wasted movement in my steps. I know exactly what to look for and where to go. I find Clarissa's diary and key in the same place as yesterday, unlock it, my hands fumbling in excitement, and open it to the last written page.

Wednesday, October 14

I can't believe he did it again. The bastard shoved me last night. And all because I refused to have sex with him. His anger seems to be getting worse since SHE disappeared. Two nights in a row and my ribs are killing me. I'm an intelligent, educated black woman with a good job and two beautiful children. This shouldn't be happening, I keep telling myself. I'm a sad statistic of a long-held racial stereotype: the violent black man.

Now that he can't be with her anymore, he's turning his wrath on me. But I won't do it. Not when he's like that. I can't do it. Even when he forces himself on me, I refuse to play along and feign pleasure and moan and groan like a beached seal. After our brief struggle last night, I lay there, my mind floating above it all, thinking of better things. Things like how nice my life would be without him. How I could be a better person and help make a difference in this world. But he knows I can't leave him. Not yet anyway.

So now we learn she was pregnant. Why am I not surprised? I'm betting anything it wasn't her boyfriend who did it. Yes, I'm fairly certain that Russell is the father. But as much as my husband disgusts me, I know in my heart that he's not a killer. Or kidnapper. Am I being naive? Is it possible to make the leap from wife abuser to killer? Emotionally, I know I'm burying my head in the sand. I wouldn't be surprised at all if he had something to do with her disappearance.

But. I. Just. Can't. Accept. It.

I must keep a close eye on him. Maybe follow him around and see where he goes. It's possible she's still alive. Maybe he'll leave a clue to her whereabouts. Mycah was only screwing him for grades and a recommendation to a prestigious law school. Her campus activism is such utter bullshit that it makes me sick. It was always about her and never the cause. She could care less about social justice. Her behavior makes a mockery of the civil rights movement. Funny that it's a complete contradiction to her private life. I'm sure this will soon come to light. LOL. Then the real Mycah Jones will be revealed as the bitch she really is.

Yet I can't say anything about this or he'll expose me. If that comes out, then I'm done in academia. All my hard work will have been for naught. But that's not my real fear. No, my real fear is that Russell will kill me if I expose his relationship with her. And that's probably why Mycah disappeared. She was planning to rat him out as the father of her unborn child.

I need to remind myself to stay strong. My time will come. One day I'll be free from him and become the person I'm meant to be. I won't

have to fake orgasms or allow him to hurt me.
Or allow him to continually berate me over
minor matters. Until that time comes, I need to
be nice, remain calm, and watch whom I speak
to. His control over me is complete and I never
know what I'm going to say after a few glasses
of wine. I don't trust my neighbor just yet, as
nice as she seems to be.

I drop the diary on my lap. Russell was having an affair with Mycah Jones and impregnated her? If true, it means that it was not a hate crime. The disappearance of Mycah Jones has more to do with lust and ambition than racial animosity.

I stuff the diary back into the drawer along with the key. A girl is missing and the town is abuzz, and I'm one of the few people on earth who know the truth.

I stand by the window and make sure the coast is clear. Certain that no one is around, I slip outside until I hit the stone path. To my surprise, I see a man jogging on the sidewalk. For a brief moment I panic. Who is he? Where did he come from?

"Hey there," he says, waving amiably as he approaches.

I wave back, frozen in place as he jogs up to me. A red sweatband wraps around his shiny bald dome. He's plump and jovial and looks like he's lost his way.

"Great morning, isn't it?"

"I was just . . . I was . . ." I point aimlessly toward the Gaineses' house.

"When are they ever gonna finish this dump?" he asks, glancing around while still jogging in place. Sweat pours down his puffy cheeks.

I shrug.

"I run through this neighborhood a couple of times a month, if you want to call this running. You're the first person I've ever seen here."

I breathe easy. He has no idea that I came out of the Gaineses' house.

"Where do you live?"

I nod toward my house.

"I live a few miles up the road. You should have moved into our neighborhood. Bustling with kids, although a lot of them are royal pains in the ass. Trample over my lawn and rose bushes."

"Sorry, but I really have to go," I say, turning back toward my house.

"Take care, lady."

He jogs toward the main road before disappearing around the corner. That was a close call. I need to be more careful from now on.

Mr. Shady barks furiously as soon as I walk through the door. He's still mad at me for leaving him alone. After he stops barking, he moves to the corner of the room and sits with his back toward me. I collapse on the sofa, exhausted, not wanting to deal with his drama this morning. After a minute of self-isolation, he plunks down at my feet and stares up at me.

What Russell is doing to Clarissa is reprehensible, but I have no evidence to prove anything. All I have are the words in her diary, which would never stand up in court. I'll need more. Maybe even follow Russell around and see what he's up to. If the girl is still alive, it's entirely possible he may be visiting her. If she's dead, he may lead me to the body.

I pull out my notebook and jot down everything I

can recall from her diary. It's exhilarating to have a concrete plan in place. I'm so excited by what I've discovered that I can barely control myself. The monotony of being a mother and wife falls away like an old winter's jacket on a spring day.

Dinner tonight will consist of two cans of SpaghettiOs slow-cooked in the Crock-Pot along with some sliced hot dogs. The laundry and dishes will have to wait.

CLAY

Thursday, October 15, 1:59 p.m.

I LOVE WALKING AROUND THE BREWERY AND TAKING in all the stainless steel equipment, as well as the endless coils of rubber and copper tubing that regulate temperature and transfer the wort to its next phase. I love the cold concrete floors that make it easy to spray down with a hose, as well as the ten-barrel conical beer fermenters that resemble inverse rockets. Damn. I love it all. Sometimes I never want to leave this place.

It's not even two o'clock and already there's a few bearded hipsters sitting in the tasting room and drinking. I want to wander in there and quaff some brews with them, talk shop, ask if they like my new selection of beers. See what's good and what needs improving on. But I have too much to do today. I look at the whiteboard and see that my calendar is full. There's a beer conference in Portland in a few weeks, and I need to find a few more bars willing to give me a tap. Business is good and getting better. I'm still in the red, but at this rate I should be making a small profit by spring. Growth needs to happen if I'm to make a go of this venture, and that means buying more equipment, canning product, and expanding the plant.

My IPA, the Information, is what customers are lining up to buy. I'm getting some interest from Portland bars and even some establishments down in Massachusetts. I rotate my beers regularly, yet customers keep asking for it, demanding more each time they come in. When I run out, they complain mightily and ask when the next batch will be ready. People come from all over with growlers and looking to buy six-packs, but I don't have the capital yet to can my product. That's the next step, assuming I can find the right investor who understands my vision and is willing to let me run the show.

Earlier in the year, thanks to Mycah, I had an exciting investment opportunity offered to me. The offer seemed too good to be true; because it was. What the hell was I thinking?

Mycah invited me to dinner soon after we exchanged our first kiss. I didn't want to go, but she said she knew someone who might be able to help my fledgling brewery. I remained skeptical, yet I drove to her apartment building that night, which was located minutes from campus. I knew what I was doing was wrong, but then again I was desperate. I blamed alcohol. I blamed the effects of loneliness and the fact that Leah had begun to drift away from me after the kids were born. I blamed greed and my lack of experience in the business world. I blamed Leah for withholding sex from me for so long. But mostly I blamed myself. In one moment of weakness, I'd given in to temptation.

But this meeting was to be different. I rationalized my behavior as operating in the best interests of the company. This was a business opportunity from a girl whose family had deep pockets. So why not take her money? It's how capitalism works, right?

I stopped at her building and debated whether or not to go up. The brewery would survive without this infusion of capital, its growth slow and steady. But why not at least hear what she had to say?

I ventured inside the lobby and pressed the button to her apartment. In my hand was an expensive bottle of Malbec from Bordeaux that the shopkeeper suggested. I'd already convinced myself that there was nothing to worry about and that this meeting was merely an investment opportunity. My mind was a steel trap; I would not make the same mistake twice.

She buzzed me in and I climbed the three flights of stairs. I knocked and a few minutes passed before the door opened. As soon as I saw her, I knew I wouldn't be able to resist. She looked stunning, even more so than the last time we met. Her long black hair cascaded in waves over her shoulders, and dangling from her ears was a pair of triangular red earrings. She wore designer ripped jeans, a green leather jacket with the sleeves fashionably pulled up below her elbows, and a ribbed black T-shirt. A silver necklace hung just above her modest cleavage with the word "*moi*" studded in diamond lettering.

I willed myself to stay strong as she invited me inside. Her apartment was clean and tastefully decorated, hardly that of a college student. She walked over and dimmed the lighting as John Legend crooned on a nearby speaker.

"I'm so glad you could make it." She took the wine from my hand. "No beer?"

"Thought I'd change it up tonight. The guy who sold it to me said it's a good one."

She looked at the bottle. "French Malbec. I'm impressed."

"Honestly, I don't know anything about wine."

"The wine is nice, but I would have rather had more of your beer."

"There'll always be more beer." I looked around her place. "This is a beautiful apartment."

"Beats living in the dorm. I shared a room with a psycho my freshman year."

"My first roommate barely spoke to me, and he hardly ever left the room."

"Chadwick requires that all students live in a dorm their freshman year. I think my first roommate was bulimic because she ate like a horse and then kept running out of the room. Her breath totally freaked me out." She passed me the corkscrew.

I twisted the cork out while she stirred something in a pan on the stove.

"So you know someone who might be interested in investing in the brewery?" I asked.

"Chill, homey. We have all night to talk business." She sipped her wine and laughed. "This is really a good Malbec."

"Glad you like it. As far as wine goes, I couldn't tell

the difference between a ten-dollar bottle and a hundred-dollar bottle."

"Trust me, this is amazing shit," she said. "So tell me more about yourself, Clay Daniels. What else do you like to do besides making beer?"

"I'm a pretty boring guy. I don't really have any other hobbies."

"What's your wife like?"

I felt horrible when she mentioned Leah, and I looked away in shame. It should have been the trigger for me to run out of that apartment and never look back, but instead I lifted my glass and gulped down the rest of my wine. At a loss for words, I gazed up at her. The sweetness of the grape assaulted my palate in a not so nice kind of way, and suddenly I wished I'd brought some beer. Why would she ask about my wife?

"You know about my family?"

"Please, I can spot a married man a mile away, even when he's not wearing his ring."

"My wife and twins are living in Seattle. The kids will be starting sixth grade in September."

"Why are they living in Seattle?"

"They're finishing school. Then we'll start looking for a house in Dearborn."

"Is your wife pretty?"

I laughed.

"Yeah, I'll bet she's hot."

"Why do you say that?"

"A good-looking guy like you wouldn't marry anything less." She laughed. "They say the pretty ones are high maintenance."

"Then you must be quite a handful," I said, feeling the wine infiltrating my defense systems.

"Do you have a picture of her?"

Despite my reservations, I took out my phone and showed her some photos of Leah and the kids. I held the phone out across the table and Mycah held my hand in her own. The sensation of her soft hands on mine titillated me. Her nails were long and done up beautifully in a French manicure. I didn't want her to ever let go.

"Yeah, she's pretty in a wholesome sort of way. Cute kids."

"Thanks."

"All-American family."

"I guess."

"You're so privileged."

She let go of my hand and I returned the phone to my pocket. Mycah went over to the stove and prepared two plates of whatever she was cooking. She placed them down on the table: steak au poivre and mixed vegetables for me and mixed vegetables for her.

"You don't eat meat?"

"Try not to."

"Animal rights activist?" I laughed.

"Activist, but not for animal rights." She sipped her wine. "The sight of meat grosses me out."

"Looks pretty damn good to me."

"Then hurry up and dig in, Clay Daniels. Hope you like it."

I carved off a strip and saw that it was medium rare on the inside, just the way I liked it. White pepper sauce oozed over the top of the meat and dripped onto the plate. I forked the chunk into my mouth and it tasted amazing, salty and unctuous. Leah had never cooked me a meal this delicious.

"You like?"

"Ridiculous. Where'd you learn to cook like this?"

"There's a lot about me you don't know."

"Yeah? Like what?"

"What would you like to know?"

"What's your boyfriend like?"

She laughed. "Does it really matter if I have a boyfriend?"

"Just trying to make polite conversation."

"Would it make you jealous if I did?"

"Of course not. I'm a happily married man." I sawed off another slice of beef and forked it into my mouth.

"You didn't seem happily married the last time we met."

"That was a mistake. I had a little too much to drink that night."

"Have some more wine." She refilled my glass. "And yet here you sit, having dinner with me."

"I came here to talk business, remember?"

"Oh yes, I forgot that you're all business tonight." She sipped the wine as if put off by me. "You're a regular wheeler and dealer. A player, in the truest business sense."

"I can talk to your investor directly and give him all the brewery's financial information."

"Wow. That's really sexist of you."

"Oh?"

"What makes you think it's a man who wants to invest in your brewery? It could be a woman for all you know."

"Okay, I'm sorry for assuming."

"The potential investor happens to be my father."

"Your father?"

"I told him about your brewery and how good your beer is. He's always looking out for a good investment opportunity," she said, forking a zucchini stick into her mouth. "How much capital do you think you'll need?"

"Figure about a hundred grand so I can expand the brewery and start canning my product."

"That's a lot of money."

"You asked."

"My father's very particular about the details. I'll mention your offer to him and see what he has to say."

"Tell him that we're going to be the next Sam Adams."

Mycah laughed. "Okay."

She smiled as she nibbled on a carrot slice. I took another bite of steak. It had been a long time since I'd had a home-cooked meal as good as this. Leah overcooked steaks, burnt chops, and dried out roasts. Since moving to Maine, I'd been eating takeout every night. Only when I flew back to Seattle and spent the weekend with the family did I get a home-cooked meal— and not a very good one at that. Usually, it would be something Leah bought pre-prepared from the supermarket and then tried to pass off as an old family recipe. Her culinary lies were all too transparent, but I never complained, seeing as how it was better than anything she tried to make herself.

Mycah walked around the table and, to my surprise, sat on my lap. She smelled heavenly and I tried not to stare into her cleavage. Her skin had the hue of toasted cumin. Feeling emboldened, I put my arm around her waist until it rested on the small of her back. I could feel her delicate spine and tailbone. The makeup and pink lipstick she wore made her look older, sexier. To my embarrassment, I could feel myself becoming aroused. It was humiliating and completely unavoidable, and try as I might, I could not hide it. I had no doubt she could feel it pressing against her bottom.

"Is that a forty-ounce stuffed in your Fruit of the Looms?" She laughed.

"I shouldn't be here."

"I'm not forcing you to do anything you don't want to do. You're free to walk out that door anytime you like."

"If I walk out that door, you might call off the deal."

"Business is business, G. That's the chance you'll have to take."

I knew she was right, but I also knew that I couldn't just walk away from this stunning creature. It had been so long since I'd made love to a woman. The sensation of her on my lap intoxicated me. Her fragrance alone made me delirious with lust. I wanted to run out of her apartment so badly, but I couldn't convince the motor part of my brain to let go.

"I really should leave."

She stood. "You might regret it. And in more ways than one."

"If I stay, I most certainly will regret it."

She laughed. "I'm not asking you to leave your wife and kids." She reached down, running her fingers over my crotch.

"Please don't," I said, not so convincingly.

"Relax, Clay Daniels." She knelt down by my side and stared up at me. "I promise it won't hurt."

"That's what I'm afraid of."

Leah calls me at the brewery around six and asks if I'll pick up some groceries on my way home. Twenty people are huddled around the oak bar and hoisting tulip glasses of beer. They're calling my name and asking me to join the fray. I most definitely don't *want* to go home. I want to stay here all night with my brood and discuss everything pertinent to beer. *Drink* beer. Luxuriate in all things related to the craft of brewing.

But I have to go.

It pains me to leave. I consider all the sacrifices Leah's made and suddenly I'm hit with an overwhelming sense of guilt. There's something about facing my family that frightens me. Raising kids is a difficult task, especially with a son like Zack. He makes me uncomfortable. He seems to know things, secret things, yet he refuses to divulge what he's concealing. I love my son with all my heart, and Zadie too, but it scares me to think about their futures. Is that why I spend so much time at the brewery? So I don't have to face the harsh realities of fatherhood?

"Are you coming home, Clay?"

"I'll be there as soon as I can."

"Please hurry. I need some time to myself."

"I'm leaving right now."

"I love you so much, Clay."

"Love you too."

I hang up and immediately pour myself an IPA. Then I join up with some bearded geeks engaged in a heated discussion about the merits of sour beers. This is my clan, the tribe I feel most comfortable around. Burly giants with thick beards, foam-studded mustaches, and wearing plaid shirts more suited for butch lesbians than urban professionals. Many are home brewers in their spare time. Others are merely beer connoisseurs. Time escapes me. After quaffing one more pint of my potent double IPA, I wobble out the garage door, climb into my pickup truck, and drive the four miles home in a state of numb resignation.

LEAH

Thursday, October 15, 6:14 p.m.

*C*LAY REEKS OF BEER WHEN HE COMES HOME, BUT I don't really care at this point. He's a little later than expected. I'm just glad he came home and liberated me from this oppressive house and all the upkeep it takes. I quickly kiss him good-bye and leave.

I learned that Cordell tends bar part-time in a French restaurant twenty miles out of town. I called the restaurant earlier in the day and found out that he's working tonight. I'm obviously not dressed for such a fancy place, but it doesn't matter. I'll have a glass of wine at the bar and wait to speak to him.

I park in the back of the restaurant and walk inside. He's not hard to recognize with his long dreadlocks and chiseled good looks. His photograph has been published a few times in the newspaper, and I've seen him interviewed on TV. The bruises on his face are healing but still evident. After a precautionary night spent in the hospital, he was released and sent back to his dorm.

The restaurant is busy tonight with people waiting at the bar. I spot a lone stool and quickly snatch it. Cordell walks over and places a napkin down in front of me. His left eye is slightly discolored and puffy. He's much darker and thinner than I expected. If he loved Mycah so much, I wonder why he isn't spending every waking minute looking for her.

"Can I help you, ma'am?"

"Chablis, please."

Cordell pours me a glass and places it down on the bar.

"Cordell?"

He turns and stares at me. "Do I know you?"

"No, you don't."

"Then how can I help you?"

"I need to ask you a few questions about Mycah," I whisper.

He leans over the bar and glares at me. "Are you a cop?"

I shake my head and he looks confused.

"I can't talk to you here," he says.

"I know that Mycah was not who she claimed to be," I whisper. "She was seeing someone else on the side."

"Shhhh," he says, looking around the room. "I can't talk about this right now."

"Then where can we go?"

"How can I trust you?"

"I give you my word."

"You going to run to the police and shoot off your mouth?"

"Why haven't you told them everything?"

"Because then they'll think I did it. But I had nothing to do with any of this. I'm the victim here."

"Will you tell me what you know?"

"I get off shift in an hour," he whispers. "There's an Applebee's down the road, next to a little Chinese joint. Meet me in one of the back booths so we can have some privacy."

I leave the restaurant and drive over to Applebee's. It's easy to find, as all chain restaurants are with their faux charm and gaudy lit signs. I park in the lot and wait patiently. I'm fearful of going inside and drinking too much while I wait for him. No way I want to run the risk of getting pulled over by the cops on my way home and arrested for DUI.

Thirty minutes pass and I'm bored to death. It's nerve-racking waiting here and listening to song after song on the soft rock station. I know I must look strange sitting in my car and staring straight ahead. Finally, after a haunting song by Adele, I get out and head to the front door. A cold wind blows through the lot, a sure sign that the seasons are changing.

The young host ushers me to a booth near the window. It's perfect; I'll be able to see when Cordell enters. The place is empty except for a few customers sitting at the rectangular bar. The exuberant young waitress comes over and asks if I want a drink, and against my better judgment, I order a glass of Chablis. I take a small sip, determined to make it last until Cordell arrives. Oh, but it tastes so cold and delicious.

The first sip goes straight to my head and gives me a false sense of confidence. I open my spiral notebook like a real journalist and gloss over the notes I've taken.

The waitress sets down my third glass of wine when I look up and see Cordell slip into the booth across from where I sit. He looks nervous as he leans over the table and glares at me. My head feels warm and fuzzy, and the wine has provided me with the impetus to see this interview through. Although this warm buzz is exactly what I need right now, it will certainly come at a cost. There's no way I'll be able to drive home in this condition.

"I'm glad you could make it," I say.

"I'm not glad at all." The waitress comes over and Cordell orders a draft beer. "Who are you and what the hell do you think you're doing?"

I'm taken aback by his hostile tone, but I will myself to go on.

"I thought you'd be happy to see me."

"Happy? Are you crazy?" he says. "You show up at my work, asking some serious shit, and I'm supposed to be *happy*? Hell, I don't even know you."

I pull out my fake badge and show it to him, thinking that he'll immediately recognize me for the phony I am. He gives it a perfunctory glance before pushing it away.

"A goddamn reporter? I don't need to talk to no reporters."

"Better you control the narrative before the truth comes out."

"Damn. I never should have gotten mixed up with that girl." He shakes his head, the dreads swinging like Tarzan riding jungle vines.

"Mycah?"

"Who the hell else?"

"What happened that night?"

"I had nothing to do with her kidnapping or whatever happened to her. That girl was trouble with a capital T. I never should have agreed to help her. And if you quote me on that, I'll deny it."

"Did you love her?"

"Love her?" He laughs. "Hell no, I didn't love her."

"She's beautiful. Smart too."

"Too smart for her own good, if you ask me."

"But so are you. I read that you received an early decision to Harvard Law."

"Wasn't supposed to find out until later in the year. After Harvard heard about that hate crime, they sent me an acceptance letter."

"With your grades and stature on campus, you most certainly would have been admitted anyway. And what about your basketball accomplishments?"

"I know what you're implying."

"Sorry, I'm not following you."

"You're implying that the reason I got in is because I'm black."

"No," I say, horrified by his accusation. "You're certainly most deserving of Harvard Law."

"My LSATs were not close to being Harvard material."

"Standardized tests aren't everything," I say. "So tell me what happened that night."

"You can't print any of this. Not right now, anyway."

"Not until I get all the facts." I realize that I'm a very good liar.

"What do you want to know?"

"Is the baby yours?"

He laughs as if I made a joke.

"Mycah was cheating on you?"

"It's more complicated than that. We had what you might call an arrangement. We just needed to be honest with each other and all was cool."

"She lied to you?"

"Not exactly a lie." He looks around nervously. "But she wasn't always forthright, either."

"Then why couldn't the baby be yours?"

"Because we never actually . . . consummated the act." He looks embarrassed.

I blush, feeling the alcohol rushing to my cheeks. It must look obvious as I sip my wine.

"The paper said you two had been together for over a year."

"The newspaper said a lot of stuff." He downs his beer and raises it for another. "Waiting until marriage, I guess you could say."

"That's very noble of you. But I thought you said you didn't love her."

He laughs as if I'm being naive. "What's love got to do with it? We were a power couple."

"I don't understand."

"My daddy happens to be an influential Baptist preacher in Mississippi. Premarital sex is seriously frowned upon down there."

"I can respect that."

"Well don't. It was the agreement Mycah and I had." He shrugs as if he's hiding something.

"And it didn't bother you in the least that she was sleeping with other guys?"

"Don't ask, don't tell."

"How about you? Were you seeing anyone else?"

"No." He blinks his eyes three times in rapid succession, which clearly tells me he's lying.

"Who exactly was she sleeping with?"

"I saw her one time with this older white dude. The two of them were standing outside her apartment building. She also told me she was seeing a professor at Chadwick."

I feel like throwing up. I want to call a cab and rush home, hug my husband and kids, and never leave them. Why did I ever get involved in this? Why am I even here? For whatever reason, all the wine is making me emotional.

"It drove me crazy to think she was sleeping with one of her professors, but Mycah told me to be cool and it would all work out. She said he might even write me a recommendation to law school."

"You were worried about your relationship?"

"About our arrangement."

"Why aren't you telling the police all this?"

"Because then they'll think I was a jealous boyfriend and that I set her up. Maybe even killed her and hid the body."

I toss some bills down onto the table and slide out of the booth. Cordell killed her, I can sense it. I need to get out of here, breathe some fresh autumn air, and collect my thoughts. Latching on to the strap of my pocketbook, I head toward the exit without saying good-bye. I feel as if I'm having an anxiety attack and might pass out. Cordell follows me until we reach the parking lot. I lean back against my car, frightened, and gulp oxygen.

"You okay, lady?"

"Did you kill her?"

"Hell no. How can you even say that?"

"You should consider talking to the police, Cordell. Tell them everything you know."

"You can't breathe any of this to no one. You hear? Promise me you won't." He stands too close to me, wagging a long finger in my face.

"I have a confession to make. I lied to you. I'm not a real reporter." I pull out my fake press badge and show it to him. "It's fake. I made it at home."

"Damn."

Tears spill from my eyes.

"Mycah asked me to write checks out of the council's budget. Said if I valued my privacy, I'd do it, and that she'd repay it once her daddy sent her a check."

I fumble inside my pocketbook for the keys as the parking lot spins around me.

"It happened a week before the attack. Before she disappeared. No one even knows about the missing funds. Not sure the college wanted that to go public for fear of appearing racist."

"How much did she take?"

"Nearly ten thousand dollars."

I start to bawl and, to my surprise, Cordell leans over and hugs me. I don't push him away or try to escape his grasp. His long dreadlocks fall around my face and chin. It's the most affection I've received in a long time, and I'm now convinced that he's totally innocent. His embrace feels warm and loving, and I press myself into his bony chest. After consoling me, he steps back and looks at me.

"You okay?"

"I'm sorry for tricking you like that. I'm just a bored housewife with nothing else to do."

"I'm the one should be crying. People don't know half the truth of this story."

"You swear you didn't hurt Mycah or have anything to do with her disappearance?"

"Swear to God. There's no shortage of people on campus who despised that girl."

"I believe you."

"You have to because it's the truth."

He leans over, parts his dreads, and shows me the stitches from the attack. They resemble train tracks running across the back of his scalp. "I'm Rasta and my daddy would kill me if he ever found out I wasn't Christian. Truth is, violence goes against everything I believe in."

Cordell walks back to his beat-up old Jeep and then disappears down the street. I look around the near empty parking lot and wonder what I'm doing here. I'm finished sneaking around and pretending to be a reporter. It's too hard. I want to go back to being a boring mother and housewife. I'll leave the investigating up to the police and let them figure out what happened to Mycah.

I jingle the keys in my hand as I collapse inside the car. My head is still spinning from the wine and I feel close to passing out. I turn the ignition only to realize that I'm too drunk to drive. Tom Petty's "American Girl" blares over the speakers. I shut off the engine, recline back in the seat, and then everything goes black.

CLAY

Thursday, October 15, 11:00 p.m.

I T'S ELEVEN O'CLOCK AND LEAH'S NOT HOME YET, which worries me. She's been acting strange as of late, and every time she acts this way it makes me wonder what she knows. Is she suspicious? Does she have any idea that I've cheated on her?

I call her cell phone repeatedly, but she doesn't answer. Has she gotten into a car wreck? Been mugged? I should drive around and look for her. A car wreck wouldn't surprise me. She's a terrible driver, already getting into two fender benders since moving here to Dearborn. And I've been finding wine bottles hidden at the bottom of the trash and under the kitchen sink. She's fooling no one. She's a hundred and ten pounds and eats like a sparrow.

Thank God the kids are finally asleep. I run upstairs and check on Zadie. Her princess blanket is pulled over her head so that only her angelic face can be seen. Zack is asleep on his back with a book open over his chest. I head back downstairs and pour another beer out of the growler I'd brought home. Despite my near panicked state, there's nothing I can do but wait for Leah to come home. I feel like an anxious parent waiting for his teen daughter to pull into the driveway.

I wish I could kick back and relax. Only I can't relax. My mind is swirling. I try to watch one of those travel shows where the host gets ridiculously drunk and makes a fool out of himself. Usually, I love watching such garbage, but for some reason I have no interest in it tonight. I watch numbly as he roams the steamy streets of Vietnam, eating pig brains and heart skewers, and getting loaded on rice wine. At one point, a young kid gulps down a still beating snake heart along with a shot of whiskey. Boy, those Vietnamese sure know how to party.

I call Leah's cell phone three times in succession, but it goes to voice mail. Where the hell is she? I envision her with another man, getting payback for the way I've wronged her. Too much beer has made me paranoid, and I curse myself for what I've done. The more worried I get, the more I drink; it's becoming somewhat of a pattern lately.

I switch to the news and run out to the kitchen for another jar. I'm anxious and drunker than I should be. While opening a bag of chips, I hear the reporter mention the missing girl. I stagger back to the couch and collapse on it. My heart races as they switch to a reporter on the scene. I pray to God that Leah's safe, vowing to never again cheat on her.

Why did I ever betray Leah?

* * *

I open my eyes and am instantly blinded by the sun filtering in through the blinds. Below me on the floor are the empty beer growlers. I can't believe I drank two of them—sixty-four ounces of IPA—and that's in addition to all the beer I consumed at work. Flamenco dancers cavort in my head, castanets snapping like clamshells against my synaptic nerves. I sit up slowly so that the blood doesn't rush too quickly to my brain. I glance at the clock and remember something.

The kids need to get ready for school.

I look around, but they're nowhere to be seen. Mr. Shady sits on the floor in front of me, his big brown eyes staring at me in adoration. I can do no wrong in his doggy eyes. The kitchen table is empty except for a single sheet of paper. I stumble over and see Zadie's perfect penmanship. *Morning, Daddy, Zack and I dressed and made our own breakfast. Since you were asleep, we walked down to the bus stop by ourselves. Hope you have a great day, Daddy. Luv, Zadie.*

I can't believe I overslept. A high-pitched whistle blows in my ears. My eyelids flutter like a pair of hummingbirds freebasing on crack. I run upstairs and notice that my bed is still made. Leah never made it home last night. Panicked, I look at myself in the mirror and see a man burdened with neglect and fear. A man hungover and guilt-ridden by a terrible secret.

Where the hell is Leah? Has she left me? Is she having her own affair? I head downstairs and grab my phone off the coffee table and dial her number. She's still not answering. I envision her lying in a ditch somewhere. Or possibly hooked up to a life-saving device in one of the local hospitals.

The news comes on. A reporter is standing in front of an apartment building. A college student from Chadwick has been found dead. When she mentions the student's name, I wonder if I'm hearing things. The man's photograph appears onscreen. His expressionless face appears burrowed beneath vines of long dreadlocks. It's Cordell Jefferson, Mycah Jones's boyfriend, star basketball player and vice president of Chadwick's student body.

Something feels terribly wrong, and Leah's disappearance only adds to my torment. This can't be a coincidence. A ton of work is waiting for me down at the brewery, yet I feel as if my world is coming apart. Outside, a car's engine roars to life. I move to the window and see our next-door neighbor. What's her name? Clara? Clarice? Claudia? She's taking her kids to school. What the hell's wrong with me? I can't even remember the name of my own neighbor.

I tidy up the area where I slept last night, making sure to toss the empty growlers in the bed of my truck. I clean up the wrappers and get rid of the empty bag of chips. A confetti of crumbs lies across the couch and I sweep them into the dustbin. I gaze into the fridge and notice that I'm completely out of beer.

Leah won't come out and say it, but she thinks I drink too much. She smells it on my breath and on my clothes. I try to tell her it's part of the job, but she doesn't buy it. And for the most part she's right. I do drink too much. It's why I've gained ten pounds in the last year. But she drinks too much too, and if I mention it, she becomes irate and says I'm picking on her.

The cops will do nothing if I call and report that my wife has gone missing. Twenty-four hours have to pass before they can declare her a missing person. So all I can do is sit on the couch and watch TV—*and wait.* I stare at the ashtray sitting on the coffee table. It's filled with cigarette butts. I must have smoked half a pack last night while waiting for her to come home. I get up and spray the living room until it smells like a bouquet of lemons. If Leah comes home—no, when she comes home—there'll be hell to pay, especially if she suspects that I've been smoking inside the house. She's allergic to cigarette smoke, among the many other things she's averse to. I notice a tiny roach sticking up out of the ashtray and realize that I was smoking more than just cigarettes last night. Hopefully, Zack and Zadie didn't see it. I grab the ashtray and dump it far down into the trash.

I turn up the volume and watch with interest about the death of Cordell Jefferson. I feel sorry for that poor kid. Great basketball player, the reporter says. Chadwick's career leader in assists. Accepted to Harvard Law and a straight A student. Had the world by the balls. Too bad he had the misfortune of dating Mycah. I wonder if he had any idea what he was up against. Or that I was screwing her behind his back? My biggest fear is the unborn child she was carrying. And I can't help shaking the sinking feeling that the kid was mine.

LEAH

Friday, October 16, 8:27 a.m.

I OPEN MY EYES AND LOOK UP. I PASSED OUT IN THE backseat of my car. Next to me is a receipt from Applebee's listing the four mango sangrias I consumed after my meeting with Cordell. What in the world was I thinking? I can't even remember going back inside after he drove off.

I sit up, my throat dry, trying to remember the events of the previous evening. The morning sun penetrates the windshield and warms my face. My neck feels stiff and creaky. Falling asleep in the hybrid is not the worst thing that could have happened to me. I could have been mugged or taken advantage of by some drunken trucker. I could have driven home and gotten a DUI.

I look behind me and see fast-food wrappers over the backseat and along the floor. *Okay, so I did drive somewhere.* Across the street is a twenty-four-hour fast-food restaurant that serves the nastiest stuff. My stomach rumbles from the grease. I'm so ashamed. All I want to do is go home and take care of my babies. It's not up to me to find the missing girl. Let the police handle that. Why can't I just mind my own business and worry about myself?

Zack and Zadie.

I look at my watch in panic. It's 8:30 a.m. They're supposed to be at school. What kind of mother abandons her children? I pick up my cell phone but the battery has gone dead. I can't call Clay and tell him that I'm all right or that I'll be home shortly. He must be worried sick. I bet he's called the police and filed a missing person report. It wouldn't surprise me if he got in his truck and started driving around looking for me.

I pick up the yellow wrappers, limp stale fries, empty shake cup, and apple pie containers, and stuff them in a bag. My head feels groggy and there's an intense pressure pushing up behind my eyes. I turn the radio on to the college station as I drive home, and hear the lovely voice of Alicia Keys.

But the song ends abruptly and I hear a student reporting the day's news. The body of a Chadwick student has been discovered just outside town. I pull over to the side of the road, next to a huge red barn in need of repairs, and let the engine idle. The police have identified the victim as Cordell Jefferson. He was shot in his Jeep as he sat by the side of the road. It can't be possible. I just met with him last night.

Tears streak down my face.

Did someone see us together? Did Cordell know the person who kidnapped or killed Mycah? Maybe the killer had been following Cordell the entire time. Or maybe the guy who impregnated Mycah wanted Cordell out of the picture. I pull the car back onto the country road and try to make sense of this.

It suddenly occurs to me that I might be in danger too. What have I done? What terrible conspiracy have I stumbled upon? Maybe it's time I went to the police and told them everything I know.

What will I say to Clay? How will I explain why I didn't make it home last night? This is completely out of character for me. Should I tell him that I met with Cordell? Tell him that I got so drunk at Applebee's that I passed out in the backseat of the hybrid?

My pocketbook is open on the front seat. While keeping my eyes on the road, I reach inside and realize that all my money is gone except for some loose change.

Clay's truck is in the driveway when I pull up and this disappoints me. I notice his empty growlers lying in the bed, growlers that were not there when I left. He thinks I don't know that he throws them in the bed in order to conceal how much he drinks. He gets defensive when I mention it to him, which is a sure sign that he has a problem. Sure, I have a glass of wine now and then, but other than last night, I'm certainly able to control my consumption.

It disappoints me that he didn't drive around looking for me. I could have been lying in a ditch somewhere for all he knew. But he didn't care enough to make an effort. He was probably too drunk to care and passed out on the couch.

I walk up the steps, let myself inside, and see him sitting on the sofa, his eyes closed and snoring. The house looks spotless, which is a telltale sign that he cleaned up his mess from last night. I peek out the window and notice that Clarissa's already left for work. Do I detect the odor of cigarette smoke? Pot? I tiptoe around, searching for any signs that he's been smoking. I open the bathroom cabinet and notice that the lemon-scented spray is not on the shelf where I usually put it. I dig around in the trash and find six cigarette butts.

"Clay," I shout, jostling his shoulder.

His eyelids open and he stares up at me in surprise. "Where the hell have you been? I've been waiting up all night for you."

"I stayed in a hotel last night."

"A hotel? We don't have money for that," he says. His expression changes and he stands to his full height, wrapping his arms around me. "I'm just glad you're home safe."

I go limp in his burly arms. The scent of mints, cigarette smoke, and mouthwash overwhelms me. I should be angry, but I have other matters to deal with right now. I realize that I can't stop looking for Mycah, especially after the death of Cordell. I glance over at Clarissa's house. She may be the key to unlocking all this.

I push Clay off me. "I can't breathe."

"What's wrong with you?"

"You got the kids off to school?"

"They dressed and made their own breakfast and then walked down to the bus stop." He grabs my elbow and squeezes it, believing this to be a sign of affection. But he's hurting me, so I step back and regard him coolly.

"What's the matter?"

"Why didn't you go out looking for me?"

"I had a few beers last night. I was waiting for you to come home."

I shake my head.

"I couldn't just leave the kids here by themselves."

"You could have asked the neighbors to watch them."

"I barely know them."

"What if it had been an emergency?" I look away in disgust. "Did you at least call the police?"

"Twenty-four hours have to pass before they consider someone a missing person. That's a known fact."

"I could have been in a ditch somewhere for all you knew. But you thought it better to lie on the couch and drink beer and smoke cigarettes?"

"I wasn't smoking."

"Don't lie to me, Clay. I can smell the scented spray. And I saw the cigarette butts in the trash." I pause for effect. "How drunk did you get?"

"Okay, so I smoked a few cigarettes last night, but only because I was nervous about you. And yes, I had a few beers."

"There are two empty growlers in the bed of your truck. They weren't there last night when I left."

He looks at me, unable to defend himself.

"Just go back to your brewery and leave me alone."

"Cut me some slack. You're the one who went out last night and didn't come home."

"I don't want to be around you right now."

He holds his arms out as if to give me a hug, but I hold my palm up to his face.

"I love you, Leah."

"Whatever."

"I'd never do anything to hurt you."

"Too late. You've already hurt my feelings."

His shoulders slump around his hangdog face as he stares at me. He looks so guilty, yet I don't waver in my conviction. He knows from years of reading my body language that I'm being serious. He shuffles out the door, a broken man like he was that day many years ago when I broke up with him. I go to the window and watch him pull out of the driveway. Once his truck disappears, I collapse on the sofa and contemplate my next move.

This is crazy. What in the world have I gotten myself into? I can't be going out and getting drunk like that, leaving the kids home alone all night with Clay. Drunk and stoned Clay.

I walk over to the window and stare at her house. I'm almost tempted to wander over there and take another peek into her diary. I bet she's added some new details about Mycah Jones. There has to be another way for me to get this information without committing a crime. I feel as if I'm being dragged into a dangerous riptide and struggling to swim back to shore.

CLAY

Friday, October 16, 9:56 a.m.

*T*HE BREWERY IS COLD AND DAMP WHEN I ARRIVE. I pull up a seat at the bar and stare at the five taps calling out my name. It's not even ten a.m. and my head feels like a mash tank where the remnants of my brain are getting sparged through a mesh filter. I can't believe everything that has happened in the last twelve hours. Leah spent the night away from home, doing who the hell knows what. She knew I'd been drinking and smoking, and the kids will no doubt rat me out as soon as they arrive home.

Cordell Jefferson was murdered last night. A shocking development. Shot in the head as he sat in his Jeep. What in God's name is going on in this small town?

The hell with it. I reach over and grab a German wheat glass and fill it with Bavarian Hefeweizen. At 3.9 percent alcohol, it's perfect for when you're having more than one. A session beer, we in the industry call it. I bring the wheat glass to my nose and allow its redolent head to fill my nostrils. The familiar scent of bananas and clove reminds me why I became a brewer in the first place. Unfortunately, it's my worst-selling beer. These ignorant asshats keep asking me to jam a lemon wedge onto the rim. I have to educate them, explain that it's not custom in Bavaria to garnish this style of beer with a lemon. I need to stay true to my mission and not give in to the lowest denominator. Purity is the key. I'll quit before I ever resort to putting blueberries in my beer or serving them with lemon wedges.

The first Weiss goes down smooth and temporarily lifts the fog out of my head. It's light and refreshing. I sit back against the wall and stare at the stainless steel equipment in the brew room. It's quiet at this hour and I'm quite content to sit here by myself rather than be at home, arguing with Leah. I suppose she's right: I do drink too much. A functioning alcoholic is the clinical term. But I can't stop myself. If I'm to continue producing quality beer, sampling is an important part of the job. It would be like a chef who refuses to taste his food before it goes out to the customer.

I remember pouring Mycah a glass of Weiss beer and watching her expression as she smelled its glorious odor. Mycah made me feel good about my career choice. She seemed to understand the brewing philosophy of this company. It made me wish that Leah could support me like that. She won't even try my beers. All she ever drinks is that crappy wine of hers.

Mycah started to visit the brewery late in the afternoon, after Ben had left for the day. We both agreed that it was best to keep our affair quiet, seeing how I was married and she had a boyfriend.

"This beer is amazing," she said one afternoon in May while we were sitting at the bar.

"I'm so glad you like it."

"This one should sell like crazy."

"Education takes time, but they'll eventually come around."

She pulled my face to hers and kissed me on the lips.

"What was that for?"

"For being a great guy." She laughed. "As well as a mighty fine brewer and patriot."

"And a living legend in the bedroom?"

"Yeah, that too." She laughed and took another sip. "By the way, I talked to my father yesterday."

"Oh?"

"After looking at your numbers, he's really excited about the prospects for your brewery. He sees a lot of growth in the industry."

"Really?"

"Don't look so surprised. You've earned it."

"How much does he want to invest?"

"He's thinking about giving you the one hundred thousand dollars in exchange for thirty-five percent ownership, which, for the sake of confidentiality, he intends to put in my name."

I mulled it over for a few seconds. Thirty-five percent seemed a lot to give up, but for one hundred thousand dollars, I could expand the brewery and get a state-of-the-art canning process up and running fairly soon.

"Sounds like a fair offer."

"It's a great offer. He said he'll have papers drawn up sometime this week."

"I can't believe this is happening."

"Well, believe it, Clay Daniels, because it is."

At eight o'clock that evening, the phone in my office rang. Mycah and I had been having such a good time that I'd forgotten about my daily call with Leah. I sat on the leather couch and placed a forefinger to Mycah's red lips. We were both tipsy and in a silly mood. Mycah tried to conceal her laughter when she realized who was on the other end of the line. I cleared my throat and answered Leah's call, trying to sound as serious and sober as I could. I wanted to end this call as soon as possible and get back to partying with Mycah.

"Hi, Leah," I said.

"How are you, honey? I miss you so much."

"I miss you too. How are the twins?"

"Good, but they really miss you. We can't wait for you to come out next weekend."

"I can't wait to see you guys too," I said, watching as Mycah knelt down on the cold concrete floor. I tried to shoo her away, but she pulled off her shirt and smiled up at me, wearing only a black bra.

"We'll find a house and be a family again?" Leah said.

"Of course."

Mycah reached for my zipper.

"You sound strange, Clay. Is everything all right?"

"Yeah." I struggled unsuccessfully to push Mycah away.

"Clay?"

"Sorry, it's hard to talk right now. I'm under a mash

tank, fixing a broken hose." I tried not to moan as Mycah unclasped her bra and lowered her head.

"It's late, Clay. Don't you think you should be getting some rest?"

"I will." I closed my eyes and took a deep breath, my fingers buried in the tangle of Mycah's thick hair, trying to push her away. "Can I call you back tomorrow night?"

"Of course. Get some rest."

"I will. See you soon."

"I love you."

"Love you too."

I ended the call and pushed Mycah off me. She stared up at me with a devilish look in her eyes, her lips moist and glistening.

"What the hell are you doing?"

"Take it easy." She sat back on her haunches, revealing her perfectly shaped breasts. "Since we're going to be business partners, I want to see how you perform under pressure."

I grabbed her arms and squeezed. "Don't ever do that to me again."

"You're hurting me."

"You could have gotten me in big trouble."

"You're drunk and acting crazy."

"We're both drunk. What does that matter now?"

Mycah covered her face and began to cry. I wrapped my arms around her as she wept. I felt guilty about cheating on Leah, but that fell away as soon as Mycah gazed up at me. Mascara streaked down her cheeks. She looked so beautiful that I leaned over and kissed her nose. It didn't take long before we moved to the couch. Soon we were making love like two savage jungle cats.

After we finished, she rested her head on my chest.

"You'll understand someday when you have kids."

"I'm never having kids."

I laughed.

"What's so funny?" She raised her head and stared at me.

"I said the same thing when I was your age."

"I mean it. Having kids will screw up my future."

"Someday you'll meet a nice guy and your priorities will change."

"Nice guys finish last—no offense to you. I want to be rich and famous. I want to *be* somebody."

"I thought you wanted economic and social justice."

She smiled. "They're not mutually exclusive. Besides, it's about time us black people got our due."

"I'm down with that."

"Do you love your wife, Clay Daniels?"

"Of course I love her."

"Then can I ask why you're sleeping with me?"

"I don't know. Being with you is exciting and much different than being with Leah." I stared into her eyes. "Do you love your boyfriend?"

"That's irrelevant."

"Then why are you sleeping with me?"

"I didn't commit myself to marriage. Not yet, anyways."

"How about we stop talking and just enjoy what little time we have left together?"

"That's cool."

I pulled her into me. "You have your whole life in

front of you, Mycah. Someday you'll be married and making big bucks as a high-powered attorney, and you'll remember these moments we had together."

She laughed. "I'll remember them, all right. Sleeping with the beer man."

"Sometimes you meet someone and make a connection, and before you know it, it spirals out of control and that person is all you can think about."

"So I'm all you can think about?"

"Mostly."

"Me and your beer, huh?"

"Pretty pathetic, right?"

"It's actually kind of sweet," she says. "In another life, Clay Daniels, I could probably love you."

I kissed the top of her head.

"I wish we could stay like this forever," she said, snuggling against me.

"We both know it can't last."

"We're going to have to find a way to coexist once we become business partners."

"I'll send you a check every month."

"You better make sure they don't bounce or I'll sue your ass." She laughed.

"I'm the president. The buck stops here."

"You pulling rank on me?"

"You're sleeping with the CEO, aren't you?"

"The boss is allowed to sleep with the help?"

"Only with minority shareholders."

"I'm a minority with a minority share."

"At thirty-five percent, you'll soon be a rich minority owner. It's the American way."

"You're a real slave driver, you know that?"

I knew I'd have to break it off with her sooner than

later. It would be the best thing going forward. Mycah would be off to law school after her senior year, hopefully far enough away from Dearborn not to be a problem. Our affair would remain a secret that only the two of us would ever know.

Or at least that was what I hoped for at the time.

I polish off the rest of my Weiss beer as I recall those heady days with Mycah. I was so stupid to think that we could have ever been business partners. The guilt of what I did weighs heavily on me, and now Mycah is missing and Cordell is dead, and the entire town is up in arms. The memories serve to fossilize my past. Only death will release me from this prison of my own making. Either that or confessing to Leah what I did.

I notice that I've consumed two giant glasses of beer while thinking about her. I need to get back to work. Get my head on straight. Instead, I pour myself one more.

The Weiss tastes better with each successive glass. On an empty stomach, it has a nice pick-me-up quality that emboldens me to return to work. Ben will be in around noon to help me brew up an Alt beer, and once I'm focused on work, it's all I'll be able to think about.

After downing the remains of my beer, I jump off the stool and start to prepare for the brewing process. Other than drinking, work is the one activity that helps me forget about my marriage and the indiscretions I've committed.

As I heft a bag of malt over my shoulder, I think of Zack and Zadie and what their life would be like without me. Maybe they'd be better off if I weren't around.

But then I think of them being raised by Leah and it gets me wondering. Maybe my occasional presence in their lives is a good thing, and it makes me realize that I should be there for Zack and Zadie in order to save them from Leah's erratic behavior. But if Zack is any indication, it might be too late. The damage may have already been done. At least Zadie's a sweet and perfect child. I thank God every day for that beautiful princess.

LEAH

Wednesday, October 21, 9:03 a.m.

*F*OR THE LAST FEW DAYS, I'VE BEEN THE PERFECT
housewife. The perfect mother. Being perfect isn't
easy. I'm practically losing my mind from the extreme boredom of this perfect life. It didn't take long
for me to get this way, especially after all the interesting things that I've uncovered in this creepy little
town. Five days of doing laundry and cleaning the
house from top to bottom, trying not to think about
kidnapping and death, watching *Ellen* and *Dr. Phil*
every afternoon. Making breakfasts and dinners from
"scratch" and then hiding the frozen-food boxes from
my family. We're a well-orchestrated theater of do-
mesticity in which we conspire to suppress the obvious faults in our narrative.

Even makeup sex with Clay proved uninspiring, although that's not unusual. I lay there in the dark the

other night as he went through all the preordained steps leading to "the act." Despite showering and brushing his teeth, Clay still reeked of beer. Sadly, I couldn't muster the energy to fake an orgasm. I just lay there like an inanimate object until he finished.

What does that say about our relationship? About me? When I can't even pretend to enjoy sex anymore? I need something to help me escape this rut I've settled into. The only thing that interests me these days is sneaking into Clarissa's house and reading her diary. It's like an alcoholic trying to quit, white-knuckling under the pressure and in desperate need of a drink. Without help, they eventually succumb to their obsession.

So when I woke up this morning, I resolved to continue with my stealth activities. So what if it's wrong to sneak into a neighbor's house. What else have I got in my pathetic little life? No playgroups, no stay-at-home mommy friends. And who knows, it might actually help the two of us grow closer. If I can discover her likes and dislikes, maybe it will give us something to talk about. Google and Amazon spy all the time in order to find out more about their customers. So why can't I do the same thing in order to make a friend; someone I can open up to and share my innermost feelings?

Frankly, I'm a bit surprised that the police haven't yet contacted me. I sort of hoped they would have tracked me down by now as a person of interest. I want to be wooed, needed, and treated as someone to be taken seriously. My rendezvous with Cordell the night of his death has thus far gone undiscovered by the police. I know I've done nothing wrong. I'm a private citizen looking into a horrible crime. It's not against the law to search for answers.

At first, I debated going to the police with my information. But what would that accomplish? Cordell and I met for drinks, two lonely souls having a private discussion. I'll go down to the station once I know all the facts. I do know this: Cordell was killed for a specific reason, and his relationship with Mycah is the only connection I can make at this point.

The kids are off to school and Clay has left for work. The dreadful laundry can wait, as can the dreadful dishes. I've already let Mr. Shady out to do his business. Clarissa won't be back until later in the afternoon (I hope). I've decided to go over there this morning and read more of her diary. I'm expecting to find some interesting new entries.

Mr. Shady scampers back inside, wagging his tail and staring up at me as if I'm truly a bad person. Why am I projecting these emotions on an innocent dog? None of this is his fault. My guilt is not appeased by scratching his chin, but it's like he's reading my mind. And this thought reminds me of my twin sister, Annie, and how I wronged her when we were young girls. I loved her for sure, but I most definitely wronged her.

I lift the diary out of the drawer, unlock it, and then open it to the page where I left off.

October 15
   I've managed to hide the bruises from my colleagues by wearing long sleeves. It still hurts though. Russell has been unusually nice to me as

*of late, swearing that it will never happen again.
He's acting all sweet and kind. Of course, he's
done this before and look how that turned out.
I'm done believing in fairy-tale endings because
I know fairy tales don't exist. This is the vicious
cycle of domestic abuse.*

*I'm frightened for my well-being and the well-
being of the children. Maybe I'm in denial about
my husband. Yes, he's hurt me in more ways than
one. But is he capable of murder? It's hard to
picture my husband as a killer. No, I don't want
to believe it despite every shred of evidence
pointing me in that direction. Even if he was the
father of her unborn child, he would have persuaded Mycah, in his usual charming way, to
abort it. That's just the way he is. A coldhearted
bastard. But maybe she refused. And he killed
her. I don't want to believe that he'd throw his
family and career away for a manipulative bitch
like her. But what if he did? And what if he did it
in order to KEEP his family?*

*I can't speak to my colleagues about any of
this. I badly need to confide in someone. But
whom? I still can't believe I went to my neighbor's house the other day with brownies in hand.
Maybe it was a good thing she wasn't home. The
one time I needed to talk to someone and Leah
wasn't there.*

*I do want to be friends with her. She seems
nice, and I think she wants to be friends with me
too. I want to get to know her better. If that's to
happen, I need to know more about her. Check*

*out her past. Make sure she's not some loony
tune before I can fully trust her.*

*Only here in my diary can I be completely
honest and forthright. Thank God for you, dear
Diary. Because there has to be someone—or
something—I can open up to and tell my most
secret fears. I'm bursting at the seams, keeping
it all locked inside me until the time comes when
I can let it all out.*

She wants to be friends with me? This is a very
good development. But what does she mean when she
says she wants to check out my past? I don't want her
to know any of that. For years I've been trying to put
my past behind me—trying to erase it from the deepest
recesses of my memory banks. But with the Internet,
anyone can do a background check and research another person. Everyone these days is an open book.

I turn to the next entry in her diary.

October 16

Cordell found dead!!! WTF??

*Now I'm seriously worried. Russell gave me a
big hug when he heard the news this morning.
Told me we were going to get some marital
counseling and that he was going to be a better
husband. I have to admit he is a great dad. The
kids adore him. If only they knew what he's done
to me, and possibly what he's done to those two
college kids. Maybe Cordell tried to blackmail
Russell. Russell's not a man to be trifled with.*

*He was a linebacker in college and earned a
black belt in jujitsu when he was eighteen.*

*I'm lucky to have a college friend working for
the FBI. She informed me that Leah graduated
from high school just outside Seattle. Leah
Green her name was back then. Earned her college degree in English from Oregon State and
then returned to Seattle for a master's degree in
Creative Writing. Worked a few odd jobs before
she met her current husband. They dated for two
years before they got married and had kids.
Haven't got all the information yet, but so far so
good. She seems pretty normal.*

*If Russell finds out I'm talking to her, he'll be
pissed. He wants to control most everything I do.
This totally sucks. I'm an intelligent black
woman living in constant fear and there's nothing I can do about it. Only Russell knows the
truth about me. It's why I need to be discreet. It's
why I must check everyone who seeks to get
close to me. The closer they get, the more anxious I become. No one can find out my secret.
NO ONE!*

*Now that Cordell is gone, I might be next in
line. I don't sleep at night, afraid I might not
wake up. I wouldn't put it past Russell. With
each passing day, I'm starting to believe that
control freak did the unthinkable.*

*I know I'm difficult to get along with. I'm
moody and easily tire of other people. I hope
Leah will find it in her heart to forgive me for
the horrible way I've treated her. Maybe one of
these days we can be friends.*

What could she have done to deserve such treatment? I drop the diary on the bed as if it's infected with a deadly virus. It makes me nauseous to think that Clarissa has asked someone to look into my past. I feel violated. What right does she have to do this? I'm not sure I even want to be friends with her now. How could I be a friend with someone who would stoop so low? What I'm doing by reading her diary is nothing like her act of betrayal. I do what I do out of love. My motive is simply to connect with another human being and develop a spiritual bond with them. Never in my life would I ever think about looking into someone else's past.

I can't go on reading these pages. Not in this condition. Yet I can't leave here without knowing what else is in this diary. I pace the room, trying to ward off the anxiety growing within me. I run downstairs and pull a Riesling out of the refrigerator.

Once back upstairs, I unscrew the bottle and take a long gulp. My hands are shaking so badly that I can barely make out her handwriting. I pace the room and try to think of a plan. Maybe I could come back tomorrow when my head is clear and I can resume reading it.

The wine calms me. I sit on the bed and rack my brain for an idea. Why didn't I think of it earlier? I pull my phone out and snap photographs of the pages. Then I close the diary and stick it back under her lingerie.

After being a teetotaler for the last five days, my body welcomes alcohol like an old friend. Fearless, I take a selfie in the bedroom and inside their bathroom. This is not a prudent thing to do, but I don't care about prudence now. I walk around the house, laughing, and take a selfie in every room. It gives me a huge rush knowing the power I wield over Clarissa and her family. How dare she look into my past. What gall that woman has.

I'm dying to know what her secret is, the one only her husband knows and is holding against her. Is this why he controls Clarissa and keeps her from making friends? It does seem cruel of him. Considering her lofty position and years of higher education, it must be humiliating to be under his thumb. It's why we can't be friends: because he's watching her every move and is controlling to a fault.

I'm developing a theory about what happened. Russell engaged in an affair with Mycah and then killed her when she threatened to go public with the news of their unborn child. An admission of an affair with one of his students could potentially destroy his career as head of the department. This is the reason he killed Cordell. Cordell knew about the affair and it posed a threat to Russell's reputation. Cordell didn't want Mycah to leave him.

Had Russell been spying on us at Applebee's? The thought frightens me. I need to expose him before he comes after me next.

I lift the bottle to my lips and take another sip. I must be careful not to drink too much lest I get drunk. My tolerance today is extremely low. I will drink just enough to take the edge off. I'm excited and slightly fearful, and the wine buzz is giving me the impetus to further investigate Russell. But other than this diary, what evidence do I have? The contents of this diary would never be allowed in court unless I could convince Clarissa to open up to the police.

I stagger downstairs and slip out the patio door, nearly tripping over the threshold. If only I'd eaten a bigger breakfast this morning I wouldn't feel so swoozy. LOL. Is that even a word? Swoozy? The air is brisk and a cold wind blows through the reedy fields. The starlings are nowhere to be seen today. They're probably sitting like statues in the tree branches, waiting for the first brave flyer to lead the way.

Mr. Shady barks as soon as I enter through the sliding glass door. I laugh at this silly little dog with the nervous tic. So what if he despises me. It takes him a few seconds to recognize who I am, and when he does, he turns and scampers off into the living room. I've read that dogs can sense a person's mood. Does that make me a bad person? I don't think so. But I do know that I'm often insecure and needy. I try to compensate for my low self-esteem by being the best wife and mother I can be, which isn't always the case. Mr. Shady is the only one who sees me for who I truly am. He knows deep down that I'm a lush and a bad seed.

I take another sip of Riesling. After placing it down on the counter, I notice that the bottle is half gone. Darn. That's way more than I planned on drinking today. My head spins as I sit down to collect my thoughts. I screw the top back on and hide it underneath the sink, behind the Tupperware, cleaning agents, and dishwashing liquid, where Clay won't find it.

It's not like I have a drinking problem or anything. Sure, I've often consumed a few more glasses than I should have since coming here, but that's to be expected. It's the stress of moving three thousand miles from home and trying to make friends and fit in. Back in Seattle I was practically a teetotaler, stopping after one or two glasses. I had plenty of mommy friends, two adorable children, and was completely happy with my life. Once we're comfortably settled here, and more financially secure, I'm sure I'll return to my old ways and be satisfied with one glass of wine at dinner.

This ordeal has taken a lot out of me. How do I stop Clarissa from delving into my past without letting on that I've been reading her diary? My alcohol-fueled brain is spinning with ideas and theories. Russell tried to make the attack on Mycah and Cordell look like a hate crime. That's why Mycah's body hasn't been found. He needed to destroy the evidence of her pregnancy so that no one would ever know he was the father. And now Cordell is dead and no one can ever testify against Russell.

I lie down on the sofa, resting my head on the pillow. A pleasant opaqueness muddles my vision as Mr. Shady jumps up on my chest and curls to sleep. A short nap will do wonders for me. By the time the children arrive home, I should be my normal self again.

I will go to the police at some point and tell them what I've learned. But not yet. I must find a way to gain Clarissa's trust. Get her to speak to me in a forthright manner. I need her to confide in me before it's too late. So that she can escape the abusive relationship she's mired in.

My eyes close and I try not to think about the twin sister I once loved. I haven't thought about her in a long time, and I don't want to start thinking about her now.

I fall asleep. The first dream I have is of Annie waving up to me from her wheelchair.

* * *

The doorbell rings, waking me out of my deep slumber. Are the kids home already? Have I slept through the afternoon? I look over at the clock and see that forty-five minutes have passed. Who could be at my door? My head feels prickly and for a brief moment I believe there's been an incident at school. A Columbine or Sandy Hook comes to mind. I rush to the front door and open it. To my surprise I see Clarissa standing there. What does she want? Does she suspect that I've been sneaking into her house during the day and reading her diary?

"Clarissa. What . . . what are you doing here?"

"I'm sorry. Am I interrupting something?"

"No." I glance around our empty neighborhood. Everything seems hazy and my head throbs from the effects of the wine. The house is a complete mess. Unfolded laundry litters the living room. Leftover breakfast plates and cereal remain on the kitchen table.

"Are you okay, Leah?"

"I don't feel so good." I stiffen up, unable to imagine how dreadful I must look. "I thought a nap might help me feel better."

"It must be nice to take a nap whenever you like." Her condescension irks me. "I hope you feel better."

"Have you heard the news? Someone murdered Mycah's boy-friend."

"I heard about it. Cordell was such a wonderful young man with lots of potential." She glances over my shoulder and takes in my messy home. "What a terrible tragedy."

"I wonder who killed him."

"This town is not as open-minded and welcoming to

black people as you might think. There's still a lot of hidden racism out there."

"Not in this house. We teach our children to value people of all races and sexual preferences."

"The reason I came over here is to invite you and your husband over for dinner tonight. It's about time we got acquainted with one another, especially considering the terrible things happening in this town."

I feel like reaching out and hugging her. Then I remember Russell. Violent and controlling Russell.

"So that's a yes?"

"Are you sure that's a good idea?"

"I'm inviting you, aren't I?"

"Of course. It's a yes then."

"Fantastic." She smiles and touches my arm. "I know it's on short notice, but I'm really hoping that you and your husband can make it."

"I'm almost certain we can. I need to call Clay and let him know."

"Can we expect you around seven?"

"Seven sounds great."

"Good. See you then."

I close the door and curse at my bad manners. Why didn't I invite her inside for some coffee or wine? Then I look around at the pigpen and am glad I didn't. I teeter over to the couch, open the blinds, and watch as Clarissa walks up her stairs. She's so elegant and refined that it's hard to believe she's a victim of domestic abuse. I see her as a strong and determined woman willing to fight for her dignity. She should take her kids and get the hell out of that house before he does something tragic.

There's so much to do before the dinner party tonight.

I run happily into the bathroom and stare at myself in the mirror. Crap. It's no wonder she asked about my health; I look like I've contracted Ebola or dysentery. My hair is frizzy like cotton candy. The right side of my face is red and splotchy from sleeping on the couch, and beneath my eyes sit two used tea bags. My lips appear pale and indistinguishable from my chin. I need to sober up before the children come home. There'll be lots more wine tonight, I'm sure of it. I call Clay and tell him the good news—that we've finally been invited to the Gaineses' house for dinner. Instead of being happy, I hear him groan on the other end of the line. It's so like him to put a damper on my good mood.

CLAY

Wednesday, October 21, 11:36 a.m.

*W*ELL, THAT'S JUST GREAT. LEAH WENT AHEAD AND made dinner plans without me. And with the Gaineses no less. It's bad enough that I'm way behind schedule, but to spend half the night with people I barely know is something I'm not exactly wild about. If it's awkward, I'll be forced to sit there and act all happy and gracious. Then I'll see them in the neighborhood on a daily basis and have to pretend to be nice.

Thank God for alcohol.

Here's something no one knows about me. I suffer from social anxiety. Middle and high school were the worst, but because of my size, I never suffered the indignities that many other kids did.

College proved to be much better for me because of the constant presence of alcohol. Alcohol helped me in most social situations and put me at ease with others.

Drinking raised my social status and gave me the confidence I needed to interact. By my sophomore year, I'd begun brewing beer in my frat house and providing the boys with plenty of suds for their weekend bashes. It provided me with an interesting hobby that eventually became my passion. Whenever I kegged a beer, our house became *the* place to party, and I the reluctant hero.

The delivery truck pulls up at the back of the facility and drops off bags of malt. I cut the guy a check, chat for a minute, and then watch as he pulls away. I dry hop the IPA that will eventually be conditioned in some old oak casks. There's too much work to do here, and I'd rather not attend a stupid dinner party with my neighbors. My head feels clear and lucid, and I vow not to have another beer until later this evening.

The Gaineses won't intimidate me. I don't give a shit if they have PhDs, higher-paying jobs, or a bigger house. Despite the precariousness of our finances, I'm the one pursuing his life passion. I'm the one who dropped out of the corporate jungle to chase his dream.

I'll bring two growlers of beer as a gift. Hopefully, they're not wine drinkers, although something tells me they are, despite Russell's frequent staff visits to the brewery. In my experience, wine people are far snobbier than beer drinkers. "Pretentious" is a better word. Maybe I'm wrong about this, but I don't think I am.

Mycah called four days after our tryst in the back office of the brewery. She hadn't received definitive word yet from her father. I tried to keep myself focused on getting the brewery ready for opening night and controlling all the unexpected construction costs that would inevitably arise. Despite the fact that we were on a tight schedule, all sorts of problems seemed to be popping up at the last minute. Zoning permits got delayed and contractors failed to show up. My mind raced with priorities, deadlines, recipes, and of course, keeping in touch with my family.

I was living two lives on two different planes and trying to juggle it all. The frightening reality that these two disparate planes might someday meet up kept me awake most nights. I knew that I'd end it with Mycah sooner rather than later. But I needed that infusion of cash. If I didn't open on time, the brewery could be doomed before it even began.

We agreed to meet for dinner at a restaurant ten miles out of town. I arrived first and sat at the bar. Mycah waltzed in thirty minutes later, wearing a white floral dress with black boots studded with silver buckles. She rushed over and kissed me on the lips. Although I'd steeled myself to be professional this evening, the kiss obliterated all my well-thought-out plans. Her lips tasted like fresh Bing cherries, and the kiss lingered long after she sat down. Even longer in my memory.

She ordered an expensive chocolate martini. I never even stopped to consider that I'd been paying for everything since we met.

"Have you heard from your father?" I asked.

"Is that all you care about? Money?"

"I thought we were going to talk business tonight."

"Well, you thought wrong."

I sipped my nine-dollar Belgian Trappist beer—brewed by celibate monks who'd taken lifelong vows of silence—and compared it to my own.

"My father's still mulling it over."

"Mulling it over? I thought he'd already agreed to invest in the brewery."

"I did too, but he says there are many details to consider before he fully commits."

"Okay." I tried not to let this setback worry me.

"He's an unusual guy. I suppose you have to know how to get on his good side."

"How would I do that?"

"You flatter him. Make him feel appreciated. He loves a good gift."

"How about I send him a nice bottle of single malt Scotch?"

"For a hundred grand, you have to do better than that."

"Would it help if I went to New York and met with him face to face?"

Mycah laughed at this.

"What?"

"No offense, Clay, but your brewery is chump change to a guy like him. My father's used to high finance and brokering multimillion-dollar deals. That's why I'm acting as a go-between."

"What do you suggest?"

"He loves going to Knicks games, but he's way too cheap to buy tickets."

"Great. I'll buy him a pair."

"He'd love that. Only problem is that he likes floor seats. Refuses to go to a game if he's not on the floor."

"How much is that?"

"Six."

"Hundred?"

"Thousand."

I nearly shit my pants. "No way I can come up with that kind of money."

"Takes money to make money. And I'm getting those tickets at a discount price because I know someone in the box office."

"Jesus, Mycah. I can't afford six grand."

"Okay, have it your way. It's something my father always appreciates and then repays in full." She sipped her martini. "You want to be a player, then you have to know how to handle important men like my father to get anywhere in life."

"You think he'll put up the money if I do this?"

"You put him on the floor in Madison Square Garden and he'll practically adopt you."

"That will make it a bit uncomfortable between us."

"A little incest won't harm anyone." She laughed.

"Okay then. I suppose I can come up with six thousand bucks if I make some cutbacks here and there." I sighed, thinking about where to cut a few corners. The price seemed steep, but I'd come this far.

"Enough business talk for now. I want to have some fun tonight."

"What do you have in mind?"

"Anything and everything you can think of." She winked at me. "Let's travel round the world and back."

"Is that really a good idea? We're going to be business partners soon."

"No one's ever going to know." She placed her hand over mine. "I'm not looking to get married, Clay Daniels, just have a little fun. We're two like-minded people blowing off some steam. At the end of the year it'll all come to an end, and I'll be off to law school. New Haven's a long ways from here."

I considered walking out of the restaurant and leaving her, but I was too weak and desperate to cut and run. And I badly needed the money.

"Let's get out of here," she whispered.

"You don't want dinner?"

"What I'm hungry for is definitely not on the menu."

After I paid the drink tab, she grabbed my hand and led me out of the restaurant. We took my truck, with the words FRESH BEER painted on the side panel. Despite feeling guilty about what I was about to do, I could barely contain myself. I was unable to resist the lustful urge coming over me. How long had it been since a woman had come on to me in such an aggressive manner? For the first time in a while, a beautiful woman had found me desirable and wanted to have sex. I realized that this might never happen again.

We went back to the hotel and wasted no time ripping each other's clothes off. This time, however, she asked to try something different. She wanted me to treat her roughly. This was a new twist in our relationship. I had no idea what she wanted me to do or in what form this rough treatment would take. I'd never done crazy sex shit like that before. The few women I'd slept with before Leah, I'd treated gently and with respect. Occasionally, they would ask me to fuck them harder during the course of events, which I happily obliged, but that was the extent of my wild side.

Leah never liked aggression and always asked that I go slow and steady. She preferred making love with the lights off, and we always did it in the missionary position, safe and boring. When we were first married, we did it three times a month. When trying to have kids, it happened maybe three times a week, sterile and mechanical. But in the last few years, it had developed into a twice-a-month pattern—if even that.

But what Mycah asked me to do in that hotel room shocked me and marked a new milestone in our relationship. I remember her emerging from the bathroom dressed in a head wrap and a plain white dress that was ripped and soiled with grease. Her feet were bare and she carried a whip in one hand, which she handed to me. I was at a loss for words when she told me how she wanted me to do her. She leaned over the bed, exposing the caramel skin on her back. Then she ordered me to whip her.

"No. I won't do it."

"You need to, governor. Treat me like the mouthy slave you've always wanted to possess."

"No."

"Pretend that you're Thomas Jefferson and I'm your humble servant Sally Hemings." She turned toward me and took me in hand. "The founding father taking control of his nigger."

Her words excited me, and though I felt confused and ashamed, I gently struck the leather straps against her back.

"C'mon, master. I know you can hit me harder than that."

"I can't."

"Would you rather suck cock? You and your assistant jerking each other off in the back of the brewery?"

"Shut the hell up."

"Then hit me. And hit me hard."

Pissed, I struck her. Not hard enough to cause welts but hard enough to hurt.

"Now rip off my dress and take me from behind." She rested her elbows on the mattress.

I pulled her dress off, in unfamiliar territory, and followed orders. I was too humiliated to turn back now.

"Call me nasty stuff. Treat me like dirt. No, lower than dirt."

"Like what?"

"Damnit, Clay, use your imagination."

"Whore."

"You can do better than that."

"Slut."

"Put more emotion into it, for Christ's sake. You're Thomas Jefferson, racist president of the fucking United States. White privilege dictates you can have any slave on the plantation."

"Nigger." The word felt horrible coming out of my mouth, and I instantly felt ashamed.

"That's better. Now slap my sorry ass around as if I tried to run away and gain my freedom."

I said it again, this time much more convincingly, and I brought the whip down hard over her back. I felt demeaned and dirty. She'd humiliated me to such a degree that I took control of my character and roughed her up good. She tried to resist, calling me every name in the book, but I managed to restrain her. We had no code word to stop in case she was really hurt, so I navigated those treacherous waters to the best of my ability.

I experienced a deep sense of shame as I drove her back into town that evening to retrieve her car. We didn't say much during the ride. Assuming the oppressive role of a slave owner had burdened me with tremendous guilt, and I couldn't even begin to imagine how the real slave owners did it. The humiliation of owning slaves hit home with me far more than reading any textbook ever had.

I thought of Leah as I drove on, thinking how mortified she'd be if she knew what I'd done. Along with my cheating ways, I experienced remorse so deep that I wanted to find a bridge and jump from it.

I dropped Mycah off at her car. We didn't kiss goodbye or say any parting words. She got out of the truck and stared at me through the window. She seemed distant and disappointed, like I'd not lived up to my end of the bargain. Had I not pleased her the way she desired? I felt like a failure on so many different levels that it depressed me. I'd made the check out for the Knicks tickets, which was supposed to go toward the deposit on our new home. Then I watched as she drove off.

But this was what she wanted. To be treated like shit. She was a liberated woman and educated at one of the finest liberal arts schools in New England. And her father was interested in investing in the brewery. Why would being degraded in such a humiliating manner turn her on? Or maybe the joke was on me, and I was the one with mud on my face. In some ways, I felt I'd let her down. Was I not good enough in the sack? I'd never been the strong, dominant male in the bedroom. Nor in my life. Most women my age wanted a sensitive

and compassionate lover. Not a pig that called them
filthy names and treated them like dirt. I'd already es-
tablished myself as a cheating pig. What would it matter now if I repeated my sin? The die had been cast, so
I figured I might as well try again to please her.

LEAH

Wednesday, October 21, 7:12 p.m.

I CAN'T BELIEVE HOW HANDSOME CLAY LOOKS TO-night. I reach beneath the table and squeeze his callused hand. What a lucky girl I am to be his wife. There's no one else I'd want by my side right now, despite his repugnant behavior the other night.

I thought it would be weird sitting across from the Gaineses, knowing what I know about their relationship. But to my surprise they appear quite at ease with each other, and after a few glasses of wine, I begin to forget about the turmoil tearing their marriage apart. Maybe I misinterpreted Clarissa's journal entries and read more into them than I should have. Russell seems quite the gentleman, kind and humorous, and full of hilarious anecdotes about teaching and the students he'd taught in class. It's funny how a few glasses of wine and some good conversation can change one's perception of another person. To my delight, I realize that I'm quite enjoying myself despite all I know.

Our banter is lighthearted and filled with humorous stories about raising children. There's one thing I've learned and that is that children are always a good icebreaker in conversation. Russell plays the polite host, continually filling our wineglasses. It seems almost hard to picture him as an abuser. Then again, I've read that many domestic abusers are charming leeches whose wives enable such rotten behavior. Maybe they'd gone to counseling or were in the process of working things out. I have to tell myself that every story has two sides. Surprisingly, Clay seems to be enjoying himself too. He discusses the progress of his brewery and is careful to point out the distinct flavor profiles of the beers he brought with him.

Clarissa's caterer works in the kitchen as we converse over wine. While things sizzle away on the stove, we sit in the dining room, laughing and joking. We polish off the first bottle of wine in no time. I take an occasional sip of beer so as not to hurt Clay's feelings. I really don't like beer. It's yucky and bitter tasting and tends to leave me bloated. I've never told this to Clay, but he knows my view on the subject and does not seem offended by my preference for wine. Complimenting him on his beer is kind of like faking an orgasm.

We've polished off two bottles of Merlot and Cab by the time dinner is served. Surprisingly, their caterer is an older white woman, and it's surprising because the menu tonight is fried chicken, collard greens, mac and cheese, chitlins, fried okra, and watermelon salad. It fits the stereotype a bit too neatly for me, but it's their culture and not for me to judge. The food is delicious, especially the crunchy fried chicken. Russell gently coaxes us to try the chitlins, and as much as the sight of them repulses me, I try a teensy-weensy bite. They crack up when I gag, and I have to spit the chitlins into my napkin while laughing hysterically. An acquired taste, Russell says. Gourmet food for the slaves.

I feel happy and content. Finally, all my hard work has paid off and we are becoming friends. But somewhere in the back of my mind I can't reconcile my feelings with the other Russell. The Russell from the diary who's a cheating abuser.

Clay goes to pour me another glass of wine, but Russell takes the bottle from him, grabs my hand, and fills the glass. His grip surprises me and I momentarily freeze in stunned silence. What is he doing? He holds it there a few seconds, smiling at me from across the table. Wearing an uneasy expression, I look up at Clarissa, but she is in deep discussion with Clay. Russell finally lets go and I feel a sense of relief. My queasiness is suddenly replaced by a sense of chagrin. I giggle drunkenly, believing that I'm imagining things. Yes, all the wine has gone straight to my head and I realize I've made a big deal out of nothing.

Russell engages me in conversation and we laugh happily. At the moment, he seems like the most erudite and nicest man I've ever met. I can see how Clarissa was initially attracted to him. Clarissa laughs loudly as Clay pours the remainder of the dark beer into her glass. She takes a sip and compliments him on concocting such a tasty porter. Her hand reaches out and rests on his, and stays there throughout my conversation with Russell.

Am I losing my mind? I turn and look at Clay and see his beer-flushed face focusing on Clarissa's face. She looks stunning tonight and it's clearly obvious Clay's flirting with her. He doesn't try to remove his hand, nor does he pay any attention to me. He has no idea that Russell is "allegedly" abusing her. I turn back to Russell, who is leaning forward and speaking to me in a low voice. I'm flustered, confused, my mind racing in so many different directions that I can't hear what he's saying. I nod repeatedly as he talks, not wanting to spoil a potentially good friendship because of my paranoia. Or because I'm unnecessarily worried about my husband flirting with Clarissa.

They laugh and look into each other's eyes. I want to run over and put a stop to their shenanigans. What the hell does Clay think he's doing?

The woman cooking our dinner sets down a peach cobbler and a sweet potato pie. She pats Clarissa on the shoulder and says good-bye to us. The four of us compliment her on such a fantastic meal as she makes her way out of the house. Russell goes back to the kitchen and uncorks another bottle of Pinot and pours everyone a glass. Looking at the others, I can tell that they are as drunk as I am.

"How you liking that Pinot, girl?" Russell asks me, a devilish grin on his face.

"Quite delicious," I say, my taste buds on the verge of neuropathy.

"Grapes grown and pressed by a black family out in Oregon. Visited that winery myself."

"It sounds beautiful."

"Nice folks too. Kind of funny that they've got a

bunch of Mexicans working for them. Have their own vineyard with their own slaves. It's the modern-day version of a plantation."

"Here's to the free market," Clay says, raising his glass.

"All labor in this market is a matter of exploitation. Because when you come right down to it, we're all slaves in one form or another."

"I'd say that's a pretty cynical view of things," Clay says, laughing in a manner that tells me he's quite buzzed. "With two employees on the payroll, that must make me one sorry-ass plantation owner."

"It's not the size of the plantation that matters. It's how you exploit it."

I find that statement odd but decide to keep my mouth shut.

"Where'd you come up with that theory?" Clay asks.

"Says in the Bible, 'If one is burdened with the blood of another, he will be a fugitive until death.' One man's enterprise is another man's plantation, plain and simple."

I sip my wine as Clay laughs in boozy consternation. For some strange reason, I sense that this cheerful mood is about to change into something dark and sinister. My only consolation is Clay: he's always been an easygoing soul with a long fuse.

"You really believe that?" Clay says.

"Don't matter what I believe. The truth is the truth, man."

"Peach cobbler, anyone?" Clarissa asks.

"I'll have some," I say cheerfully, trying to remain upbeat.

"Does that make your caterer a slave?" Clay asks.

"You familiar with the old saying about 'calling a spade a spade'?"

"Play nice, Russell," Clarissa says playfully.

"I find it ironic that you hired an elderly white woman to cook us this soul food," Clay says.

"Judge a person not by the color of their skin but by the content of their character—unless they can cook like Miss Judy." Russell roars with laughter.

"Miss Judy cooks the best soul food in the area, right, baby?" Clarissa puts a hand on her husband's arm.

"Where would we be in this town without Miss Judy? My dear wife here is a working girl and can't cook a lick. Not like her forebears, anyway."

"That's because I'm not your slave, dear."

"I love a modern girl." He turns to his wife and caresses her cheek with the back of his knuckles. Clarissa smiles awkwardly. "As for being a slave, you're not going to find anyone makes a better peach cobbler in these parts than Miss Judy. Of course, my momma made the best cobbler I ever ate, but my poor old momma's not around anymore."

"I so enjoyed that meal," I say. "Except for the chitlins. They tasted like shit." I break out laughing, so happy with my witty and edgy banter.

"That's because chitlins are a lot like my husband," Clarissa says, laughing. "Completely full of shit." We all laugh drunkenly.

"I'm so glad you enjoyed my people's food," Russell says, placing his large hand over mine. "It's a reminder of our heritage. It's a sure sign of the times when the children of slaveholders can break bread with the children of the slaves they once oppressed." He holds up his glass and we all toast.

I take a sip of wine, let a few seconds pass, and clear my throat. "So what do you make of this missing girl?" I say, changing the subject.

"A real tragedy," Russell says, sneaking a look at his wife before turning back to me. "There's haters everywhere in this country. Haters are born to hate. The only difference today is that it's hidden behind the facade of civility and good manners. When it emerges, it erupts from the bowels of this earth in the most violent fashion and in the unlikeliest of places."

"Can you say 'lacrosse team'?" Clarissa says.

"Why do you think they attacked her?" I ask.

"Mycah was outspoken in her support for civil rights and economic justice," Clarissa says. "Maybe too much so for her own good."

"It's a plantation mind-set," adds Russell. "People around these parts don't like an uppity, intelligent black woman getting in their business and pointing out the hidden racism that exists here in Dearborn. Everyone knows that Chadwick College has a long and shameful history of racism. So when they see someone like her on campus, speaking her mind about economic justice and police brutality, they fall back into their old tribal patterns."

"Then why did you come here to Maine if you think it's such a bad place?" I ask.

Russell laughs. "What's the difference where we live? Racism is everywhere you turn. Police stopping and murdering young black men for no other reason than the color of their skin or that their britches are riding too low. Young black men turning to gangs. Higher rates of incarceration and poverty in the inner cities." He turns to Clay. "Born the right color in this country, you've

been granted a privilege denied to the rest of us. Whoever killed Cordell and kidnapped Mycah Jones is
sending a message that the Confederacy is alive and
well in these parts. Wouldn't even be surprised if it's
someone on campus."

"Then why didn't they kidnap Cordell?" I say.

"Why do you think? Trying to humiliate an upstand-
ing black man by absconding with his woman. It's a
form of emasculation. It's how the plantation owners
asserted their dominance over those proud slave men,
by selling off their women."

"I certainly hope the police find the creeps who did
this," Clarissa says. "I want those racist bastards to pay
for what they've done. In this day and age, no black
person should have to walk around in fear because of
the color of their skin."

I study Clarissa's face to gauge if she's being authentic or merely spouting platitudes. After reading her
diary, I feel that something is off about this dinner.
Have we been invited here to listen to them pontifi-
cate? The strange thing is that they're preaching to the
choir. If only Russell knew that I was on to him. That
he abuses Clarissa in private and has been unfaithful to
her. What a messed-up marriage these two are mixed
up in. Despite Clay's occasional missteps, it makes me
thankful to be married to him. He's not perfect, not by
any stretch of the imagination, and neither am I. But at
least we love and respect each other.

"Do you think they've hurt her?" I ask. "Assuming
she's still alive."

"Who knows what they've done. But I can tell you
this: if it had been a white girl who'd gone missing in
Dearborn, the police would have surely found her by

now." Russell once again places his hand over mine as if to emphasize his point.

I try to remain calm and not let Russell intimidate me with his physical prowess. Clay's face turns noticeably flush at the sight of Russell's hand over mine, or maybe it's because of all the beer he's consumed. I remain still, slightly nauseous from all the wine and rich food. Russell's thumb gently massages a circle in my palm. Clarissa looks over at me with an uneasy smile. Is it possible that he's trying to make me uncomfortable? Or am I once again overreacting?

"Funny how history defines us. We're all descended from Adam and Eve, but then some of our ancestors took a detour to get where we are today," Russell says.

"Do you believe in God?" I ask.

He laughs. "You?"

"Yes, but we haven't gone to church in some time."

"Going to church has nothing to do with believing in God," Russell says. "How about you, Clay?"

"Of course I believe in God," he says. "To quote Ben Franklin, 'Beer is proof that God loves us and wants us to be happy.' "

Russell laughs and lifts his glass. "I'll drink to that."

"Did you grow up Christian?" I ask, pushing on for some meaning.

"Well, I suppose you could say that. Grew up in a Southern Baptist family, so I suppose that qualifies me as a Christian man. Like you, it's been a while since I been to church. My great-great-grandfather on my momma's side was a Southern preacher in Mississippi during the Civil War."

"My relatives fought on the side of the Union," Clay says rather smugly.

"Well, I sure do thank your people for their sacrifice. But it still is not enough to remedy all the wrongs done to us black people."

"How so?" Clay asks.

I try to gently pull my hand away, but Russell refuses to let go.

"Tell him what you mean, baby," Clarissa says.

"Why don't you tell him, hon? You the one with the silver tongue."

"Russell believes that only reparations will settle the score and make our people right again," Clarissa says, looking uncomfortably at me.

"Reparations?" Clay's expression changes in a manner that worries me.

"It's the only right thing to do. You wrong me. I sue for damages. Eye for an eye, like the good book says."

"Payback to every black person in this country?" Clay asks.

"Unless you got a better way to repay that debt, that's the ticket."

Clay laughs. "That's absurd. My family never kept slaves. In fact, they fought to emancipate your people."

"My people?"

"Yeah, your people. Besides, the two of you don't look as if you need reparations," Clay says, his words stinging with acrimony.

"Reparations don't have to be just money, my good man. It can come in many forms. Maybe you the one that needs reparations."

"From what?"

"From the damage slavery has done to your own family. The guilt. The sins of the father passed on to the son."

"I don't need shit," Clay huffs. "Look, I'm sorry that your ancestors were slaves, Russell, but that has nothing to do with us, right now, sitting here at this table and enjoying a nice meal."

"It has everything to do with us. The past affects everything we do. We're all slaves in this goddamn country because of the past."

"Come on, man, be real. You know what I'm talking about."

"For your information, Mr. Clay, my ancestors were not even slaves. Okay, maybe way back on God's dark continent they were once slaves, but in the Deep South my people were the masters who owned slaves."

"Your ancestors were white?" I blurt out, confused.

Russell laughs. "Hell no, they were as black as Georgia molasses and some of the richest folks in the Charleston area. My great-grandfather on my daddy's side raised crops and sold off his slave women for profit. He was known as the harshest taskmaster in the South, and his slaves were the worst fed and most poorly clothed of them all. Those poor slave bastards hated that mean old son of a bitch more than any of the white masters. In fact, they wanted to wipe that old geezer off the face of the earth. He ruled his plantation with an iron fist and kept his niggas in line. Cross him and you got a whipping you'd not soon forget."

"I never even knew there were black slave owners," Clay says.

"Lot of black folks owned slaves. Part of history a lot of people don't know about," says Russell.

"Why did his slaves hate him more than the white plantation owners?" Clay asks.

"Because he was black like them *and* he sold off their women. Kept a ratio of one woman for every twenty men. How do you think them boys felt when they got a little frisky? Before you know it, they started turning against each other, the plantation owner, and then the system in general. Many resorted to homosexuality like the cats in prison. By the time the Civil War started, William had more than one hundred slaves. His kids branched off and had their own slaves too. Sort of a family business. That old dog even managed to produce a commercial gin mill as well."

"Then why would you want reparations?"

"Because it was the system that failed us. Failed us all. Caused black people to turn against each other. Led to all this black-on-black crime. The paper bag test. Turned many a proud man homosexual. Those wrongs must come home to roost, Clay. It's inevitable," Russell says, still gripping my hand.

"I'm still not buying it," Clay says.

"Now, I'm not saying that I or my family require financial remuneration. Sure, we done good. But reparations can come in more ways than money. Take this get-together, for example. My wife and I invited you two over for a nice meal. Good food, conversation, and plenty of wine. Neighborly stuff like that. Pay our respects."

Clay laughs as if amused by this. I simply want my hand back but am too afraid to appear ungrateful. Maybe Russell is just being affectionate, and this is his way of showing it. But for some reason it feels creepy and strange and makes my skin crawl.

"We'll certainly repay the debt and invite you two over sometime," Clay says.

"There you go. Or we could become closer in other ways." Russell's hand moves slowly up my forearm.

Clarissa reaches out and touches Clay's hand and he immediately recoils at the touch.

"What? You're telling me that you're not attracted to a beautiful, intelligent black woman like my wife?" Russell says, a sly smile creeping over his face.

"You're crazy," Clay says, knocking over his chair as he stands. He grabs my hand and pulls me up, saving me from further humiliation.

"Sure, I'm crazy. But that doesn't take away from the truth of the matter. Which is that I'm taken aback by your antipathy toward my African queen."

"See this." Clay holds up his ring finger. "I'm a happily married man."

"As am I," Russell says, holding up his own ring finger. "Why the hell do you think I'm so happy?"

"We're not like that."

"That's not what I heard," Russell says.

"Let's go, Leah." Clay pulls me by the hand. "We don't need this bullshit."

"Are you implying that I'm unfaithful because, on occasion, I step outside the lines?" Russell says.

"Take it any way you like," Clay says, helping me on with my coat.

"Swinging's enhanced our marriage."

"Good for you."

"What about those poor slaves who were forced to share their precious women. Would you accuse them of being unfaithful?"

"They didn't have a say in the matter."

"But you and I have choices, Clay. We have free will, according to our loving and just God."

"We don't swing, Russell, and that's final. That's the choice *we* made."

"It don't mean a thing if you ain't got that swing," Russell replies in a singsong voice.

"I'm sorry how this turned out, Leah," Clarissa says. Russell shoots her an angry look. "Let them be, Russell. They're not up for it."

"I guess we can forget about being neighborly, then," Russell says as he opens the front door for us.

Clay stops at the threshold and glares at him.

"I was just playing with you, Clay. My ancestors were never slave owners. They were house niggas just like the rest of them poor folks."

"I guess the apple don't fall far from the tree then."

"Best of luck with that white privilege thang."

I'm sobbing as we make our way back to the house. What a disaster. My head is spinning and I feel like throwing up. What just happened? How can I ever face our neighbors again, especially Clarissa? But I'm proud of Clay for standing up to Russell and declaring his commitment to our marriage. I've not been the ideal wife, especially in the bedroom. But that's more about my own issues than a blank rejection of Clay. It amazes me that he's stayed by my side for so long, waiting patiently for me to come around.

Clay pays Molly and then we fall back drunkenly on the couch. I rest my head on his lap as Clay runs his hand through my hair and massages my tingly scalp. I feel so lucky to have such a loving and faithful husband.

Now I'm convinced that Russell is a monster. I feel terrible for Clarissa and more sympathetic to her plight than ever. She needs to leave him right away. He's the one pushing her to do those terrible things like swapping partners. I'll bet anything that she has no interest in swinging or serving his prurient interests. She's with him for the children and to keep the family intact. Russell is charismatic, handsome, and highly manipulative. A man like that tends to develop an overinflated sense of his own ego. I remember running into pretentious jerks like that during my college years. Professors who invited me out for coffee or drinks, only to try to lure me back to their bed.

Clay massages circles into my warm scalp. His gentle touch puts me at ease and makes me feel safe. Even lying on his lap, drunk, I can smell his stale beer breath. I'm nearly asleep when I feel something pressing against my cheek. I keep my eyes closed and pretend not to notice. I'm much too upset now for that. I don't have the capacity to go through with it. Clay will never come right out and ask me to have sex with him. It's just not his style. He'll wait for me to make the first move. Always me. And I rarely make it these days.

"I didn't overreact, did I? Tell me I did the right thing," he says.

I pretend to wake up. "Of course you did the right thing, dear. What kind of silly question is that?" Something that Russell said suddenly troubles me.

"I know how badly you wanted to be friends with them."

"Not enough to do that." I stare up at Clay in consternation. "Why? Is that something you'd like to try?"

"Of course not."

"Do you find Clarissa attractive?"

He hesitates for a brief moment before saying, "Not

really. I mean, some men might find her good looking."

"So you do find her attractive. What is it you like
about her?"

"Jesus, Leah, is this an interrogation?" He laughs.
"I'm just saying that some men might find her attractive."

"Because she's black?" I lift my head off his crotch
and turn to face him.

"Jesus, I'm not saying that she's attractive because
she's black. Or that I'm in any way attracted to her.
What difference does the color of her skin make?"

"I saw the way you and Clarissa were holding each
other's hands."

"You're crazy."

"Am I?"

"Yes. We were just having a conversation." He
pushes my head aside and walks upstairs. I feel like
such a jealous fool for goading him, but I can tell when
he's lying. I suddenly realize that it's not me who caused
him to become aroused. It was her. He was thinking
about Clarissa the entire time I was here with him.

I lift myself off the couch and stagger upstairs. Clay
is lying in bed, turned away from me. I climb in and
apologize profusely to him, but it doesn't seem to make
much difference. My head is drowning in wine and I'm
so tired I don't even take off my clothes. I reach
around under the blanket and grab his member, give it
a gentle squeeze, but there's no response. I feel terrible
about the way I've treated him.

"I love you, Clay."

"Love you too."

"I'm very lucky to have you."

"Thanks."

"I know you'd never cheat on me."

He grumbles something under his breath.

"What do you think Russell meant when he said, 'That's not what I heard'?"

"I have no idea what you're talking about."

"He said it as if we were cheating on each other."

"Forget Russell. He was just talking smack."

"I wonder what he could have meant by that."

"Who the hell knows with that guy? He's obviously a loose cannon."

I laugh, the wine making me bold and adventurous. I suddenly want to fulfill my marital duties to this wonderful man. "Would you like to make love to me, Clay? Would you like me to pretend I'm your slave? A young girl that you trapped behind the barn one night and had your way with?" I giggle girlishly.

He spins around and glares at me. "What did you just say?"

The look on his face scares me, but I don't want to back down now. "I thought you might like that. Something different."

"Are you messing with me, Leah?"

"No. I just thought I'd step out of my comfort zone for once and change it up for you. Do something 'edgy.'" I make quotation marks with my fingers.

He seems to think it over, and as he does, I suddenly realize that I don't want to assume this role anymore. Why did I even offer myself up in such humiliating fashion?

"You'd do that for me?"

"If that's what you really want."

"If it's what you want."

I gulp nervously. "Okay then."

Clay begins to rip off my shirt and panties, a bit rougher than I would have liked. This isn't how I thought it would proceed. I can't even begin to imagine how a poor slave girl must have felt back then.

"Clay?"

"Hold still."

"Please," I mumble, but he thinks I'm assuming the role.

He pins my wrists down on the pillow and begins to push into me, with each successive thrust calling me names I've never been called before. It hurts, bad, but I close my eyes and keep my mouth pressed tight. Hopefully, it will be over soon. I shouldn't complain. I'm the one who offered myself up. I'm the one who volunteered to be his sex slave for a night.

His beery breath blows on me and makes me sick. I turn my head into the pillow and bite my lower lip until the skin breaks. A trickle of salty blood makes its way into my mouth. Although I don't resist his entreaties, I feel dirty and violated. He flips me over roughly and takes me from behind. This is something we've *never* done. I bite down on the pillowcase, fighting back the tears. This act is entirely new and most assuredly not welcome. Finally, he groans and climbs off me, falling back onto the mattress. I begin to sob quietly as he huffs and puffs, trying to catch his breath.

I don't want him to see me crying, and so I turn away from him until our backs are touching. I'm sore all over. There'll be no cuddling or affection tonight.

He took advantage of my good nature to punish me, and there is no way I can protest. He treated me like the lowest piece of dirt on the planet. A nonentity.

Like a lowly slave.

And I'm the one to blame. . . .

CLAY

Wednesday, October 21, 11:30 p.m.

I TURN OVER IN BED, WIPING THE TEARS FROM MY eyes. I'm pissed at myself for doing that to Leah, and I'm pissed at her for suggesting it. What was she thinking? Our backs press up against each other in stubborn defiance. Although I know I should turn over and embrace her, tell her how sorry I am for what I've done, I don't. I can't apologize. It would be an admission of guilt. Of not understanding her mixed message. And I have to stay strong, deny any plausibility that she wasn't role-playing. She was the one who suggested it. What the hell did she expect? Of course, I'm lying to myself if I think that what I did was right. I took liberties. My behavior was the action of an angry, vindictive husband who feels guilty for having cheated on his wife with a girl almost half his age. A husband fed up with his wife's passive-aggressive bullshit, and because of that turned elsewhere for intimacy.

So why did she want me to treat her like a slave? Does she know something about my relationship with Mycah? It's almost as if Mycah's ghost returned and whispered something nasty in her ear.

Here's the sad irony. Mycah appeared to enjoy the rough sex. She couldn't get enough of it. Name the sexual act and we did it. She encouraged—no ordered—me to smack her around. There was no holding back. Grab her hair and pin her wrists down. Nothing I did or said seemed to upset her, no matter how demeaning. She performed the most bizarre sexual acts I'd ever seen, things I'd only seen in movies. And hell yeah, I began to enjoy it. It opened my eyes to a new avenue of pleasure. It felt liberating, exciting, and way too cool to be true. To be the sole object of a beautiful girl's desire made me feel like a man again.

I wipe the tears from my eyes. What I'm thinking right now is shameful and wrong, and it has nothing to do with hurting my wife. A plutonium grade of sadness buries me to the core. Something inside me whispers that I'll never experience such sexual pleasure again. I cringe at the notion that that part of my life is over. Forever. I miss the curves of her body as well as the caramel hue of her skin. I miss running my hand over her smooth, strong stomach, and fingering her symmetrical belly button and perfectly shaped ass. There were nights I made love to her for hours at a time and into the early morning. Three or four sessions a night until I was spent. Delirious with love or lust, I seriously contemplated leaving Leah and the kids to be with her.

What a damn fool I was.

Then I woke up one day and learned that Mycah had gone missing. And I can't help but hope that she is dead and buried.

LEAH

Thursday, October 22, 7:45 a.m.

I WAKE UP AND FEEL SORE FROM LAST NIGHT. THERE are bruises on my upper arms and thighs. Clay has already left for work. I envision him down at the brewery, holding test tubes and flasks up to the light as if he's a Nobel Prize–winning chemist. My head hurts, although I can't be sure if it's from the wine or from our late night tryst. I remember my skull smacking repeatedly against the headboard. I smile cheerfully, reminding myself that what we did last night was based on love. It confounds me at times how worked up I get over absolutely nothing. Our lovemaking was consensual. I gave him permission to role-play because I'm a dutiful wife who loves her husband. This is what normal couples do to keep their marriage fresh and exciting. It says so in all the women's magazines. Although I'd prefer not to do that sort of thing again, maybe what we did will end up strengthening our bond.

I down three Tylenol with a glass of water and then limp to the kitchen. There's so much I need to do today, and it all involves tracking down this missing girl. I can't wait to ship the kids off to school so I can take out my phone and read the rest of Clarissa's diary. Maybe she'll drop another clue as to what Russell did to her. Because if she won't report him to the authorities, then I certainly will.

As I make the kids breakfast and bag their lunches, I try to recall the events from last night. Unfortunately, Zadie is gabbing away at the table and trying to get my attention. My mind shifts gears like a badly tuned racing car, and I feel myself jerking from one speed to the next. If only she would stop talking for a few seconds so I can hear myself think. Zack sits quietly at the table, reading a book I can only assume is one of those weird science fiction novels he's always nose deep in. This one's titled *A Scanner Darkly*.

Once the kids are out of the house and on the bus, I rush back inside and open my phone. The soreness radiating throughout my body spreads up my arms and into my shoulders. I remember how Clay pinned me down last night, an expression of mock rage over his face.

I open up the jpg file, hoping that I might learn something about that girl's whereabouts.

October 19
   Still no word about Cordell's death. Russell
seems unfazed about it, as if nothing has
happened. I still find it hard to believe that he

killed Cordell, but what else am I led to believe?
What else can I do?

We all have secrets, every one of us has them,
whether we know it or not. Maybe it's best to
bury these nuts as deep as possible and never go
back. Shoot any rival squirrel that tries to dig
them up. He holds it against me. My own husband.

I followed him today when he left during
lunch. His department secretary tells me everything. Seems he's been leaving every day around
noon. Today I finally worked up the courage to
follow him. He drove around some. Then he
headed toward Carver, a few towns away. After
thirty minutes of driving, he stopped in front of a
house in a neglected part of town. The house
was a run-down bungalow located next to the
river that used to feed the nearby mill. I heard
the waterfall before I saw it. He sat in his car for
about ten minutes before he got out and went
inside. Fifteen minutes later he emerged from
the house. Then he drove back to campus for his
afternoon class.

What was that all about? Whom was he seeing? I wanted to stay and find out, but I had a
meeting to attend that afternoon.

I need to go back at some point and find out
who lives in that house. I want to know why he
visited it. Is one of his mistresses hiding inside
that bungalow?

Somehow I convinced Russell that I should
invite our neighbors over for dinner. He wasn't
too happy about it. Not in the least. But he

*agreed to go along in order to appease me. The
question is, will he behave or will he spoil the
dinner with his usual arrogant bullshit?*

*Leah confounds me. I find it odd how her his-
tory abruptly stops at the age of thirteen. I've
looked into her past and there's no record of her
attending grade school or middle school. It's like
she appeared out of nowhere. Or disappeared
from someplace else. Was she adopted later in
life? Did her parents die and her relatives in
Seattle take her in? My friend in DC is supposed
to call any day now and tell me her full story.
I'm extremely curious to know who this woman
really is. Or who she was as a girl. Honestly, I
find it rather comforting to realize that I'm not
the only one with a secret. Then again, her secret history could end up being nothing at all.
Or maybe just as bad as mine.*

I slam my phone down on the table and Mr. Shady
scampers out of the kitchen with his tail between his
legs. What is this woman doing to me? Why is she
checking out my past? I pace around the room in a
state of agitation, wondering what to do about it. I debate going over there and demanding that she stop this
nonsense. But if I do, she'll know that I've been sneaking into her house and reading her diary.

My hands are trembling so bad I can barely hold my
glass of juice. I'm visibly shaken by this development.
Mr. Shady runs back into the kitchen and starts barking
furiously at me. There's one more diary entry on the
phone, but I'm not sure I can read it. The coffee has
made me jittery. I take the phone into the living room

and settle on the sofa, staring at it, working up the courage
to read it.

I've made up my mind about all this. I'll confess to
Clarissa what I've been doing and beg for her forgiveness, and pray that she'll keep this secret between us.
But what if she doesn't? What if she tells Clay? Clay
cannot know that I've been sneaking into her house
and reading her diary or he'll think I'm crazy. I'd be
willing to do almost anything to keep him from finding
out about my past.

I scroll down to the next journal entry, almost too
afraid to read.

October 20

*I still can't believe it!!! WTF! When my con-
tact informed me about Leah, I nearly spit out
my wine. Who would have ever guessed? She
seems so quiet and unassuming. It's amazing she
can even live with that hanging over her head.
Then again, she was only a child.*

*The invitation will be made tomorrow. I'm
going to feel weird sitting across from this
woman, knowing what I know about her. So
creepy. But in some ways it's a relief to know
that someone else has a past stranger than my
own.*

*Despite my shock, I managed to sneak out of
the office just before Russell's lunch break. I
drove over to that house and parked across the
street and then waited patiently. I wrote down
the address. 26 Peavey Terrace. Fifteen minutes
passed before I saw his BMW pull up. He sat in
his vehicle for a few. Then he approached the*

*front door. He rang the bell and waited. A few
minutes later the front door opened. Was that a
woman I saw? I was a good distance away. Is
she still alive? OMG! I can't be sure it's her, but
it looked a little like her.*

*Should I call the police? Then again, if I'm
wrong, I'll look like a complete fool. It could
possibly jeopardize my career and rip me away
from my children. Russell will surely file for divorce, take custody of the kids, and then reveal
my true identity.*

*But what if it's really her? What the hell
would that mean? Did these two lovebirds conspire to get rid of Cordell?*

*There's only one way to find out. I'll need to
go over there at some point. If it's her, then
maybe I can get her to tell the truth about what
happened that night and see if it was really a
hate crime or whether Russell had anything to
do with it.*

Shit! Russell's coming up the stairs. Gotta go.

I grab my coat and car keys and run out to my Prius.
I Google the address and head toward Carver. It takes
me twenty minutes before I pull into this broken-down
mill town. The GPS leads me to Peavey Terrace and I
slowly cruise down the street. I search for Russell's car
and am relieved to see that it's nowhere in sight.

My entire body is shivering as I let the engine idle.
An Aerosmith song comes over the radio: "Dream
On." I put on my sunglasses and pull the knit cap over
my scalp. It takes me a few minutes before I work up
the courage to shut off the engine. I take a couple of

deep breaths. It takes me another five minutes before I get out of the Prius. The street is quiet, the neighborhood depressing and run down. A lone dog barks savagely in the distance. I make my way up the stairs until I find myself standing at the front door. The sound of rushing water fills my ears, reminding me that my heart is like an overflowing creek. I reach up and ring the doorbell. A minute passes before the door opens and the harried face of a woman appears in the crack, her head wrapped in a grimy white towel.

CLAY

Thursday, October 22, 10:34 a.m.

*E*VERYTHING FEELS RIGHT IN THE WORLD ONCE I'M back at the brewery, busy with the day's activities. It feels more like home than my actual home. Keeping busy eases my mind and allows me to forget all that I've done.

I try not to dwell on that disastrous dinner last night and the events that followed in the bedroom. What was I thinking? Yes, I was drunk and angry. But hurting Leah in that manner is the last thing I want to do. She's essentially a good woman. And for once she was trying to make *me* happy. Unfortunately, she triggered a response that I couldn't control.

I scoop grains into the plastic bucket, thinking about Zack and Zadie, and how I've wronged them. They seem almost foreign to me since moving here. It's as if our brief separation has irrevocably altered the parent-

child balance of power. Zack is becoming more estranged, isolating himself in his room most nights and
reading his weird books. I worry about him. I worry so
much about him that I end up spending twenty hours a
day at the brewery—worrying.

Once eleven o'clock rolls around, Ben prepares our
coffee in the French press. But it's not coffee I want.
My yearnings have shifted and not for the better. I
crossed a line with alcohol and now it seems as if I
can't walk it back. From morning to night I have this
powerful urge to drink. Drink, drink, drink. It temporarily fills some deep vacuum in my wretched soul. I
watch as Ben pours me a piping hot cup of black coffee. I drink it with urgency as Ben sits across from me
and looks on. The coffee tastes good and strong and
momentarily quells my need for alcohol. But sooner or
later it will return—and when it does, it will do so with
a vengeance.

What the hell was up with that dinner last night? It
felt like I was starring in some awful B movie with the
evil couple from next door. The woman didn't seem so
bad. In fact, she seemed rather pleasant. Attractive too,
although I could never admit that to Leah. I sensed at
the time that she was flirting with me, however gently.
Her husband was a bona fide asshole, though, and I
wanted to rip his head off when he grabbed Leah's
hand and held it in a suggestive manner. But when he
went on about slavery and reparations—that was when
I really lost it.

Leah is acting strange as of late, stranger than she
usually acts. I wonder if she has any idea about me. I
know I'm being paranoid, because if Leah harbored
any notion of my infidelity, there'd be hell to pay.

She'd have left me long ago and taken the kids with her. Sometimes I think that splitting up with her wouldn't be the worst thing in the world. Hell, I'm not even sure she loves me anymore. She says the right things, plays the role of the perfect housewife, tries to make everyone happy. But it's mostly for the kids' sake. Aside from the other night, she rarely wants to have sex. A lot of wives throw up the white flag when it comes to sex. But I need it more than ever. I need intimacy and affection and adventurous excitement. I yearn for more sex.

Just not in the middle of the day when I should be working. Scheduled, boring lovemaking that occurs in the dark is never any fun. Merely seeing it scrawled on the calendar takes me completely out of the mood.

It's hard to believe that Mycah still occupies a good deal of my waking thoughts. She's ignited something inside me that I never thought existed. And now that she's gone, I know with absolute certainty that I will never again experience that kind of heightened sexuality.

Mycah and I drove down to Boston one day and stayed at the Park Plaza Hotel. After strolling around downtown, we passed through the Boston Common until we arrived at the Public Garden. The duck boats were cruising around the pond, so we stopped to watch. Only a few passengers were out for a ride that day. It was nice to be out with this beautiful young girl on my arm, the sun shining, a radiating glow filling me with a joy one could only experience in the moment. Skyscrapers glistened in the backdrop. Old brick architecture appeared everywhere. Ye olde pubs beckoned us to stop in and quaff a beer by a warm fire. We walked around openly, no fear of being seen by anyone we knew. No fear of being judged or gawked at. We didn't need to worry about age or racial disparity as we walked hand in hand through downtown Boston.

After watching the duck boats for a few minutes, Mycah dragged me by the hand to the periphery of the park, laughing in hysterics. I had no idea what she was doing, but I allowed myself to go wherever she wanted. In broad daylight, she pulled me into a bramble of thick bushes, unzipped me, and dropped to her knees. The notion terrified me and I couldn't believe what she was doing in the light of day. People were everywhere, walking along the streets and through the park. Fearful we might be seen, I made sure to keep my eyes glued to the duck boats paddling through the pond.

The first of August arrived and there were only a few weeks before Leah and the kids were set to arrive in Maine. Mycah and I were supposed to meet up at a hotel outside Dearborn, but she sent me a brief text canceling our meeting. There'd been no explanation or reason why. At the time, I'd been trying to work up the courage to tell Leah about the affair and ask for a divorce.

Mycah's father had not yet cut the brewery a check, but she assured me that he was still committed to investing in the brewery, especially after I'd coughed up six grand for Knicks tickets. She even said that her father, after looking at the brewery's numbers, might be willing to invest more money for an additional ten-percent stake. It was a lot to give up, but the extra money would allow me to significantly increase production—and I'd still be calling all the shots.

But then a few days passed and I didn't hear from her. I texted and called but heard nothing. It wasn't like her not to return my calls—or what little I knew of her in the four months we'd been seeing each other.

I parked in front of her apartment and waited for her to arrive. After an hour passed with no sign of her, I returned to the brewery. I was way behind schedule and planned to work late into the evening. Ben usually stayed late if I asked him, but then I had to pay him overtime, which I really couldn't afford.

My cell phone rang around ten that night. It was Mycah. She wanted to meet me at some Podunk bar on the outskirts of town. I pulled up to it forty minutes later and sat in the parking lot, listening to a live concert on the college radio station. The squat, windowless bar supported a neon sign on the roof that said Rodeo Red's. A dozen choppers sat in front of the building, which in normal times would have been enough to keep me motoring down the road.

I went inside and sat at the bar. A song by some country rebel was playing over the overhead speakers. I looked around the dimly lit joint and saw a small stage and two pool tables off to the side. A few of the bikers—real hard-ass types—sat across from me, staring sullenly into their drinks. Draped over the far wall was a huge Confederate flag.

This was the last place I ever expected to meet Mycah, but then again she'd proved to be adventurous and unpredictable. I ordered a draft beer, which tasted like shit. Dive bars rarely clean their beer lines and the lines eventually start to collect yeast and sugars, which kill the taste of the beer. I finished it and ordered a rum and Coke instead.

Laughter went up and all heads turned as soon as Mycah walked in. I could have sworn a few of the bikers were snorting coke behind one of the pool tables. She removed her leather pocketbook from her shoulder and sat down next to me. She was dressed casual chic, but the cumulative effect was, as usual, stunning. She looked totally out of place in this shitty juke joint. Every head in the bar glanced up from their muddy cocktail or stale beer to take her in. Were they staring at her because she was hot or because she was black? Or both?

"Would you rather sit at a table?" I asked.

"No, the bar is fine." She ordered a Sea Breeze and the grizzly- looking bartender laughed.

"What the hell is a Sea Breeze?"

"For God's sake, just give me what he's having," she said.

"One rum and Coke coming right up for the little lady."

"Why'd you pick this dump?" I asked.

"I find rednecks entertaining. There's not many bars like this where I come from."

"Seems a little dicey choosing this place."

"These inbreeds don't scare me." She laughed in a weird manner. "Why? They scare a big guy like you?"

"A little." I laughed and sipped my awful drink, gazing at all the hard eyes staring in our direction. One bad-ass wore a leather vest and a red bandanna and had a long scar running across his cleft chin, making it look like a cross.

"Don't be such a pussy, Clay. A big strong brewer like you could probably kick all their asses."

"Ya think?"

"I asked you here for a reason. I'm afraid I have some bad news."

"Forget to bring your whip today?" I gently tickled her stomach and she backed away.

"I'm being serious."

"Okay." I lifted the straw to my lips.

"The loan from my father is not going to happen."

"What?" Her words stunned me. "Why?"

"I advised him against it."

"Why the hell'd you do that?" A few of the bikers noticed my reaction and began to wander in our direction.

"Don't make a scene."

"What the hell do you mean you advised him against it?" I grabbed her shoulders and squared her to me. "Goddamnit, Mycah, what are you doing?"

"We can't be together anymore, Clay. I think it's a bad idea to go into business with someone who you are absolutely crazy about."

Her words floored me. All I could taste was that god-awful rum poisoning my taste buds. Not getting the loan seemed pale in comparison to losing her, especially after admitting that she was crazy about me. I knew the end of our affair was coming, but the sudden reality of it hit me hard. Why was she breaking up with me? I'd thrown everything away to be with her, and now she was tossing me aside like a wet rag. I sat on that stool, heartbroken and at a loss for words.

"Please, Mycah, give me another chance."

"This is what you wanted, Clay. Now it's over between us. We were two people having a little fun and then it turned serious." She slung her purse strap over her shoulder and stood to leave. I moved in front of her, blocking her exit.

"Tell me why?"

"We have no future—you said so yourself."

"Tell me you don't love me."

"I don't need to tell you shit. Now, get out of my way."

"Please, Mycah, I'm begging you to rethink your decision."

"Don't be an asshole about this, Clay. We both knew it was going to end sooner than later."

"I'm not moving until you give me a reason."

She pummeled my chest and face, and I staggered back in shock at her ferocity. "Loser. Go back to your skinny-ass wife."

I grabbed her hands and pushed her back on the stool. She screamed as I restrained her. One of the bikers, a scrawny guy with wavy blond hair and a diamond earring, approached while the others looked on. Mycah struggled to escape my grasp, but I squeezed her wrists so tight that I could tell it hurt. I didn't care. I seethed with indignation at the thought of her leaving me. In that moment, all I wanted to do was to wrap my arms around her and tell her how much I loved her.

"Get your hands off me, motherfucker."

"Damn you, Mycah. You can't just play with my emotions like that."

"Take that shit outside," the bartender barked.

"Mind your goddamn business," I snapped, pushing Mycah back against the bar.

"Maybe I'll tell your wife about what we've been doing," Mycah shouted. "Bet she'd like to know how good you are with a whip."

"You better shut your mouth."

I felt something tapping against my shoulder and realized that the blond biker had his hand on me. I let go of Mycah and stepped back, taking in the biker's amused expression. He was at least six inches smaller than me, but he looked as if he'd gone through a ten-year gang war with the Bandidos. His thinning blond hair swept back over his scarred scalp, making him look like a model for the Aryan Nation.

"This asshole bothering you, sweetheart?" the blue-eyed biker said as he grabbed me by the throat.

"Mind your own fucking business, hillbilly," Mycah shouted, punching the man in the shoulder. The blond man laughed as the other bikers surrounded us.

"Hear how that bitch spoke to you, Drifter?" one of the bikers said.

"Sure are ungrateful." Drifter eyed her warily. "But goddamn, you're a fine piece of ass."

"We don't want any trouble." I raised my hands as he squeezed my throat.

"Shut up, Gomer."

"Get your filthy hands off him," Mycah said, punching the man in the arm. The compact biker backhanded her across the face with a lightning-quick flick of his wrist, and Mycah went sprawling against the bar.

"Look, sir, we apologize if we got carried away," I said, eyeing the long knife attached to his belt. "Please, just let us go our way and we won't bother you again."

"But you already done bothered me, boy," the man

said, moving his face closer to me. His eyes were Bermuda blue and penetrating. "Problem is you don't know how to deal with your woman."

"I'm not his woman, asshole," Mycah shouted.

"Shut up, nigger." He turned to Mycah. "What's a welfare queen like you doing in this honky-tonk joint anyway? Trading your EBT card for booze?" The other bikers laughed.

Mycah cleared her throat and spit in his face. While still gripping my neck, the biker wiped the spit off his cheek. Then he jabbed a straight right into Mycah's face. Her head snapped back and she grunted. Blood trickled from her nose as her knees buckled. She reached over the bar and grabbed a napkin to staunch the flow.

"Come on, Drifter, let these two assholes go," the bartender said. "Not like you never fought with your old lady before."

"Watch your mouth, Rusty. You the one let these two come in here and offend our sensibilities." He leaned over the stool and glared at her while gripping my neck. "This here ain't the ghetto, girl. Your homeboys ain't gonna drive by and save your pretty ass tonight."

Mycah unhooked the strap from her shoulder and rested her pocketbook on her lap.

"What do you know about the ghetto?"

"I grew up worse than you monkeys ever did, so don't tell me about how hard your fucking life was collecting welfare checks, drinking forties, and smoking crack on the street. Boo-fucking-hoo."

"You grew up with a privilege denied to me," she said. "Your greedy ancestors enslaved my people and profited from them."

"This," he says, letting go of my neck and holding up his knife, "is all the privilege I need in my life. It's how I protected myself in prison against all those homeboys."

"Dumb-ass redneck. Didn't your white-trash momma teach you to never bring a knife to a gunfight?"

"Can you believe the balls on this one?" Drifter said, laughing.

Mycah reached into her purse, pulled out a handgun, and pointed it at the biker's head. My heart churned as I stood in stunned silence, wondering what this crazy girl was capable of doing. She jumped down off the stool, ignoring her bloodied nose, and pressed the barrel into Drifter's vein-riddled forehead. The man smiled and held up his wiry arms as if to mock her.

"Hands up, don't shoot."

"You disgust me."

"You gonna shoot me, hon? Come on, let's see if you're brave enough."

"You gonna stand there and let him talk to me like that, Clay? You gonna let these rednecks push me around?"

"Jesus, Mycah, put the gun away and stop acting so crazy," I said.

"I want so badly to shoot this inbreed." She moved close to Drifter until her face was mere inches from his. He was smiling from ear to ear, clearly enjoying this encounter.

"Be a good little monkey, babe, and pull the trigger," the biker said. "That way Uncle Drifter won't oppress you in the back room with his enormous white privilege."

She stepped back, lowering the gun until she was aiming it at his crotch.

"How about I blow this off instead?"

"You want to blow off my dick?" Drifter looked around at his associates before breaking out into a fit of laughter. "Why don't you get down on your knees and blow it off instead."

"Suck this." She kneed him in the balls, and Drifter crumpled to the floor. Mycah pointed the gun at the other bikers. "Any of you other hillbillies want a piece of me?"

Mycah grabbed my hand and walked us backward toward the door. Once we reached our vehicles, she turned to me.

"You're not a real man, Clay Daniels. You're just a useless faggot like all the others out there."

"Mycah?"

"Stay away from me from now on. Go back to your pale wife and kids, and don't ever call me again."

She jumped in her car and sped off down the road. As I climbed into my truck, I saw a few of the bikers straggling out the door and into the overhead light. I didn't wait to see what would happen next. I stepped on the gas and got out of there as soon as possible, kicking up dust and dirt in my wake.

By the time I made it back to the brewery, I was a wreck. What kind of man would allow a biker to hurt his girlfriend and squeeze his own neck like that? Never had I felt so humiliated in my life. It made me realize how desperately I wanted to return to the good graces of my family. How could I have ever considered leaving them? I was willing to do anything now to win

Leah back, even though I'd never really lost her in the first place.

I staggered into the brewery that night, depressed and alone, and poured myself a beer. The investment opportunity was gone and so was my six thousand bucks. I quaffed the first one down in no time and then poured myself another. I knocked back beer after beer until I could barely stand. Someone called during my marathon drinking session, but I didn't pick up.

The next morning I lifted my aching head off a sack of grain and wondered if it had all been a dream. Then I felt Drifter's phantom hand around my neck, remembered Mycah pointing the gun at his crotch, and knew instantly that it was no dream.

LEAH

Thursday, October 22, 1:27 p.m.

"*W*HO ARE YOU?" THE WOMAN ASKS THROUGH the crack in the door.

I freeze, wondering if it is truly her. The room behind her is dark and I can barely see her face, a face I'd only glimpsed on the evening news and in the newspaper. In them she resembled a glamorous model or famous actress. The girl in front of me, without makeup, looks anything but.

"I asked who you are. What do you want?"

"You're Mycah Jones."

"Sorry, but you have the wrong house."

"No, I'm fairly certain that I don't."

"You're wrong, lady. Now, get the hell out of here before I call the cops."

"Please do. In fact, I'll call them if you'd like." I take out my cell phone.

"No. Wait." The girl puts her face up to the door and looks around to see if I'm alone. "How did you know I was here?"

"It's complicated." I can barely contain my excitement at finding her. "May I come inside and talk to you?"

She closes the door and leaves me standing there, wondering what to do next. A thousand thoughts run through my mind as I debate whether to call the police. Will she escape out the back door? What led her to this godforsaken house in the worst part of this depressing town? I call Clay, but it goes to voice mail. Mycah undoes the bolt lock and the door swings open.

"Come in," she says, looking around to make sure no one sees her.

I stash my phone away and enter the dark living room. Clothes lie strewn everywhere and a suitcase sits on the floor next to the battered sofa. Greasy blotches soil the green shag carpet. A water stain spreads out over the ceiling and down across the wall. The inside of this house smells of mold and cat dander. A white bathrobe wraps around Mycah's slim body. Although it's dark inside, I can clearly see the hint of a bruise on her face. Without the benefit of makeup and a nice outfit, she looks nothing like the glamorous college girl they've been showing on TV and in the newspapers. Her look is hard and edgy, like someone with a chronic drug problem, although I can make out her remarkable beauty beneath it.

"Okay, so you've found me. What the hell are you going to do about it?"

"May I sit?"

"Be my guest." She pulls out a cigarette. A glass

ashtray sits on the floor and she kicks it back toward the ratty couch. "Mind telling me who you are first?"

"My name is Leah."

She takes a long drag on her cigarette and seems to study me. "Okay, Leah. So now you know who I am."

"I certainly do."

"What are you, a cop or something? How did you even find me here?"

"I'm a housewife with a couple of kids who took an interest in your disappearance."

Mycah laughs as she sucks smoke into her lungs. "So by your lonesome, you accomplished what the police and all those newspeople couldn't? You found the missing girl?"

"Yes," I say, quite proud of myself. "I was worried about you."

"Why would you give a shit about me? You don't even know me."

"We're all God's children," I say. "Do I have to know you to care about your safe return? Or the fact that a hate crime has no place in Dearborn?"

"And you're simply a bored housewife with nothing else to do than to look for a missing college girl?"

"I guess you could say that." Is she mocking me?

"Wow. That's so fucked up it's actually kinda sweet."

"If that's the way you want to see it."

"You wanted to be a hero. Save the poor black girl from all these backwoods racists."

I stare at her, wondering why she's being so mean to me. When did doing something kind become a crime?

"I suppose you're curious as to why I'm here." She flicks ash into the tray.

"I wouldn't have come otherwise."

"I know, right? Why else come to this shit hole of a town?"

"So why *are* you here?"

"Why are any of us here? What's the meaning behind the universe and our existence in it?"

"You know what I mean. Why are you hiding away in this house?"

"Why should I tell you? I don't know you from that hole in the wall," she says, pointing at the hole punched in the living room wall.

"Because for starters, your boyfriend was found murdered the other night."

"You think I don't know that? I've been watching the news every night." Mycah massages her temples, the cigarette still burning between her fingers, the nails of which are painted with chipped red polish.

"You don't seem overly concerned about his death."

"What do you want from me? Crocodile tears?"

"I guess I was expecting more of an emotional reaction."

"You want me to break down and cry? To prove to you that I'm a good and moral human being? Well, don't hold your breath on that, sister. You don't know half the shit I saw growing up in the hood. Niggas being shot and stabbed in broad daylight."

"But your boyfriend was murdered in cold blood."

"That's precious. A privileged white bitch like you telling me how to react to my own boyfriend's death." She laughs bitterly. "You white folks have no idea how racist you are even when you think you're being cool."

"I'm sorry, I didn't mean to imply—"

"Bullshit. You knew exactly what you meant to imply."

"I swear to you I didn't."

"Then you did it on a subconscious level, by making reference to the stereotypical 'strong black woman.' The woman who appears not to grieve and who's assumed to have developed a decreased sense of loss and suffering. It's textbook racism and so demeaning to me as an intelligent black woman."

What is she talking about? "That was not at all my implication."

"That kind of thinking is so inherent in white people's sense of entitlement. The notion that a 'strong black woman' can recover from trauma much faster than white people because she's numb to poverty, pain, and violence. It's bullshit. We feel pain too. Next time check your privilege at the door, lady."

"Of course you feel pain."

"Such ignorance."

"I'm a college-educated woman and I can assure you that I've never heard of this stereotype, nor was I in any way trying to offend your sensibilities."

"Going to college means nothing to me. The biggest racists in this country sit in those ivy halls of whiter learning."

"I don't care about any of that," I say, regretting the words as soon as they come out of my mouth. "I mean to say, I care greatly about race relations in this country and about avoiding negative stereotypes, and I'm terribly sorry if I offended you. But right now I just want to know how you ended up in this house."

Mycah grinds her cigarette in the ashtray and stares up at me. "Because I'm afraid he's going to kill me."

"Who's going to kill you?"

"Who do you think? The same person who killed Cordell."

"And who might that be?" I need her to say Russell's name.

"Listen to me, this whole thing is messed up—and dangerous as hell. You sure you want to get involved?"

I think of my kids and husband. Do I really want to insert myself in a murder case, especially knowing that the killer is still out there and that he might actually live next door to me?

"I'm not so sure."

"Then go home, lady. Go back to your comfortable life, your exclusive country club, your tea parties and white privilege."

"No, I do want to get to the bottom of this."

"You sure about that? Because I'm not going to ask twice."

"Yes, I'm sure of it."

"Can I trust you?"

"Of course you can trust me."

"You need to know my history before you hear what happened the night I went missing. You need to know about the real Mycah Jones."

"Okay."

I realize I've been waiting a long time to hear Mycah Jones's side of the story.

CLAY

Thursday, October 22, 1:32 p.m.

I IGNORE LEAH'S CALL, HAVING NO DESIRE TO TALK to her. I know she wants to talk about what happened last night, in a roundabout way. "Process" her feelings. She'll mention for the millionth time how we must listen to one another and work to develop our communication skills. This is the last thing I want to do—communicate with her. Or listen to her talk for the next thirty minutes while there are a million other things I need to do. I'm a black-and-white sort of guy. The what-you-see-is-what-you-get type. I take things literally. I don't read into words and discover different meanings as if I'm "deconstructing" a James Joyce novel.

Today has already started out bad. And it's only getting worse. A batch of IPA spoiled when some lactic acid bacteria infiltrated it, and now Ben and I must dump the entire tank down the drain. I try not to go all ape shit on Ben, although I certainly have reason to. Once again it's his fault the batch spoiled. Damn kid failed to properly sanitize the equipment on the day I left work early. It does no good to bitch about it now, especially when we're way behind schedule. I can't afford to have Ben quit because good workers are extremely hard to find in this small town. I already had three walk out on me before I found Ben, and none lasted more than a week. Yes, I'm hard on help. Brewing beer is not the glamorous job people make it out to be. It's hard work. Cleaning tanks and humping sacks of grain and sweeping floors. Ben, for the most part, has been dependable and loyal. He shows up on time and doesn't give me shit. He still has a lot of maturing to do, but he's got loads of potential and a good head. I'll walk him through every step of the process until it brands into his primitive monkey brain.

The lingering aftertaste of that horrible dinner last night replays in my mind. I still can't believe that Russell wanted to swap wives. What a sick bastard. Reparations can kiss my ass.

Detective Armstrong is at the door again, knocking, wanting to ask me questions about Mycah. Hasn't he harassed me enough already? I've told him everything he needs to know. Correct that: everything I'm willing to tell him.

I want a beer so bad it's making me miserable. The pulls call out to me like a bugler playing taps at Camp Lejeune. I yearn for its sudsy goodness, cold and delicious with a slightly bitter aftertaste, to dampen my lips.

I let the pestering cop inside and then reluctantly

make my way back to the storage tank where the spoiled beer waits to be drained.

"How's the beer business?" Armstrong says cheerfully.

"Bitter, at the moment."

He hesitates for a few seconds before saying, "Oh, a beer joke. Good one."

"Look, Detective, I don't have time for idle chitchat today. What do you need?"

"I'm following up on that missing college student and her dead boyfriend."

"I heard about that. Real shame. Looked like he had a bright future."

"Star hoops player and accepted to Harvard Law. Worked a few nights as a bartender in a fancy joint down the road. That was in addition to his many social activities on campus. He was quite the political activist."

"Aren't most college kids activists?"

"What do you mean by that?"

I wished I hadn't said that because I want to get this meeting over with as soon as possible.

"It just seems to me that college kids these days are always protesting one thing or another. Wait until these brats get into the real world."

"I spent most of my free time in college chasing girls."

"Whatever happened to the good old days? Chasing skirts and drinking beer." I unscrew the cap under the tank. "Watch your feet, Detective."

"What are you doing?"

"Skunked batch. It's all going down the drain."

"They say dumping beer is enough to make a grown man cry."

"Trust me, you wouldn't want to drink any of this gnarly shit."

He takes out his notebook and stares at it. "We still have no fix on the missing girl, but we've discovered some interesting things about Cordell."

"Oh? Like what?" I look up at him as I unscrew the cap.

"Seems he had quite a few partners."

"He was a college kid. What do you expect?"

"We searched his Internet history and didn't find any evidence that he dated women. All his partners were men."

"But I thought he and Mycah were an item?"

"People get together for different reasons. Take the Clintons, for example." He stares at his notebook. "Think of any other reason why she called the brewery the night she disappeared?"

"Nope." I remove the cap and the spoiled beer drains onto the concrete floor and down the drain. Armstrong jumps back, but it's too late. The beer splashes over his loafers and pant legs.

"There has to be some reason she called here."

"Maybe she was trying to reach someone inside."

"Then why wouldn't she call their cell phone?"

"Maybe they forgot their phone," I say, watching my profits spiral down the drain. "Or their battery died."

"Did you talk to Mycah on the phone that night?"

I laugh, trying not to sound bitter—no, trying not to sound *guilty*. "I told you already, I barely knew the girl. I have no idea why she would call the brewery."

"You admitted to being here the night she disap-peared."

"Yeah, like I already told you, I was working out back."

"You said it was busy in the tasting room that night. Can anyone vouch for you?"

I can feel my blood pressure rising as the splashing sound fills the room. I grab a squeegee and begin to direct the noxious stream toward the drain. Suds begin to grow around it, and the overwhelming stench of skunked beer permeates the facility.

"Just my pourer, as I told you before. Ben went home earlier in the day. Is there anything else, Detective?"

"Unless you've got something else to tell me."

"I have nothing else."

"Are you sure about that?"

"Positive," I say, not bothering to look up from my squeegeeing.

"Okay then, I'll see you around town. And sorry about the spoiled batch."

"Not your fault," I say, looking over at Ben.

Armstrong lets himself out, and when he's finally gone, I throw down the squeegee and make my way over to the tasting room. The sound of beer gurgling down the drain screams of Chapter 11. Ben stays in the back, scrubbing one of the kettles with a long brush and a gallon of sanitizing solution. Time for a coffee break. I go behind the bar and grab one of the tulip glasses and fill it with coffee porter. By the time the storage tank finishes draining, I look down and notice that my glass is empty.

I pour myself another, trying to permanently erase the memory of that troubled girl. Holding the beer up to the light, it appears like a black hole in some strange universe. I study its color and viscosity. The porter sports a thick white head lingering just below the rim, thanks in part to the nitrogen used to carbonate it. It's one of the best porters I've ever made. I break momentarily from my admiration and think of her. My mysterious black hole where nothing good ever escaped.

LEAH

Thursday, October 22, 2:29 p.m.

"*I*'M NOT REALLY FROM A WEALTHY FAMILY. I grew up in the Queensbridge, one of the most dangerous housing projects in New York City," Mycah says. "Ghetto poor, and unless you've grown up in that environment, you don't know about what I've had to go through to get this far in life. Trading food stamps for money and drugs. Avoiding the gangs and drive-by shootings. Fortunately, my grandmother pushed me to study and get good grades, and it paid off. I got into one of the best high schools in the city. Then Chadwick gave me a full scholarship to come here."

"You should be quite proud of your accomplishments."

"Are you listening to me? Because what I'm telling you has nothing to do with my accomplishments." She bites her lower lip and bounces her knee in nervous anticipation. "You have no right to judge me."

"I'm not judging you, nor do I have any intention to do so. I just want to know how you ended up here."

"It's complicated, is what I'm trying to say."

"So it wasn't a hate crime that caused your disappearance?"

"Every act and every thought in this society is a hate crime. Until we completely overthrow the system and undergo a revolution, hate is the only crime that exists."

"A hate crime in the traditional sense," I say. "A racially motivated act of violence."

Removing the towel wrapped around her head, she swipes her long black hair into a ponytail and then releases it. "It didn't go down that way."

"Then how did it go down? Because Cordell claimed that his attacker shouted out a racial slur before he was knocked unconscious."

"Yeah, I know what Cordell claimed to hear."

"Then you must also know that everyone was out looking for you and that they even held a candlelight vigil on campus. Why didn't you go to the cops?"

"Let me break it down for you," she says. "I couldn't just go to the cops or I would have ended up like Cordell."

"Who would have killed you?"

"Russell."

"Russell Gaines, my neighbor?"

"Lady, if he's your neighbor, I'd seriously consider moving to another neighborhood."

"What do you know about him?"

"He's been a professor at Chadwick for about three years now. All the students know what a hound he is. I tried to stay clear of his classes, but on such a small campus, that's damn near impossible to do, especially if your major is in the African-American Studies Department."

"So you ended up taking a class with him?"

"And his useless wife. She's the director of diversity on campus, but she also teaches a class there every semester." She stood, her robe flitting open and affording me a brief view of her stomach and cleavage. "Want something to drink?"

"No, thank you."

She disappeared into the kitchen and returned a minute later with a tall glass filled with a dark liquid.

"Captain and Coke helps chill me out. You should try one."

"You were saying?"

"Right. The first course I took with him was Sociology of the Urban Black American. Hell, I grew up in that lifestyle. But it was a requirement, and he was the only prof teaching the course that semester, so I had no other choice."

"Did he come on to you?"

"Not at first. He was intimidating and hard to engage. All the students feared him, knowing his reputation as a tough grader. I did everything in my power to get to know him, never having met my own father. I volunteered answers in class. I turned my assignments in on time and showed up during his office hours to discuss the material. Was I flirting with him? Hell yeah, I don't deny it. He was smart and amazing, and with incredible charisma. But it was nothing serious.

The harder I tried to be friends with him, the more standoffish he became."

"He didn't make a pass at you?"

"Not right away. I aced his class, which made me eager to take another one with him."

"And that's when it happened?"

"What happened?"

"When he came on to you?"

"Chill, girl, and let me tell the story." She takes a sip of her drink. "I took his wife's course next: Race, Class, and Gender. Now, that woman was a total bitch. Terrible teacher too."

"What did she do to make you feel that way?"

"She played favorites. If you disagreed with any of her opinions, she held it against you. The hell with free speech. She wanted us to parrot back her lectures on the exam, and if you didn't toe the line, she'd grade you down."

"I remember having professors like that. For me it was just a matter of giving them back what they wanted to hear."

"Not me. I got this far on my own terms and I wasn't about to become someone else's bitch. We often butted heads in class. She would say one thing and I would refute it from my experiences growing up in the hood. It sounded to me like she'd never lived in the ghetto or knew what it was like to be a black woman and experience racism and real poverty."

"So she treated you different?"

"Yeah. She would call me out in class and try to humiliate me in front of everyone, but I never backed down. Up until that time, she gave me the only B I've ever received at Chadwick."

"You didn't appeal it?"

"Hell no. I wouldn't give her the satisfaction of groveling for a higher grade. But I got the last laugh."

"How so?"

"As part of our final exam, we were required to submit an essay to a national contest on the poem 'Dream Deferred,' by Langston Hughes. She used her essay as the teaching model and gave mine a B minus."

"So how did you get the last laugh?"

"My essay went on to win the contest." She breaks out into laughter. "Best part about it, I won fifteen hundred bucks and a free trip to DC."

"She must have been shocked."

"I went back and showed her the check, and all she did was shake her head in disgust. It felt good to shove it in her face." She takes a gulp of her drink. "I felt sorry for her husband, knowing he had to live with such a spiteful bitch."

"So you took another class with him?"

"Prejudice and Racism in Modern Society."

"What happened?"

"I threw myself into the work and continued to visit him during his office hours. Midway through the semester, he noticed that I was serious about his class, and he began to engage me in discussions after hours. I loved it, and I think he loved talking to me too. It was only when we ran into each other one night that he took it to the next level." She lights a cigarette.

"Go on?"

"He invited me to sit and have a drink with him. Yeah, it was flattering. He treated me like a total equal. The time flew by and we ended up having a few more drinks. I was pretty drunk by the time the night ended.

Russell was wasted too, and in no condition to drive. So we ended up having a nightcap at a hotel down the street. One thing led to another."

"So it was by consent?"

"If you define consent as sleeping with your drunk student and then treating her as if she never existed when she shows up to your class the following day. He gave me a B on my next paper and it pissed me off."

"He probably felt guilty for cheating on his wife."

"Then why did he hold me after class? Or ask me to go out with him the following night? I didn't realize at the time that he was grooming me. Breaking me down only to build me back up. Dude made me feel special despite the fact that we could never be seen together on campus."

"Because it's against the college's rules?"

"He said something about a code of conduct and that he could get fired for sleeping with one of his students."

"Did you love him?"

"I'm not sure it was love, but I fell hard for him. He even changed that B into an A."

"Then it got worse, I assume."

"Hell yeah, it got worse. He became obsessed with me. Kept trying to convince me to break it off with Cordell and be exclusive with him. Cordell and I had an arrangement. We could see other people. We were both young and free-spirited. We made a great power couple on campus and didn't want to limit ourselves, especially seeing how Cordell was on the down low."

"Down low?"

"He liked guys too. Maybe even more than he liked girls."

"Cordell?"

"No big deal. I was totally fine with him being bi. We had no sexual hang-ups."

"So Russell wouldn't take no for an answer?"

"Precisely. He followed me and sometimes waited in his car outside my apartment. Promised that he'd help advance my career. He also said that if I reported him to the administration, he would run me out of Chadwick and ruin my good name. What choice did I have? It was his word against mine, like that black woman we studied who testified against the Supreme Court judge."

"Anita Hill?"

"Yeah, that's her."

"I was in middle school when that happened and always believed Anita Hill's version of events. Look at the damage Thomas has done to the Supreme Court."

"Right-wing asshole. Reminds me of Russell."

"In what way?"

"In the way some powerful black men are no different than whitey," she says.

I don't feel compelled to respond to her comment, but I understand the gist of her complaint. It reminds me of the privilege I carry around by the mere virtue of my skin color.

"I wanted to break it off with him for good, but I was scared. After all I accomplished just to get into Chadwick, I didn't want to jeopardize everything. My academic scholarship was on the line. In the back of my mind, I figured I could wait him out and that maybe he'd move on to another undergraduate. Besides, it wasn't all that bad between us. There were some good times too. He took me on some nice trips and we dined at fancy restaurants. Once in a while he even gave me money."

"But then something changed."

"I pleaded with him one night just to leave me the hell alone and to stop checking up on me like I was his slave. I was drunk and sobbing hysterically and swinging fists at him. The asshole surprised me with a backhand. I fell back on the hotel bed in shock. He'd never hit me before, and it stung coming from someone you respect. Seriously, that abusive shit doesn't sit well with me. My lip was bleeding all over the place. He warned me in a low voice to never again threaten him or he'd kill me, and I believed him."

My phone goes off. I look at the caller ID and see that it's the kids' school. I answer and am informed that Zack has been in another confrontation. What sort of confrontation? I ask, but they won't tell me until I get there. The timing of his behavior pisses me off and so I call Clay to see if he can go down to the school and talk to the teacher, but he isn't answering. Once again the burden falls on my shoulders. I'm the old standby in the family who must drop everything for someone else. It's never about me. My needs always seem to go unmet.

"I have to go," I say.

"Everything cool?" she asks, looking genuinely concerned.

"It's my son." It suddenly occurs to me that I forgot to ask about her pregnancy.

Mycah walks over and grabs my hands. "Are you going to call the cops on me?"

"You can't expect me to look the other way while Russell walks around a free man."

Tears form in her eyes. "I'm the victim here. Do you know what the police will do to me if they find out I've been hiding out in this dump? They'll blame me for all this and then his lawyers will dig up my past and ruin me. Please don't turn me in just yet."

"I need to think it over."

"Just give me some time. Swing by tomorrow and we can talk again. Come up with a plan."

"You'll stay right here?"

"Where else am I going to go? The cops would pick me up in a heartbeat if I ever left."

I gather my bag and slip out the door. Once behind the wheel, I think about all that I've uncovered. Although it's scary and dangerous, I'm proud of what I've accomplished. This could open doors for me. With my creative writing degree, I've always dreamed of finishing one of the many novels I've started. Maybe one day I might even write a true crime book about this case. But then I wonder about my culpability in the matter. Does my relative silence make me an accessory to these crimes?

Russell had both the motive and the means to kill Cordell, and Clarissa's diary is concrete evidence of his violent nature. If only I can convince Clarissa to speak with me, to get her to talk about what she has penned.

My mind-set totally changes as soon as I park in the school lot. I sit in my car for a few minutes, not wanting to face Susan with her withering gaze and impatient stare. Although I've never laid a hand on my children, I'm almost tempted to give Zack a good spanking once he gets home. Maybe that's what he needs. God knows I've tried everything else and have read every book on the subject. Maybe it's Clay's turn to step up to the plate. Why am I always the one to take the blame for Zack's erratic behavior?

I walk inside the office and immediately see Susan, arms folded and gazing at me as if I'm the villain.

"Where's Zack?" I blurt out. Heads in the office turn and look up at me. "What did he do this time."

"Follow me, Mrs. Daniels," Susan says.

CLAY

Thursday, October 22, 2:47 p.m.

I REMEMBER THAT STICKY DAY IN EARLY AUGUST when Mycah called out of the blue and said she needed to see me. It had been weeks since we'd gotten together at that redneck bar, and I knew I should have turned her down. But like an idiot being led to his own slaughter, I agreed to meet her. She showed up later that evening after Ben had gone home, an hour later than we agreed upon. I'd been drinking quite a bit while waiting for her to arrive. The tasting room was closed for the night and my only companion was the foam-webbed jar of the Information in front of me. I was well into my fourth beer when I heard her come in through the back door.

She walked through the darkened brewery and sat down at the bar next to me. I was almost too afraid to turn and face her, fearful of how I might react. As much as I tried to forget her, she'd been all I could think about since our last meeting.

"I'm sorry for treating you that way, baby," she whispered.

"I can't do this anymore."

"I know."

"My wife and kids will be arriving soon."

"Never wanted to take you away from your family."

"I could lose everything. You, on the other hand, have nothing to lose."

"Losing you is hard enough. Why do you think I broke it off with you?"

"Then why did you treat me like that?" I said, swiveling on my stool to face her. "Why'd you make me spend six thousand bucks on those Knicks tickets?"

"I was confused. I didn't know what to do."

"And to think I was considering leaving my wife for you."

"Don't be mean to me. I came here to apologize."

I sipped my beer, trying not to succumb to her charms.

"I realized how bad I'd missed you, Clay. It was torture not being with you."

"Could have fooled me."

"No one makes me feel the way you do. We were amazing together."

"And now we're done."

"I need you one last time before we call it quits."

"I can't do it."

"One last time, baby. Give me something to remember you by. Then I promise you'll never see me again."

"One last time and we're done?"

"Swear to God."

We agreed to meet at a rural hotel ten miles away. I

practically broke the sound barrier in my attempt to get there. I saw her car parked in the lot and so I rushed up to the room. She was waiting under the covers, and she made it clear that she wanted to make this last experience memorable, as if the previous encounters were not. It took me seconds to undress. Despite consuming many beers throughout the day, the alcohol had little effect on my libido. I slipped into bed with her, swearing this would be the very last time we ever made love. My hands roamed her smooth, smoky skin and over her breasts and rounded ass. So different than Leah, who was all skin and sharp angles—the body of a runway model.

"Please, I need you to do me like you did before," she said.

I bit my lip. I could barely control myself, kissing her neck and her ears as she pushed herself away from me.

"Make me pay for being such a bad girl."

I continued to kiss her neck and down to her nipples.

"One last time, please. To remember you by."

She grabbed my hands and placed them around her neck. She wanted me to choke her while we made love, and to slap her and call her all sorts of despicable names. Role playing. I agreed, as it had long ago ceased to offend my sensibilities. It helped that I was pissed off at her, and this time I went above and beyond the call of duty.

Hours later, I collapsed in exhaustion. She looked up at me, her face bruised and red welts spread over her upper arms and body. Her lip was split and bleeding. Fingerprints encircled her throat like a necklace. I apologized profusely for what I'd done, but she merely smiled at me as she snuggled against my body.

I awoke the next morning and she was gone. The curtains were open and the sun's rays poured into the room. I felt as if a considerable weight had lifted from my shoulders. The sex last night had been crazy good, but at least I was free of her. Free at last.

I took a hot shower, soaping away the powerful odor of sex from my body. I promised myself to never cheat on Leah again. From then on I would be the best husband I could be and the best father to my kids. Nothing would ever come between us again. My turbulent midlife crisis was finally over.

I truly believed I had closure on Mycah.

LEAH

Thursday, October 22, 3:30 p.m.

Z ACK GOES STRAIGHT UP TO HIS ROOM ONCE WE AR-
rive home, and this is fine by me. We drove home in
silence after all my questions about the incident went
unanswered. I kept looking back in the rearview mirror and staring at the shiner given to Zack by the other
boy. As much as I abhor violence, maybe a fist to the
face will finally put a stop to all his crazy behavior.

The black boy claimed that Zack called him a bad
name. Do I believe it? I don't know what to believe at
this point. Zack had been teased pretty badly by some
of the black boys in his previous school. Susan recom-
mended he see a counselor, giving me a few names to
call in case it hadn't already occurred to me. I didn't
have the heart to tell her that Zack was already seeing
a counselor and that it appeared not to be helping.
Maybe I'll call one of the other therapists on the list.

I momentarily put Zack out of mind. He'll be all right in his room, alone with his books. It's where he feels safe from all the craziness in his life. All the change and turmoil must be hard for him to deal with: his dad working at the brewery all day, moving cross country, a new school, and making new friends (not that he had many friends in Seattle). It's been hard on me too. I can't imagine what must be going through his young, formidable mind.

My head is still buzzing from my rendezvous with Mycah. I know I should go straight to the police and tell them everything I know, but I can't. Not just yet. They'll take all the information I gathered and then forget about me, and then I'll be back in the same miserable place where I started. Besides, there's more to learn from her. If I don't get to the bottom of this matter, Russell could walk away scot-free, leaving Clarissa and the kids in harm's way. Violence only begets more violence, and I'm afraid he might soon explode with rage.

I check on Zack before I sneak over and read more of her diary. He's sitting at his desk and reading a book, one hand cupping his bruised cheek. I ask if he's okay and he turns and regards me oddly before turning back to his book. My maternal instincts prevail and I rush over and kiss the top of his head. He shies away from me, and it hurts when he does this. It makes me feel unloved and unwanted. I wish he had some friends to hang with instead of going up to his room day after day and reading his stupid books. It makes me sad that we ever moved from Seattle and into this cursed neighborhood.

"I love you."

"Love you too," he says, not looking up from his book.

"You okay to be alone for a little while, buddy?"

"Yes."

"I'll be back soon."

"Where are you going?"

"I'm just going to take a walk."

"But it's supposed to rain."

"I'll be quick."

He looks up at me, and his freckled face makes me so sad that I run out of the room before I break down in front of him.

I head outside and notice that the sun has completely disappeared behind the mass of dark clouds. The neighborhood takes on an especially ominous hue in bad weather. I sprint over to the Gaineses', covering my head with my jacket as the raindrops begin to fall. Once safely on the porch, I remove my shoes and carry them inside. Without warning, it begins to downpour,

The carpet along the stairs tickles my feet as I climb up to their master bedroom. I plop down on the mattress and stare up at the recessed lights, imagining what private horrors Clarissa must have to endure in this room. After five minutes of doing nothing, I reach into the drawer and pull out her diary and key. My body trembles as I open it. What has she learned about my past? And what terrible act has Russell inflicted upon her this time. I can't believe how much progress I'm making on this case. For a relative newcomer in town, I've accomplished far more than the police have.

I open the diary to the last page and begin to read.

October 21

   Still can't believe what I found out today from my contact in the Justice Department. It's hard for me to believe. Leah seemed like such a kind and caring person. I nearly coughed up my breakfast when I read it. Who knows about any-one anymore? Does the entire world consist of monsters waiting in the lurch? Like Leah? Like Russell? Then again, maybe Leah's changed her ways. Maybe she's made her peace with God and has moved on from the sins of her childhood.

   Does Clay know? I'm betting he doesn't. Maybe he should know whom he's sleeping with each night. Maybe it's my responsibility to tell him.

   I'm thankful they left when they did after that miserable dinner. To think that my husband would want to have sex with Leah disgusts me. Yes, Russell was quite upset when Clay rebuked him. I take no pleasure in sleeping with other men, except that, in the early days, it made Rus-sell happy. It spiced up our sex life. I initially did it for the sake of our marriage. To please him. But now I do it out of self-preservation. So that he doesn't rage on me. It's my fault for agreeing to do it in the first place. I never should have agreed to his outrageous sexual demands.

   I was madly in love with Russell when I first met him. Although fifteen years removed didn't seem so bad at the time, I understand now how it has put me at a disadvantage. That and the fact

*that he was my professor, and I his eager
student. But that's in the past now. Our marriage
is at a crossroads and no amount of cooperation
on my part may be able to save it. Sadly, I
believe that once an abuser, always an abuser.*

    But a killer?

    *What am I to do? Where am I going to go?
I'm living a nightmare that I can't wake up from.*

I slam the diary shut and lie back against the pillow, clutching it to my chest. I'm furious. My cheeks melt like hot candle wax. How everything could change for me if this comes out. She *knows*. I've been repressing this part of my life for so long now that it feels like reading a horror novel penned by Stephen King. It doesn't seem a part of me or part of my history. In the years since, I've completely rewritten my life story, and in its absence patched together a much happier narrative. I've created, on the surface anyway, a much happier version of the Leah I present to the world.

I close my eyes and scream into the pillow. It takes ten minutes before I'm able to calm down and my breathing becomes normal. Focus, Leah, I tell myself. I understand now what I need to do: confront Clarissa and admit to her that I've been sneaking into her home and reading her diary. I'll say that it was an act of desperation, a silly idea that I came up with in order to befriend her. I'll fall to my knees and beg for forgiveness, and plead with her not to divulge my secret to anyone. It horrifies me to think what might happen if Clay finds out. What would people around town say if they knew? I'd never be able to show my face in Dearborn again. In exchange for her silence, I will tell Clarissa everything I've uncovered about this case and about Russell. Maybe she can use that evidence in her divorce proceedings and try to maintain custody of the children.

I peel the curtain aside and look over at Zack's window, hoping to catch him red-handed doing something naughty. How bad have things gotten when you're peeping into your own home? I run downstairs in my bare feet and grab a half-empty bottle of Riesling out of the fridge, take a healthy sip, and then return upstairs with the bottle. My grief needs to be tamed like a wild stallion galloping on the beach. I sit against the headboard, drinking straight from the bottle, feeling sorry for myself. The alcohol makes me feel better, but I know I'll pay dearly for it come morning.

I don't want to think about anything. For so many years I've convinced myself that my marriage is strong. But is it really? Because what would Clay do if he learned the truth about me? I'm not that young girl anymore and haven't been in a long time. Although I apologized in front of the judge, I've never really been contrite for what I did. In many ways, I'm still glad I did it.

I close my eyes and, through the spatter of tears, tell myself that it's okay to sleep. I lift the bottle, but it's already empty. My head swims in a weed-infested pond of cold Riesling. I let my mind drift to sloped vineyards, arid Tuscan fields littered with grapes, and virile men walking along dusty paths carrying woven baskets. I slip further under the blanket, reminding myself to make the bed up as soon as I'm ready to go. Zack has his book. He'll be fine by himself. There's no one else in the neighborhood to worry about.

* * *

I'm awakened sometime later by footsteps coming up the stairs. I sit up in shock. How long have I been out? I toss the covers aside and run over to the window and see Russell's blue BMW parked in the driveway. *Darn.* There's not enough time to make the bed, hide the empty wine bottle, and slip under the mattress. I'm woozy and unsteady on my feet. It suddenly occurs to me the danger I'm in—Russell might kill me if he finds me here. He killed Cordell and now he will kill me. I look around for something to defend myself as the footsteps approach the door. The knob turns and I stagger against the wall. My knees buckle and I ball up into a fetal position, ready to scream. I suddenly realize that I don't want to die just yet. I close my eyes and mumble the Lord's Prayer.

Then the door bursts open.

CLAY

Thursday, October 22, 3:35 p.m.

*A*s I sit drinking in my office, I can't help but think back about how it all unraveled with Mycah.

The end of August was fast approaching and I looked forward to welcoming my wife and kids back into my life. Two weeks had passed since I'd last seen Mycah. No calls, no visits or texts. We'd quit each other cold turkey, although the temptation to call her was strong, especially after I'd consumed more than a few beers. Somehow I managed to be a good boy during that time.

Then the day came and Leah and the kids stepped off the plane and into my arms and I felt whole again. The missing pieces of my life fell neatly into place. They moved into my small efficiency and planned to stay there until we found a house that appealed to

Leah. Zack and Zadie slept on an air cushion in the middle of our compact hotel room. I even took time off from the brewery to take them to Old Orchard Beach to enjoy the last days of a gorgeous Maine summer.

But after a few days passed, something didn't seem right. We were slightly off as a family unit. My absence from their daily life had created a subtle but noticeable distance between us. We circled each other like suspicious cats. At the time, I chalked it up to the newness of our situation. I figured that everything would return to normal once we settled in to our new home and got reacquainted with one another. It felt awkward at first, but so did everything back then. In retrospect, I underestimated the emotional toll that moving three thousand miles away had on all of us. And my affair with Mycah had irrevocably changed me as a person.

Not a week after Leah and the kids arrived, I received a text from Mycah, pleading with me to meet her. What the hell was this? I deleted the message, got back to work in the brewery, and did my best to ignore her. I'd finally come to grips with my reckless behavior and needed to move on. The guilt still tortured me, and I knew that I'd need to forgive myself in order to get on with life. On the worst of days, I thought about ending it all. Yet, oddly enough, the memories of those sexual trysts kept me going, and night after night I replayed those sizzling trysts in my mind.

She continued to text and harass me, and I promptly deleted her messages without reading them. No way did I want to chance Leah seeing them. One Sunday, as I walked out of a restaurant with Leah and the kids, I saw Mycah sitting on the hood of her car and watching us. Three nights later the doorbell to our hotel room rang. I opened it and saw Mycah standing there with a pizza in hand, dressed in a blue delivery uniform, her hair tied up in a bun.

"We need to talk," she whispered.

"Shhh. What are you doing here?" I said.

"It's important that I speak to you."

"You and I are finished."

"Who's at the door?" Leah sang out from the bathroom.

"Pizza delivery," I called back to her.

"But I thought we were going out for dinner," Leah replied.

"Yeah, I figured we could save it for later," I said, turning back to Mycah. "Meet me at the brewery tomorrow night."

"No. I can't risk being seen there with you."

"Then where?"

She mentioned a motel thirty miles away, and I agreed to meet her the following night. I took the pizza from her, slammed the door shut, and tossed the box onto the wrinkled bedsheet. Zack and Zadie immediately made a beeline for it, seeing as how we kept little to no food inside the mini-fridge. But when they opened the box, there was only half a pizza left.

"Oh, Clay. You'll ruin their appetites." Leah walked out of the bathroom, wearing a white towel wrapped around her head. She stared down at the four remaining slices. "Where's the rest of it?"

I shrugged.

"They only delivered half a pizza?"

"Looks like it."

"What a rip-off."

"They must have made a mistake."

"Pesto?" She snatched the slice out of Zack's hand before he could bite into it. "Why would you order pizza with pesto on it? You know that Zack is allergic to pine nuts."

"They must have screwed up the order. I would never order a pesto pizza."

She walked over and sat down at the foot of the bed, picking up the phone. I suddenly remembered a night, after we made love, when I told Mycah about Zack's allergy to pine nuts and how we once had to rush him to the hospital.

"What are you doing?" I asked.

"Calling the pizza place to complain. Give me their number."

"Put the phone down, Leah. It's no big deal."

"Of course it's a big deal. We can't let them cheat us."

"I don't have the number."

"Then how did you call in the first place?" she said, holding the phone aloft.

"Put the phone down," I said firmly.

"Why?"

"Because the owners are thinking about giving me a tap in their restaurant. That's why I don't want to make a big deal out of this."

"They should at least give us a free pizza."

"Trust me, they've given me more than a few free pizzas when I was working late nights at the brewery. That's why you need to let this go."

Leah put the receiver down. She crossed her arms and sulked. A few moments passed before she skittered into the bathroom to get dressed.

We went out to an Italian eatery that evening. I was facing the door when I noticed Mycah walking in with a skinny young black man. He wore his long hair in dreadlocks, and from her description of him at the time, I assumed it was Cordell. They sat on the far side of the bar, Mycah facing me. Our eyes met at one point during dinner and she smiled seductively.

"Are you okay, honey?" Leah asked, sitting across from me.

"I'm fine. Why do you ask?"

"You look weird. Like something's bothering you."

"Why would I be upset now that you and the kids are here?" I reached over and cupped her hand. "I was just thinking about the house we're going to visit tomorrow. It's priced to sell and I really think you and the kids might like it."

"You say it's a big neighborhood and that there'll be lots of families moving in?"

"That's what the agent says. It's a large cul-de-sac with a big field and at least twelve other homes being constructed for families just like ours." After blowing six thousand bucks on Knicks tickets, I searched around and had found a much less expensive development.

"Hooray. I can't wait to see it," she said, clapping excitedly.

The mention of a new house in a busy neighborhood immediately put Leah in a good mood, and she squeezed my hand throughout dinner. As much as I tried not to look over at Mycah, I couldn't help but notice when she kissed Cordell on the lips. She looked amazing and at that moment I jealously coveted her.

Zadie talked nonstop throughout dinner, giving me a nagging headache and forcing me to drink more beer than I should have. Despite Leah's protest, we skipped dessert and I hustled them out of the restaurant before Mycah did something foolish.

"You seemed a bit distant tonight," Leah said on the drive home.

"No, I'm very happy to be back with you and the kids. It just feels as if the honeymoon is finally over."

"I'm not following you." She put her hand on my lap. "Aren't you glad we're here?"

"Of course I am. You don't know how hard it's been for me without you guys around. Now the pressure is really on me to make this brewery work."

She smiled and rubbed her hand against my thigh in a nonsexual manner. "Then just be happy, silly."

"I am happy. It's just that you've made such a huge sacrifice by coming out here that I don't want to let you down."

"You'll never let me down."

"I'll be spending long days at the brewery, trying to get this business off the ground."

"Don't worry, Clay. Everything will work out now that we're a family again. You'll see."

Once we arrived back at the hotel, we put the kids to bed. Leah took a long shower while I sat in the darkened living room, staring at the muted flat-screen. I glanced occasionally at Zadie sleeping next to me in her duck-themed pajamas. Then at Zack on the air mattress, his thin little hands folded over his chest. I couldn't believe that I'd jeopardized my relationship with these precious creatures by sleeping with that whore.

I guzzled the first growler of beer and went to the

mini-fridge and retrieved the second. By the time I got back to the pullout, my phone started to ring. Who could be calling me at this hour? I stared down at the caller ID, instantly recognizing the number I'd deleted from my contact list. I couldn't believe that she had the nerve to call me after the way she'd been stalking me.

"What?" I whispered.

"I need to see you right now."

"We agreed to meet tomorrow night," I said, listening for Leah to emerge from the bathroom.

"It has to be tonight."

"What if I say no?"

"I wouldn't if I were you. You know what I'm capable of doing."

I held my tongue, trying to restrain my anger. "I wish I'd never gotten involved with you."

"Well, you did, asshole, so fucking deal with it."

"Where?"

"Your brewery. Be there in fifteen minutes. I'll wait for you to go in first."

"Okay."

"I have something important I need to tell you."

"And it has to be in person?"

"Yes."

I went over to the bathroom and informed Leah that I had to make an emergency trip to the brewery, making up some lame excuse about a fire alarm going off. Thankfully, she never questioned me about my business dealings.

Despite being drunk, I took the growler with me, sipping it through a straw while driving across town. The brewery was only ten minutes away, and at this time of night, there were not many cops patrolling the roads around Dearborn. My head felt as if it might explode. I kept telling myself not to do something I might regret. Never in my life had I maliciously laid a hand on a woman, but Mycah had sorely tested my resolve. If she happened to drive off a cliff that night, her body mangled and torn beyond recognition, I would have pumped my fist in celebration.

The center of town had long been deserted, and the streets were bathed in an eerie darkness. I pulled up to the back door of the brewery and wobbled inside. Pitch blackness greeted me. I turned a light on in the back, sipping from the growler as I made my way to the tasting room. Then I collapsed on one of the stools—and waited. Fifteen minutes passed. Thirty. Forty-five minutes later, as I was about to leave, the back door opened and Mycah appeared.

She looked less glamorous than when I'd seen her at the restaurant earlier in the evening, all dolled up for a night on the town. She wore a gray wool cap and a long dungaree jacket. As soon as she saw me, she made her way over to where I sat. Fortunately, the alcohol had a calming effect on me, but in my head all I wanted to do was wrap my hands around her throat and throttle her.

I'd seen friends destroyed by manipulative women like her. Bitter divorces involving alimony and custody fights. Fortunately, I'd never been the target of a vindictive girlfriend. There weren't any domestic arrests or battered girlfriends in my past. I'd always been the good guy, the dude everyone wanted to party with and have a good time around. The girls I dated were not harlots, but nice girls. Like my mother. Like Leah.

I seriously wanted to hurt this girl, which scared me. I told myself to stay calm and not do anything stupid. Feelings of unmitigated rage and hate had been utterly foreign to me until now. Fueled by my growing alcohol consumption, I needed a way to process these emotions before I did something I might regret.

"Hey." She smiled, and for a brief second I remembered why I'd been so attracted to her. Then I noticed her bruised cheek. Like the kind of bruise I gave to her the last time we made love. "You look good, Clay."

"Don't give me that bullshit. I'm drunk and look like shit."

"I've missed you." She walked over and put her hands on my lap. "I couldn't take my eyes off you tonight at that restaurant."

I remained perfectly still.

"Your boyfriend give you that shiner?" I pointed toward her bruised face.

"Cordell?" She laughed. "Hell no. And FYI, he's not my boyfriend."

"I saw you kissing him at that restaurant."

"You were watching me?" She laughed. "Did that make you jealous, Clay Daniels? Did that make you desire me even more?"

"Not in the least." I felt confused. "Why did you say that Cordell was your boyfriend when he's not?"

"I wanted to make you jealous." She pressed her hip into my knee. "Besides, Cordell has plenty of others to keep him busy."

"He likes to play around?"

"Yeah, if sucking cock's your thang." She reached

for my fly. "His daddy's a big preacher in Mississippi, so he doesn't want people to know."

"Cordell bats for the other side?" I laughed. "Who would have thunk?"

"You say that like it's a bad thing."

"It's not a scandal these days to be gay. Far from it."

"It is if you're a basketball player with a Baptist minister for a daddy, who's connected to some important politicians in the Deep South."

"Is this why you desperately needed to meet me? To tell me that your boyfriend's in the closet."

"Someone else gave me this shiner. Like you, he gets all crazy whenever I try to break it off with him."

Did this other guy treat her like a sex slave too? I realized that I was not the only lover in her life and it pissed me off.

"A black girl with a black eye. Quite an irony, isn't it?"

She stepped back from me in anger. "It's obvious that I wasn't screwing you for your wit."

"Who is he?"

"A professor at my college."

"Jesus, a professor? You do the rough stuff with him too?"

"I don't kiss and tell. Let's just say he happens to be the lucky guy who grades my exams."

"So he's the one who beat you up?"

"More or less the way you did."

She took notice of my aroused state and began to massage it through my pants. For a moment, under the spell of alcohol and the allure of her beauty, I briefly considered letting her seduce me. But at what cost? I thought of Leah and the twins sound asleep back at the hotel and so I pushed her away from me, and she fell back against the concrete floor.

"Fucking asshole."

"How many times have I told you to leave me alone?" She buried her face in her hands and sobbed.

"I told you that we can't do this anymore. You and I are done."

"You wouldn't have been with me if you were happy with that skank."

"That skank is my wife, and I mostly did you for the money," I said, walking over to her. "Look, we made a mistake. We should have never hooked up in the first place."

"Fuck you." She looked up at me from the concrete floor, hate filling every inch of her face. I thought she might leap up and punch me.

"You played me by offering up that loan. You pocketed my six grand, now it's time to move on."

"Get over yourself." She stood, wiping away the tears on her sleeve. "I didn't come here to mess around. I have something important to tell you."

"Then hurry up and say it because my wife and kids are waiting for me back at the hotel."

"How could you have married that pathetic scarecrow?"

"Don't *you*, of all people, make fun of my wife." I made a threatening move toward her and she stepped back in fear.

She laughed. "You going to hit me for real this time?"

"Bet you'd like that."

"You're all talk, faggot. And a total loser in bed."

"Get out of my sight." I pointed at the door.

"Forget you. We're not done until I say we're done."

"And how's that?"

"Because I'm pregnant with your child, Clay Daniels."

LEAH

Thursday, October 22, 4:12 p.m.

*T*HE SOUND OF A WOMAN'S VOICE STARTLES ME. I open my eyes and, to my bewilderment, see Clarissa standing next to the bed. She glances around in stunned surprise before staring at me. Her open diary lies on the bed along with the empty bottle of wine. On the nightstand sits the key I'd used to enter her private world.

"I can explain," I say, pushing myself up to a sitting position.

"What the hell are you doing in here?"

"It's not what you think."

"Oh? You break in to my house, violate my privacy, and then you have the nerve to tell me that it's not what I think. What kind of monster are you?"

"What about you?" I say, a sense of righteousness

filling me. "What kind of person goes snooping around into another person's past for no apparent reason?"

"You're the one breaking in here and reading my diary."

"I didn't break in. You left your door unlocked."

"It's still unlawful entry."

"Tell me, Clarissa, what reason do you have for calling the FBI and running a check on me? What kind of person does that to their next-door neighbor, a neighbor whose only crime is that she tried to be friends with you?"

"That's why I was checking you out. So we *could* be friends. I've been burned in the past by my so-called friends."

"How dare you snoop into my childhood."

"How dare you break in to my home and read my diary and drink my wine."

"What you did is a breach of trust."

"You're entirely missing the point," Clarissa says, clearly exasperated.

"Which is?"

"You never would have known about it had you not snuck into my home in the first place. I have a right to privacy. I have the right to say or write anything I please."

I realize that she's right and that I have no answer for this. My righteous indignation has clearly been trumped by her legalistic argument. My dam of tears bursts and I break down sobbing. My chest heaves uncontrollably until I find myself hyperventilating. Wine bubbles tickle my nose and make me sneezy. Will she call the authorities on me? File criminal charges? If she does, it'll be the end for me in this town.

"Take it easy, Leah." She grabs some tissues off the dresser and hands them to me.

"Are you going to report me to the police?"

"I'm not sure." She sits down on the bed next to me. "Tell me the real reason you snuck in here and read my diary."

"I've been so bored and lonely since I moved here. I thought I was going crazy, and for whatever reason, you seemed to want nothing to do with me, no matter how hard I tried to befriend you."

"Oh, Leah."

"It confused me. I didn't know what I was doing wrong or how I offended you. Then a crazy idea came to mind. I thought if I got to know more about you, then we could become friends." I dab at the tears spilling down my cheeks. "That's why I broke in here."

"You really got to know me all right." She turns to me, hand gripping her diary. "Did you read *all* of it?"

I nod in embarrassment, recalling the morning I lay under the bed while she pleasured herself with the white dildo.

"It's partly my fault." She strokes my hand, which surprises me. "I suppose in hindsight I should have been nicer to you."

"I prayed every day that you would call and invite me over for coffee. I pictured us lunching together and sharing picnics with our families."

"Poor thing."

Her pity irritates me. "Poor me? How about poor you?"

"Why do you say that?"

"I've read your diary, remember? I *know* the hellish things you've been going through with Russell."

"Yes, I can see how you'd think that."

"Now that you know my secret, Clarissa, don't you think it's time I know yours?"

She mulls it over. "No. I'm not ready to disclose that just yet."

"But why?"

"It's a very personal issue."

"That's not fair."

"No, it's not, but that's the way it's going to be for the time being."

"But we can still be friends, right?"

She laughs. "Why wouldn't we?"

"I thought you'd hate me after learning about my past."

"I won't lie to you. That shocked me when I heard about it."

"I was so young when it happened."

"You must have had your reasons." She squeezes my hand. "I believe in second chances, Leah. I believe that people can change their lives for the better."

"Can I ask you something?"

"Of course."

"Was it your idea the other night to swap partners?"

"No." She looks away as if humiliated. "I hate the way Russell makes me sleep with others. But then I realized that I could lose my kids if I didn't agree to his demands."

"He'll reveal your secret. The one you don't want to tell me."

"Yes."

"That's why you refuse to report his abusive behavior to the police?"

She thumbs a tear from the corner of her eye. "Does Clay know what you've done?"

"He has no idea."

"Will you ever tell him?"

"I hope I'll never have reason to," I say. "So will you stay with Russell?"

"What other choice do I have?" She moves closer to me. "His behavior has been getting much worse as of late."

"Clarissa, you can't go on like this. It's too dangerous."

"I know. It's to the point where I'm scared for my life and the safety of the children."

"We both know that he's somehow involved with those two college kids."

"There's a part of me that doesn't want to believe it."

"Can *you* keep a secret?"

"You know I can."

"I found Mycah Jones and she's alive and well."

"You're kidding."

"It's no joke," I say. "I drove over to the address you wrote down in your diary. I knocked on the door and discovered that she's been there the entire time."

"But why?"

"Your suspicions have been confirmed. Russell has been sleeping with her."

"Maybe there's been a misunderstanding. Russell could have been helping her with her class work. After all, she was one of his students."

I laugh at this. "Trust me, there's no misunderstanding between those two."

"How can you be so sure?"

"She told me as much. He struck her and she's quite scared of him."

"And you believed her?"

"Yes, and she has the bruises to prove it. He preyed on her by abusing his role as a professor."

"Preyed on Mycah?" She laughs bitterly. "Please, Leah. How well do you know that girl?"

"Not well. I talked to her only that once."

"She's got a reputation as the most manipulative student on campus."

"Mycah's scared and convinced that he killed Cordell."

"Of course she is. She's a drama queen and pot stirrer. Russell certainly has a temper, but he's no killer."

"You just admitted that he's become more abusive to you."

"I know Russell better than anyone and I seriously doubt that he killed Cordell."

"How did you meet Russell, anyway?"

"He was my professor."

"Just like Mycah."

"Yes, just like Mycah. But we were in love with each other."

"Was he married at the time?"

"Yes."

I grip her hand for support. I feel important, like a true friend. It's been a long time since anyone confided in me and made me feel like I was needed. We embrace and she sobs quietly against my shoulder.

"I'm frightened, Leah."

"As am I. I think the three of us should go to the police and tell them what happened."

"No." She stands, throwing my hand down. "The cops can never be involved in this."

"Why not?"

"I'm not going to risk having my past come up in court and then watch as my life is destroyed and my children whisked away from me."

"You'd rather die than fight back?"

"Don't worry, I'll fight the way I know best."

Her response seems irrational and pigheaded. What is it that would warrant such a drastic reply? Without the police involved, what other options do we have? I think about my own history and suddenly understand what's at stake. I've buried the memory so deeply into the recess of my mind that what I did feels like a distant dream. Yet it happened, I know it did, and its long shadow has colored everything I've done since. A therapist once told me that if I didn't deal with the issue, the psychological ramifications would manifest in unforeseen and possibly dangerous ways.

"I understand that you're scared," I say.

"I don't think you really do."

"We have to work together if you want to escape from his grasp."

"What do you suggest?"

"The three of us should sit down and formulate a plan."

She shakes her head. "I don't think I can face that girl after what she's done to me."

"We have no other choice, and she seems ready and willing to help us."

"If only Russell would drive his car off a cliff, then everything would be fine." She laughs and I laugh with her.

"I seriously doubt that he's going to kill himself for your benefit, Clarissa."

"Then maybe there's another way we can go about this."

"Oh?"

"He threatened me the other night, Leah. He held me down on the bed with his hands around my neck. I honestly thought he was going to kill me."

"Oh my God. What set him off?"

"It doesn't take much to piss Russell off these days." She lets go of my hands and picks up her diary. "I asked him to his face if he was seeing one of his students."

"And what did he say?"

"He told me to mind my own business."

"So what are you going to do?"

"I can't take it anymore. I'm seriously thinking about using a gun to protect myself and the kids."

"A gun? Now you're talking like a crazy woman."

"Maybe to you, a privileged white woman living in the suburbs, it's crazy talk. You don't have to live with him day in and day out. What do you think will happen if I die and he gets custody of the kids?"

"It can't be all that bad. But whatever you do, Clarissa, I will support you."

"You're the best friend ever, girl." She walks over

and fingers away a strand of my hair. "I feel so much closer to you now."

"I just pray you and your husband one day have the kind of marriage Clay and I have."

Clarissa laughs hysterically at this. "You think Clay's any better than the rest of the dogs out there?"

"Clay's a devoted husband and father. He loves us dearly."

"Don't kid yourself." She laughs bitterly. "Every man will stray if presented with the right opportunity."

"No, he's different than the others."

"Tell me this. How would you ever know if he was cheating on you?"

"You saw how mad he got the other night when Russell proposed that swap."

"Seriously? That's the basis you're judging him on?"

"Clay was furious when he got home. I thought he was going to explode."

She laughs as if I'm being naive. "I guess you're a lucky girl, then."

"Yes, I most definitely am lucky."

"Some of us aren't so."

"My daughter will be home shortly," I say.

"When can we pay Mycah a visit?"

"How about tomorrow? Can you take the morning off?"

"I'm the director of diversity. I can do whatever I like at that school."

"Can I ask you one other question, Clarissa?"

"Of course."

"Can you see it in your heart to forgive me for what I've done?"

"Leah, you inadvertently came to my rescue by sneaking in here and reading my diary. Now, I can't condone such behavior, but for the first time in a while I feel like I have someone I can talk to and confide in."

"Like a real friend?"

"Yes, like a real friend indeed."

LEAH

Thursday, October 22, 5:17 p.m.

I'M IN A DAZE, UNABLE TO DEAL WITH THE KIDS' messy issues. There's so much that needs to be done around here that I can't seem to function in any normal capacity. I'm an emotional wreck. My mind races frantically, trying to process everything that has happened recently.

I should have forced Clarissa to go to the police. What if Russell comes home this evening in a foul mood and does something terrible to her or the kids? I'd never be able to forgive myself if that happened. But she insisted that I not call the police, and I can't bring it upon myself to defy the wishes of someone who I hope will one day be a dear friend.

Zack hangs around downstairs, reading on the couch, which is unusual for him. Zadie's playing on her tablet, most likely messaging one of her schoolmates. The fireplace crackles as soon as I flip on the switch. It feels cozy and safe, protected from the evil lurking just outside our door. I make some hot chocolate and a batch of sugar cookies while listening to Andrea Bocelli. The fragrant odor of baked goods wafts throughout the house. I want to feel happy and unburdened. I want this intense yearning in the pit of my stomach to go away.

A car pulls up in the driveway. I peek out the curtains but do not recognize the man getting out. He walks up to the front door and rings our doorbell. Neither Zack nor Zadie can be bothered to answer it. Who is this man, and why is he here? Is he a solicitor who has found himself lost in this vacant neighborhood? A Jehovah's Witness looking to make converts out of ghosts?

"Who is it?" I ask through the locked door.

"Detective Armstrong, ma'am. I'm holding up my badge for you to see."

I close one eye and take a look through the peephole. It certainly looks like an official police badge, but who knows these days.

"What do you want?"

"I'm investigating the murder of Cordell Jefferson and the disappearance of Mycah Jones."

My heart skips a beat. If I refuse to let him in, he may suspect me of something. Yet if I answer his questions, I fear I might incriminate myself. Or at least appear as if I'm withholding valuable information. The problem is that I'm a terrible liar and always have been.

I open the door and stare at him through the storm

door. Clay has not yet installed the glass, so the cold autumn air rushes inside. I cross my arms to keep warm, a gesture meant to demonstrate my extreme discomfort.

"How can I help you?"

"May I come in and ask you a few questions?"

"I suppose, but I'm not sure how I can assist you. I didn't know either one of those individuals."

"I promise you I'll be quick."

"My children are inside, Detective. I don't want to frighten them with all of this crime business."

"I suppose we could talk down at the station if you prefer."

The notion of being interrogated at a police station terrifies me, and I realize that talking to him here is my only hope of staying calm and telling my version. "No, it's okay. Give me a minute to escort the children up to their rooms."

I let him inside, telling Zack and Zadie to go upstairs. Zadie's sitting at the table with her cup of hot chocolate and a cookie and complains about having to get up. Zack follows my direction, but not before stopping to look up at the impeccably dressed detective. After a brief but contentious confrontation, I allow Zadie to take her tablet, hot chocolate, and cookies to her room despite our strict rule about eating in bed.

"Who are you?" Zack asks the detective.

"Detective Armstrong. And who are you, young man?" He holds out his hand to shake but Zack ignores it.

"Are you here to arrest me?"

Armstrong laughs. "Arrest you? Why in the world would I do that?"

"I've been getting into a lot of trouble at school."

"I'm sorry to hear that, but we don't arrest students unless they do something really bad."

"Like bring a weapon into class? Or attack their teacher?"

"Yeah, something like that."

"Bad stuff like that happens all the time in the inner cities. I read on the Internet where one kid stabbed his teacher."

"That's terrible." The detective looks up at me before returning his attention to Zack. "Fortunately, we don't have those kinds of problems here in Dearborn."

"I also read that most crimes in the inner city are black-on-black crime."

"Sometimes you have to look deeper into the statistics."

I grimace at Zack's words and usher him upstairs before he says any more embarrassing things. What's gotten into that boy? And where has he learned all this crazy stuff? Once he's safely ensconced in his room, I check on Zadie. She's sitting at her desk, brushing her doll's hair and speaking softly to it.

Detective Armstrong is sitting at the kitchen table when I arrive downstairs. Across from him is a platter of cookies.

"Would you like a cookie with a cup of coffee, Detective?"

"I thought you'd never ask."

I put the plate down in front of him, trying to steady my shaking hand. I pour him a cup of coffee.

"I'm sorry for showing up so suddenly."

"It's not a problem." I sit down across from him and

pour myself a cup. "Have you had any luck locating the missing girl?"

"Not as of late. This case has been a total head scratcher. But the reason I came here is to speak to you about Cordell."

"What about him?" I try not to panic.

"Did you know him?"

"No."

"Then could you explain to me why you met with him the night he was murdered?"

I sit perfectly still and stare at him. How does he know about that?

"You want to talk about it, Mrs. Daniels?"

"How did you find out?"

"The restaurant has the two of you on security tape. You entered the restaurant first and then Cordell came in later. Prior to meeting him there, the hostess at the restaurant he works at said you showed up at the bar where he worked."

"Yes."

"Why in the world would you meet with him?"

"You're going to think I'm a stupid woman, Detective."

"I promise you I will not. It's merely a procedural question that I'm required to ask."

"My family and I moved to this neighborhood a little over two months ago. My husband owns the new brewery in town."

"Yes, I'm familiar with your husband's brewery," he says.

Has he already spoken to Clay? "I've been so lonely and bored, and I thought if I could help the police solve this case, then I might make a name for myself in town. I was only trying to help."

"You were trying to track down the missing girl?"

"Yes."

"Which is why you also went over to the college, passing yourself off as a reporter, and interviewed members of the lacrosse team?"

"Is that illegal?"

"No, but it does complicate things when you interfere with an ongoing investigation. It also demonstrates a lack of confidence in your local law enforcement."

"Oh no, it had nothing to do with your competence. I'm sure you're a very good detective. Searching for that girl gave me something to do. A reason to get up in the morning."

"These cookies are fantastic, by the way. Ever think of opening your own bakery?" He smiles and takes a sip of his coffee.

I look across the kitchen. On the granite counter sits the plastic blue bowl and the empty pouch of premade cookie mix. Did he see it and is now mocking me? Cops often notice such small acts of deception.

"You know that Cordell and Mycah were not really a couple. Not in the traditional sense," he says.

"Oh?"

"It appears that he was sexually attracted to men as well."

"Hmm." I try to act surprised.

"We checked his computer. He was involved in many dating sites on the Internet. Two or three times a week he met with one of these strangers in Portland for what, I assume, was a 'hookup.'"

"Hookup?"

"Casual sex."

"Do you think Mycah knew about this?"

"I'm almost certain she did, but that it was not much of an issue between them."

"Cordell told me that Mycah was involved with a lot of activist groups."

"Mycah was a controversial figure on campus. She was elected president of the student body and started the Black Lives Matter group. Although she had a good deal of support, she was also despised by many students."

"If you call advocating for social justice controversial, Detective, then I think that's where you and I part ways."

"I suppose that being an officer of the law gives me a certain perspective about these things, especially when it comes to the Black Lives Matter movement."

"That's because there's not the same level of anxiety out here in rural Maine as there is in the inner cities."

"I suppose," he says. "As for Mycah, she was constantly attacking the administration for what she perceived as white privilege on campus. Many people believe that she went too far by posting pictures of herself on Facebook, mocking Chadwick's alleged racist culture. Seems odd, considering all the men she dated."

"People have the right to do whatever they please. This is still America."

"True, but don't you find it a bit curious that she was secretly dating the captain of the lacrosse team—the one group on campus most students associated with white privilege?"

"If it was a man sleeping around, no one would say boo about it."

He bites into another cookie. "These are delicious. What did you put in them to make them taste so good?"

I drop all pretenses. "They came premixed from the supermarket. Just add water and bake." I point to the empty blue package on the counter.

"Wow, some detective I am." He laughs. "Still, they're very tasty."

"My children need to come down shortly and finish their chores, Detective."

"Of course. I have only a few more questions to ask," he says, flipping through his notebook. "Did your husband know the missing girl?"

"Not that I'm aware of."

"How long have you two been married?"

"Fourteen years." His questions confound me. "Why are you asking me this?"

"I can't understand why Mycah Jones made so many calls to the brewery the night she went missing."

"What are you suggesting?"

"I'm not suggesting anything. Just asking a question."

"Maybe she wanted to know what sort of beers were on tap that evening."

"That must be it."

"Clay rotates his beers on a regular basis."

"I didn't know that."

"See? That wasn't so hard."

"Or it could have been something else," he casually remarks.

I stand and give him a cold glare. "What are you implying?"

"Maybe she had a . . . a thing for your husband. He is a very good-looking guy."

"That's the craziest thing I've ever heard," I say, laughing. "Clay is a dedicated and loving husband. He would never cheat on me."

"I never implied that he was cheating on you."

"Please go, Detective. I can't take any more of this crazy talk."

"I have one more question to ask," he says, taking another cookie. "What did you and Cordell talk about that evening?"

"He told me exactly what he told you. That some white guys had attacked him and Mycah as they were walking home. He remembers them shouting out a racial slur before he was knocked unconscious."

"How did he know they were white if he never saw them?"

I shrug. "Maybe he just assumed."

"Did he tell you that Mycah was his girlfriend?"

"He did."

"Did he tell you where they had just come from the night of the attack?"

"I don't recall."

"You don't recall?" He looks puzzled. "They spent part of the night in your husband's tasting room."

"Clay never told me that." I hate lying.

"You didn't think to ask Cordell such an important question?"

"Honestly, I don't remember much. I had a few more margaritas than I should have had that night."

"A detective should never drink while on the job." He smiles coyly.

"It's obvious that my skills are far inferior to yours, Detective. Now, if that's all."

"It is. For now."

He thanks me and leaves, driving out of the neighborhood in his unmarked car. I collapse on the sofa. My hands are shaking, I'm so upset. What is happening to me? There has to be a reasonable explanation for why Mycah called the brewery so many times that night. I'm not worried in the least about Clay's loyalty. I remember when we first met at that protest march, and how he called me for days on end after we met at that dog park. His mild manner was what I found most attractive about him. He seemed to lack the alpha male gene that most men use when wooing a girl. It's how I knew early on that he'd never betray me.

I broke up with Clay after a year of dating. It felt like he was smothering me and always around. He reminded me of a lost puppy nipping at my ankle. My old boyfriend called out of the blue and we went out a few times, but it wasn't the same as before. I realized that I missed Clay more than I thought, and when I went over to his Capitol Hill apartment one day I was disappointed to learn he wasn't there. His roommate answered the door instead and informed me that Clay was out drinking. In fact, he'd been drinking heavily every night since I'd broken up with him. His roommate claimed that Clay was depressed and missed me terribly. He'd had every opportunity to cheat on me with one of the girls at the bar, but Clay couldn't even think about anyone else. It was then that I knew we were meant to be together. I asked his roommate what bar he frequented, and then I went over there and claimed him. He cried drunkenly on my shoulder when I told him that I'd take him back.

From then on I knew he would always be true to me.

LEAH

Thursday, October 22, 5:56 p.m.

A BIT LATER MY PHONE RINGS, AND I HEAD UPSTAIRS to get the kids. It's Clarissa. I feel overjoyed that she thinks enough to call me. I lift the phone to my ear and the first thing I hear is the sound of her sobbing.

"Clarissa? Are you okay?"

"Russell's home. He's in the bathroom and in a bad way."

"Do you want me to call the police?"

"No, promise to take care of my children if something bad happens to me."

"Don't talk like that. You'll get through this, and I'll be with you the entire way."

"I fear he'll hurt me if I don't go along with his demands."

"What would you like me to do?"

"You can see into my bedroom, right?"

Sheepishly, I admit that I can.

"Keep your lights off and record it on your phone in case he gets violent. It may be the only evidence I have against him."

"Are you sure?"

But the line has already gone dead. I run downstairs, grab some chips and cupcakes for the kids, snatch my phone off the kitchen table, and then head upstairs to my bedroom. All the lights are off. I slip the curtain aside and peer through the shutters.

The light to the Gaineses' bedroom is on and I can see Clarissa lying on the bed, wearing pink lingerie and with her legs splayed. She doesn't look happy. I raise the phone up to the window as Russell walks into the room, dressed only in his boxers. He stands off to the side and takes in his wife. I zoom in as far as the lens will allow and watch the scene through the video. Russell climbs on the bed and forces her to her stomach, twisting her arm up behind her back. I try to control my rage and keep my hand from shaking. He reaches under her belly and pulls her up so that her behind points toward the ceiling. He slaps it three times in succession before reaching down toward her face, which is buried in the pillow. His large hands wring her neck as he enters her from behind.

It brings me to tears. I look away so as not to witness this humiliating offense. I feel sick to my stomach. When I look up, I see something that shocks me.

This can't be happening.

CLAY

Thursday, October 22, 6:04 p.m.

*T*HE TASTING ROOM IS SLAMMED TONIGHT. PEOPLE sit at the picnic tables and line up against the bar, waiting for Bree to pour them drafts. I should be happy at all the money filling the till, and I am, but I can't seem to rest easy. The meeting with Armstrong this morning worries me. Does he suspect me of anything? The thought of that extramarital affair continues to haunt me. I will lose everything if that comes to light: my family, the brewery, and all that I've worked for.

Mycah's calls to the brewery didn't worry me at the time. Who had any idea that she would go missing and that her boyfriend would end up dead? I assumed that our affair would fizzle out quietly and without notice, and then we'd go our separate ways. The burden of this guilt will be my lifelong albatross.

I walk among the crowd gathered in the tasting room. Happy customers slap my back and tell me how awesome I am and how wonderful the beer tastes. Although I don't usually crave such attention, it feels good to be praised by others. And all because of my talent for brewing beer. If not for that, these people could care less about me and my myriad of problems.

I sit down and have a beer with a group of young hipsters who frequent the brewery. We engage in the usual small talk, and I tell them about my brewing philosophy and how I craft my beer. But in the back of my mind all I can think about is Mycah. If I wake up tomorrow and hear that her lifeless body has been found in pieces along the riverbank, it wouldn't bother me in the least. No, I'd probably cheer her squalid demise with a rousing toast. Drinks on the house. Then maybe I could get on with my life. There'd be no witnesses to our affair. Only an unborn child from an unnamed father, unless she'd aborted it like I asked her to. But what if she's alive somewhere? What if the demon seed is still churning in her belly? What then?

After consuming three beers, I go behind the bar and fill up my growler with an IPA. Then I go back to my cluttered office, put my tired feet up on the desk, and drown out the empty chatter filling my head.

LEAH

Thursday, October 22, 6:15 p.m.

I FALL TO THE FLOOR, CLUTCHING THE PHONE TO MY chest. My body is on fire and painful to the touch, as if I've suffered third-degree burns. Angry screams echo inside my skull. What do I do now that Russell has seen me?

How did he know? It's dark in my bedroom and almost impossible to make anything out. Or is it? I examine my phone and wonder what gave me away. A flash? I swipe my hand over my scalp and curse at myself for being so stupid. Mr. Shady sneaks in through the bedroom door and begins to bark madly. I gently push him aside, whispering for him to go back downstairs. He growls for a few seconds before leaving the room. I want to climb under the covers and stay there forever. But I can't. Someone is ringing the doorbell.

I ball up in a fetal position. But then I hear footsteps

and realize that either Zack or Zadie is going to answer it. I drop my phone, jump off the floor, and sprint downstairs, leaping past Zack until I'm in front of him. Thankfully, the front door is locked. Through the peephole I see Russell pounding on the door and jabbing his finger on the doorbell.

"You fucking pervert," Russell shouts. "You better erase that video or there's going to be trouble."

"Is that man trying to break in to our house?" Zack asks, looking scared.

"No, he's just upset about something."

"Upset about what?"

"I don't know." I stand with my back against the door.

"Is he going to kill us?"

"No, Zack. Now, go up to your room."

Instead, Zack walks toward the living room window.

"It's our neighbor, Mr. Gaines," he says. "Why is he banging on our door?"

"Go back up to your room."

"Better erase that video," Gaines shouts.

"What video?" Zack asks. "What is he talking about?"

"Goddamn peeping Tom," Russell shouts.

"Is that true?" Zack asks.

"No." I look out the window and see Russell stomping back down the pathway. When I look over, I notice that Zack is running upstairs.

I scamper after him, practically out of breath. I run into Zack's room and notice that he's not there. I check Zadie's room and see that she's buried under the covers. Poor girl. Where else could Zack be? My mind is racing, adrenaline fueling my righteous anger. Upon entering my bedroom, I notice that my phone is gone. The brat took it. I stomp around, looking for him, pissed at this invasion of my privacy. He's not in the closet or behind the dresser. I fall to the floor, lift the covers, and see him. The light from the phone's flashlight temporarily blinds me, and I realize that I must have switched the flashlight app on by accident. I reach out to grab him, but he slides away from me, his eyes trained on the screen.

"Give me that phone, young man, or you're in big trouble."

"They have no clothes on and his wiener's huge," Zack says, eyes glued to the video.

I crawl under the bed, but he slides out the other side.

"Give me that right now."

"He's choking Mrs. Gaines and hitting her. Is he trying to kill her?"

I slither out the other side as Zack leaps over the mattress. But he is too slow and I grab him by the elbow and push him onto the bed. His terrified eyes gaze up at me as I snatch the phone out of his hand. I'm so angry now that I feel like slapping his face.

"Why did you disobey me like that?"

"I'm sorry." Tears fall down his freckled cheeks. "Why were you spying on them, Momma?"

"You should have listened to me." I squeeze his elbow.

"Ow! You're hurting me."

"You're lucky that's all I do to you."

"He'll come over here and kill us. He knows you were spying on them."

"Stop saying that."

"Why'd you do it?"

"That's none of your business."

He sobs. "When his hands are around your neck, I won't stop him. I'll let him kill you."

I push him hard against the mattress and then let him go. He sprints back to his room, bawling. What have I done? It's the first time I've ever laid a finger on my children and now I've scarred him for life.

I collect myself, wondering what to do next. Something seems not right. I don't enjoy spying on people. I was only trying to help Clarissa in the event he tried to kill her. I hold up the phone and watch the video. As much as I want to turn away, I keep my eyes glued to the screen. Russell walks in and sees his wife lying on the bed. He flips her over and places his large hands on her waist. His back is to me as he chokes her with one hand and slaps her with the other. His hips start to grind back and forth. But then he stops for no apparent reason and turns one hundred and eighty degrees, looking in my direction. He approaches the window and starts to lean forward when the video shakes and goes black.

How did he know I was filming them? Did a feeling of being watched suddenly come over Russell? The only other explanation is that Clarissa told him. But why would she do that? She's scared of her husband. It makes no sense for her to tell him this. I watch it again and am just as confused the second and third time.

The remainder of the evening passes in a blur. The mood in the house feels dark and scary. I go in the bedroom and comfort Zadie. She smiles at me from her bed as she repeatedly combs her doll's long blond hair.

The doll squeaks some bland comment whenever she pulls its hair hard enough. Zadie makes the doll speak while I'm sitting next to her. "You're an evil person, Leah," I imagine the doll saying. Zadie laughs at the doll's droll comments, but it freaks me out all the same. Am I losing my mind? I reassure Zadie that I care about her and that everything is all right. It doesn't concern me that my eleven-year-old daughter still plays with dolls at her age. I suppose she'll move on to other things when she's ready.

I go into Zack's room, bearing milk and cookies. He's sitting in his rocking chair and reading a book with a red cover and with the words *The Turner Diaries* in the title. He's wearing earbuds attached to his tablet. The cover portrays a man and woman shooting rifles, and I assume it's one of the many action novels he enjoys reading. I try to talk to him, but he wants nothing to do with me. He doesn't even look up from the pages of his book to acknowledge me. I apologize profusely for hurting him. Tears stream down my face, but they have no effect. I hesitate for a moment before confessing to him that I was fearful for Mrs. Gaines's safety. Something clicks and he looks up. A flicker of hope ignites inside me.

"You should have said that before you pushed me," he says, coolly removing one earbud.

"I'm so sorry for doing that."

"It doesn't surprise me about the Gaineses."

"Excuse me?"

"I read on the Internet that one out of every three black men have served time in prison."

"I don't want to talk about this right now, Zack."

"It's the facts, and the facts don't lie."

"There are historical reasons for these problems. Black people's ancestors were enslaved and oppressed."

"But the Gaineses were never slaves. And their house is way bigger than ours."

"History casts a long shadow on certain people in our society. Slavery's destructive force still affects black lives to this day."

"President Obama?"

"That's different."

"LeBron James?"

"Please, Zack."

"Oprah Winfrey?"

"I came here to apologize to you, not argue."

"A race war is coming and we must be prepared."

"Don't talk like that."

"You didn't just put your hands on me, Momma. You pushed me very hard. You humiliated me." He replaces his earbud. "And that's inexcusable."

"I'm sorry."

"Not accepted."

"Will you ever be able to forgive me?"

"I can forgive, but I'll never be able to forget what you did to me."

I force a smile and lean in to kiss him, but he stiffens up as my lips press up against his clenched cheek. I hear something coming out of his earbuds and it's not music. A man is screaming about Second Amendment rights. Do I dare say anything? Punish my son for listening to right-wing radio? He's too young for ideology. Can an eleven-year-old identify with a radical political movement designed to enslave us?

He returns to his book as I walk out of his room. For the remainder of the night, I allow the children their privacy, delivering treats to their rooms and apologizing for my disgraceful behavior. Then I sit on the couch and think about my next move. Clay will not be home until midnight, if tonight is like most nights. I feel vulnerable and scared. For the first time in my life—I can't believe I'm even thinking this—I wish I had something to protect myself and my family.

I sit on the couch, with my feet tucked under my haunches. On the coffee table in front of me sits a full bottle of Pinot. The first glass goes down easy and calms my nerves. The second glass takes a bit longer as I savor the fermented grape on my tongue. Tomorrow we'll go see Mycah. Tomorrow we'll get answers or else I will go to the police with my findings. It has to be this way.

CLAY

Friday, October 23, 6:21 a.m.

I DRAG MYSELF OUT OF BED AND SWALLOW THREE Tylenol for my hangover. The house possesses a weird vibe this morning. Forgoing a shower, I put on the same clothes I wore yesterday. They smell of yeast and fermented fruit.

I stagger downstairs and am ambushed by a messy house and Leah asleep on the couch. Laundry and dishes lie everywhere. An empty bottle of Pinot sits on the floor. What a disaster. What is she doing all day? Sitting around and reading her stupid chick novels while getting drunk?

I climb in my truck and drive away, picking up a coffee on my way to work. No way I want to sit around and hear her complain about this thing or that problem. I fear what I might have said if she woke up and saw me there. With each passing day, I find myself wanting to leave that depressing house as soon as possible.

LEAH

Friday, October 23, 7:44 a.m.

I WAKE UP TO THE SOUND OF A TOASTER POPPING. Lifting my muddled head off the couch, I see the children sitting at the kitchen table and eating in an orderly fashion. An empty wine bottle lies on the floor beneath me. I pick it up and stuff it under the cushion so the children can't see it. Then I stagger toward them, a pained smile over my face. Oh, how I wish I had eaten something last night to counter the effects of the alcohol.

A car door slams shut, and it's like a gunshot going off in my head. I stagger over to the window and see Russell sitting in his BMW. He turns back and says something to his children, who sit buckled in their seats. Then he backs out of the driveway and leaves the neighborhood. Clarissa's car is still parked in the driveway. Is she staying home today? Is she all right?

The kids eat quickly, gather their backpacks, and get

ready to head out. I hand them their Lunchables, seeing how I'm too sick to make them a proper lunch.
They seem quiet this morning, begrudgingly accepting
my parting kiss. But I am glad to see them heading toward the bus stop, leaving me to my own devices. I
blow them kisses and shout good-bye like a forlorn
mom, but they don't even turn to look at me.

Mr. Shady barks when I reach for his leash. I gulp
down a couple of aspirin with a swallow of wine. Then
I grab my coat, a paper bag, and head out. The sky is
overcast this morning with flecks of rain. The starlings
must have moved on to warmer climes, their flights of
fancy finished for the year. The neighborhood looks
more desolate than ever, maybe because of the scarcity
of light. Or maybe because of my dark mood.

Mr. Shady lifts his hind leg and pees on one of the
unfinished foundations. It leaves a dark stain that resembles Mount Fuji. A little further on he squats and
poops on a scruffy thatch of grass. I scoop it up with
the bag and follow Mr. Shady until we arrive at the
Gaineses'.

Do I knock and check in on her? Or call her on my
cell phone? I want to see her, to comfort her, and find
out what happened last night. My head hurts, and not
for a brief moment do I suspect her of betraying me.

I walk up the steps and ring her doorbell. After a
minute the door opens and I see a wedge of her face.
Her left eye looks slightly bruised and puffy. An over-
powering sensation radiates from the center of my
being as soon as she sees me.

"You're taking quite a risk coming over here," she
whispers, cinching up her robe.

"I saw Russell drive away. He won't return until evening."

"How do you know that? Unless you've been keeping tabs on us?"

"It's just something I've observed."

"Would you like to come in?" She opens the door to let me inside.

"What should I do with Mr. Shady?"

"Tie him up along the back deck. He'll be fine."

I walk through the house and out onto her deck, and loop the leash over a post. Mr. Shady glares at me as I go back inside. I sit across from her in the living room. She pours me a mug of coffee, but it's not coffee I want. A container of cream and a bowl of sugar cubes sit on the table.

"He's really angry with me right now," she says. "And with you too."

"I saw what he did to you."

She looks away in shame.

"Did he hurt you bad?"

"Bad enough. He slapped me around afterward. But it was the emotional abuse that hurt much worse. The name-calling and the way he put me down like I was a piece of garbage."

"I'm so sorry, Clarissa. Why can't husbands and wives treat each other with respect?"

"Like your husband?"

I hesitate before saying, "Yes."

"You've at least opened my eyes to the possibility of a life without Russell."

"Good. Now, you must find a way to get away from him if you want a normal life."

"Yes, you're right. I can see that more clearly now."

"You're a wonderful person, Clarissa. You deserve to be with someone who makes you happy."

"It's taken your friendship for me to see that."

"Come with me and hear what Mycah has to say?"

"I don't know if that's a good idea, the way Russell is acting right now."

"Should I be worried?"

"You might want to protect yourself, Leah. Who knows how Russell will react when he sees you?"

"But how can I protect myself?"

"Have you ever thought about owning a gun?"

"A gun?" The word "gun" sounds foreign and frightening to my ears. "Is that really necessary?"

"If he suspects that you know about Cordell or Mycah, then your life could be in danger."

"I don't think he suspects me of anything except filming him."

"I'm just saying, Leah, it wouldn't hurt to have one. Considering what he's capable of—what he's possibly *done*."

"But I don't believe in gun ownership. I've never owned a gun in my life."

"I'm just saying that you should consider it. Think about the safety of your family."

"If you're so concerned about it, why don't you have one?"

She sipped her coffee and replaced it on the saucer. "What's to say I don't?"

I can't believe my ears. "Clarissa, you're the *last* person on earth I'd suspect of owning a gun."

"That's how frightened I am. I haven't yet worked up the courage to use it. But if that bastard ever lays a hand on the kids . . ."

"Oh my God, I can't believe this."

"I can't quite believe it either." She smiles. "You must think I'm a raving lunatic."

"Hardly."

"Do you think any less of me now?"

"How could I think less of you?" I say, trying to calm my emotions. "Do you know how to use it?"

"It's a Ruger nine millimeter with a seven-round, single-stack magazine. You just aim and pull the trigger." She lifts her coffee cup off the saucer. "I keep it hidden away so he doesn't find it."

"You're so bad."

"Would you like to see it?"

I don't want to, but I nod anyway, feeling giddy about our dangerous little secret. She runs upstairs and returns a few minutes later with the gun. It looks big and scary as she places it in my palm.

"Oh wow, it's really heavy." I let its weight rest in my hand.

"You should take it," she whispers. "Keep it in the house for protection, just in case."

"I can't even." Just looking at it scares the daylights out of me.

"You have your family to think about."

"But what about your family? You have children too."

"I bought two just in case."

"Two?" I pause to consider this. "Do you really think he'd come after me?"

"I don't know my husband anymore or what he's capable of doing. Clearly, he's not the man I married. Moving here to Maine has made him crazier and more unpredictable."

"I don't think I could ever pull the trigger."

"You could if it comes to protecting your family," she says. "Go on. Take it. It will make you feel safe."

"Okay. I'll hold on to it for just a little bit," I say, slipping the gun into my coat pocket. "But I hope I never have to use it."

"I think I would like to go with you to see Mycah."

"Will you tell me your secret during the drive?"

"I suppose it's not fair that I know yours and you don't know mine."

"Not if we're going to be friends, it isn't."

"Then again, life's not fair." Clarissa rises off the sofa and walks toward me instead of going upstairs.

She reaches into my pocket and takes out the gun. Pressing it into my slender hands, she lifts it as if to aim at something off in the distance. Her shimmering hair brushes against my cheek as she guides my forefinger over the metallic trigger. I close one eye and take aim at a carving of an African peasant woman.

"Close one eye and imagine that Russell's coming at you."

I do as instructed.

"No one would ever blame you, Leah, especially if he broke into your house and tried to kill you."

"You'll back me up?"

"Of course I will. We're best friends now." She lowers the gun and places it back inside my pocket. Then she heads upstairs as if angry with me.

What do I do now? I'm sitting in her living room, all alone, and with a gun in my pocket. Do I leave or wait for her to come back downstairs? Now that we're best friends, I suppose I should wait.

LEAH

Friday, October 23, 11:55 a.m.

I CALL CLAY AND TELL HIM TO PICK THE KIDS UP FROM school this afternoon.

"You picked the worst day to ask me. I'm brewing a beer as we speak."

"I'm not asking, Clay."

"I just can't pick up and leave whenever you want me to."

"I don't ask for very much, do I?"

"Can't you get a sitter to pick the kids up this once?"

I feel my blood pressure rising. "After all I've sacrificed for you and your stupid brewery, you can't even do this one favor for me?"

"Leah?"

"Go to hell."

I hang up, confident that he'll call back. My phone rings a few seconds later. It's him, but I refuse to answer. He sends me text after text, apologizing profusely for his rude behavior and promising to pick up the kids.

Clarissa walks back downstairs, fully dressed and with a bag slung over her shoulder. She guides me over to the back door. Where are we going? I follow her onto the deck. The autumn sun peeks through the ocean of clouds. She gently closes the sliding glass door behind her, and I follow her downstairs and onto their perfectly manicured lawn. Mr. Shady barks madly at me.

We leave the yard and walk along the adjacent field and along the border of the unfinished homes. I have no idea where we are going, but I follow anyway. The gun feels weighty in my pocket, its lethal presence heightening my awareness of everything around me, which is not necessarily a bad thing.

Clarissa stops behind one of the unfinished homes and stares at it as if she's a prospective buyer. I pull up next to her and study it. The contractor had finished the exterior, but the inside is all studs and two-by-fours, kinetic space waiting for a family to complete it.

"Why are we stopping here?" I ask.

"Take the gun out of your pocket, Leah. I'm going to teach you how to shoot."

I laugh. "Oh no, you're not."

"Oh yes, I am."

"But we'll get in trouble."

"No one will ever hear us out here. The nearest home is a mile down the road."

Reluctantly, I reach inside my pocket and take out the gun. Clarissa loads it before instructing me to point it toward the empty house.

"Now, close one eye and choose something as your target."

"Like what?"

"I don't know. Pick something."

I close my left eye and aim at one of the windows on the first floor. Clarissa moves behind me and reinforces my grip in her hands. Her head is next to mine, and I can feel her hot breath waxing against my cheek.

"Good." She readjusts my finger on the trigger. "So why did you kill her?"

"Kill who?"

"Okay, I can see that you're aiming for the kitchen window. You need to raise your aim just a tad."

I zoom in on the pane, my concentration never more focused. Fear and excitement zip through my veins as she helps me nudge the gun up a smidgen.

"There you go. When you're ready, pull the trigger."

I bite my lower lip and hesitate for a few seconds before doing as instructed. My hands fly back as the gunshot explodes in my ear. The powerful kickback surprises me, and I fall back into Clarissa's awaiting body. Upon looking up, I notice that the window is still intact. How in the world did I miss?

"That's okay, hon. You need to aim a little higher next time. Now, grip the gun and try again."

"Okay." I feel as if I've let her down.

"So why did you kill her?" she asks.

"I don't know what you're talking about."

"Your sister. You killed her, right?"

I clench my teeth in an attempt to stop my hands from shaking. I want to pull the trigger and fire nonstop, but in the condition I'm in, I'd miss an elephant two feet in front of me. I'm Annie Oakley suffering from Parkinson's. Calamity Jane with a bad case of the DTs.

"You pushed her into the pool when no one was looking."

"You're making me extremely nervous, Clarissa."

"No worries. Just aim a little higher this time." She taps the gun upward ever so slightly. "Now, close your eye and concentrate on the window. Put everything out of mind."

I close my eye, which is now bubbling with a tear.

"When you're ready, I want you to pull the trigger."

I focus on the pane of glass before pulling the trigger. The window shatters in a burst of crystal fragments. I did it. Happy, I jump up and down as if I've just won a teddy bear at the town fair. Clarissa grabs my hands and joins me in celebration, and I momentarily forget about the terrible words she just uttered. Despite my lifelong aversion to firearms, the rush that fills me is like nothing else I've ever experienced. Who knew playing with guns could be this thrilling? I don't want to stop. I want to keep shooting. I want to blanket that home in bullets until it looks like a house made of Swiss cheese.

"Can I do it again?"

"You can shoot as many rounds as you like. I have plenty of ammo," she says. "There's no one here who'll hear us."

I smile, wiping the tears out of the corners of my eyes. I look at her, my spirits soaring. For some reason I think I'm happy. A paralyzing, infatuating sense of joy has overwhelmed me.

"Do you want to tell me about it?"

"It was easy. I just closed my eyes, aimed like you said, and pulled the trigger."

"I mean about what happened to your sister. How you drowned her."

I shrug and stare at her as if to ask why.

"The truth will liberate you, Leah. You'll become a better person because of it."

"How did you ever . . . ?" Then I remember her friend in law enforcement. "Why would you even . . . ?"

"You and I are just alike. We're victims of the past. In order to be free, we need to be true to ourselves."

"I will not let Russell hurt you anymore." I hold up the gun.

"Now that you know how to do it, the second time should be easier."

"You don't know the whole story about my sister and me."

"Then tell me, Leah. Let me help you unpack."

"I'm not the monster you're making me out to be."

"Did I ever say you were a monster? I'm sure there was a good reason why you did it."

"There's always a reason for the things we do." I spin around, brimming with confidence, and point the gun at an upstairs window.

The window appears as if it's right in front of me, and I close my weak eye and fire. The glass explodes in a burst of shards. Yes. I swivel like a pro and pull the trigger. The next pane explodes as well, and I feel like I'm getting the hang of it. The vibration of the weapon shoots up my arms and into the nether regions of my cerebral cortex. I feel invigorated and strong. Maybe I've been mistaken about owning a firearm. It's empowering and visceral and a totally thrilling experience. It gives me a newfound confidence in myself.

"You're a regular Stagecoach Mary," Clarissa says, high-fiving me.

"Do you really think?"

"I know it."

"We're going to be best of friends, Clarissa."

"Of course we are. It's about time we get real with each other."

"I couldn't agree more. Where should we begin?"

"We begin with you telling me about your sister. Then I'll tell you my secret." She places her hand over mine, the one holding the gun, and squeezes it affectionately.

"I'm so happy I met you, Clarissa."

"Likewise, girl. It's about time to break free of these chains holding us down."

CLAY

Friday, October 23, 1:27 p.m.

*T*HREE POLICE CARS PULL UP ALONGSIDE THE BREW-
ery as Ben and I transfer one of our beers to the fermenting kettle. It doesn't surprise me. Actually, I'd
been expecting the day to come. Armstrong enters first,
followed by four uniformed officers. I nod to Ben; he
knows what to do from here. I see his startled expression and wonder what he's thinking. Did I rob a
bank? Commit murder? Drink a domestic beer? (We
constantly joke that drinking Budweiser's a crime.)

"Everything okay, boss?" he asks.

"Yeah. Bit of a misunderstanding." I slap him on the
back. "You can handle it from here, right?"

"I suppose."

"Make sure to clean the tank out good. I should be
back later today."

"Aye, aye, captain."

I walk toward Armstrong with hands raised, smiling. They have nothing on me yet, but I must play their game. This game is all that's separating me from my fall from grace.

"We're taking you downtown for questioning, Clay."

"Am I under arrest?"

"Not yet."

"I want to call my lawyer," I say. The only lawyer I know in town is the goofy real estate attorney who helped us purchase our home. Hopefully, he can recommend a good criminal attorney, but I don't expect to find many crackerjacks in this area.

"You can call him once you're down at the station."

"I'd rather call him now."

"Let's go down to the station and you can call him. Trust me, this is in your best interest."

I laugh. "Since when have you had my best interest at heart?"

"Either that or we can question you at home."

"Let's go down to the station."

They seat me in the back of one of the police vehicles and we ride into town. I'm led into the interrogation room, which looks a lot like the grubby rooms seen on all those crime shows. Armstrong asks if I want a coffee and I take him up on his offer, although what I'd really like is a cold beer.

Despite my apprehensiveness, I feel relieved knowing that my lies are coming to an end. I'm prepared to unburden myself if necessary and tell him everything that has happened. Whether he believes me or not is another matter entirely. I sip the coffee and wait for him to ask the first question. I fiddle with the Rustic

Barn coaster I brought with me to keep my hands busy. He asks about wanting to call my lawyer and I tell him I've decided to hold off on that for now. I have nothing to hide—or at least I manage to bluff a good game.

"You haven't been telling us everything, Clay," Armstrong says.

"What else is there to tell?"

"Tell me more about the calls she made to your cell phone."

I'm screwed. He's done his homework. I have no answer for this.

"Or the fact that we have witnesses who saw you dining with her one night."

"Either they're lying or you are."

"I'm not playing a game of beer pong with you." He passes me the phone records. "A mixed couple dining in these parts is something people tend to remember."

"Racist assholes," I mumble under my breath.

"It's an observation, not an act of racism."

I pass him back the phone records. I don't need to look at it to know I'm in trouble. My whole life feels like it's crashing down on me. So why do I feel so calm? So relieved? Almost happy to be unburdened of this secret.

"I didn't kill her."

"Thatta boy."

"I want to call my lawyer."

"Okay, but here's the thing. We're still going to file charges against you."

"I said I didn't kill her," I snap.

"Obstruction of justice, perjury. You've lied your ass off to me the entire time."

"Not under oath. I know my rights."

"It's your choice, Clay. We can file murder charges later if we need to," Armstrong says, standing to leave. "We both know she called your cell phone the night she went missing. We also know you left the place shortly before she disappeared."

"And shortly before her boyfriend was assaulted."

"Yes, that too."

"I may have slept with the girl, Detective, but I didn't hurt her." Not intentionally, anyway.

"Then what happened?"

"I fell in love with Mycah. Sure, it was stupid, but I couldn't stop thinking about her. I finally wised up and broke it off with her, but she kept calling and begging to see me. I was weak. I was a lonely, dumb ass who just couldn't resist a sexy girl, especially when I'd been drinking. My wife and I . . . well, we weren't doing so well." I stop myself.

"You were having an affair and she broke it off with you, and you became angry and lashed out at her?"

"That's where you're wrong." He looks like he doesn't believe me. "She wouldn't leave me the hell alone."

"You expect me to believe that?"

"Believe what you want." I slouch down in the chair. "I had nothing to do with her disappearance."

"But you left the brewery that night to go meet her, right?"

"I'd never been unfaithful to my wife until I met Mycah. Yes, I left the brewery to meet her one last time."

"Because she told you she was pregnant with your child?"

"Wouldn't you do the same? Convince her to terminate it."

"I've never cheated on my wife, so I wouldn't know."

"I never cheated on my wife either until I met this bitch."

"And I'm supposed to believe that?"

I bang my fist on the table, pissed that he doesn't believe me. "I'd like to see how strong you'd be if some hot twenty-something-year-old made a pass at you while you were drunk."

"Some guys have all the luck."

"I don't need your sarcasm. I need a lawyer."

"So she called to talk to you that night about the baby and you agreed to meet her. You got angry when she told you about it, so you assaulted her boyfriend and then killed Mycah in a fit of rage. You panicked after realizing what you'd done and then hid the body somewhere."

"No," I shout. "That's not at all what happened."

"Then you better start telling your version once your lawyer arrives," he says, holding out his cell phone.

"I hate lawyers."

"You're waiving your rights to an attorney?"

"Why not? I've got nothing to hide."

"Duly noted," Armstrong says. "The floor is all yours."

I sip my coffee and think about that fateful night. I explain that she called me just before eleven that evening. She badly needed help. She was hysterical and threatened to expose me as the father of her unborn child if I didn't meet her along the wooded trail that led to campus. She said her boyfriend had found out about the affair and was furious. She said he was drunk—

they both were, which I thought very irresponsible for a woman with child—my child. But then I figured she'd already decided to abort the fetus, which meant that any drinking she did would only harm herself. Cordell had struck her, she told me over the phone, and was taking a piss in the woods. She wanted me to protect her so that he wouldn't hurt her again. She claimed she loved me, but I could tell that she was drunk. Still, somewhere in the back of my mind, I thought she still loved me.

I'd been drinking pretty heavily that night too. I had a very nice buzz that evening when she called, and was eager to help, especially knowing that she was pregnant with my kid—a kid who would never see the light of day. Chivalry rules, especially when it's a hot college girl who makes love like a porn star. I rationalized my decision to leave the brewery and meet her. I would show up as a white knight in shining armor—no pun intended—to save her from her abusive black boyfriend. In return she would abort the fetus. Who knows what women find attractive these days?

People saw me leave the brewery. Despite it being closed, there were still a few hardcore beer geeks in the tasting room. I jogged through downtown just as some of the bars were letting out. The wooded path leading to Chadwick College was only a quarter mile from downtown and I knew many students took the shortcut back to campus, mainly to smoke pot and drink. Sometimes for other purposes.

The woods were quiet that night. I remember it being very dark, and my footing unstable thanks to the combination of alcohol and the gnarled roots flaring up out of the path. The only light came from the moon's reflection. She told me to meet her by the painted rock: a famous landmark on Chadwick's hallowed grounds. Much of the forested path was owned by the university, and it took me about ten minutes before I reached it. I stopped twenty yards from the path when I saw someone leaning against that infamous rock, his back to me. Despite the darkness, my eyes adjusted and I saw a white guy with long blond hair and a lean muscular build. He looked to be a college student. Sitting on the dirt at his feet was a red and black bag: Chadwick's school colors. Leaning against the giant boulder was an oversized lacrosse stick that players on defense used to protect the net. Over his hunched shoulders, I saw a faint glow emanating from his palms.

Was he waiting for someone? Texting? I approached him, but he didn't look up from his phone until I was almost on top of him. He was a few inches taller than me, athletically built, and with a surfer's good looks. He glanced up tentatively, caution in his eyes. I could tell from his demeanor that he'd been drinking. I pictured him as an asshole stockbroker in his next life, thanks to his connection to Chadwick College and the lacrosse team.

"Can I help you?" he said.

"Are you waiting for someone?"

"What's it to you?"

"I don't know. Seems kinda funny hanging out this late at night around the painted rock with your lacrosse gear."

"Dude?" He shot me a look of disgust.

"Mind if I join you? I'm supposed to meet someone here."

"Whatever," he said, looking back down at his glowing screen.

"Who is this Gardiner dude and why'd they name a rock after him?" I asked.

"Why do you assume Gardiner's a dude?"

I laughed. "Aren't all these old monuments around New England named after some fat old white guy?"

He laughed. "Thaddeus Gardiner graduated from Chadwick back in the nineteenth century. Legend has it that he was the first student to deface this rock."

"What a rebel."

I leaned back against the boulder and pulled out a smoke. I only smoked when I was drinking, and rarely ever at home. An army of crickets chirped in the woods. I looked up and saw a ribbon of stars shimmering between the canopy of trees. It looked like a river of liquid gems moving through the sky. In a way, I was glad this college guy was standing next to me, because being there all alone, that late at night, would have spooked the hell out of me.

"Later, dude," the guy said, grabbing his bag and stick and wobbling down the path toward the college.

"Hey, where you going?" I called out. "Aren't you going to wait for your friend?"

"Hell no," he said, swinging his stick so hard against a nearby tree that it broke in two. "I'm going to kill the bitch next time I see her." He left the jagged, broken stick along the path before disappearing into the darkness.

"He just left you there?" Armstrong asks.

"Yeah. And I didn't like being out there all alone. So

I headed back to the brewery. I shouldn't have been meeting her anyway."

"And you didn't see Mycah or Cordell walking along the path that night?"

I shook my head.

"Were you angry with her?"

I shrugged my shoulders. "She was constantly late whenever we met. Sometimes she wouldn't even show and so I got used to being stood up. But yeah, I was pissed, but not as pissed as that lacrosse player. I wanted her to terminate that pregnancy."

"Did it ever cross your mind that the guy with the lacrosse stick was also waiting to meet Mycah?"

"Never occurred to me."

"It's the same lacrosse stick we found with her blood on it."

"I would assume."

"Don't you think you should have come forward with this information?"

"In a perfect world, Detective, but I have a wife and kids to think about. I moved them all the way across country at great expense so I could chase this stupid dream of mine of opening a brewery. My life would have been ruined if I'd come forward."

"It still might be ruined."

"True. Sometimes you bite the dog and sometimes the dog rips your throat out."

"You really think she'd leave you?"

"Like you really give a shit." I laugh bitterly. "I have no doubt my wife would leave me. She and the kids would move back to Seattle and I'd never see them again."

"Next question," he says, looking down at a stack of papers on the table. He pulls out a book. "Could you identify this lacrosse player if you saw him?"

"I don't know. It was dark that night and the only light was the moon and his cell phone. And as I mentioned, I'd been drinking pretty heavy all day."

"How much had you consumed?"

I shrug, embarrassed to admit the truth. "I drink throughout the day, so I can't really give you a hard and fast number."

"If you had to guess."

"Ten, fifteen beers maybe, throughout the course of the day."

He whistles. "Can't be a very good thing to own a brewery and have an alcohol problem."

"Who said I had a problem?"

"Denial's the first sign."

I laugh, because to deny it even further would only strengthen his hand.

"Maybe if I showed you a few photos of the lacrosse team, you might be able to identify him?"

"Maybe," I say. "Do you think he's the murderer?"

"It's possible." He opens the book and slides it across the table.

I examine all the photographs of the players and struggle to recognize the guy. They appear to me as good-looking jocks with affable smiles. The minorities and dark-haired individuals I rule out, leaving me with a couple dozen others who could be the one. The more I look, the more I realize that I don't really know which player I saw that night.

"You said he was tall," Armstrong says.

"Little taller than me."

"And you're about six two?"

"Two and a half."

"That eliminates all but five players." He uses his pen to put an X next to the remaining players. "Two of these guys were not in town that night, which leaves us with these three guys."

"Still can't be sure. I was very drunk that night."

"What about this one?" he says, circling the photo.

I lean over and examine the profile. His name is William Allen Price and he's listed as six four. In the photo, he has short blond hair framing a movie-star face. He's smiling in it, revealing perfectly white teeth.

"Yeah, that might be him," I say. "You think this guy did it?"

"Not sure." He closes the book. "I'm almost certain that he was the guy waiting for Mycah that night."

I feel my ire rising. What the hell is he talking about? Mycah had called this lacrosse player as well?

"They were hooking up, or at least that's what college students call it these days. A euphemism for casual sex. They managed to keep it a secret for some time."

"Booty call."

"How's that?"

"The ghetto term for casual sex."

"Booty call. Learn something every day."

"Whore," I mutter under my breath.

"If she were a guy, everyone would be congratulating her."

"She's still a whore."

"Not really."

"Is there a difference?"

"The method of payment, I suppose." He sits back and smiles. "Did you really think she was in love with *you*?"

I look up and clench my fists under the table.

"It seemed puzzling to me that she was dating a gay guy."

"Mycah was a user," I say offhandedly.

"Somebody made her pay, because the blood on that lacrosse stick was definitely hers."

"It was that college kid's lacrosse stick, so it has to be him."

"The kid said he left you standing against that rock after he snapped his stick against the tree."

"You knew who it was all along. This is bullshit." I slap an open palm on the table, causing the papers to jump. "I went back to the brewery and drank."

"All the beer geeks were gone?"

"Yeah. They locked the place up and left."

"How do I know you went back? The place was empty, and you certainly had the motive to kill her."

"So did that lacrosse player. She obviously screwed him over too. Maybe the kid she was carrying was his."

"Yes, he had as much motive to kill her as you did. In fact, she might have tried to get her revenge on him and the team."

"Revenge for what?" I ask.

"There were reports that the lacrosse team held a 'ghetto party' last year at one of the frat houses. The college looked into the matter, but no one confessed to having been involved. Everyone held their tongue."

"So the college didn't punish them?"

"They put the frat and the team members on probation, despite having no evidence that this 'ghetto party' ever occurred. Many of the alumni cried foul and threatened to hold back their donations to the school unless the administration reversed their decision. Naturally, the school caved in, and when they did, all hell broke loose on campus. Students blamed the administration, specifically the director of diversity. They called for her ouster, saying she failed to keep them safe from these micro-aggressive behaviors."

"What are micro-aggressive behaviors?"

He shrugs. "Behaviors that cause hurt feelings. Being racially offended by certain statements or actions. College kids are offended easily these days."

"What did they want this diversity director to do?"

"Shut down the lacrosse team. Completely obliterate all forms of racism and sexism on campus, no matter the method. Basically do away with the First Amendment. The students even made signs with their demands and paraded them around campus."

"Sounds like fascism to me."

"Call it what you will," he says. "I bet you can guess who led the protests against the college."

"Mycah Jones."

"And her boyfriend Cordell."

"Maybe Mycah was secretly a racist who only liked to screw white guys."

Armstrong sat back in his chair, put his hands behind his head, and laughed. "That's a preference, not racism."

"Discriminatory, to say the least."

"Not in the legal sense, or any sense."

"But when you go around throwing stones . . ."

"I hate to tell you this, but everyone on that ivy campus lives in a glass house."

"Can I go now?"

"You fell madly in love with Mycah."

I stay perfectly still, trying to remain calm despite my animosity toward this guy. He already knows this and is rubbing it in my face.

"She gave you the best sex you ever had and then became pregnant. I bet she did things in the bedroom you secretly desired. Things you might only see in movies."

"You should really watch what you say, Detective."

"Liked to role-play. I bet she even pretended to be a runaway slave. She asked you to be rough with her. Slap her around and whip her as if she'd tried to run away from the plantation."

I glare at him in stunned silence. How did he know all this? Having an affair was one thing, but if Leah ever found out about the kinky stuff . . .

"Did she let you use the whip?"

"Surfer Boy tell you all this?"

"Doesn't matter how I know, Clay, it only matters that I do."

I'm unable to take any more of this conversation. "Am I free to go?"

"It might be better if you told us what you did with her."

"I told you, I didn't harm a hair on that girl's head." I get up and move toward the door.

"The truth will eventually come out, and when it

does, the consequences will be much worse. Better to talk about this now."

"Am I free to go?"

"Sure, Clay, but don't go very far. We'll be keeping an eye on you."

I storm out and make my way back to the brewery. Ben is taking a coffee break at my desk when I walk in.

"Everything all right, boss?"

"Yeah, fine," I say. "How'd the transfer go?"

"Peachy. I cleaned that son of a bitch out so thoroughly that not a living organism could thrive in there."

"Good." I grab a mug and pour myself a beer. I kick him out of my leather chair and sit down. "I have a lot of paperwork to do."

"Little early for the Information, isn't it?"

"Say what?"

"Shit's a beast, boss. She'll kick your ass."

"You my mother now?"

"Hell no. Just one knowledgeable motherfucker when it comes to getting drunk."

"Okay, Einstein, go unload those pallets of grain like I asked."

I watch him saunter off, coffee cup in hand. I grab the tall stack of unpaid bills and start to go through them. It takes my mind off everything. I sip the beer, a circular glow running counterclockwise in my muddled brain. It helps me forget about that humiliating interrogation. But not for long.

Recently, I've been suffering moments of panic when I feel as if my whole life is crashing down around me. Mycah deserves to die for what she did. I hope she's buried deep in a ditch somewhere.

I finish the mug and pour myself another. I gaze at the framed picture sitting on my desk of Leah and the kids. Jesus. It suddenly hits me what I've done to them. Poor little bastards. I collapse into the leather chair and contemplate my limited options. I'm fairly certain now that I'll lose everything that's near and dear to me.

LEAH

Friday, October 23, 2:22 p.m.

I CLIMB BEHIND THE WHEEL AND DRIVE UNTIL WE AR-
rive at the house where Mycah has been staying. I
park along the curb and stare up at it. Everything is
moving so fast that I'm not sure if I'm doing the right
thing. Clarissa rests her hand on my arm and it gets
me thinking. What am I doing here? With my next-
door neighbor? But I know I must help these poor
women before something bad happens. So my life
can return to normal.

We exit the car and make our way up the stairs. The
gun feels like a grenade in my pocket. I know that
these two women are familiar with each other, and that
there's considerable hostility between them. But to
what extent?

I knock on the front door and after a few beats it
opens.

Mycah's eyes gravitate toward Clarissa. "What is she doing here?"

"Let us in, Mycah. We need to talk," Clarissa says.

"Maybe I don't want to talk to either of you."

"This is important. It could save your life," I say.

"I don't care about my life anymore."

"Then consider my life and all the other lives that may be in jeopardy," I say.

She shuts the door. After a few seconds pass, she lets us inside. Clarissa and I sit on a soiled sofa pushed back against the front window. Every window is covered with curtains or bedsheets, blocking the light from entering the room. A chipped coffee table separates Mycah from the two of us. She goes into the kitchen and returns moments later with three cans of Coke.

"I can't believe you're still alive," Clarissa says.

"Have a soda. They're cold." Mycah places the cans down on the table. She opens one and then settles on the couch with a cigarette.

"Have you been sleeping with my husband?" Clarissa says.

"Wow." Mycah laughs. "How to ease into the conversation."

"I need to know before we continue on," Clarissa says.

"Your husband's a pig. Why did you even marry a guy like him?"

"I was a young college student just like you when I met him."

"Isn't that a delicious irony," Mycah says. "The pot calling the kettle black."

"I was in love. What's your excuse?"

"That husband of yours harassed me, and he didn't stop until I finally agreed to sleep with him."

"I don't believe you."

"Of course you don't believe me," she says. "You berated me constantly in class and called my essay a joke."

"I was mad at you for fawning all over my husband," Clarissa says. "You think I didn't notice you shaking your ass at him every chance you got?"

"That first night we went out, he must have slipped something in my drink, because I woke up the next morning with my head fuzzy and barely able to remember anything."

"Why didn't you go to the police?" I ask.

"I don't trust the police. They're all racist bastards anyways. Besides, it was his word—a highly respected college professor—against mine."

"You've been trying to get me fired for months now," Clarissa says. "And now to find out that you've been sleeping with my husband."

"Damn straight you should be fired. You let the lacrosse team wear blackface and host a ghetto party."

"I've been working my ass off to change the culture at that school. Change doesn't happen overnight," Clarissa says. "Besides, there was no evidence that party ever occurred."

"There was plenty of evidence. You should have talked to more students and then demanded they shut down that frat house. You should have threatened to step down if they didn't meet our demands and dump the lacrosse team. But no, all you care about is your paycheck and your social standing on campus."

"How well do you two actually know each other?" I ask.

"Mycah led a student protest on campus to get me fired," Clarissa says.

"The lacrosse players held a secret 'ghetto party' last year and this traitor took no action against them," Mycah says. "How much more of this shit can us black people take?"

"What was I to do? We couldn't get anyone to admit that it took place. Then the alumni association got involved and threatened to sue the college, as well as withhold their annual donations. It was completely out of my hands."

"You should have insisted they be disciplined."

"Sometimes you have to live to fight another day."

"You were supposed to be on our side. Instead, you sat on your sorry black ass and maintained the status quo."

"This is crazy," I say. "We're supposed to be supporting each other, not bickering like children."

"Then let's be real," Mycah says. "Her husband is the reason we're in this terrible situation. He's the one who murdered Cordell."

Clarissa stands, her fists clenched. "You manipulative whore. You'll sleep with anyone to get what you want."

"I don't have to sit here and be attacked by Uncle Tom's wife," Mycah says. "Her husband threatened to run me out of school if I didn't sleep with him. He said I would lose my scholarship and any chance of attending law school if I turned him down."

"Why would Mycah lie about this?" I ask Clarissa.

"That's what snakes do, Leah. They lie coiled in the grass, waiting to strike."

"Look at the way Russell abuses you. Look how he forced you to have sex with other men. Face facts, Clarissa. The man's a scoundrel," I say.

Clarissa fights back the tears.

"He attacked Cordell that night with a baseball bat. He was furious after I broke it off with him, jealous that I'd decided to stay with Cordell. He threatened to kill me, like he killed Cordell, if I didn't stay in this house and wait for him to return. He told me he was trying to work out a plan for me," Mycah says.

"We still have time to go to the police," I say.

"No police or I'm out," Clarissa says.

"Jesus, Clarissa, whatever you're hiding can't be that bad," I say.

"I told you, my life will be ruined if my past is revealed. No police or I walk."

"We all have secrets," Mycah says. "You shouldn't be ashamed to admit yours."

"It's the reason we should be working together," I say, "as a team."

"Working to get rid of that lowlife so he doesn't hurt any other women," Mycah says.

"I don't know."

"We have to be honest with one another if we're going to solve this problem," Mycah says.

"What do you say, Clarissa?" I ask.

Clarissa sits back on the sofa and crosses her arms, and the three of us sit quietly for the next few minutes. It feels strange to be here with these women—wife and mistress. Victim facing victim. All three of us have something to confess. For me it's been a long time coming.

"What about you, Mycah? Do you have anything to get off your chest?" Clarissa says.

Mycah puts her cigarette in the ashtray and stares down at it.

"Go on, we're here for you."

She turns to Clarissa. "As I've already told your friend, I'm not really from a wealthy family. I grew up in the ghetto, and my mom turned tricks to pay the bills. It's humiliating, you know, to have that as your life story when you're going to a prestigious school like Chadwick. Who wants to admit growing up dirt poor in one of the worst projects in Queens? So I lied and said my daddy owned a big company in Manhattan, and right away everyone started looking at me different. I finally felt like I was someone important. As long as I was out there walking the walk and pushing for social justice, no one seemed to question my past."

"At least your experience growing up is authentically black," Clarissa says.

"Call it what you will, it was a hard life," Mycah says.

"See, Clarissa, your secret can't be anywhere near as bad as Mycah's," I say.

A long pause ensues.

Mycah gestures with her soda. "You going to trust us with your secret or not? I'm not going to beg."

"Okay." Clarissa sits quietly for another few seconds before saying, "The truth is, I'm not really black."

"Excuse me?" Mycah spits out her cola. "What the hell did you just say?"

"She means to say that she's lost her identity as a

black woman living in this small Maine town," I say, staring at Clarissa. "Right?"

"No, I'm saying that I grew up in a white family just outside Boston. We lived in a predominately blue-collar, Italian-American neighborhood. All my friends in school were black, so I began to identify as black. After a while, I began to wonder, why can't I be black too?"

"Because you're not actually black," Mycah practically shouts.

"What does being black mean, anyway? Look at my skin color." She holds up her arm. "I'm darker than most black and brown people out there."

"That really offends me," Mycah says.

"I'm sorry if you feel that way, but who are you to judge, especially after misrepresenting your own past?"

"It's not just a person's skin color that defines them. Blackness encompasses the entire experience of our being, our history of oppression, and for you to steal that is wrong on so many different levels."

"I believe that race is an issue of identity and that being black is as much a state of mind as it is a skin color. Somewhere back in time my Sicilian ancestors were oppressed, and I have no doubt they intermingled with black folks at some point in history."

"I can't believe what I'm hearing. That's the most messed-up, insulting thing I've ever heard," Mycah says, lighting a cigarette. "You can't simply become black. You either are or you're not. That's why they have boxes on job applications."

"Even as a young girl, I related to the black experience. I was totally into black music and black culture. I went to a public high school in Boston where all my friends were black kids from Roxbury and Dorchester.

I feel it on such a deeply personal level that it's now an integral part of my being."

"That may be the case, but it's based on a false premise," Mycah says.

"But your hair and skin color." I'm stunned by this admission.

"I was always dark-skinned as a kid, being of Sicilian heritage. I first began transitioning after college. I colored and treated my hair, and later in life had a minor surgical procedure on my nose. It was very easy to convince people that I was black, especially after I moved out of state."

"And to think I've been accused of not being black enough," Mycah says bitterly. "Your own husband even questioned whether I was dark enough for his liking."

"It's obvious you passed the test."

"Lucky me."

"How did Russell find out about you?" I ask Clarissa.

"It was only after we married that he suspected I wasn't black. He paid an investigator to look into my past."

"Just like you delved into mine."

"Where do you think I got the idea?" she says. "Once Russell confirmed that I wasn't black, he set about to use it against me."

"Were you surprised?" Mycah asks.

"To say the least, but what was I going to do? In some ways it was my fault. I kept an important part of myself from him. Worse, I took a job as an equal opportunity specialist in the Department of Education."

"Let me guess," Mycah says. "You checked the box?"

"What do you mean she checked the box?" I say.

"She's right. I checked the box on my application listing myself as African-American."

"You stole food out of my people's mouths," Mycah says.

"This is what he's been holding over your head?" I squeeze her hand supportively.

"It's why I put up with his abuse for so long. If he informed the authorities about my past, I could go to jail for providing false information. I most certainly would lose my job at Chadwick."

"You *should* go to jail for stealing a people's cultural identity," Mycah says. "Black people get pulled over and imprisoned for a lot less than that."

"I'm sorry," Clarissa says.

"That job should have gone to a brother or sister instead of you."

"But don't you understand? In my mind I've always believed I'm a black woman," Clarissa says. "I know it may be hard for you to fathom, Mycah, but that's how strongly I identify. Being black resonates in my soul more than anything else. It's literally who I am."

"Let's put aside the racial divide and skin color for the moment," I say. "We're all women here. The question we need to be asking ourselves is what are we going to do about Russell?"

"We should do to him what he did to Cordell," Clarissa says, her face coiling into a mask of pent-up fury. "But we have to be smart about it."

"Are you saying what I think you're saying?" Mycah asks.

"Precisely," Clarissa says. "We're defending ourselves, our children, and potentially other women from his violent behavior."

"Are we talking about . . . *murder*?" I say.

"No, it's clearly a case of self-defense," Clarissa responds.

"I don't know about this," I say, not quite believing my ears.

"Think of your family, Leah. Do you want to be living in fear for the next few years, knowing that a cold-blooded murderer lives next door to you and your kids?"

"Of course not," I say.

"Then this is our only option."

"This is insane. How would we even do it? Or get away with such a thing?"

"I'll call Russell Monday at work and tell him that you're sorry for filming us having sex. I'll tell him that watching it turned you on and that you've had a change of heart about sleeping with him. Russell will take the bait when he hears this."

"You filmed your neighbors having sex?" Mycah says, turning to me in disgust.

"Clarissa asked me to do it. She hoped to get proof of his bad behavior," I say.

"I'll tell Russell that you're ready and willing and that you can only do it while your husband is at work. I'll say that you plan on leaving the front door open so that he can slip inside. Once he enters, you wait for him to undress, then you shoot the bastard. Make damn sure he's dead, call the police, and tell them you shot him in self-defense."

"That's brilliant in the most devious way," Mycah says. "A black man illegally entering a white woman's house. No jury would ever convict her. It reinforces the stereotype of the promiscuous black man desiring a white woman."

"Precisely why it will work," Clarissa says. "Are you game, Leah?"

"I'm not so sure. All this talk of killing someone is frightening me."

The prospect of actually murdering another human being is antithetical to how I've lived my life post-Annie. And yet I know that killing is sometimes justified in life. It says so in the Bible. It doesn't make me less scared to do it. Just thinking about pulling the trigger terrifies me. It makes me want to run out of this room and never return. But the sad fact is that I know it needs to be done. How many times have I read about some chronically battered woman who was murdered by her husband, and then wish someone had killed him before it got to that point? Too many times to count. Because of this, I know I can kill him. My friendship with Clarissa means everything to me and I'd be devastated to lose something so precious.

"We need to act quickly, before someone else gets killed, Leah, and you're the only one who can do it."

"I'm so tired of everything," Mycah says, lowering her head on the couch.

"Don't you want to hear Leah's secret?" Clarissa asks.

"It can't be any worse than yours."

"Trust me, it is."

"Really?" Her eyes bug open and she sits up. "What could be worse than impersonating a black woman?"

"How about killing your twin sister."

"For real? How?"

"She pushed her into a pool."

"Her sister couldn't swim?"

"She was confined to a wheelchair."

"Damn, girl, that's cold."

"I told you it was bad."

"It's bad, all right. Still, it's not worse than passing yourself off as a sister."

CLAY

Friday, October 23, 3:49 p.m.

I'M WELL INTO MY THIRD BEER WHEN MY CELL PHONE rings. It's deep into the afternoon and I'm in no mood to take calls from angry vendors requiring payment for this service or that product. My mind floats above the fray, and for good reason. I've fallen way behind on the bills, having squandered the money on one thing or another. There's money in the bank but not much. I owe, I owe, off to drink I go. At least there's free beer here and plenty of it. And while the brewery's doing far better than I ever anticipated, it's still operating in the red.

I whip out my phone and pray it's not Leah. She can always tell when I've been drinking—unless she too has been drinking. Little does she know that drinking helps me deal with her wild mood swings and obsessive worrying. She's high maintenance in many ways.

She wears me down with her compulsions and frequent demands.

I look at the number on the text. Restricted. It's probably junk mail. I open the message and begin to read.

Are you that fucking stupid, Clay? Did you really think that bitch you call your wife didn't know about our affair? She loves you so much that she was willing to kill for your sins. After she jumped out of the woods and hit Cordell over the head with a baseball bat, she turned on me. She's much stronger than she looks. There hath no fury like that of a woman scorned—or something like that.

Your crazy wife pulled a gun on me that night, Clay, and threatened to shoot me in the head. I fell to my knees and literally begged her to spare my life. For a brief second, I really thought she would do it. I'd never felt so scared in my life. But I kept talking to her, appealing to her better nature, until I finally persuaded her not to kill a poor black girl from the ghetto. She had demands, though. Are you listening to me, Clay? I was supposed to leave town that night and never return. She said if she ever saw my face again, she'd kill me. Said she'd killed once before and could easily do it again, especially considering I slept with her husband. I believed the crazy bitch. That's why I disappeared.

So what a shock it was to read in the newspaper that someone murdered Cordell. I knew right away your wife did it. Did you know that she was out with him that very night? Dined at Applebee's. Don't you see, Clay? Your crazy wife went back and killed Cordell—and she did it all for you. To save

your pathetic marriage. And if you don't believe me, go ask the cops. They have video of the two of them eating together in Applebee's. She killed him for you, Clay Daniels, because she plans on forgiving your sorry ass.

I need money. Bad. Sorry to have lied to you about that phony loan. I was never rich, as you probably know by now. Hell, I grew up so poor that I thought every family ate at soup kitchens. Please don't hate me. I really did like you. I'll always remember the times we had together in bed and how manly you were with the whip. It's making me wet just thinking about it.

Here's the deal. I need five thousand dollars and I'll be out of your hair forever. Promise this time. I'm leaving town and I'll never breathe a word of this to anyone. Then you and your crazy wife can get on with your lives as if nothing ever happened. Please don't make me go to the police and tell them what she's done. I really don't want them to put her away.

Text me back and I'll tell you the time and place to meet.

Mycah's still alive? Is this a hoax? It's laughable to believe that Leah was the one who assaulted the two of them that night. She's not strong enough. She doesn't possess the temperament or will to hurt another living creature. She's delicate and fragile: a hundred and ten pounds after a long swim in the Puget Sound. Besides, Leah's had a lifelong aversion to guns. She hates firearms and believes the Second Amendment should be abolished from the Constitution.

I call Armstrong. "Is my wife a suspect?"

"Everyone's a suspect. Why do you ask?"

"My wife doesn't own a gun."

"You know as well as I do that it's easy enough to get one in these parts."

"She wouldn't even let our son have a toy gun."

"How well do you really know your wife?"

"Is it true she met Cordell the night he was killed?"

"I can't comment on that, Clay."

I hang up and stare ahead in disbelief. She did meet with Cordell. It's hard for me to believe that Leah knew about my affair and never let on. She couldn't possibly hide her emotions for any length of time. It's so unlike her. Then again, how well do I know this woman? I find it hard to believe that she's taken matters into her own hands just to save this Hindenburg we've been calling a marriage.

Something tells me not to go home. How will I face her, knowing what we both know? Do I dare confess my infidelities and get it all out in the open? Part of me still doesn't believe that Leah committed these crimes. Or even knew about the affair.

I pour myself another IPA, my second in less than thirty minutes. With no food in my stomach, it goes straight to my head. I rather like the way it eases the dull throb of existence and makes everything appear brighter.

Ben comes in my office and asks what needs to be done. I tell him to pull up a chair, grab a mug, and have a beer with me, but he says he can't. He has too much work to do. The kid knows when I'm feeling funky and when to stay clear of me. I don't blame him. Drinking with me can only lead to bad things.

I send a text back to Mycah, asking her where she wants to meet. I tell her I don't believe Leah killed Cordell and that I think she's messing with my head. There had to be another reason she met Cordell that night. I wait anxiously for her reply. A few minutes later I receive this text:

How well do you really know your wife? Do you have any idea what she did before she met you? If you only knew her history, Clay Daniels. She was a very bad girl.

What is she talking about? Why have I never been told what Leah supposedly did before she met me? Really, how bad can it be? Did she steal some pencils in the fifth grade? Tattle on a friend? I laugh at the notion that Leah is somehow a dangerous criminal. But I need to know what happened if I'm to believe that my marriage has not been a sham all these years. If we are to have any future at all.

LEAH

Friday, October 23, 4:01 p.m.

*C*LARISSA LOOKS COMPLETELY DIFFERENT TO ME now. I can't wrap my head around the fact that she's not really black or that she visits tanning parlors and has had plastic surgery to widen her nose. It completely changes my perception of her. Then again, who am I to judge? Maybe she really did identify as a black girl growing up. I imagine it's like a young transgender girl trapped in a boy's body. Yet in some ways it sets my mind at ease and explains why she's been so standoffish to me all these months. It was never about me. We were a reminder of her past: a privileged white family living comfortably in the suburbs.

The woods fly past us as I speed down the country road. The sky has turned gray and overcast. I'm scared about what Clarissa wants me to do tomorrow, but I know it needs to be done. I remind myself that it will save lives, primarily my own and that of my family.

I turn on the windshield wipers, visualizing Russell entering my bedroom with lust in his eyes. He will remove his tie once he sees me reclined on the bed, but he won't see the gun I'm holding beneath the pillow. The one I'll have aimed at his chest. I see myself lifting the gun out and pulling the trigger. I hear the shot go off, watch as he collapses to the floor in agony, and then stops breathing.

Clarissa doesn't want to go home just yet. She points to a road leading out of town, explaining that she wants to go somewhere to talk. I'm in no mood to resist her temptations, especially since I can't get the memory of that shooting lesson out of my head. She has many questions to ask me, questions that I haven't thought about for years. My memory about that time in life is hazy, and I wonder if it will even come back to me.

I speed past a wall of sheer granite cliffs, water dripping down the sides like a leaky faucet. Ahead is a series of rolling hills. To my right I see three large windmills, blades spinning slowly and churning out energy for all these rural towns. I don't care about any of that right now: clean energy, climate change, rising oceans. All I can think about is Annie and that terrible day we shared.

We emerge into a small town and I park along the sidewalk. We enter a quaint Italian bistro and settle in to one of the back booths. I know I shouldn't drink this early, but I order a glass of wine anyway.

"The police are going to ask where I got the gun," I whisper. "What do I say?"

"You bought it for protection after you heard about the attack in town. You tell the police that you were scared to be all alone in that new house because your husband was gone most of the day, working at the brewery. It made you feel scared and vulnerable."

"But whom did I buy it from?"

"Someone told you to go down to Portland with three hundred dollars. Park Street, you tell them. You purchased it from an anonymous seller on the street."

"This is really frightening me."

"Stay strong, Leah. It'll be over soon."

"I don't think I can do it."

"Don't you want to protect yourself and your family? Isn't it crucial that we prevent others in the community from being terrorized by him?"

"But I've never shot anyone before."

"It's easy. All you have to do is pull the trigger like you did at that abandoned house," she says. "And it's not like you haven't killed before."

"Yes, but I had my reasons for doing that."

"I'm sure you did. There are also very good reasons for shooting Russell, don't you agree?"

"I suppose." I do wholeheartedly agree. The man's a monster not deserving of such a beautiful soul as Clarissa.

The waitress appears out of nowhere, smiling and cheerful to a fault, calling us "honey" and "dear," which sounds so silly coming from someone barely out of high school. She sets down our glasses of wine before lunch arrives, and I can't drink mine fast enough.

"So are you ready to talk about it?" Clarissa asks while I butter a yeasty roll.

"What if I'm not?"

"You need to get it off your chest, Leah. Look how much better I feel."

"But my memory is so hazy after all these years."

"We need to be brutally honest with each other if we're going to pull this off. I confided in you, didn't I?" She sips her wine and waits for me to respond. "You need to confess your sins if we're to be friends."

I never want to revisit those days again. But there's something in her eyes that tells me I have no choice in the matter if we're to pull this off. If I'm going to kill another human being—in self-defense—I need to tell my story. I can't care about appearances or how she'll perceive me. It's time to strip naked and bare my soul. I gulp down the rest of my wine, order another, and prepare myself for what is to be a painful admission.

We sit quietly until the waitress returns with my second glass of wine. I take a healthy sip and let the alcohol fortify my brain cells.

"Now are you ready?" Clarissa asks.

"Yes."

This is what I tell her.

From my earliest memories, I knew that my twin sister was different. But it didn't matter. I still loved her. It didn't bother me when Annie refused to maintain eye contact when we huddled together as toddlers. Or that she failed all the earliest tests of childhood. None of that mattered because she seemed completely normal to me. To a young child who didn't know any better, Annie seemed like the most normal, wonderful sister in the world.

By the time I reached school age, we'd developed a close bond. It was a bond that only twin sisters could form. Although she'd never uttered a single word, apart from shouting and occasional startled cries, I understood everything about her. In fact, I thought her a brilliant and rare creature.

We had our own way of communicating, which utilized body language, grunts, and hand signals that only I seemed to understand. As time wore on, I grew to understand how others perceived her. Most thought Annie an imbecile with a low IQ. But I knew better and believed she was far more intelligent than anyone could begin to imagine.

I loved Annie more with each passing day. She was my best friend and confidante. I raced home after school each day to confer with her about what I did and whom I spent time with. Annie would lay reclined in her chair, rolling her head around on her neck and jerking spastically. Saliva often drooled from her lips, and her hands were perpetually bent at the wrists. She laughed at my jokes, and many days I would read one of my books to her. Whenever I stopped or got up to use the bathroom, Annie would cry out in protest. Before I left for school in the morning, she would make a fuss, and I would have to go over to her chair and give her a big hug so she'd settle down.

Our mother refused to let Annie leave the house unless we were going to church, so protective was she of her youngest daughter. The summer before I started third grade, the state had agreed to pay for a special school for girls like her. My father was all for it, arguing that the school could do far more for Annie than we could in Oregon, but thankfully my mother wouldn't hear of sending her to California. Being separated from Annie would have killed me.

As the years passed, my father became more embittered because of Annie's condition. He began to drink heavily. He argued constantly with my mother about the merits of sending her away. I could hear them shouting as we huddled in Annie's room with the door closed. I tried to block out the noise for Annie's sake, but sometimes it became too much, and I would need to calm her down. She hated all the yelling and screaming, the banging of doors and smashing of pans. She hated hearing our father complain about her "uselessness." Or how our mother was neglecting his "needs."

If the weather was nice, I would wheel her out to the backyard patio so we didn't have to listen to them fight. I'd place the life jacket over her, secure it around her waist, and then gently guide her into the pool. Her body had grown thin and slender as the years passed, and she loved to be submerged in the cool water. She had long legs, allowing her to kick freely once inside.

I was ten when I first noticed my father making his way into her room. What was he doing in there? I knew he resented Annie for how she'd ruined his life. The first time it happened was early in the morning after he'd been drinking whiskey all night. Annie slept on the first floor because of her disability. I happened to be downstairs, pouring a glass of milk, when I saw my father stagger inside her room and close the door. It aroused my curiosity and made me suspicious.

I woke the next morning and heard Annie screaming. She was hysterical, jerking and convulsing, and nodding her head spastically. I'd never seen her like this. Was she in pain? My mother consoled her as I got ready for school. I didn't want to leave Annie, but my mother insisted I go.

"What's wrong with her?" I asked.

"She's becoming a woman."

"What does that mean?"

"Just because she's handicapped, Leah, doesn't mean she won't go through all the same stages as a regular woman."

"You mean she's having her . . . ?"

"Yes, she's spotting."

"Oh my God. Poor Annie." I hadn't had my period yet, but I'd heard all about it and both feared and looked forward to its arrival.

"She probably has no idea what's going on inside her body. All the changes taking place are scaring her."

I went to school that day in a sour mood. I found it odd that Annie's strange behavior occurred the exact day after my father paid her an early morning visit. I vowed to monitor his behavior and see what he was up to. Was he hurting Annie? He rarely interacted with her during the day other than to occasionally feed her or carry her to bed. I knew poor Annie would never be free from my parents until death separated them. My father must have come to the conclusion that he would never live the life he wanted: golf, retirement, and travel.

It was around this time that my mother started drinking as well, although she did it much more secretly than my father. I never actually saw her put a bottle to her lips, but after watching my father, I knew why she'd been acting so strange. They argued constantly, slurring words, often for hours at a time. His job as a maintenance man with the city paid the bills and kept our family afloat, but once he got home he couldn't wait to hit the bottle.

It happened again a month later. I watched from my bedroom door as he made his way downstairs. I waited at the top step until Annie's door closed. For some strange reason, I had it in my head that he was going in there to pray with Annie. Maybe he was going to pray that she might recover from her condition and become a normal girl like me and marry a nice boy and leave home. My parents were devout Catholics. Maybe I was selfish, but I didn't want Annie to change. I didn't want her to marry a nice boy and have kids and a house with a white picket fence. I loved her as she was. But to my father, she was a constant reminder of his failure as a parent.

I snuck downstairs and stopped at Annie's door. I could hear my father making a shushing sound, although I couldn't understand why he'd want to pray with her at such an early hour. Annie was probably mad about this intrusion. I didn't think that Annie liked to pray in that manner.

Why hadn't my father tried to pray with me? We all went to church together on Sunday, and my father constantly prayed for a cure for Annie. Wasn't that enough praying for one week? Jesus would eventually tire from our supplications. Or were we required to pray as much as possible for Annie's well-being?

I gently pulled open the door, closed one eye, and peered into the dark room. The window was open and I vividly remember seeing a full moon in the distant sky. The illumination allowed just enough light for me to see what was happening. My father was lying on top of

Annie. His hips were moving back and forth, and his pants were halfway down his legs. I could see Annie's head swiveling wildly on her neck, her arms splayed across the mattress, strange noises emanating from her mouth. It took me a few full seconds to realize the sick thing he was doing to her. I'd often overheard the boys in school talking about this sort of behavior in the recess yard.

This was certainly no prayer.

I ran back up to my room in tears and dove into bed, covering myself with blankets. I sobbed into my pillow, not knowing what my sister was suffering at the hands of my father. I swore in the morning to tell my mother what I saw. Once he left for work the next morning, I would tell her the truth about his "prayers" and watch happily as she kicked him out of the house.

But to my disbelief, she disregarded my words. She said I must have been walking in my sleep and imagining things. I insisted that I hadn't and she called me a liar and a troublemaker. She was forceful in her claim that he was a good man and that he went in there to pray for my sister's health.

"Are you trying to break up our family?"

"He wasn't praying, Mom. I saw what he was doing," I said.

"You're a liar, Leah. You're just jealous that Annie gets more attention than you do."

"No, I love Annie."

"You want her all to yourself. You think you're so special because she's your twin and that you're the only one who understands her. Well, you're wrong about that. Annie's got the brain function of a two-year-old."

"That's not true. Annie's smart and funny."

"I'm sick of your lies. All the doctors say that Annie's retarded."

"They're wrong. She's brilliant and smart and witty. Annie understands way more than you know."

"Someday you'll leave home and we'll be the ones left to take care of her. It's all on your father and me. We're her only caretakers in this world when you leave for college."

"Then maybe I'll never leave."

"Oh, you'll leave all right."

I hated my father after that day. I hated my mother even more for not believing me. I wanted to kill him for what he'd been doing to Annie—and what he would continue to do in my absence. That evening, I went into his bottom drawer and stole the grimy nine-millimeter handgun he kept hidden there. I stashed it under my pillow and would wait for the next time he tried to hurt my sister.

For the next two weeks, I stayed awake in bed, waiting to hear if he left his bedroom. My grades suffered and I began to get in trouble at school. There were times I could barely stay awake in class. I was becoming emotionally abusive to other students and getting into fights. Annie seemed more distant and estranged as well, as if my father's "prayers" had inextricably broken our close bond. It nearly destroyed me that Annie would not laugh or communicate to me in our uniquely designed language.

Then one night I heard my father's door open. I grabbed the gun stashed beneath my pillow and walked gingerly down the stairs. The door to Annie's room clicked shut. I moved alongside it, trying to work up the courage to confront him. His soft groans nearly made me sick. I became paralyzed with rage and revulsion. He slipped out of the room at some point and I sat behind the door, pointing the gun at him as he staggered drunkenly upstairs. But for some reason I couldn't pull the trigger.

Tears streamed down my face as I heard his bedroom door shut behind him. I raced up the stairs, walked into his bedroom, and crawled over to his side of the bed. He was snoring loudly by the time I got up on my knees. His breath reeked of sour lemons and spoiled meat. I lifted the gun and pointed it at his head. A second, unfamiliar yet noxious odor emanated from his wretched body, which later in life I would come to associate with sex. My hands trembled. It seemed as if I had been pointing that gun for a long time. But once again I couldn't do it. I couldn't kill the man who'd raised and then destroyed me, in such a short time.

I believe that's when my aversion to firearms began. The gun had let me down. It had let my sister down. Or maybe it was the other way around. My cowardice fed into my growing sense of self-loathing and hatred for men like my father. All I knew was that I never again wanted to touch another gun. Or "pray" in that method.

The next month proved catastrophic. No one else could see it, but Annie had retreated deep into her shell. She refused to laugh or interact with me. She wouldn't listen to me read books or sing to her. I stayed home from school for days at a time because of my disruptive behavior. Her spasms and tantrums worsened. It was almost as if she'd been trying to tell the world about the abuse she'd suffered at the hands of our father. But she was unable to do it in her condition. I was the only person who could communicate her thoughts to the world and tell the authorities what had really happened. But I knew they wouldn't believe me. Or Annie. Every doctor claimed she had the mental capacity of a two-year-old.

I came to believe that Annie wanted to escape from the catatonic flesh jail that kept her captive. Stuck in a body that enslaved her, and with two dysfunctional, drunken parents who were broken beyond repair, her only hope was to transcend. This was what I believed she was trying to tell me at the time. That she wanted to transcend her body.

It was a gorgeous Sunday when I wheeled Annie out to the pool. Her symptoms seemed worse than ever that day, and when I tried to pull the life jacket over her, she screamed louder than I'd ever heard. Her one good arm pointed toward the pool. I pushed the chair to the water's edge and listened to her usual grunts and shrieks. It took me a few seconds to understand what she was trying to say. She wanted to be liberated from the shackles of disability and dysfunction. The water was the one place she felt safe and free, her useless body unhindered by the crushing heft of gravity.

I didn't want to do it, but she persisted until I had no other choice. I knew what I had to do. Tears dripped down my freckled cheeks as I spoke to her. Annie kept jerking and pointing toward the pool. For a brief second she looked me in the eye and held my gaze. I could see this was how she wanted to go. I embraced her for a long time. I kissed her on the lips and told her how much I loved her. My tears dripped over her face and made it look as if she too was crying.

After I'd said my good-bye, I made sure she was

buckled in. The seat belt had been installed so that she wouldn't tumble out during a spasm. I grabbed the two handles, prayed to God for strength and forgiveness, and then gently pushed her over the pool's edge.

The chair hit the water and began to sink. Annie shouted something before her voice got drowned out. Her head went under and she began to descend. Soon she would be free. I watched as the chair fell to the aquamarine bottom. She kicked her legs and waved her hands. Bubbles rose up to the surface. After a few minutes her body went slack and began to oscillate in the ripples of pool water. I gazed down at her and for a brief second caught a glimpse of my own reflection. I was smiling. But so was Annie.

I sat at the pool's edge for a while, dangling my feet in the water and staring down at her.

Annie was free at last.

"Oh my God, Leah. You must have felt terrible," Clarissa says.

"Actually, I felt very much at peace with myself. I knew she'd be in a better place."

"What did you do next?"

"I just sat there until my parents came out."

"How long was that?"

"About twenty minutes. My father dove into the pool and tried to save her, but it was too late."

"What did the judge give you for a sentence?"

"The court gave me two years, with six months suspended. When I got out of the juvenile correctional facility, my parents shipped me off to finish high school with some relatives in Seattle."

"That's such a sad story."

I nodded.

"Not necessarily the full truth, but sad nonetheless."

"It is the full truth."

"I think you've conveniently forgotten certain details."

"You weren't there, Clarissa. You don't know anything about what happened that day."

"Now is not the time to argue about what's true and what's not. The important thing is that you're in the right frame of mind for doing this."

"I did what I had to do. I only wished I'd killed my father instead."

"All the more incentive to get rid of Russell."

"I assure you, I won't fail to pull the trigger this time."

"I know you won't, honey." She reaches over and pats my hand. "It's very important that you shoot him as soon as he enters, before he utters a single word."

"Why?"

"Russell is a very persuasive man. I've seen him talk himself out of many crazy situations."

"He won't be able to talk his way out of this one."

"I mean it. Under any circumstances, don't let him sweet-talk you into letting him go. He's charismatic and charming when he wants to be."

"Don't you worry, Clarissa. It'll soon be over, and you won't have to worry about him hurting you any longer."

CLAY

Monday, October 26, 6:46 a.m.

I WAKE UP TO THE SOUND OF MY PHONE RINGING. My head hurts, another throbbing hangover. I look down and see that I'm lying on the cot in my cluttered office. The smell of yeast, fermenting grapefruit, and warm bread fills my nostrils. Usually, I love this particular smell, but today it's making me sick. How many beers did I consume last night? It must have been quite a few if I've got a carpenter banging nails in my head.

The phone continues to ring. The clock on the far wall tells me it's 6:46 a.m. Someone has sent me a text message with an audio recording attached. I press play and hear the sound of a woman speaking. It takes only a few seconds to recognize that high-pitched voice as Leah's. She's telling a story from her childhood, one that I've never before heard. In fact, now that I think about it, I know little to nothing about her life prior to our meeting.

I lie back on the cot and listen to her speak, quaffing the remainder of warm beer swirling in my glass. It immediately takes the edge off the table saw buzzing in my head. I wait a few seconds, hoping the carpenter might take a coffee break.

LEAH

Monday, October 26, 7:20 a.m.

C LAY IS NOT BESIDE ME WHEN I WAKE UP THIS morning. How many nights in a row does that make it? Nothing else matters to me. I don't care that he gets drunk and decides to sleep on the cot in his office. Not like it's the first time that's happened. He's turning into a lush and I'm starting to wonder if I'm better off without him. I miss home and have arrived at the conclusion that it was a bad idea to move here. Bad for me and bad for the kids.

Of course I want to try and make our marriage work. It's all that I have. Clay needs to show more interest in me, to love me the way I've always needed to be loved, to look me in the eyes and let me know that he truly cares about me. I've repeatedly told him that this is what I need, but after a few weeks of good behavior, he typically reverts back to his authentic self. The problem is he's found his one true love in life—and it's not me.

I make breakfast for Zack and Zadie, fill Mr. Shady's bowls with food and water, and prepare their school lunches. The kids sense my ambivalence this morning, my dispassionate efficiency while doing chores, and eye me warily.

"You seem weird this morning," Zack says.

"I'm fine." I make an effort to flash them a fake smile. "Now, the two of you get your stuff together and head down to the bus stop."

"But the bus doesn't come for another ten minutes," Zadie complains.

"It won't hurt you to wait a few minutes."

"But, Momma—"

"I don't want to hear it. Go."

I grab their backpacks and lunches and hustle them out the door. They don't complain. They sense my urgency, understanding that I'm in no mood to negotiate with them.

Once they're out the door, I grab Mr. Shady's leash and race him around the neighborhood. He wants to stop and sniff every rock and stick in the cul-de-sac, but I move him along with an assertive grip on the leash. The Gaineses' driveway is empty. I stop in front of their house and stare up at it, my entire body trembling at the prospect of what I'm planning to do.

Clarissa instructed me to wait in the living room after I finish my walk. I return home and unhook Mr. Shady. He barks furiously at me, as if he knows something's amiss. I go upstairs and take the gun out of the bottom drawer. Then I go downstairs and pour myself a glass of wine. If I'm going to pull this off, I need all the fortification I can get.

CLAY

Monday, October 26, 9:58 a.m.

I'M STILL IN A STATE OF SHOCK, UNABLE TO BELIEVE that my wife could have done such a horrible thing. Who recorded this crap? Is she reading off a script? If true, why has Leah decided to confess to this crime now? In some ways it makes perfect sense. It's the reason she never talked about her childhood or enjoys having sex with me.

I rise from the cot, my head groggy and my knees creaking in agony. I feel old before my time. I pour myself a cold beer. I'm about to take a sip when another text message arrives. It's from Mycah. Bitch wants to see me again and collect her money. Says she misses me and that I don't deserve to be married to a woman who drowned her own sister. But how does she know about this? Was she the one who recorded Leah's confession? She tells me that she plans on having the baby after all. *My baby.* She's changed her mind and wants us to be together. To be a couple and live happily ever after. But hell no, I can't let this happen. I don't know how she wrangled such a confession from Leah, but then in the next sentence it all starts to make sense.

Mycah claims that she's holding Leah at gunpoint. She says that if I go over and profess my love for her, she promises to spare Leah's life. But if I call the cops, she guarantees that Leah will die.

As disgusted as I am with Leah, I have no choice but to save her. She's the woman I vowed to honor and protect. The mother of my two kids and, if true, the sadistic killer of her disabled twin sister.

Furious, I chuck my phone against the concrete wall and watch as it shatters into many pieces.

I toss on my wrinkled clothes and chug down the rest of my beer. Sporting a nice buzz, I jump into my truck and race over to the address she has given me, praying that Leah is still alive.

After thirty minutes of driving, I pull up to the address. A set of concrete stairs leads to a dilapidated bungalow. I get out and take them two at a time. At the stoop, I ring the bell until the door opens. Nearby, water rushes loudly over some crappy-ass falls.

As soon as I go inside, I feel something smash against my skull. My knees go weak, my vision blurry, and I collapse on the shag carpet. I hear a woman's voice speaking. Drool flows from my lips. The pain in my head is wicked, worse than I've ever experienced. I feel like I'm going to die. Then everything goes black.

LEAH

Monday, October 26, 10:56 a.m.

I SIT QUIETLY FOR OVER AN HOUR, THE GUN RESTING on my lap, trying not to think about what I'd done to my twin sister those many years ago. In the ensuing years, I'd managed to convince myself that I'd done the right thing, but now I'm not so sure. My father should have been the one to die instead of Annie. It's my fault. I deeply regret not shooting that bastard when I had the chance. I never saw him again after being released from that juvenile correctional facility. We spoke over the phone a few times, out of necessity, but that was the extent of our contact. He died ten years ago, five years after my mother passed. I prayed every day that God would sentence him to eternal damnation for his sins. Even thinking about him now makes me furious.

The sound of a car door slams, followed by a second

door. I stare out the window and see Clarissa and Russell walking up the driveway to their home. They're arguing about something, their voices echoing throughout the cul-de-sac. When they reach the stairs to their porch, Clarissa turns and starts pounding on Russell's chest. He grabs her by the arms and tries to restrain her. Then he pushes her inside the house. Why would she do such a stupid thing, knowing Russell's violent temper? The only reasonable explanation I can come up with is that he threatened her. Or maybe threatened to take the children from her. Something must have precipitated her reaction.

I collapse on the couch in panic, wondering what to do now. Mr. Shady stares up at me with consternation in his eyes, ears raised and spine arched. I hate when that dumb dog trains his eyes on me. It's almost as if he can read my mind.

What if Russell strikes her? Or, God forbid, kills her? Isn't it my responsibility to save Clarissa from this monster?

But the plan was for me to sit tight and not make a move until he walks through that door.

I call their house and hear Clarissa's voice.

"Do you need me to come over?" I say.

"No. Stay put and do as I've instructed." The line goes dead.

I gaze out the window, trying to see what's happening. The lights are on, but I can't see a thing. I run upstairs and enter the master bedroom. I lower the shutter and peek outside. Clarissa and Russell are standing in the bedroom and arguing. I gently prop up the bedroom window to try to hear what they're saying, but all I can make out is the muffled sound of their voices.

He pushes her onto the bed and climbs on top of her. They appear to be wrestling atop the mattress. Their hips move in opposite directions as their arms flail about. He's forcing himself on her. I grip the gun, wondering whether I should go over and put an end to this nonsense. But Clarissa gave me explicit instructions.

Do. Not. Leave. The. House.

They grapple on the bed for a minute before he attempts to rip off her clothes. He's big and strong, and I can see that Clarissa is having a difficult time fighting him off. She pummels his chest to no avail. His hips begin to grind back and forth. I can see her tortured face up against his shoulder, and for a brief moment it appears as if she's staring directly at me. I close the shutter and step back in shock, clutching the gun against my chest so that the barrel's pointed at my chin. I realize that if I pull the trigger now, my brains will splatter against the ceiling. Maybe that wouldn't be such a bad thing.

I return downstairs and wait on the sofa. Ten minutes pass before I hear someone outside shouting my name. I glance out the window and see Clarissa half naked on her lawn. Her clothes are torn and she's barefoot and cold. Her long arms stretch across her bare breasts. She sprints past the driveway and heads to my house. Russell emerges out the front door and begins to chase after her, dressed only in his boxer shorts. He doesn't seem to be in any hurry. The doorbell rings. I open it and let Clarissa inside. She's breathing hard and looks scared.

"Are you okay?"

"He's coming after me, Leah. I'm certain he wants to kill me this time."

I slam the door shut. "This was not the plan. I thought we were going to stick to the plan."

"The hell with the plan. He wants to *kill* me."

"I saw the whole thing from my bedroom."

"I specifically instructed you to wait downstairs."

"Plans are only good intentions, Clarissa."

"At least now you see what I've been up against?"

"I'm ready to do this."

"Good." She puts her hand on my cheek. "You're an amazing person."

"So are you," I say. "You better go now. He'll be here any moment."

"Be strong. You know I'd do the same for you."

"I know you would."

"Thank you, Leah. You can do this, girl."

She gives me a big hug before sprinting out the sliding door and onto the deck. There's a loud banging noise and suddenly my front door opens, and I see Russell standing in the doorway. He's big and strong, muscles padded upon muscles. He seems to take up the entire space. His thighs look as if they're padded with sandbags. I move calmly to the center of the room, gripping the gun behind my back. He's wearing a pair of black Nike shorts and nothing else. His arms and shoulders shimmer in the light, and his abdomen is sectioned off like a ladder leading to a three-alarm blaze.

"Where's Clarissa?" he says, slamming the door shut behind him.

"I have no idea."

"Don't lie to me. I saw her run in here." He starts to walk slowly toward me.

"I know what you did to her."

"Stop fucking spying on us. What we do in private is none of your goddamn business."

"Then close your curtains if you don't want me to see."

His face wrinkles up in a show of disgust. "I thought I warned you about that last time."

"After all the harm you've done, Russell, I hope you're not going to stand here and lecture me on good behavior."

"Harm I've done?"

A car screeches out of the driveway. I look over and see Clarissa's Mercedes speeding through the neighborhood.

"What the hell?" Russell throws up his arms. "That's just great. She's taken off."

"You're a disgraceful excuse for a man who deserves to be punished." I pull out the gun and point it at him.

"Whoa. What do you think you're doing?" He raises his arms and it looks like two softballs have taken up residence on his biceps.

"You make me sick."

"Take it easy with that."

"I saw the way you treated her."

"Maybe you should put that gun down and chill."

"Maybe I should, but I won't."

"You're the one spying on us."

"Oh, you think you're so smart because you're a worldly professor. Did you really think you could kidnap Mycah Jones and kill her boyfriend?" I know I should follow Clarissa's plan and shoot Russell, but I can't. I want him to suffer just a little bit longer.

"You're crazy if you think I did any of that."

"She said you'd deny it."

"Who did?"

"Clarissa."

"You're making a terrible mistake." He takes a baby step toward me.

"Don't move. And put your hands up where I can see them."

"Why don't you call the police if you think I'm the one who killed Cordell and kidnapped that girl?"

"Because Clarissa insisted I not call the police."

He shakes his head in confusion. "So are we just going to stand here all day?"

"No, I'm going to kill you, Russell. I'm going to do what I should have done many years ago."

"Many years ago? But the two of us have only known each other for a few months."

"I'm going to kill you so that you'll stop hurting other women. I won't allow you to hurt Clarissa by revealing her secret."

"What secret?"

A voice in my head is telling me to stop this bickering and just shoot him.

"Stop playing dumb, Russell. You know full well what her secret is. You've been holding it against her for years."

"Seriously, I have no idea what you're talking about."

"Clarissa was right. She told me you'd deny everything and play dumb."

"You going to tell me or not?" He laughs.

"No, I'm going to shoot you instead."

"How do you plan on getting away with it?"

"I'm going to tell the cops that a black man broke

into my house and tried to rape me. The same man who wanted to sleep with me after our dinner party the other night. What jury would ever convict?"

"You really believe what you're saying?" He takes another step closer.

"I'm done talking." I raise the gun up with two trembling hands.

"I'm begging you to at least hear me out."

"Clarissa said you'd try to sweet-talk your way out of this."

"My Clarissa said that?" Another tiny step.

"I said stay where you are."

Russell shakes his head in disbelief and then sprints head-on toward me. He catches me by surprise, but I manage to fire off a quick shot. The bullet strikes him and he collapses to the floor. He stares up at me in shock, not quite believing that I pulled the trigger. Blood begins to pool along his stomach. He lifts himself up into a sitting position and crab walks until he is resting against the far wall. In his wake, he has left a smear of blood streaked across the oak floor.

The lingering effect of the gunshot reverberates in my ears. Gunpowder residue singes the insides of my nasal cavities, causing a burning sensation whenever I inhale. I can't quite believe that I did it. I shot him.

Russell's groaning in pain. I hadn't anticipated that he'd still be alive after the first shot. I thought killing him would be quick and easy, and that the deed would be done, like in the movies. Now I have to finish him off, which is a lot harder to do when your victim is groaning in pain and pleading for his life. I'm not sure I have the will to shoot a wounded, defenseless man in cold blood.

Russell leans back against the wall and squeals in agony, his hand over the wound on his belly, unable to staunch the flow of blood pouring onto the floor. I walk toward him, keeping the gun trained on his head, wishing I had the courage to put him out of his misery.

"What have you done?" he gasps.

"No one else will get hurt because of you."

"Please call nine-one-one. I'm bleeding."

"You should have thought of that before you abused Clarissa and took advantage of Mycah. You deserve to die for what you've done."

"Sleeping with Mycah was Clarissa's idea."

"Do you think I'm that stupid, Russell?"

"It's true. Clarissa and I have an open relationship. I never wanted that arrangement, but she insisted we see other people. She gets off on that kinky shit."

"I don't believe a word you've said. Clarissa is a good woman and doesn't deserve a husband like you. You frighten her."

He laughs. "I frighten her? How so?"

"You threatened to expose her past."

"Her past?" He laughs through the pain. "Bear with me, please, because this bullet in my gut hurts like hell. But what past are you talking about?"

"You knew she grew up in a middle-class white family. You threatened to expose her real identity if she didn't do exactly what you wanted."

"She told you that?"

"We've become close friends, Russell. She tells me everything now." I lower the gun. My arms are tired and he's not going anywhere in his condition.

"Then she lied to you." He squeals in agony. "Her

parents live in Baldwin Hills out in LA. You know what they call that neighborhood?"

I have no idea. My head is spinning and feels out of control.

"The Black Beverly Hills. And trust me, her folks want nothing to do with her. In fact, they cut her out of the will."

"She told you this?"

"I went out there and spoke to them myself. This was a few years after we got married." He winces, pausing to let a few seconds of pain pass. "Clarissa and I eloped at her insistence. A Vegas wedding. She didn't want her folks there and now I can see why. Because they wouldn't have gone anyway."

"Why?"

"'Cause they know she's a manipulative bitch who uses people like toilet paper. Took me a while to find this out. Of course, I never expected her to convince someone to kill me."

"But I saw you beating her in your bedroom."

"What you saw was us role-playing. She likes it rough. If I don't play by her rules, she's threatened to turn me in to the administration."

"For what?"

"For sleeping with Mycah Jones. I'm starting to believe that Clarissa and that girl made some sort of pact." He coughs up more blood. "We been played, girl."

"I don't believe you."

"Chadwick instituted strict rules against professors fraternizing with their students. Seems they once had a big problem with it. I should have known better, goddamnit, but that girl got the best of me."

"Are you absolutely sure Clarissa's not white?"

"Hundred percent. They showed me all her childhood pictures. Told me she had work done to become *lighter*. Like Michael Jackson." He lifts his hand and examines the warm blood, and I can see the perfectly round bullet hole funneling into his belly.

"She said you would lie to me."

"Wouldn't anyone manipulating you say that?"

I reflect on his words for a moment, trying not to let doubt creep into my head. It starts to make sense. I remember Russell turning around and pointing at me when I filmed them having sex. It was Clarissa who tipped him off.

"Please call an ambulance."

"I've been sneaking into your house during the day and reading her diary. She wrote that you were becoming increasingly violent toward her."

"Please, lady, I'm in pain and losing lots of blood." He presses both hands against the wound. "It's bad."

"What about the diary?" I ask.

"She insisted we install a security monitoring system in the house a few months ago. I had no idea why, seeing how we're the only ones living in this shit hole. It requires one of us to turn it off whenever we go inside."

"A monitoring system?" I say, trying to connect the dots. "Could she see me the entire time? Even when I was standing on your porch?"

"Everywhere. She had a camera installed in the peephole so she could see who was at the door."

"Then it had to be Clarissa who sent me that letter about my sister?"

"What letter?"

"Forget about it."

"Clarissa was watching you from her computer screen at work. Whenever you came onto our porch or snuck inside our house, an alarm went off on her phone and she could see what you were doing."

"I can't believe it. She knew what I was doing the entire time?"

"Of course she knew. She saw you sneaking inside and doing whatever you were doing. Then she obviously scripted her diary in order to manipulate you. Turn you against me."

I try to process his words. Thinking back, it all seems to make sense. I feel like such an idiot. She planted the diary and used it to trigger my most vulnerable emotions. Of course, it was my own fault. I never should have gone inside and snooped around in the first place. In many ways, I got what I deserved.

"What about the wife swapping you proposed at dinner?"

"That was humiliating. She insisted I talk about slavery and get you two all hot and riled."

"You really seemed like you wanted to sleep with me."

"I won't lie. You're an attractive woman, and I'm a man with strong urges. You know as well as I do that marriage is a compromise." He grimaces and lets out a groan. "Do you believe me now?"

I remain silent.

"She fucked us over. Get it through your thick head."

"But why?"

"Money, celebrity, who the hell knows with that evil bitch?" Sweat beads up on his forehead. "Please call nine-one-one and get me some help before I bleed to death."

"How can I be sure you're telling the truth?"

"You need to trust me."

"She said you're a persuasive man and she's right. I need more proof."

Russell shakes his head and sighs. "Then how about this. Chadwick's alumnus offers every tenured professor a three-million-dollar life insurance policy. I die, bitch gets to cash out. You want someone that evil getting three million bucks and raising my kids?"

I grab my cell phone, call 911, and report what happened. Will I go to jail for shooting my neighbor in cold blood? In my defense, I'll say that I feared he might attack me. The dangerous black man preying on an unsuspecting white girl. The black man as sexual predator. Rapist. But how will this play out if Russell dies? He is, after all, a well-regarded professor at Chadwick.

In contrast, I'm your average, overeducated housewife with nothing better to do than shoot her next-door neighbor.

I stare at the carnage. A large puddle of blood pools along the floor. There are red handprints on the wall as well. My kids will be home soon from school and I don't want them exposed to this horrific crime scene. Russell's eyes close and he appears to be slipping into unconsciousness. His breathing is labored and he's making a wheezing noise out of his mouth.

I place the gun down on the kitchen table and grab the nearest towel. I moisten it with some iodine and then press it against his wound, praying the medics will arrive soon. He glances up at me and smiles, too weak to move. Thick beads of sweat bubble up on his forehead. Gently, I guide his head to the floor so he can rest. Then I go into the living room and grab a pillow off the couch and place it under his head.

"I'm sorry for shooting you, Russell."

"She fooled us bad," he says under his breath.

"I should have known better."

"Black-on-black crime." He laughs, which turns into a bloody cough.

"I only wanted to be her friend. I wanted so bad for her to like me."

"Same here."

"Who knew she could be so evil?"

"And I'm the sorry son of a bitch who married her."

"She's going to think I killed you."

"Let's pray to God she's wrong."

The ambulance pulls up outside the house. Russell gestures for me to lean down. Once I do, he whispers in my ear, "If I make it through this, we need to give Clarissa a taste of her own cooking."

"Yes," I say as the police and medics rush inside and shout for me to freeze.

CLAY

Monday, October 26, 10:48 a.m.

I OPEN MY EYES AND SEE A FOREST OF GREEN SHAG. I'm lying facedown and staring into the kitchen. From this angle, it resembles some bizarre jungle terrain deep in the South American rain forest. A daddy longlegs lumbers past my nose and disappears. A blistering, pounding juggernaut fills my head. I know from experience that no hangover could ever produce such thundering torture. So what did?

Where am I? I blink my eyes. Where is Leah?

I pull myself up to a sitting position, groaning in agony. I close my eyes to manage the pain ricocheting through my head. It feels like protons smashing in a Hadron Collider that had been installed in my brain. Tidal waves of blood crash against the seawall encapsulating my skull. I try to remember the events that led me here, but I can't recall a single thing. I reach up to my head and feel a golf-ball-sized lump of wetness. Shit, it hurts even to the touch. I bring my hand back down and open my eyes and notice that my palm is covered in blood.

What the hell happened? I close my eyes again and try to remember something. Anything.

I'm afraid of opening my eyes, but when I do, my worst fear is confirmed. Ten feet away a woman's body lies sprawled on the carpet. She's situated between the living room and the kitchen, which are separated by a common dividing wall. From where I sit, I can see up to her waist. I push myself up and stagger over to the corpse, half expecting to find Leah's bloodied body. But it's not Leah. It's Mycah, and there's no question she's dead.

The horror of this scene hits me on impact. Was I the one who killed her?

Mycah stares vacantly up at the ceiling. A large pool of blood encircles her head. There's a pea-shaped hole between her eyes. I look around the living room until I see a handgun lying on the carpet. It's right next to where I passed out. Something tells me my fingerprints are on it.

Do I flee the crime scene? Call the police? Then I think: what the hell am I even worried about? I don't own a gun. Never was allowed to, thanks to Leah.

I look at my watch and realize that I was out for at least fifteen minutes. Suddenly the events of the last hour begin to trickle back. I remember Mycah texting me. I remember leaving the brewery to come here and save Leah. I remember walking through the front door. Then I remember everything segueing to black.

Sirens cry out in the distance. I pull the dingy curtain aside and notice that a crowd has gathered down on the street. I debate whether I should run out the back door and make a getaway, but realize that would be pretty useless now. My car's parked on the street. It would make me look guilty as sin if I took off running, especially since I'm fairly certain that I didn't shoot Mycah. I can't say I'm disappointed she's dead. In some ways I'm ecstatic. Her death has wiped away a myriad of problems. On the flip side, it has also created many new ones.

I try to rationalize my predicament. I know I'm not a killer. A cheating asshole, yes. A drunken louse, for sure. But I don't have the fortitude to kill another human being. I don't possess the mental toughness and go-for-the-jugular mentality that killing takes. My weakness is that I'm a weak man. Those who can murder another person in cold blood are a rare breed.

I fall back on the couch and laugh at the absurdity of my situation. The police will be here any minute and I don't even have the balls to wipe my fingerprints off the gun. A life in prison seems abstractly pleasant at the moment. Three square meals a day, time to read and relax, plenty of respite from all that is Leah. Isn't that pathetic? Prison suddenly seems more appealing than spending the rest of my life with Leah.

A car door slams. I hear footsteps coming up the concrete stairs. I push the coffee table out of my way and fall to my knees, then to my bloated stomach. I place my hands behind my pounding head and scream into the shag carpet. Someone shouts something vaguely policey. The door swings open. Cold steel closes around my wrists and cuts deep into my leathery skin. A cop reads me my rights. Then another cop pulls me up by the cuffs and leads me down to the awaiting car. I see people below taking pictures and pointing at me. Laughing. They shout my name as if I'm a movie star or famous Bavarian brewer.

This is the American way.

I'm a reluctant crime celebrity.

LEAH

Monday, October 26, 12:23 p.m.

*B*UT IT DOESN'T GO THE WAY WE PLANNED. RUS-
sell falls into a coma at the hospital and is immediately put on life support. The police question me
endlessly about every pointless detail that happened
during the ordeal. I envision the crime scene—my
bloody home—being analyzed and photographed
from every angle. Lightbulbs popping like in one of
those old detective movies. They can't charge me
with a crime. For all they know, I was a defenseless
woman shooting a black man who barged into my
house to rape me. Any jury in these parts would believe this scenario. I'm white and he's black. He
walked into my house practically naked. I tell the police half-truths. I tell them some of what Russell and I
discussed after the shooting. I've incriminated myself—but in a good way.

Try as I may, I can't get in contact with Clay. I call the day care and ask if they can pick up the children from school and keep them until five. I try to call Clay again, but to my disappointment, he doesn't pick up. No one is answering at the brewery either. Where is he?

"So you shot Mr. Gaines in self-defense?" Detective Armstrong asks me.

"Yes."

"But then after speaking with the victim, you realized that this whole crazy scenario was set up by his wife?"

"Exactly."

"And you're telling me that she was the one who advised you to kill her husband?"

"That's correct."

"And the reason she asked you to kill him was because he was abusive to her and having a sexual relationship with Mycah Jones."

"Not quite. She said I needed to protect myself in case he came after me. She believed he killed Cordell."

"You believed your life was in jeopardy?"

"Yes, but why are we rehashing all this? I told you everything that happened over an hour ago."

"I just want to make sure we have your entire story down."

"I can tell by your tone, Detective, that you don't believe me. You're testing me. You're trying to see if there are any discrepancies in my story."

"Of course. We need to be thorough in our investigation."

"What other reason would I shoot him? I was genuinely scared for my life."

"There's the matter about the gun you used to shoot him. You claimed that the victim's wife gave it to you."

"Yes," I say, trying to make him understand. "Look at me. I'm a white, middle-class housewife. How in the world would I know where to get a gun?"

"You're assuming that just because she's black she knows where to get a gun?"

"No, but it's the truth. She gave it to me."

"A lot of people in Maine own guns, especially out here in the country. It's not that hard to get your hands on one."

"Guns disgust me. I've been advocating for gun control my entire life. In fact, I hadn't even considered using one until my family was placed in danger."

"We talked to Mrs. Gaines and she's visibly upset about her husband's condition."

"Of course she's upset; that's because he's not yet dead." I pound my fist on the table. "She's faking it. She set this whole scenario up for her own benefit."

"We sent some officers to check out the surrounding homes. They reported finding bullet holes and broken windows in your neighborhood. A bullet was lodged in the plywood of one house and it matches the gun you used to shoot the victim. In addition, the victim's wife claimed to have heard gunshots out there."

"That's because she and I went back there to practice. She was teaching me how to shoot."

"Again, because all black people know how to use a gun?"

I laugh. "Please, Detective. Don't you label me a racist."

"Did you know that Clarissa heads the local chapter of the Coalition to Stop Gun Violence?"

"It's all a pretense. The woman's a cold-blooded liar. First she told me she was white and grew up outside Boston. Then her husband told me she grew up in a rich black neighborhood in LA."

"Baldwin Hills, just outside LA."

"I know that now."

"She called the station that day and reported hearing gunshots. The police even went out to your neighborhood and checked everything out."

"She's playing off stereotypes for her own benefit."

"You say she told you she grew up white?"

"That's what she claimed, and at the time I believed it."

"Take a look at these," he says, pushing a pile of photographs across the table. "She claims that you were obsessed with her husband and extremely jealous of her and her family."

"Jealous? That's the craziest thing I've ever heard."

"Well, we have security videos of you breaking in to her home and reading her diary. And drinking her wine and stealing her art. The only reason she didn't report the crime was that she felt bad for you."

"Yes, but . . ." I don't know what to say to this. This information deeply embarrasses me and puts me in a bad light. Because the truth is I was jealous of her.

"She believes you were the one who killed Cordell."

"Oh, that's so silly. Why would I want to kill Cordell?"

"You were in the restaurant with him the night he was murdered. You admitted to taking an unusual interest in the case."

"Yes, but I was merely a concerned citizen looking for answers to a racially motivated crime. I wanted to help find the girl before something bad happened to her."

"Forensics has determined that the same gun was used to kill Cordell."

Checkmate. Clarissa has thought of everything to cover herself.

Armstrong barely suppresses the urge to laugh, but I catch it.

"Do you think this is funny, Detective?"

"Mrs. Gaines said you were obsessed with black culture and it was all you wanted to talk about when she bumped into you in town or in the neighborhood."

"Of course I was interested in her culture, but not to the point where it consumed me. I was simply trying to express my solidarity with the plight of black Americans in this country. The way they're discriminated against and harassed by law enforcement."

"Oh really?"

"Social justice is something I've been passionate about for years."

"I hate to get on my high horse, Mrs. Daniels, but based on the statistical evidence, your assumptions about police brutality are completely misguided."

"If you've forgotten, Detective, it was I, and not the police, who tracked down Mycah Jones and discovered her holed up in that dilapidated house."

"And it never occurred to you to inform us about her whereabouts?"

"The girl was scared. She believed Russell was out to kill her. She believed he killed Cordell. I was waiting until I had all the facts before I came to you."

"I think you had an obligation to tell us."

"I'm sorry," I say, near tears.

"Why did she believe Russell wanted to kill her?"

"She was his student and having an affair with him."

"That seems odd, considering that she was never formally enrolled in any of his classes. Of course, in his current medical condition, we may never learn the truth."

"Then why don't you go over there and ask Mycah yourself? I have the address in my purse if you need it."

"There's no need for that, Mrs. Daniels."

"Why not?"

"Because Mycah is dead."

The word "dead" reverberates in my head. My entire face flares up as if I'm gazing into a crackling bonfire on Alki Beach.

"We found her this morning, a gunshot wound to the head."

"No, I don't believe you."

"We found her boyfriend in the apartment too. It appears they had a fight just before she died, evident by the cuts on his scalp. She also had his skin and blood particles under her nails."

"But that can't be true. Russell was at my house this morning."

"It wasn't Russell, Mrs. Daniels. It was your husband."

CLAY

Monday, October 26, 3:03 p.m.

*A*FTER THE DOCTOR STITCHES UP THE CUT ON MY head, the police lead me to a solitary cell. I fall back on the cot and stare up at the stained cinder-block wall. They've confiscated my belt and all my personal belongings. I'm depressed, yes, but not that depressed. Not enough to kill myself. In some ways, I feel a sense of relief. My lies have finally come full circle. Two negatives multiplied always equal a positive. Now the truth can come out.

I'm tired but can't sleep, thanks to the trace remnants of beer still circulating in my brain. Time passes in a vague and indeterminate manner. My mind races beyond control, in shuffle mode, stopping randomly wherever the roulette ball of memory lands. At some point I notice an officer standing outside the cell, watching me, making sure no harm comes to my person. It feels like an intrusion at first, but then I simply ignore him, forget he's even there. He becomes invisible to me. A ghost of the future. I don't want to die just yet. Not when I feel perversely freed from all social conventions. Freed from the bonds of marriage and raising a family and paying off the Twin Tower–like stack of bills.

Occasionally, I hear someone shouting inside the facility. I stay calm until the sound of keys jangling stirs me. The door swings open and a burly officer appears. He beckons and I find myself being led in handcuffs down a narrow hallway and into a spacious conference room.

"It's been an interesting day," Detective Armstrong says, clutching his tie as he sits across from me.

I ignore him and sit quietly, listening to the rush of blood pounding against the golf ball teed up on my brain.

"You want to tell us what happened?" he asks.

I laugh. "You want a confession? With no lawyer here to represent me?"

"I didn't say confess, Clay. I asked if you want to tell me what happened."

"You'll laugh if I tell you."

"Or your version of it."

"At least what I can remember, which isn't much."

"Sampling too much of your own inventory lately?"

"Not nearly enough, but that's another story."

"You can certainly call your lawyer if you like."

"I'd be crazy to talk to you without my lawyer present, but then again, I've done worse things in the last few months."

"That's because you have nothing to hide. Or so you believe."

"Oh, I have plenty to hide, Detective, but murder isn't one of them."

"I'll wait until you call your lawyer."

"Forget about it. I'm waiving my rights."

"You absolutely sure?"

"Positive. I want to get my story out."

"Okay then. Let's hear what you have to say."

"As I previously told you, Mycah did things in the bedroom that you only see in movies. It's why it was so hard to break it off with her."

"I suppose you know that she's dead."

"I'm not going to lie to you and say I'm all broken up about it, but the truth is I didn't do it, unless I blacked out and killed her in a fit of rage."

"You don't strike me as a particularly violent person, Clay. Then again, I've seen other scorned men kill for less."

"I tried repeatedly to break it off with her, but she kept pursuing me."

"So you felt compelled to see her one last time?"

"Someone struck me as soon as I walked into that house. When I came to, I saw her lying in a pool of blood, a bullet wound between her eyes."

"How did you know she was staying there?"

"She sent me a text saying that she was holding Leah hostage and that my wife had made a life-changing confession."

"And she told you what that confession was?"

"She must have recorded it and then played it back for me over the phone. I recognized Leah's voice instantly."

"Where's your phone, Clay? It wasn't in your possessions."

"I smashed it against the wall after hearing Leah's confession."

"And that confession was?"

"That as a child she drowned her twin sister by pushing her into the family pool."

"Is it true?"

I shrug.

"And you never knew this about your wife?"

I laugh. "Do you really think I would have married her, had kids with her, had I known she was a murderer? Someone sick enough to kill her own sister?"

"A child killing a child," he says, shaking his head. "There must have been a reason why she did it."

"Even assuming that's true, what difference does it make what her reason was?"

"Every story has another side."

"And you're going to sit here and charge me with murder?"

"Honestly, Clay, as bad as this looks for you—and it does look bad—I don't believe you killed her. I don't think you're foolish enough to kill someone, nor do I think that you're prone to violence. Moral failings aside, you're like most other guys out there."

"Does that mean I'm free to go?"

"Unfortunately not. The DA is not as convinced of your innocence as I am. The evidence against you is strong, almost too strong for my liking."

"What are you saying?"

"I'm saying you're not in the clear yet. Besides, you have lots of other things to worry about."

"Such as?"

"There's a media shit storm out there waiting to ask you about the two crimes that occurred today."

"Two crimes?"

"This is going to come as a surprise, Clay, but your wife came very close to killing Russell Gaines a few hours ago."

"Come again?" The words come as a shock to me.

"She shot him in the stomach."

"Are you screwing with my head? Leah would be the *last* person on earth to use a gun. She wouldn't even let me buy a rifle to shoot trap."

"The facts are the facts. She shot him as he entered your house and then claimed self-defense. When we arrived, she made up this convoluted story that the entire scenario was set up by his wife. Russell couldn't back up her story because he was unconscious when we arrived on scene."

"Bullshit!" I slam my fist down on the table. "Russell Gaines wanted to have sex with her."

"How can you be sure?"

"Because we went over to their house for dinner one night and he asked if we would swing with them. He grabbed Leah's hand during dinner and wouldn't let go."

"So you think he went over there to have sex with your wife?"

"Why else? Leah would never cheat on me."

"You're certain about that?"

"Detective, my wife barely wants to have sex with me, never mind our African-American neighbor. It's probably why I was unfaithful to her."

"Maybe she just didn't want to have sex with *you*."

"I doubt that very much. She's one of those women who are puritanical about sex."

"Then why is she blaming the shooting on the victim's wife, saying she orchestrated the whole event?"

"Because my wife is a bleeding heart liberal and forgiving to a fault, especially when it comes to people she feels have been historically oppressed. As for getting a gun, I have no idea how she obtained it."

"She's claiming that she was fearful for her life and believed Russell might attack her."

"Then that asshole deserved it. But I still have no idea how she got that gun."

"She said his wife gave her the gun and encouraged her to shoot him."

"But why?"

"Your wife is claiming that Clarissa was being physically abused by him, and that she witnessed this abuse one day while staring out her bedroom window. But then after she shot Russell, he told her a completely different story."

"Wait a minute. All of this is confusing the hell out of me."

"She said Russell admitted to her that he was, in fact, the one being abused in their relationship. He told your wife that Clarissa forced him to participate in an open marriage, and that's why he engaged in the affair with Mycah Jones."

"You mean to say that Mycah was screwing him as well?"

"Seems that way."

"And screwing that lacrosse player too?"

"Girl got around."

"Maybe I've been played more than I realize."

"It's certainly starting to look that way."

LEAH

Monday, October 26, 4:17 p.m.

"YOU MUST BE MISTAKEN. THERE'S NO WAY CLAY would ever cheat on me, Detective. I know him better than anyone else in the world," I say.

"He confessed that he was seeing Mycah Jones while you and the kids were living in Seattle."

"No, I don't believe you." I shake my head, tears at the ready. "Clay is no cheater. He would never do that to me."

"He admitted to being lonely and said that the two of you had been having some marital problems. He also admitted that he'd been drinking quite a lot during that time."

"He's a brewer. He needs to be constantly sampling his beer."

"He was doing more than sampling."

"That's the most absurd thing I've ever heard. We've been happily married for years. Clay would never go out and chase a girl nearly half his age, never mind a black girl."

"You don't think he found black girls attractive?"

"Please don't twist my words, Detective. You know what I mean."

"According to your husband, she pursued him."

The folly of this makes me laugh. Now I know it's not true. "What would a twenty-year-old black girl from the ghetto see in Clay? He's in his late thirties, for goodness' sake."

"We're not entirely sure." Armstrong clears his throat. "She did things to him that he'd . . . he'd never before experienced."

"What sort of things?"

"Do you really need me to spell it out for you?"

"Like what?" I shout hysterically. "Tell me what she did to him."

He pauses for a few seconds before whispering, "Oral. Role-playing, to name just a few things."

I break down at this. "But I'm the mother of his two children."

"I'm sorry."

"I was good to Clay. I sacrificed and agreed to move all the way across country so he could chase his dream."

"Mycah was young and attractive, but we're now learning that she had a dark side to her as well."

I begin to hyperventilate in violent gasps. "Clarissa suspected Mycah of having an affair with her husband. Mycah said Russell harassed her until she finally agreed to sleep with him. But Russell told me a different story. He said that Clarissa was the one who convinced him to date her."

"We're still trying to put together all the details, Mrs. Daniels, but with Mycah dead and Russell in a coma, it makes solving this case that much harder."

"Am I being charged with anything?" I ask, wiping my eyes clear. "I need to pick up the children from day care."

"No, you're free to go."

I head to the door but stop before leaving. "Do the doctors believe Russell will come out of his coma?"

"They don't know yet." He gathers his files together. "He's lost a lot of blood."

"If only I called nine-one-one sooner."

"Why didn't you?"

"I was afraid to turn my back on him. Then he started to explain what happened, and I realized what a fool I'd been."

"Let's hope he survives. Then maybe he'll be able to corroborate your story."

"You better not let Clarissa in his room or else you'll regret it."

"You think Clarissa might try to kill him?"

"I wouldn't put it past her." I turn one last time. "Are you charging Clay with a crime?"

"Not at the moment. He'll be released shortly."

"You mean he's here? In this station?"

"Yes. In one of the holding cells."

"Can I see him?"

"Not yet. Go home and rest, Mrs. Daniels."

"What makes you so sure my husband is not guilty if you found him in that house with the gun nearby?"

"A gut feeling. Also, the ballistics don't make sense to me. He was struck hard enough to render him unconscious, yet he still managed to shoot her. It just doesn't add up."

I walk out of the police station and see a crowd of news reporters, cameramen, and spectators. They converge on me like a pack of hungry lions. I push them away and struggle out to the parking lot where my car is parked. They follow me, shouting questions, cameras clicking away. It takes me a few seconds to pry the car door open, but once I'm inside, I feel relieved. Slowly, I make my way out of the parking lot. I drive over to the day care, pick up the kids, and grab some fried chicken. To my chagrin, there's a group of reporters waiting outside my house.

"Do you people have any scruples?" I shout out to them. "My kids are with me."

"Did you intend to shoot Russell Gaines?" a man's voice says.

I push the children through the front door and then lean back against it in fear. Is this how the rest of my life will be? Evading pesky reporters?

"Mommy," Zadie asks, looking up at me, "why did that man ask if you shot Mr. Gaines?"

"They must have made a mistake, honey," I say.

"Did you really shoot him?" Zack asks, a devilish grin forming over his face.

"Go upstairs and clean up, the two of you. There'll be no more of this crazy talk. After dinner I'll make some popcorn and we'll watch a movie together."

"*Frozen*," Zadie calls out.

"*The Incredibles*," answers Zack.

"*Finding Dory*."

"*American History X.*"

I collapse on the couch, exhausted and numb, but thankful that they've hired someone to clean up the bloody mess. There's no visible signs that a crime ever happened here. Being in this house raises my anxiety to another level, and I replay the shooting over and over in my mind. What if Clay comes home tonight? How will we ever recover from the terrible secrets we've kept? Will our marriage survive these betrayals?

I badly want out of this house. Out of this godforsaken town and state. But will I ever be able to leave Dearborn? Or live with the repercussions of what we've done? I need a glass of wine. Maybe an entire bottle. I suddenly can't shake the long-repressed memory of pushing my twin sister into that pool. Or watching as her wheelchair sank to the aquamarine depths, her arms waving before gently rippling by her sides. I remember feeling at peace when she stopped breathing, knowing that I had relieved my sister of all her pain.

Or did I?

CLAY

Monday, October 26, 5:44 p.m.

TO MY SURPRISE, ARMSTRONG ARRIVES AT MY CELL and releases me on my own recognizance. They don't have a strong case. Not yet anyway. He tells me not to wander too far. But where am I going to go? I have a brewery to run. A family to raise.

A huge crowd awaits me as soon as I walk out the door. This is the new way of achieving celebrity in America: commit a crime. Get used to it, I tell myself. This could be the end of my life or the beginning of a whole new chapter. I wave to the reporters as I pass, answering their questions with non-questions, the tone of which is meant to sound vague but pleasant. I admit to having an affair with Mycah Jones and showing up at the house where she was shot dead. But I proclaim my innocence.

I politely ask the reporters to let me open the door to

my pickup truck. Surprised by my civility, they move back and allow me to climb inside. I slowly make my way out of the parking lot until I turn onto the street. Then I accelerate.

For a brief moment I see myself starring on a hideous reality TV show. The thought of it repulses me, but I may need the money. Buckets of money. Money to keep my brewery afloat. Money to fend off lawsuits. Or to start a new brewery somewhere else if this one doesn't work out. Money, money, money.

I drive home, listening to the oldies station and not thinking about all that has happened in the last twenty-four hours. Men like me are simple creatures. We accept reality. We have the ability to adjust to our shifting environment and make the most of it. Compartmentalize, plan, and prioritize. The future is murky, but somehow I know I'll survive.

Leah's car is parked in the driveway when I pull in, but there are cars parked all around the development and in our neighbors' driveway. A car pulls up as I sit listening to the end of a song by the Police: "Every Breath You Take." A well-dressed black couple gets out and walks toward the Gaineses' front door, a casserole dish in one hand and a bottle of wine in the other. They don't turn to look at me.

I'm not even sure I want to go inside and face Leah and the kids. What will she say? It's possible she won't let me stay the night after how I've betrayed her. But she lied too, and in many ways her lie is worse than mine. If true, it's likely that I never would have married Leah had I known about her past. I would have run away as fast as possible.

After the song ends, I get out of the pickup and walk

to the front door. A few reporters ask me questions, but I ignore them. I go inside. After all, this is my house too. I'm part owner of this monumental debt. As soon as I make my way inside, I see Leah and the kids sitting at the kitchen table and eating fried chicken out of a red and white box. Zadie jumps off her chair and runs over to greet me. She jumps up in my arms and squeals. Leah gives me one of her fake-ass smiles, and I know I'm in for a long night. I can barely return her gaze after recalling the terrible things I've done. The terrible things she confessed to doing as a child.

How could she have pushed her disabled sister into a pool? What kind of person does such a thing? Or claims to have done it?

Zadie grabs a plate and dishes me up some macaroni and cheese, chicken legs, and corn. It all seems so weird that it feels dreamlike. Zadie pretends to feed some to her doll. So surreal. Zack says grace, a generic version of the prayer that Leah has approved. I'm not hungry, but I bite into some extra-crispy skin.

"How are you?" she asks me.

I laugh. "Been better. You?"

She places her hand over mine. "We all make mistakes."

"Some worse than others."

"We'll get through this, Clay. We still love each other, right?"

"Yeah."

"One forgives to the degree that one loves."

"I suppose."

I want to run out and never come back. Everything feels sickly and wrong. I'm not even sure I love Leah anymore or if she loves me. It feels staged. Forced.

Everything has changed in our lives. I cheated on her, and she lied. A good friend once warned me not to marry her. Only now do I realize how right he was.

So why did I marry her? I married her for the same reason most men marry their wives. Love blinded me to the dark sides of her personality. When she broke up with me after a year of dating, I thought my life was over. I thought I'd never again meet such a beautiful woman who accepted me for the person I was, faults and all. And I had plenty of faults, which later in life made me believe that love had blinded Leah as well. We looked past the real person and married the ideal of who we wanted our mate to be. I had little insight into my superficial nature, believing that if I'd lost Leah, I'd never again get a woman as beautiful and altruistic as her. So I told that friend off and never laid eyes on him again. His words of warning, however, still reverberate in my head.

A car door slams. I look out the window and see people gathered in the Gaineses' living room, comforting the injured man's wife and family. The gulf between our two homes seems vast now, and our lives forever entwined. Yet we're so close. How long will we coexist like this? The Hatfields and McCoys. Spy versus Spy. What will happen if Russell doesn't wake up?

Worse, what will happen to all of us if he wakes from his coma and tells the truth? Or at least his version of it.

LEAH

10 Months Later
Monday, August 17, 7:47 a.m.

I WAKE AS USUAL, THINKING THAT THIS DAY WILL BE like all the others since our life changed ten months ago. Clay has left for the day. He now works at a welding shop forty-five miles out of town. I pop my head out the front door and grab the newspaper off the stoop. A bulb flashes and a lone reporter shouts out a question that I can't understand. It's been a while since these leeches have showed their faces around here. So why now?

The coffee timer goes off and it begins to brew. I bake banana muffins and blend healthy smoothies as Mr. Shady wags his tail and stares up at me. I pull back the sliding glass door and let him out to do his business. The air feels warm and humid this morning. Summer has hit Maine with a vengeance. Soon the starlings will be here to put on their annual aerial acrobatics.

I hear the news bulletin on the radio and understand almost instantly why that reporter was camped outside my front door. It's the most wonderful news I've heard in some time. Mr. Shady disappears from sight, but I can hear him barking at something in the shrubs. I walk out onto the deck and search for him, hoping he hasn't rooted out an ornery skunk.

"Get that filthy mutt off my property."

I turn and see Clarissa standing on her deck in her bathrobe. The sight of her sends a chill down my spine despite the fact that we've been reluctant neighbors all this time. Has she seen the news? She must have.

"And pick up that dog shit or else I'll throw it back on your deck."

I grab a bag and run over to where Mr. Shady has wandered. A drainage ditch separates our properties, and I leap over it and pick up Mr. Shady's fresh mess. Then I scoop him up in my arms and turn to Clarissa, who stands on the deck with her arms folded, glaring at me.

"You must be so happy about the news," I say in my most smarmy voice.

"Why are you even talking to me? Look at the way you ruined our lives and destroyed this community."

"Don't act so holier than thou, Clarissa. It's just you and me here. Let's be real."

"I have nothing to say to you."

"You don't need to lie anymore or plant those fake 'stories' in your diary. What's done is done."

"You're a very good liar, Leah. You even lied to

your own husband, for God's sake. All those years and he never suspected that he was sleeping next to a murderer."

"At least we have that in common."

"You make me sick." She turns to go inside.

"Isn't it wonderful about Russell?"

She stops and turns toward me. The shocked expression on her face lingers for a few seconds before she forces a strained smile.

"What about Russell? I've had my phone off this morning."

"They just announced on the radio that he's woken from his coma. He may even be talking soon. Looks like you'll have your husband back."

She rushes inside the house, leaving me standing with Mr. Shady. I can't stop smiling. Russell is conscious and hopefully talking. That terrified look on her face will make me smile all day. It will help me forget about the injustices my family has had to put up with over the last ten months. The name-calling and racist taunts from strangers. Having to transfer the kids to a private Christian school ten miles away. My husband having to sell the brewery. Gone. All of it is gone.

The children are not down from their rooms yet. 10,000 Maniacs comes on the radio. As much as I love this song, I switch to the local news station. I dump cereal into the kids' bowls, take out the muffins, pour myself a coffee, and then fill Mr. Shady's bowl with dried dog pellets. A car door slams outside. I peek through the shutter and see a bunch of reporters standing outside our home. A woman photographer stands on my property, crouched down and leaning against the tired FOR SALE sign planted on my lawn. For some reason I'm not mad at them today. In fact, I'm glad they're back.

Once Zack and Zadie finish their breakfast, I guide them out the front door. Back when the bad news first started, Clay and I would park in the garage so as not to deal with these pesky reporters. But today I wave and say good morning to them. The kids enter the car and buckle themselves in, unfazed at the sight of all these leeches. I tell them to wait a minute, and then I stand at the foot of the driveway. Shutters click as the reporters fire off questions in rapid succession. I quickly shush them with a raised hand. Once it's quiet, I begin to speak.

"As you all probably know by now, Russell Gaines woke up from his coma this morning. This is wonderful news for my family. Hopefully, we'll finally be vindicated once the truth comes out. You'll see that we are not bigots or racists, but innocent bystanders to a terrible crime. Then you can report the real story and we can get on with our lives. That's all I have to say for now."

They will not let this go and keep peppering me with questions and snapping pictures. Where before this would have bothered me, today I'm quite happy with the attention. I'm happy to drive the kids ten miles to their Christian summer camp. I'm happy to have my busybody job at Goodwill, working in the back and tagging donations out of the public eye. If Russell's conscious, he will talk. And I'm confident he will point an accusing finger at his manipulative wife.

CLAY

Monday, August 17, 9:56 a.m.

I WATCH AS THE DRILL BIT LOWERS AND THEN PIERCES the metal. Minute after minute, hour after hour, day after day I perform this mindless job. I suppose I should be happy that I'm employed. At least I'm not in jail—not yet, anyway—and I'm able to pay some of the bills. Our family remains together, although the dynamics have certainly changed. My dream of opening and running a brewery has been dashed. Of course I'm not giving up on my dream. There's always hope for the future.

I take my "coffee" break in the lunchroom with a few of the other guys. The TV is on the local news station. I polish off my messy breakfast sandwich while listening to the top story being reported: Russell Gaines has emerged from his coma.

The other guys in the break room pay no attention to

the story and continue playing cards or staring dumbly at their cell phones. This is a primitive lot. Neanderthals who drive oversized American pickup trucks, drink cases of Bud on the weekend, and prefer to listen to classic rock or country music. They know me as Skip. I've grown a beard and gained fifty pounds in the last nine months. Still, I pray my face doesn't come up on the TV screen.

A buzzer goes off and my coworkers begin to file back into the plant. I stay behind after they all leave and stare up at the television. A man's face appears next to that of an attractive woman. It takes me a few seconds to realize that the photo is of Leah and myself. I look washed out. Bug-eyed with only one chin. I look unrecognizable from my current bloated version.

I don't want to go back inside that plant and press drill bits into metal plates all day. But I don't want to go home and face Leah, either.

The two of us are locked in a cold war of our own making, neither of us coming to grips with the past. We haven't talked about our indiscretions or even acknowledged the terrible things we've done to each other. There's been no family counseling or therapy sessions. Leah simply refuses to go. She thinks we can heal ourselves with love. And in that vein we've managed to continue on as if nothing had ever happened—and it feels surreal, as if we're living in a fishbowl that's getting murkier by the day. She doesn't want to face the truth, but then again, neither do I.

The day drags on. The hands of the clock seem to never move. How I wish I had a cold beer next to me. When I was running the brewery, I could quaff a porter or pale ale whenever I wanted. But my life now hangs in the balance. The DA hasn't formally charged me with a crime. Of course, that could change at any moment. The prospect of murder still hangs over my head like a French guillotine. If I end up behind bars, I can all but forget about ever quaffing a beer again.

My shift ends. I wait in line and punch out. Something tells me that my life is going to get a lot more complicated in the coming days.

LEAH

Monday, August 24, 8:36 p.m.

I POUR MYSELF A GLASS OF WINE AND GRAB A BOTTLE
of beer for Clay. Then I sit next to him on the couch.
The dishes have been put away and the kids are upstairs in their rooms, where we can momentarily forget about them. The news is about to come on. I put
my hand on Clay's thigh and wait for him to recipro-
cate, but he doesn't.

The lead story is about the Gaineses. Ever since
Russell returned home in a wheelchair, I've been on
edge. I keep having to remind myself that I shot him in
self-defense and that Clarissa tricked me into doing so.

I have to give the woman credit: she's played her
hand perfectly. Although she hasn't gotten to collect on
his life insurance, she's parlayed her victim status into
something more profitable. She's been a guest speaker
on a few of the cable news shows, decrying all the hid-

den racism in society. Where else could a black man helping his troubled neighbor be shot in cold blood? Her speaking engagements have grown considerably and she's become somewhat of a celebrity on campus. From what I've heard, there's been a stampede to get into her classes, and she's even being considered for tenure.

I stopped reading all the stories in the newspapers and magazines about us. It pained me to see Clay and I portrayed as bitter-clinging racists. They made Clay out to be a heavy drinker and philandering frat boy. He's put on a lot of weight in the last six months. At least fifty pounds because of the stress of it all. I typically skim over the bad articles when I see them. I change the channel whenever our names are mentioned. I was waiting for the day when they would bring up my past and refer to me as a child killer. But for some reason, they never did. Clarissa must be holding this back for a reason. Her ace in the hole in the event she ever has to use it.

A news reporter appears on screen. It takes me a few seconds before I realize that he is standing in my front yard. The screen transitions and I see Russell sitting on a sofa in his living room, surrounded by their diverse collection of African art. He looks gaunt and tired, but with the red bow tie and wire-rimmed glasses, he appears professorial. He resembles one of those POWs being held against their will, forced to parrot the Islamic propaganda fed to them for fear of being decapitated. And for a brief second I feel sorry for him, even as he begins to spew the hateful words that Clarissa is forcing him to say.

"I owe my life to the doctors and nurses who kept

me alive all those months and never gave up. And of course, to my family, who also never gave up hope that I would one day pull through. My wife has been my rock, and were it not for her, I may not be here today.

"Let me just say the atrocity committed against me was a blatant act of racial hatred. The Danielses have been hostile to our family ever since they moved in to this neighborhood. Leah Daniels invaded our privacy on a regular basis and illegally entered our house. She became obsessed with me and desired a sexual relationship. Despite how it appears, I had absolutely no interest in a relationship with her. Who knows what her motives were? Some people speculate that she was obsessed with black men. Others say that she wanted to get back at her husband because he had an affair with a black student who attended Chadwick. Whatever the reason, I know in my heart that she tried to kill me that day. Thankfully, she didn't finish the job. Why else would she call my house just before the shooting happened and tell me that she was going to kill herself?

"There's more that will come out. I only pray that the police will be able to gather enough evidence to convict the Danielses for their crimes. Mycah Jones and Cordell didn't deserve to die like that. I didn't deserve to be shot because of my skin color and because I was willing to help a deeply troubled woman. I think it's terribly sad that black people must live in a society where this attitude is so prevalent. While many prejudiced folks would never act out on their racist beliefs, the Danielses showed their true colors."

Clay sips his beer and shakes his head. I clutch his hand and squeeze it. We've been beaten and battered for so long now that our defense systems have been honed down to a double-edged blade. We're a team now with an "us against them" mentality.

"Can you believe this bullshit?" Clay says. "I thought you said he would back you up?"

"Didn't you see his eyes? He's being forced to say all that nonsense. Clarissa's controlling his every utterance."

"Or maybe he's suffered so much trauma that he actually believes what he's saying."

"You mean her version of the events that happened," I say, pointing to the screen. "I can tell by his body language that he's lying."

"How can you tell?"

"He blinked a lot during his statement. And did you notice the way he kept touching his right ear?"

"Is it true you called him before he came over?"

"I called their house to see if Clarissa was all right."

He turns to face me. "Why did you break in to their home and read her diary?"

The question surprises me. We haven't yet talked about any of this. "Do we really want to go there?"

"I can't continue with this hanging over our heads, Leah. We have to get things out in the open if we're to stay married."

"Why did you sleep with that girl?"

"I asked you first."

"I needed a friend, someone I could talk to. I needed to feel loved and be loved in return, and you weren't giving that to me in the way I needed. I read her diary so I could become closer to her."

"We need to have a serious talk."

"Now?"

"What better time is there to do it?"

"How about I get us some drinks before we start." I grab his empty beer bottle and my wineglass. My hands are shaking as I carry them to the counter. I grab another beer out of the fridge and fill my glass to the rim with Chablis. I knew this day was coming. But am I ready to confront my past and spill my guts to Clay? I return to the living room and hand him his beer.

"We need to be completely honest with each other," he begins.

"I understand."

"If we're to stay together, this is something we need to do."

I grab his hand and we begin to peel away the layers of our complicated past.

LEAH

Tuesday, August 25, 8:12 a.m.

I WAKE UP WITH A MIND-CRUSHING HANGOVER. CLAY'S side of the bed is empty. It's hard to believe he could get up so early for work after the marathon drinking session we had last night. I vaguely remember the kids coming downstairs, saying good night, and watching as Clay broke down in tears while he hugged them. We slurred our good nights and then watched as the kids slumbered back upstairs.

Despite my hangover, I feel optimistic this morning. I get the kids off to summer camp and call in sick to my job at Goodwill. The media has stopped camping out in our neighborhood, but that won't last long if new charges are filed.

I stand by the kitchen window, waiting for Clarissa and her kids to leave the house. I have a small window before Russell's caregiver arrives to assist him with his physical therapy. I know this because I've been making detailed notes about their daily habits.

Clarissa rushes out of the house with the kids in tow. Just the sight of her enrages me and makes me wish I never tried to befriend her. She buckles them in, climbs into the driver's seat, and zips out of the neighborhood. I stare into their quiet house and see Russell, thin and depressed, staring out the shutters. I imagine he's relieved now that his draconian captor is finally gone for the day.

Five minutes pass before I slip out the patio door. Mr. Shady barks as I slide it shut. He wants to come with me and sniff out the neighborhood, but I ignore his entreaties and move to the neighbor's backyard. Once I arrive at their deck, I pick up a few small pebbles and pepper the sliding door. I stay out of sight of the security cameras. After I've thrown pebbles against the window for about a minute, Russell's dour face appears. He looks around until he sees my eyes peeking above the decking. He shoos me away, but I don't budge until he opens the sliding glass door and sticks his head out.

"Get out of here," he whispers before disappearing inside. Is he calling the police? I debate whether to stay put or run back inside my home. He returns a minute later and pops his head back outside. "What the hell are you doing here?"

"We need to talk."

"Are you nuts? About what?"

"Did you go back inside and call the police?"

"No, I temporarily shut off the security system. Come inside. We have about ten minutes before it alerts the monitoring company."

"Are the cameras on?"

"Nah, everything's off. Now, hurry up and get inside before any of those reporters come by and see you."

I run up the deck stairs and slip inside the house. He motions me to the kitchen table and sits across from me.

"You can't be coming over here." He looks around worriedly.

"Why'd you lie about me on TV?"

He paws his strong jaw. "Look, I'm sorry about that, but I had no other choice. This is the way it has to be from now on."

"If you give in, Russell, she'll push you around for the rest of your life."

"It don't matter now. We can't prove a damn thing."

"We can if we work together."

"Besides, they got you on tape sneaking in here and reading her diary and taking liberties with our wine. Then you made up that crazy story about her being white. It'd be madness if I came out now and told the God's honest truth. I'd look like a damn fool."

"The truth being that your wife wants you dead?"

"Wanted, as in the past tense. Everything's cool now between us."

I laugh at this. "Please, Russell. Do you really believe that?"

"There's too much at risk. I could lose everything."

"She's on her way to achieving everything she's wanted in life: celebrity, money, legitimacy. She'll leave you in a heartbeat if it'll benefit her."

"Says she truly loves me now."

"Sure, until you become a burden on her. Then she'll find someone else to knock you off."

He looks down at his watch. "Why you have to ruin my good mood?"

"Are you going back to Chadwick?"

"What else am I gonna do? Sit around the house all day and bake cookies like you?"

I let this insult pass. "She'll set you up again. I bet she has a lot of dirt on you."

"Enough to ruin my life and take away the kids."

"Then you have to work with me so she doesn't destroy both of our lives."

"She was an undergrad when I first met her. Girl played me perfectly. I bet she taught Mycah everything she knew about men and how to please them, sexually speaking. How to control your man."

"She took Mycah under her wing and the two of them devised this plan. She used Mycah to get to us. Only Mycah didn't realize how dangerous your wife was."

"Hateful bitches."

"I bet she made Mycah trust her and feel wanted before she set out to kill her."

"She's good at that—being your best friend when she wants something."

"Please help me put her away, Russell."

"Tell me, what should we do? And hurry, the security alarm will go off soon if I don't restart it, and then Clarissa will become suspicious."

"We set her up like she did to us. We beat her at her own game."

"Jesus, get on out of here before we get caught. Come on now, scoot," he says, rushing over to the panel located near the front door.

"You'll help me, Russell?"

"Yeah, I'll help you. Now, get the hell out of here before she finds out you were here."

"Tomorrow morning, I'll leave an envelope with instructions on your deck. We need to do this as quickly as possible."

"Okay, okay. Just go."

I slide the door shut and then scamper back to my house. Upon seeing me enter through the patio door, Mr. Shady lowers his head and runs into the other room. I immediately see why. The poor little guy has pooped on the floor. I clean it up and then sit quietly at the kitchen table, racking my brain to come up with a plan to ensnare Clarissa. The pain in my head has been reduced to a dull thump thanks to the three Tylenols I gulped down this morning. The urge for a glass of wine is strong, but I resist the temptation. I need to have all my wits about me if I'm to pull this off.

LEAH

Wednesday, August 26, 9:56 a.m.

I WATCH THROUGH THE WINDOW AS RUSSELL STEPS out onto his deck. He moves gingerly, looking around to make sure no one sees him. The air is warm this morning and he's dressed in tan cargo shorts and a polo shirt. Being in a coma has changed him. He's lost a lot of weight and muscle, and isn't nearly as intimidating as before. In fact, he looks rather harmless.

He snatches up the manila envelope I left for him and slips back inside. I trust that he'll follow my instructions to a tee. Clarissa is no doubt monitoring his every move on social media and through the surveillance camera.

At ten o'clock I make my move, praying that he's shut off all the security systems. I tiptoe over to their backyard and enter through the sliding glass door. It's eerily quiet inside and I wonder if I've done the right thing by coming here. My phone is charged and at my disposal.

I scamper up the steps until I reach the master bedroom. I practically know the layout by heart now. Russell is waiting inside and motioning for me to scoot under the bed. I fall to my knees and then to my back and slide beneath the mattress until I'm staring up at the cross boards.

"I'm going to turn the security system back on and then call Clarissa," Russell whispers. His face is parallel to the floor.

"Make sure you and your wife speak up so I can record it all on my phone."

"Oh, we'll raise our voices all right. We usually do when we get into a big-ass fight."

"You don't deserve to be treated like that."

"Tell me about it. After all the crazy shit that woman put me through, I should be treated better."

"Good luck, Russell."

"Don't need luck when the wind's at my back. I'm filled with righteous indignation."

I place my hands over my belly and wait, thinking about everything that has led me to this point in time. Things will need to change after this is over. I need to develop a goal in life. A passion that will give me meaning and purpose. Clay has agreed that when we sell the house we will move back to Seattle. It's expensive out there, but I know we can make it work. I'll land a full-time job doing something or other. Clay's a talented and resourceful man. He'll find a way to make ends meet even if he has to go back into the computer industry. Zack and Zadie will be okay with the move. They've gone through so much in the last few years that nothing seems to faze them. Maybe moving home will be beneficial to them and they'll make more friends.

I close my eyes and envision how great our life will be in the near future. My relationship with Clay will grow stronger and deeper now that we've opened up to one another. It feels like a turning point in our lives. I've forgiven him for his infidelity and he understands why I did what I did. A smile forms on my lips and I drift off, lulled by the prospect of better days to come.

CLAY

Wednesday, August 26, 10:16 a.m.

*T*HERE'S A FIERY VORTEX INSIDE MY HEAD THAT RE-
fuses to die. The beers I knocked back last night
aren't helping matters any. I've had four cups of coffee this morning and I still don't feel right. Something
seems off-kilter about my life. Everything just seems
so messed up that I'm convinced that life is crazier
than fiction.

Leah's words continue to haunt me as I lower the
drill press over and over and over. Eight mind-numbing
hours of this shit. Overtime if I want it, which I don't.
The thought of working here for any length of time depresses me, especially after opening my own brewery.

My mind feels like a soda can used for target practice. I simply can't get past the fact that my wife pushed
her handicapped sister into the family pool. I went on-
line and researched it in the Oregon newspapers and

found her sister's obituary. Leah claimed that she witnessed her sister's abuse at the hands of her father and
did nothing about it. She served eighteen months in a
juvenile facility before moving in with her aunt and
uncle just outside Seattle. I didn't ask Leah directly,
since we swore to be brutally honest with each other,
but I got the distinct feeling that she was the one who
was victimized by her old man.

Why do I believe this? Because all the pieces seem
to make sense now. She displays many of the behav-
ioral symptoms that result from sexual abuse. She drinks
too much, obsesses about every small thing, and completely shies away from sexual intimacy. I can't be
totally sure, but it seems obvious to me. Leah's miserable, drunken father is the root of all her insecurities.
She needs intensive therapy if she's to put her sister's
death in the rearview mirror.

But will that be enough to save our marriage?

The notion that she murdered her own sister in cold
blood frightens me. There's Zack and Zadie to think
about, and I worry constantly about their safety. I feel
like I can't trust her with the children anymore. I have
nightmares about coming home one day and seeing
their mangled bodies sprawled on the living room
floor. Or floating lifeless in the bathtub.

There's no way I'm moving back to Seattle with her
and resuming our old lifestyle. It's a fantasy, a sick
dream she harbors in order to make her believe everything's fine. Well, forget her and her sick mind. As
soon as I save up enough money, I plan on hiring a
lawyer and suing for custody of the kids. She's crazy
and completely deluded, which is how we ended up in
this situation in the first place. Yes, I'm partly to blame

for the destruction of our marriage, but after comparing our respective crimes, I think hers is far worse in the greater scheme of things.

I'm not paying attention when I lower the drill and the bit breaks. *Damn.* It's the second time I've ruined a piece of equipment this morning. The supervisor comes over and rips me a new one, telling me that there's lots of guys out there who'd like this shitty job. The economy in rural Maine sucks and good jobs are hard to come by. But I don't care right now. Screw this job and the inbred supervisor who lords over me. I rip my gloves off and throw them down to the floor.

"Where you going?" the supervisor asks.

"I'm done with this place."

"Get your shit and get the hell out of here."

"You think I'm going to run a drill press the rest of my life?" I laugh.

"You're a loser, Skip. With an attitude like that you'll never hold down a job."

"Open your mouth again, asshole, and I'll close it for you," I say, towering over this short little prick clenching a clipboard.

He turns and walks away, and I'm glad he did. My frustrations are mounting and I feel like I'm going to explode at any minute. My fuse has grown shorter in the past year and I'm more prone to temper tantrums and explosive outbursts. I can see myself hurting someone if they say the wrong thing.

I clean out my locker and head to the parking lot. My brain is screaming inside my skull and I can't shake the feeling that I'm losing my sanity. The days of making beer in my own brewery bring back memories, both good and bad. I get in the car and head home.

It's all I can do not to swerve off the road. Up ahead I see a dingy roadside tavern. I pull over in the near-empty parking lot. A neon-red sign flashes. It's dark inside and smells of mold and mildew. A country song is playing over the speakers. I saddle up to the bar and order a Budweiser, as there are no craft beers on tap. Three more beers and a shot of Jack Daniel's follow in rapid succession. The alcohol numbs my mind and reduces the voices in my head to a murmur. I feel better now with a few under my belt. I feel like I can go home, play the role of "husband" I auditioned for many years ago, and think of a way to end this troubled marriage. Maybe I can start searching for a good divorce lawyer, one who will ensure that I get full custody of Zack and Zadie.

I grab a beer for the road and then head back into town. Everything is lush and green, and the air conditioner blows a cool breeze over my fat, sweaty face. I pass my old brewery, which has been taken over by a friendly rival. Ben's still working there, and probably ripping off my recipes, but I don't begrudge the kid. Good luck to him. I hope he falls in one of the fermenting kettles and drowns.

I stop momentarily at the gates of Chadwick College and stare at the quaint buildings and meticulous landscaping. Summer classes are in session and a few students stroll lazily across campus. The gates in front of the college have always struck me as exclusionary and pretentious, and I realize that the biggest hypocrites on the planet take up space within those ivory towers.

I continue on until I arrive in my deserted neighborhood. I live in a ruined development that I can't escape: underwater on the mortgage and a turnoff to prospective buyers. Trying to sell it has been a nightmare, and for more reasons than the obvious fact that the neighborhood resembles the Gaza Strip: two ancient enemies at war and living side by side.

I park haphazardly in the driveway and stagger up to the front door. A nice buzz counters the hangover still plaguing my brain. I look around the first floor, but Leah is nowhere to be found. Yet her car is parked outside. She's probably upstairs, once again spying on the neighbors. What a nosy bitch. She thinks I don't know that she goes upstairs and spies on them every chance she gets. It irked me at first to learn that she'd been peeping in on the Gaineses, possibly watching them make love. But I never dwelled on it, having too much to worry about at the brewery. But after hearing her confession, it all makes sense now. Her sickness is much worse than I thought, and I fear not only for the safety of Zack and Zadie, but for my own life, especially when she learns that I plan to leave her and file for full custody of the kids. It's why I need to act fast, before she discovers what I'm doing. If I have to borrow money from my parents, then I will.

It feels eerily quiet inside. Needing to fuel my addiction, I grab a bottle of beer out of the fridge and pop it open. Ahhh, the taste of a good craft brew still pleases me to no end. I guzzle it down in one swoop, savoring the heft and body.

Fortified with a good buzz, I run upstairs, hoping to catch her in the act. But she isn't there. So where is she? I move to the window and see the bedroom light on in the Gaineses' house. One of the shutters is slightly bent from her fingers repeatedly pushing down on it. Her spyglass stands vertically on the nearby dresser. I grab it and push the lens through the opening.

What I see surprises the hell out of me.

LEAH

Wednesday, August 26, 11:44 a.m.

*T*HE FRONT DOOR CLOSES AND MY EYELIDS SPRING open. Fortunately, I've always been a light sleeper, able to wake up at a moment's notice. Footsteps scurry up the stairs and I hear the pitched tone of Clarissa's low voice. I turn on my phone, hoping to record her confession.

"This better be an emergency, Russell. What's so important that you had to call me away from the office in the middle of the day?"

"I shut off the security system so we can discuss this in private."

"You what?" Her voice sounds suspicious.

"I know you wanted me dead, Clarissa, so it makes this conversation very hard to have."

"Don't be ridiculous, Russell. That white bitch next door is crazy and you know it."

"Please don't try to deny what you've done."

"Okay, I won't. But look how everything turned out. I'm moving up in the world and making a name for myself, and you'll soon be back at Chadwick, a celebrity professor in your own right. It couldn't have turned out better for us."

"But how can I ever trust you again?"

"Don't be so dramatic, Russell. It's not like you didn't want to screw every female student who waved her ass at you." She sits down on the mattress.

"Sure, I fooled around a little. It's how I met you, isn't it?"

"Lucky me."

"It's no reason to kill a man."

"Come on, babe, there's no need for you to worry about that. I got what I wanted and now I'm done."

I hear her push off the mattress, but Russell pushes her back down on it.

"You were ready to cash in on my life insurance policy."

Clarissa laughs. "You're telling me you wouldn't have done the same?"

"You killed that poor girl and her boyfriend and made it look like our neighbor did it. Do you really think the cops are going to buy that story?"

"I taught that girl everything I know. I coached her how to handle these fools in the bedroom so that she could wrap her little finger around them and do what she wanted. She thought I was her friend, and with you out of the way, we would have been rich. Now that she's dead, Russell, it's just you and me."

"Then why were they over here this morning asking me all these questions about you? I'm worried, Clarissa."

"Who was here?"

"That Detective Armstrong fellow and another gal. He's quite a hound when he gets on a scent."

"You better not have told him anything."

"No, of course not. I want to make this marriage work, especially for the kids."

"I once adored you, Russell. Despite all that has happened between us, I'm sure I can love you again."

"Why'd you stop in the first place?"

"As soon as we got married, you went back to your old ways, sticking your dick into every undergrad who'd let you. I wasn't going to stand for that. You were mine. So I figured I'd give you my blessing of an open marriage and then take advantage of it when you slipped up. You can't really blame me now, can you? I absolutely worshipped you. Little did I know that you would cheat on me so soon after we married."

"You shut me off in our marriage, Clarissa. A man has his needs, goddamnit."

"I was your trophy wife until the next young, hot undergraduate came along. Then you'd dump me like you did your last wife." A long pause. "Look, Russell, I know what I did to you was wrong, but we're in a much better place now. Things will get better, I promise."

"How can I ever trust you again? I can't even sleep at night."

She laughs. "You have no other choice but to trust me."

"Maybe I'll go to the cops and tell them the truth."

"It's your word against mine. Now that I'm a celebrity on campus, they'll be less likely to believe a cheating dog like you." She laughs. "Haven't you been watching my performances on the cable news shows?"

"Maybe it's not just my word, babe. Maybe I got a collaborator, and maybe me and this other person go on CNN and tell them what their civil rights guru has really done."

"What are you talking about?"

"Come out from under the bed, Leah."

The shock of hearing my name stuns me. This wasn't part of my well-thought-out plan. Clarissa was supposed to go back to work, and I was to take this information to the police and prove once and for all that she was the brains behind everything. Instead, I crawl out from under the bed and stand sheepishly in front of Clarissa, who is seated on the mattress and staring at me with hate in her eyes. Russell takes a gun out of his pocket and points it at his wife. I want to gently remind him that this is not what we agreed upon, but I'm too stunned to speak.

"What's the meaning of all this?" Clarissa says.

"You were right all along about this bitch, babe. She's been spying on us and trying to break us apart," Russell says, pivoting to aim the gun at me. "I had to draw her out first."

"This is not the plan, Russell," I say.

"The hell with your stupid plan," he says.

"But she was the one who tried to kill you. She's the one who set you up by telling you to go over to my house," I say.

"Yeah, and you agreed to go along with it. You knew all along that you were going to shoot me in cold blood. Another innocent black man taking the fall for whitey."

"Only because she convinced me that you'd been abusing her."

"And you agreed to play judge and jury. Where were my constitutional rights? My due process?"

I turn to Clarissa. "Please, I have young children to care for."

"If you'd minded your own damn business, this never would have happened. But no, you had to get all high and mighty on us. Try to keep the black neighbors from going ghetto," she says.

"You killed Mycah and Cordell. You even orchestrated the death of your own husband. Haven't you done enough damage?" I say.

Clarissa laughs. "So sue me, bitch."

"Russell, you can't be serious," I say. "You'll never get a good night's sleep with her by your side."

"All my wife ever wanted was to be someone. A spokesperson for black people just like Jesse and the Reverend Al. Now that she's got what she wants, I'll be able to rest easy," he says.

"So you're just going to shoot me in cold blood?"

"No different than what you had in mind for me."

"How will you ever get away with it?"

"Seeing how you have a history of breaking in to our home and harassing us, I have probable cause for shooting you." He lifts the gun higher, looking as if he's about to pull the trigger. "And once you're dead, the cops will pin all those murders on you."

"Too bad, dear," Clarissa says, caressing my cheek with the back of her hand. "And to think how badly you wanted to be my friend."

Russell lifts the gun and points it at me. I close my eyes, say a quick prayer, and hear the gun go off. Then I fall back against the dresser in agony.

CLAY

Wednesday, August 26, 12:15 p.m.

*T*HROUGH THE WINDOW I SEE CLARISSA SITTING ON the bed and staring up at Russell. His back is facing me and it looks like they are having a vigorous discussion, judging by the way Clarissa is gesturing with her hands. I know I should put the scope down and walk away, but for some reason I can't, and it makes me realize that I'm no better than Leah. A scumbag Peeping Tom loser. Maybe it's the alcohol in my system. Or maybe I'm laboring under the belief that they might provide me with a clue about what happened that day.

Russell pulls out a gun. I stumble backward in fear. Clarissa's expression changes as soon as she sees the gun in his hand. It takes me a few seconds to realize that there's someone else in the room with them. But I can't see this person. A figure rises up from the side of the bed and comes into view. Holy shit. It's Leah!

What is she doing there?

Am I drunk and seeing things? I blink my eyes to make sure I'm fully conscious. When I open them, I see Leah standing there with her arms raised. What is she doing in their bedroom, especially after nearly killing Russell in our own home?

Russell swivels around and points the gun at Leah.

I pull out my phone and get ready to dial 911. Russell and Clarissa will get off scot-free if they kill her. Then they'll be liberated from her obsessive spying, her wild accusations and personal intrusions. They'll be spared her pathetic attempts to save the planet and spread racial harmony.

And then I realize something so profound that it causes me to rethink dialing 911. If Leah dies, I too will be free of her. We will all be free from Leah. The world will be free from her. There'll be a nice little life insurance policy at the end of the rainbow. Possibly enough to kick-start another brewery. I'll be able to raise the kids in a safe environment and without worrying about them. No divorce lawyers or fighting for custody. There might even be a few bucks left over for college. I'll never again have to worry about whether she'll harm them while I'm at work. All I have to do is stand here and do nothing. Pretend I'm downstairs being a slug and let nature take its course.

A shot goes off and I realize that Russell has fired the gun. Clarissa falls back against the mattress, blood oozing out of her left eye. Leah kneels by the side of the bed, sobbing at the sight of her dead neighbor.

Then Russell turns and points the gun at Leah.

LEAH

Wednesday, August 26, 12:18 p.m.

"**Y**OU KILLED HER," I SAY IN A STUNNED VOICE as he points the gun at me.

"I know. . . . It wasn't part of the plan."

"Please don't kill me."

"Sorry, but I have no other choice now."

"What about my children?"

"Didn't bother you when the shoe was on the other foot."

"You won't get away with killing both of us."

"Sure I will. You broke in here to try to kill us, and I had to protect myself. Everyone knows you're a busybody and have a history of violence."

"That was different. My sister was being abused."

"That's not how I heard the story."

"Well, I'm sorry to disappoint you, Russell, but that's what happened."

"A little bird told me otherwise," Russell says, nodding toward his dead wife.

"What did she tell you?"

"Clarissa was good at getting people to do what she wanted."

"Those court files were permanently sealed."

"When that woman had her mind set on something, watch out."

"I don't want to hear this."

"Of course you don't. But you're going to."

"No one was supposed to know about that."

"Know about what? The fact that you were the one being abused and not your sister, and that you resented her for it?"

"That's a lie."

"It's in the court documents. Your sworn testimony as part of the plea agreement. Pushing your sister into that swimming pool was no mercy killing."

"Annie was the lucky one. They doted on her and ignored me. I resented her for that. I loved her as much as anyone could love a sister, but then I began to hate her as time wore on."

It causes me unbearable pain to admit this. I've been burying that emotional aspect of my life for quite some time, and for it to come out now stings. Loving and hating Annie were not mutually exclusive. Because as I was busy hating her, I knew in my heart that I had literally loved her to death. I loved her to her final breath, when her useless body stopped functioning at the depths of our family pool. I justified it as a mercy killing. In my head, hate was no part of the calculation. But it was. It was there all the time.

"Don't matter to me that you're a coldhearted killing machine."

"Don't shoot and I'll testify that you killed Clarissa in self-defense. Better yet, I can return home and no one will ever know."

"But that will mess up my well-thought-out plan."

"What plan?"

"I'm a fragile man still recovering from my gunshot wound. You broke in here and tried to assault me."

"Please, I beg for you to think about my kids."

"Why? So you can push them into the pool too? Or maybe smother them with a pillow when they fall asleep?"

"I would never do that."

"It's always different on the opposite side of the grass." He stares at his wife's corpse. Sticky blood pools over the floor and around her body. "Looks like I can take an early retirement now. Three-million-dollar life insurance policy ain't nothing to sneeze at."

"You two snakes were meant for each other."

"Like you and Sam Adams weren't? You kill your disabled sister, and then he goes around fucking the dark meat while you're out of town. Great role models the two of you make."

"He made a mistake and paid dearly for it."

"Lady, once a dog always a dog. And I should know, being the leader of the pack."

"How will you explain her death?" I ask, nearly throwing up at the sight of blood spattered over the bedcovers. Clarissa's one eye remains open as if she's studying the ceiling pattern.

"You broke in here and killed her. I wrestled the gun away from you and then shot your sorry ass."

Tears fall from my eyes at the prospect of never seeing my kids or husband again. I never should have had
the twins to begin with. In that way, they'd never have
to experience all the evil that exists in this world. But I
truly believed at the time that I was game for raising
kids. I lived under the deluded notion that someday I'd
be a great mother, and Clay would be a devoted husband and father. So I decided to keep the pregnancy.
Twins. Poor Zack and Zadie never had a chance.

"And that's how this ends?" I ask.

"Maybe for you it ends. I envision a nice life in
Bermuda, sipping rum swizzles on Elbow Beach and
sailing out in the bay. Little golf here and there. Get me
and the kids as far away from this racist state as possible."

Russell's phone rings just as an alarm goes off. He
answers it and begins speaking in a panicked voice. He
forgot to reset the security system. Seconds pass and
the alarm blares in my ears. He turns momentarily, and
when he does, I leap over the bed and tackle him. The
gun goes off as I grab his wrist in one hand, jerk his
earring down with the other, and tear it out of the lobe.
His screams of agony fill the room as we wrestle over
the bloody mattress. I manage to pull him down with
me, and we fall over Clarissa's lifeless body. Blood
sticks to my hands and hair like wet paint. He raises his
head up and glares at me, nostrils flaring and out of
breath. I open my mouth and sink my teeth into his
thick nose and bite down as hard as I can. He squeals
in pain as the gun falls out of his hands and lands next
to Clarissa. I bring my knees to my chin, place my feet
on his chest, and kick him off me with all my might.
He staggers back against the far window, landing hard

against the pane of glass. I grab the gun off the bed and hold it with two shaking hands. Blood gushes from his torn ear and the bridge of his nose.

"You won't do it," he says, standing to his full height.

"I've killed before, remember? I can certainly do it again if I need to."

"Stupid white trash. How anyone could possibly love you is a mystery to me."

"Yes, my husband made a mistake when he married me, but he still loves me, and for that I'm grateful."

"Your husband's not going to save you now." He pushes off the wall and sprints toward me.

I close my weak eye and pull the trigger until it clicks. The momentum of his bullet-riddled body causes him to collapse on top of me. It takes me a second to realize that he's dead or seriously injured. I roll him off me and sit on the edge of the mattress, trying to calm myself down. The security alarm begins to blare in my ears. My body is drenched in blood and sweat, and the powerful stench of dead flesh begins to permeate my nose.

I raise my head up and catch something outside the window. Is someone watching me from my own bedroom? I wipe the blood from my eyes and take a closer look. Yes, that's Clay's face peering out from behind the blinds. He sees me. Thank you, God. Now I have a witness to my story, along with Clarissa's taped confession. I stand happily, weeping, and blow kisses to my love.

I know my marriage will survive.

CLAY

Wednesday, August 26, 12:20 p.m.

THE GAINESES ARE BOTH DEAD AND SHE'S BLOWING me kisses?

I push back against the window in shock. My skin feels cold and prickly and I feel like I'm going to throw up. I try to convince myself that I imagined this entire scenario and that it's not real. But I know it happened, and because of that I'm screwed. I need to act fast if I want to make things right. If I don't want to be known as the coldhearted husband who failed to come to his wife's rescue.

I sprint into the bathroom and throw up. The bathtub is filled with water and at the bottom I see Zadie's baby doll staring up at me. The arms and legs have been cut off, and there are slashes in the doll's abdomen. But what gives me chills are those plastic eyes staring up at me.

The sight of it causes me to heave until my stomach empties and my throat is left burning.

I bolt downstairs and out the front door just as three police cars pull up in front of the Gaineses' property. A security alarm blares from inside their home.

"What's going on?" a young cop asks.

"I heard gunshots going off," I say, trying to look concerned.

"Stay back, sir. We'll check it out."

But just then the Gaineses' front door opens and Leah staggers out like Carrie after the prom, her face, clothes, and hair drenched in blood. The cops shout for her to put the weapon down and drop to her knees. She glances at me and smiles in an unnerving manner. Three cops sprint over, cuff her, and then lead her to one of the police cars.

"Leah," I shout, running toward her. I want to explain and to apologize for not calling 911 and saving her life.

"Hold on, buddy," a cop says, blocking my path with a raised arm.

"That's my wife."

"Why was she in your neighbors' house?"

"Please," I snap angrily. "I need to speak to her. We have young children."

"Make it quick."

The cop opens the door, lowers Leah's head, and then guides her into the backseat.

"It's okay," Leah says to me. "Everything will be fine now."

Her calm demeanor creeps me out.

"Thank you so much, Clay."

"For what?"

"For watching out for me. For calling the police

when you did. You are my witness to it all. You can tell them everything that happened."

"Sure."

"You really do care about me, Clay, don't you?"

I pause before answering. "Of course I care about you."

"We'll soon be together again, Clay. You, me, Zack, and Zadie. Then we can move back to Seattle and get on with our lives."

I can't begin to envision such a bleak future. I must now accept the inevitable or counter it with a lie. I could tell the cops that Leah was the aggressor and that she shot them in cold blood. They would have no reason to doubt me. Then the kids and I could live happily ever after. Yes, I decide that is what I'll tell the police.

"Don't worry, dear. I'll be home very soon."

"How can you be so sure?"

She lifts her cuffed wrist and shows me the cell phone in her hand. "I've got their confessions. I've recorded every last word that was uttered in that room. The truth will set us free."

The cop slams the door shut. I see Leah waving to me as the car circles around our depressing cul-de-sac. A neighborhood of one now. The car speeds onto the main road and disappears. I suddenly realize that I'm the only one left standing. Alone and numb and afraid. Sweat pours down my face and chest. I feel dead inside as Mr. Shady runs out and scrapes his paws against my shin. I look up and stare numbly out at the barren fields behind our home. Then I see them.

Those damn starlings.

Joseph Souza, acclaimed author of **The Neighbor,** *brings readers into the dark heart of a small town in this riveting, relentlessly twisting new novel . . .*

Lucy Abbott never pictured herself coming back to Fawn Grove, Maine. Yet after losing her lower legs to a roadside bombing in Afghanistan, then years spent as a sous chef in New York, she's realized her only hope of moving on from the past involves facing it again. But Fawn Grove, like Lucy herself, has changed.

Lucy's sister, Wendy, is eager to help her adapt, almost stifling her with concern. At the local diner, Lucy is an exotic curiosity—much like the refugees who've arrived in recent years. When a fifteen-year-old Muslim girl is found murdered in the woods, difficult memories of Lucy's time overseas come flooding back and she feels an automatic connection. At first glance, the tragedy looks like an honor killing. But the more Lucy learns about her old hometown, the less certain that seems.

There is menace and hostility here, clothed in neighborly smiles and a veneer of comfort. And when another teen is found dead in a cornfield, his throat slit, Lucy—who knows something about hiding secrets—must confront a truth more brutal than she could have imagined, in the last place she expected it . . .

Please turn the page for a sneak peek of Joseph Souza's PRAY FOR THE GIRL coming soon wherever print and ebooks are sold!

1

THE GIRL'S BODY WAS FOUND AFTER A DAYLONG search, her frail corpse discovered not far from the banks of the Alamoosa River. She was nestled between two unmovable boulders rising up out of the ground. I heard my sister say that a kayaker paddling down the river saw what looked to be a body protruding from the ground and called the police. The girl, later identified as a refugee from Afghanistan, was fifteen at the time of her death. Rumor had it that she'd been buried up to her chest and then stoned. Wendy said that the trauma to her face was so devastating that she was almost unrecognizable to her family and friends.

The news of the girl's death startled me when I first heard it. Things like this didn't happen in Fawn Grove. Or at least they didn't happen when I grew up here.

Then again, I left this place fifteen years ago—and I've seen a lot of bad since.

I'd roused myself from a long bout of self-imposed hibernation when I heard the news. My sister and her husband were discussing it at the dining table over lunch, although it could have been breakfast for all I knew. I was standing upstairs and holding on to the railing for support, unsteady and fighting off a stubborn case of vertigo. Time had lost all meaning to me. It seemed not to exist in the sorry state I had gotten myself into.

To say that I was in a bad frame of mind during this conversation was an understatement. My current woes included PTSD, anxiety, and depression, and they were all acting in unison to cloud my thinking. I hadn't experienced such helplessness in a long time. As much as I tried to disassociate myself from the conversation my sister was having with her husband, I ended up hearing every last word of it.

I stumbled back to my room, numb, narcoleptic, not wanting to hear any more of this. Depressing news seemed to be all I ever heard while living in New York City. Murders, rapes, greedy Wall Street types ripping off investors, stabbings, shootings, terrorist attacks, to name just a few of the heinous crimes that occurred there. The sound of police sirens became like elevator music to my ears. But now that I was back home in Fawn Grove, I just didn't care. Hope seemed like some long-lost campaign slogan from a bygone era. I'd lost track of my med schedule and started taking whatever pills lay in front of me that day. Sometimes the shape or size appealed to me. Other times a certain color reflected my ever-changing mood.

Whatever I took, it wasn't helping the situation.

On the bureau sat a vial and next to it a syringe wrapped in plastic. I was supposed to administer a shot to myself every day. I ripped the syringe package open with my teeth and gazed at the troubled woman staring back at me in the mirror. The eyes were accusatory and judgmental. In another time I would have run from this red-haired witch, but instead I drew the liquid into the syringe and stared back at her with an adversarial snarl.

It infuriated me that my mirror image couldn't or wouldn't share in the emotional pain I was feeling. But the shell she wore that day was certainly beautiful. Or had been beautiful at one time. Maybe she still had the capacity to be beautiful under the right conditions. I pulled out the bottom drawer, rested my toes on the wooden lip, lifted the robe up to my waist, and plunged the needle into my scarred thigh. The quick burst of pain never failed to thrill me, and I shivered with excitement as the juice wormed its way into my system. It was the one time each day that I felt alive, and it made me envious of the addict's ritual.

But back to the girl's murder. I'd allowed a girl to die while serving as a combat medic in Afghanistan, and I vowed never to let that happen again. Not on my watch, anyway. It still weighs on my conscience. It's part of the reason I left New York City and returned to Fawn Grove. The pain of that memory lingers long after I left the battlefield. Healing both body and mind takes time as well as effort. I thought if I could only confront my past and let it go, everything would be better. But I found that I couldn't. It was too painful. There's a toxic hostility seeping through me that I can't quite cast out.

Something *has to* give.

Here's the deal. That Afghani girl is a part of me now. Forgetting her death, as well as the voices that continue to cry out in my head, would destroy me far sooner than coming to grips with their existence, especially now that a girl has been killed in my hometown. I feel compelled to act, or it'll eat away at me until whoever committed this crime is caught.

They say everything happens for a reason. This must be the reason I wigged out one night in my bug-sized efficiency and returned to Fawn Grove: the veritable armpit of Maine. I feel I was brought back here for a reason.

To find out who killed this girl.

2

WHEN I LEFT NEW YORK CITY, I LEFT WITH A suitcase filled with my best clothes (admittedly, not many), some personal stuff, a canvas roll of professional knives, and my ego in splinters. Heather was not exactly a happy camper when I gave my notice, which took effect immediately after saying "I quit." She was eight months pregnant at the time but looked ten, and most of her line cooks were junkies, alkies, or whack jobs. I felt bad about leaving like that. But shit happens in this business. I tried not to stare down at her pumpkin belly as I said the dreaded phrase. I tried not to dwell on the fact that her body would soon burst with life, something mine would never do. She was already short-staffed on the line, and the restaurant was packed to the gills night after night.

Heather was a victim of her own success. If I could have stayed and helped her until she found a replacement, I would have. But in the fragile state I'd descended into, I knew I wouldn't last another minute in that place. Dropping the ball in that fashion was a terrible thing to do, and considered one of the worst offenses in our profession. But what choice did I have? When the inner demons awaken from their deep slumber, there's not much one can do but let fate run its course.

So I returned home to Fawn Grove, a town best known for two things: its paper mill and the plane crash that occurred there in 1975, which took the life of hard-partying rock star Angus Gibbons and all his band members. They were on their way to Bangor for a concert when the Convair they were flying in ran out of fuel. Sensing a financial opportunity, the town quickly erected a memorial at the sight of the crash, and just like that, a small cottage industry was created, celebrating the life of a guitar god taken too soon.

Returning to Fawn Grove was never in the cards for me. Then again, not much in my life has gone as planned. It's been a little over fifteen years since I've been back here, and every day that went by I missed this town a little bit less, until one day I forgot it ever existed.

I stare at myself in the bureau mirror, under the soft light of a faux Tiffany lamp my sister has a fondness for collecting. The skin over my face appears remarkably smooth, considering all that I've been through. I lift the brush and dust a light smattering of rouge over my cheekbones. Putting on makeup is something I've become quite adept at. I pencil in black eyeliner, apply a swathe of lavender across my lids, and then draw a thin sheen of glossy pink over my lips. A quick pucker and I'm ready to go.

But go where?

It's three-twenty in the morning when I look up. The old Victorian is deathly quiet at this hour. I swear it groans under the considerable weight of my family's history. I move gingerly through the room, the floorboards warped and weathered with wear. Being nocturnal has its advantages. It also has its downside, and considering that I've barely left my room in the last few weeks, I'd say everything's evenly matched.

I'm all skin and bones. Lying in bed for over a week tends to do that to a girl. Still, most women would kill to have my svelte figure and razor-sharp features. I know this because many women have come up to me on the street and said as much. I'm not trying to brag by saying this. In fact I've never had much in my life to boast about. But women definitely yearn for the smooth skin along my cheeks; my long, thin legs; and my perfectly shaped nails. If they only knew what I had to do each day to look this beautiful, maybe they wouldn't feel so envious. If they only knew about the capricious panic attacks that strike out of nowhere. The constant anxiety I experience over my weight. Or the fact that I eat like a hummingbird on an Atkins diet, despite being an accomplished sous-chef in New York City. But worst of all is the insomnia.

The main reason I can't sleep is because of the voices. They fill my head when I least expect it, beseeching me for help. They cry out for me to do something. *Anything*. They plead for me to save them from the terrible fate that awaits them. But I don't know how to help them. I'm forced to listen to their high-pitched pleas with a hopelessness bordering on resignation. I hear chains scraping and pulling from their mooring. I hear men's stern voices. And screams. It's one of the reasons I became a chef, so I could avoid them by working late into the night. Then stay up until dawn when the light rectifies the anxiety and puts the voices to bed. I'm a vampire infected by my own past.

But today I'm up and about, casually outfitted in a sleeveless white sundress imprinted with a pretty floral pattern. It's the first day since I've arrived that I feel good enough to leave the house. It's time I do something productive. Like find out more about that dead girl.

I unfurl the canvas bag and run my hand across the collection of knives I've amassed throughout the years. After caressing the black walnut handles, I slide a finger over a razor-sharp blade until a papery layer of skin splits apart like a white rose in bloom.

I traipse down the stairs, trying not to make the floorboards groan. Holding the polished rail for support, my eyes struggle to adjust to the dark. I see photographs of my family on the wall as I descend. Near the bottom, there's a portrait of Jaxon taken in his high school days. In it he looks serious and reflective, which is completely different from the Jaxon I remember. The sight of him hiding behind that long mane makes me want to cry. Despite all the years that have passed, and my conflicted feelings about him, I still miss that boy.

I make my way into the kitchen and see the keys to the '94 pickup hanging by the light switch. Before grabbing them off the hook, I slip into my sweater, checking to make sure my sunglasses are still in my pocket. Then I make my way into the darkness.

Not a week after I'd arrived in Fawn Grove, the girl was found dead. At the time, I was in no condition to reflect on this crime. I had my own problems to deal with, and it took all my energy just to care for myself. I buried my head under the covers, hiding out from the world, and stayed in that state for over a week. During this period of self-imposed isolation, time ceased to have any meaning. Two weeks could have been two days. I staggered out of bed for minutes at a time to nibble on stale toast left over from the previous day's breakfast. I ignored whatever dish happened to be brought up to my room. All I could stomach was toast, charred and tasteless, in nibbles that fooled my stomach into believing it was full. And sips of water. Or else plain tea, in order to swallow the random pill I had chosen that day.

But today I feel more like myself. Not 100 percent, but better.

I leave the house and climb inside the pickup my sister has allowed me to use during my extended stay here. It starts without hesitation, and the engine has a nice rumble to it that travels up my spine and warms me with a nostalgic glow. A chill hangs in the air this morning, my breath visible like powdered sugar flung haphazardly in the air. I let the engine idle. After a few minutes, the steady stream of defrosted air clears the fogged windshield and allows me to see the road ahead.

The inside of the cab is warm and cozy as I punch the clutch and shift into first. The truck jerks forward, tossing my head back.

Now to see what's become of my old hometown.

It never occurred to me that I would in any way miss Fawn Grove, or accept the fact that it had changed during the fifteen years I'd been away. There's the paper mill on the north side of town, still hanging on by a thread. At one time, the mill employed half the town, providing good wages for the people who lived here. Not so much anymore, as their line has shrunk down to producing one specific product: catch-and-release papers. On the south side of town, up on the hill, sits Dunham College for the Deaf. The school is, without a doubt, the quietest forty acres in Fawn Grove. In the event one ever needs a bit of solitude, Dunham is the place to go. On the western part of town, by way of the grubby train terminal, is the development of townhouses where the Afghani immigrants have settled. This is where the murdered girl lived.

I drive past the mill, smoke billowing out the tall brick stack. Even with the windows up, I can still detect the sour stench of rotten eggs, a natural by-product of the papermaking process. My grandfather always said that smell was a good thing. The smell of money, he'd announce with pride. A skeletal crew works around the clock struggling to produce these catch-and-release papers, which are used to create synthetic textured finishes for certain manufactured goods. These skeletal crews keep the plant afloat one ream at a time. I try not to stare at the plant as I pass, but the smokestack has become somewhat of a landmark in these parts. Mention Fawn Grove to anyone outside of the town, and depending on who you ask, they'll either mention Angus Gibbons or the paper mill.

The mill has taken up a good chunk of real estate in my mind. Even when it's not in sight, it looms large in my consciousness. My dad worked there for over ten years, as did his dad, overseeing the lines of print news, when print news was the shits. Newspapers put a roof over our heads and food on our table. These days no one my age reads newspapers.

I turn off Mill Road and head back to the main artery that cuts through town. Past the grimy strip mall with the sad bowling alley, the Bennie's Original Steak Burger, and the town's lone movie theater. Taking a right on to Beardsley Road, I drive toward the townhouses where the new arrivals have settled. Even in the dark, I can see that they're poorly constructed. Officially, they call this neighborhood Blueberry Hill, but I heard from my sister that some people in town refer to it as Mecca. The rows of drab gray townhouses run up and down and along the back side of the hill. An aerial view might mistake it for a series of Marine barracks. At one time this area was populated with trees and brooks and places for townie kids to play. Everyone came here to pick the wild blueberries that grew naturally. We used to race bikes up and down the dirt paths, making ramps out of discarded plywood boards, and cutting trails through the woods so that we could get from here to there. We'd play Relievio, hide-and-seek, and any other adventurous game that could occupy us until dinner.

I cruise slowly through the narrow streets, mindful of the speed bumps, eyeing the broken-down cars and porches littered with junk, wondering which unit the missing girl had once lived in. The shabbiness of it all depresses me. It makes me wish they'd just kept it the way it was. It's a reminder that not all change is for the best.

But who am I to say what's best? To the refugees who've settled here, this town might seem like paradise. Or hell. I can't imagine escaping from some shitty war-torn parcel of dust only to be moved halfway across the world to Fawn Grove. To arrive upon our frigid Maine shores and realize that in many ways America is a more dangerous and depressing country than the one they left. A place where children die for no good reason.

Not a soul is out at this ungodly hour, and so I cut short the tour and head back to the center of town. Surprisingly, I discover that I'm famished, which is a good sign. I haven't been this hungry in weeks. Maybe such hunger pangs are a sign that I'm finally getting better and will soon be able to face my sister and her family.

I glance at the clock and notice that it's almost four A.M. I've been driving for nearly forty minutes. It's way too early to return home and start chopping potatoes, frying bacon, and scraping sweet cream butter across slightly charred squares of toast. My only hope is that The Galaxy is open at this hour.

Back in the day, when the mill was going full steam, The Galaxy used to be open twenty-four seven. You could find people in there at all times, especially on weekend nights after the local bars and pubs let out. It was a place for workers to go after a long night toiling in the mill. At one time it boasted about having the best corned beef hash in Maine. Come fall, there would be lots of burly, bearded men dressed in camouflage, oftentimes a freshly killed moose or deer lying bloodied in the bed of their pickup.

The road I travel on is dark and surrounded on either side by woods and gentle hills. As I speed past, I see a police cruiser hiding between a grouping of trees. A quick glance at the speedometer tells me I'm doing nearly seventy in a forty-five mph zone. Lights flash and the siren blips. I peek in the rearview and see a cop car racing in my direction. I pull over and watch as the cruiser comes to a stop behind me. The officer steps out of his car and ambles toward the truck, one hand on his holster (this never used to happen here). I place both hands on the steering wheel and pray that I've never crossed paths with this cop. My long blue nails tap nervously on the hard plastic. I admire their shape and hue as he approaches, but I try not to focus on the many scars and burns dotting the back of my hands. Women who make their careers in kitchens rarely have smooth skin.

A knock on the window and I roll it down by hand.

"Good morning, ma'am. Out for a drive?" he asks in a low voice that sounds vaguely familiar. He leans forward so that his face can be seen through the open window. I continue to look straight ahead. A distrust for authority once ran strong through these veins.

"Something wrong, Officer?"

"You tell me."

"I couldn't sleep, so I went for a drive." I turn and notice that it's Rick Dalton. How could I forget those magnetic blue eyes and butt cheek chin. Or the barest trace of acne scars over the lower half of his face. Pinned to the breast of his uniform is an American flag. Underneath it, it says AMERICA FOR AMERICANS.

"Going a little fast in this old truck, wouldn't you say?"

"Honestly, I didn't realize I was going so fast." I stare nervously at the road ahead, praying he doesn't recognize me. I've changed since those days. I'm not the same dorky kid he once bullied.

"What's your name?" He breathes a cloud of smoke.

"Lucy."

"Well, Lucy, I'm going to need to see your license and registration."

I pull the registration out of the glove compartment, pluck my New York City license out of my purse, and hand them to him.

"Wow! All the way from New York City." He stares at my license before breaking into his most charming smile. "Now, don't go away, Lucy. I'll be right back."

I'm a wreck and can barely hold myself together. As I wait patiently for him to return, I pray he doesn't make the connection between my current and former self. But how could he? I'd changed my name and my appearance since moving away. After a few minutes pass, he gets out of his car and walks toward me. I apply another shade of gloss over my lips, pop a breath mint into my mouth, and toss my hair back over my shoulder. I can't help but notice that he's aged well since I last saw him.

"Well, Lucy Abbott, it appears you have a very clean driving record."

"Do I get a sticker for that?"

He laughs. "Not quite."

"I'm sorry if I went over the speed limit, Officer. Honestly, I didn't intend to."

"No one ever intends to. But the law is the law."

"I'll make sure to pay attention to the road signs from now on."

"Probably not the best idea to be driving around here at this time in the morning. Especially the way this town is changing."

"Changing?"

He leans in a bit closer. "You haven't heard?"

I shake my head.

"Just passing through town, are we?"

I laugh. "Something like that."

"Where're you staying?" He leans on my door a bit too close for comfort.

"Is this an official interrogation?"

"Just making polite conversation."

"Good, because for a moment there I thought I might need to call my attorney."

"This used to be a good, law-abiding town. Unfortunately, a girl was recently kidnapped and killed here. I'm concerned for your safety."

"Don't go worrying your pretty face, Officer. I know how to take care of myself."

"Didn't you hear what I said? A girl was murdered."

"Girls are murdered all the time in New York City. That doesn't stop me from going out and living my life."

"Fawn Grove is definitely not New York City," he says, laughing. "I've always wanted to visit that place."

"You definitely should. The restaurants there are to die for."

"Listen to me, Lucy. This girl's murder was different than most murders you hear about."

"Are you trying to purposefully scare me? Just because I went over the speed limit?"

Dalton stares at me for a few seconds before breaking into laughter. "Maybe I am."

"What's so funny?"

"You."

"Me?"

"Big-city girl like you cracks me up." He reaches for something down by his pocket. "You plan on staying long in Fawn Grove?"

"I'm not sure just yet."

"Well, whatever you decide, I hope you have a pleasant stay here." He rips off a pink sheet and hands it to me. "Today's your lucky day. I'm letting you off with a warning. So take it easy on the gas, okay?"

"Trust me, you won't catch this girl speeding through town again." I laugh in spite of myself.

"Maybe I'll see you around."

"Not if we're meeting in this fashion."

"Something tells me that with a lead foot like yours, this speeding thing could be habitual."

"Habitual," I say. "Good word."

"Never underestimate the intelligence of a Mainer." He raps his knuckles against his temple.

"I would never."

"Maybe we can grab a coffee sometime."

"Did you become a police officer to spice up your love life?"

"A guy like me doesn't need a badge to get a date in this town."

"Maybe we'll run into each other one of these days."

"I'd like that," he says. I start to roll the window up, but he stops it with his fingers. "My friends call me Rick."

"You have friends?"

"I have one now." He winks at me. "Have a great day, Lucy."

I watch as he walks back to his car. The headlights in the rearview flash in my eyes, momentarily blinding me. I sit quietly, overcome with emotion, trying to keep my hands from shaking. A fine line exists between police work and criminality, and Rick Dalton is no exception to the rule. I half expected to learn that he was behind bars or out on bail. Or that maybe someone had killed him in a fit of rage. Nothing would have pleased me more than to have spit in his face and sped away.

His car does a U-turn and heads back down the long, dark road. Thankfully, he won't be following me back into town. He'll be setting a trap for some other poor sap.

By the time I get to the diner, I'm in a much better space. My stomach growls for pancakes, sausages, and bacon. Or maybe a cheese omelette as plump as a princess's pillow. There's only a few cars parked in the lot. I pull up in front of the stainless steel caboose, remembering all the times I spent here in my youth. A dilapidated sign over the caboose says THE GALAXY DINER in neon pink lights. It's the same sign from my youth.

I walk inside the brightly lit dining room, slipping on my sunglasses as I make my way to the counter. My heels click loudly against the chipped and moldy tiles, announcing my presence. The sun will soon start to rise, which will cause me to retreat back to the safety of darkness. If I fail to return to my room by then, the headaches might return with a vengeance. Then I'll be right back where I started when I first arrived here.